THE RUSSIAN GIRL

Also by Kingsley Amis

Kingsley
AMIS

THE RUSSIAN GIRL

VIKING

VIKING
Published by the Penguin Group
Penguin Books USA Inc., 375 Hudson Street, New York, New York 10014, U.S.A.
Penguin Books Ltd, 27 Wrights Lane, London W8 5TZ, England
Penguin Books Australia Ltd, Ringwood, Victoria, Australia
Penguin Books Canada Ltd, 10 Alcorn Avenue, Toronto, Ontario, Canada M4V 3B2
Penguin Books (N.Z.) Ltd, 182-190 Wairau Road, Auckland 10, New Zealand

Penguin Books Ltd, Registered Offices: Harmondsworth, Middlesex, England

First American edition
Published in 1994 by Viking Penguin,
a division of Penguin Books USA Inc.

1 3 5 7 9 10 8 6 4 2

PUBLISHER'S NOTE
This is a work of fiction. Names, characters, places and incidents either are the
product of the author's imagination or are used fictitiously, and any resemblance
to actual persons, living or dead, events, or locales is entirely coincidental.
ISBN: 0-670-85329-1
LIBRARY OF CONGRESS CATALOGING IN PUBLICATION DATA AVAILABLE

Printed in the United States of America
Set in Sabon

THE RUSSIAN GIRL

ONE

The man who was acting as chairman of the small assembly, though of course he was called something else, seemed about to conclude the proceedings. 'So when it surfaces at the overall objectives forum,' he said, 'I'll give 'em what I take to be the general view, that as a body we're right in there pitching in the tradition of supplying the needs of society, but that there is a minority position which I'll call upon . . . Dick to address, and then you sock it to 'em, Dick. Is that agreeable to everybody?'

The speaker had spoken in what were once known as cultured or cultivated tones, diversified by an occasional moment of roughness, when he would throw in a colloquialism, if not a piece of what he took to be fashionable jargon or current patois. Chair-of-department Hallett felt he had better not talk here in his natural style, that of an old-fashioned academic, any more than he could have afforded to wear a jacket and tie, so he fancied at least, or to have shaved off his beard.

From where he was sitting at the long table, a couple of places down from its head, naturally, Hallett caught the eye of a short-haired, moustached young man in a sleeveless undervest that revealed an irregular cylinder of bangles piled up one arm. The eye of his that Hallett had caught, while the other wavered towards the ceiling a metre above their heads, had an aggrieved look, but that was standard.

'Yes, Duncan,' said Hallett, 'would there be some additional . . . do you have a beef?' Now and then the patois took on a mildly disrespectful edge.

'This is not a representative gathering.'

'Ah, you mean Jenkins isn't here. But he never was going to be here. He's off, the lucky – '

'As you know I do not mean Jenkins. My point is that among those qualified no women are in attendance.'

1

'Indeed. Er, they appear to have played hookey.'

'Eh? I understand they took a collective decision to boycott this gathering.'

'You're saying they've stayed away as distinct from not coming. I see. I clock it. All four of them?'

'Grant-Fellowes has never recognised this gathering.'

Managing just in time to identify the verbal tandem as a surname and to recall from distant memory the scowling female face that went with it, Hallett said, 'Quite so,' and hastily added, 'But there's enough of us rolled up to, er, validate the proceedings, know what I mean?'

'Affirmative. Only wanted the record straight.'

'Okay. Right. Check. Will do. Anything else?'

Evidently there was not, for the time being at least. The meeting broke up. The young man who had said his say gave a perceptible smile beneath his tubular moustache and his singlet was really quite clean, considering.

Or so Hallett might have said if put to it. As it was he waited a moment and asked an older man, the one he had earlier addressed as Dick, to stay and have a drink with him. 'I'm as sorry as ever about calling you Dick, Richard,' he added when they were alone. 'One has to be careful about élitism here. Or have I said that before?'

'Why isn't your beard élitist?' asked Richard Vaisey. 'I may not have said that before but I have thought it. After all, none of them, that lot, have one. A weak whisky and water if I may.'

'Certainly. Well, they expect it, you see, my beard. It shows I'm out of date.'

'What about me? Surely I'm out of date?'

'Oh yes, don't worry about that, but your case is different. You're out of date because you know a lot. They really think you do, Richard.'

'You don't mean they respect me for it?'

'Of course not, but they don't mind. They take it for granted, they've learnt to live with it. Every department is likely to include somebody who knows a lot, even now. You get that, as they say.'

The two had walked over to the small private suite that adjoined the administrative office-cum-conference-room. Here, in the style of a local-government potentate, Tristram Hallett could have offered his guest a specially cooked and served meal

2

as well as a drink, could have run with no great trouble to a shower, a shampoo, a shave, indeed every facility for a sexual romp, if anybody could have seriously felt like such a thing within the walls of the London Institute of Slavonic Studies. These luxurious appointments, unused by Hallett except for occasions like the present, were the result of a bygone surge of funding that the present decade would never see approached. The authorities wondered what to do about them and meanwhile huddled new senior lecturers into a sort of partitioned common-room.

Hallett settled himself with his drink in or on one of the grossly fat lounge chairs, with cylindrical arms like plastic-covered bolsters, that seemed to offer themselves at such times. Opposite him Richard Vaisey did much the same, though to sit there properly, shoulders against back of seat, a man would have had to have thighs a couple of metres long.

With a glance that deterred all banter, Hallett said, 'I take it you will actually be telling the – what are we supposed to call it? – the overall objectives meeting that your overall objective is the retention of full study of Russian texts in the original for all A and B candidates?'

'In Russian. Of course I will, Tristram. What else?'

'Nothing else. Of course. I was merely raising the point.'

'You mean in the hope of getting me to think again? Change my mind?'

'No, also of course. Just for me to have a brief gloom about the *overall* look-out. With somebody civilised in attendance. Whatever you do or say – even you, Richard –, in fifteen years or less Russian texts as such will be read by a tiny minority of students here, if by any at all. Or don't you accept that even now?'

'The old system should see me out, then, especially if I go at fifty-five.'

'Richard. Please. Consider which is better and by how much.' At this stage it seemed likely that Hallett would have sprung up and paced the room, or some of its vast expanse, if that had seemed possible, but in fact he merely thrashed impotently about on or in his chair for a short interval. 'Damn it,' he continued. 'Anyway. Try to pretend you haven't heard it all before. It is not just very slightly better, it is a great deal better that some young people should read *Crime and Punishment* in English than not read it at all, have no acquaintance with as much as its title, which will infallibly be the state of affairs everywhere else but here and a relatively few other such places.'

'The knowledge they'll have will be of information only.'

'Oh, a little more than that, surely, at a place like this. And the information in this case is interesting and important. So much so that the odd one might go on to read the book in Russian.'

'Having learnt the language at one of those crash-course joints, presumably.' Richard drained his glass. 'You know as well as I do that every word Dostoevsky writes is written in a way only he can write it. A translation, even the best imaginable, has got to leave all that out.'

'Then may I ask you what you were doing when you translated Alexander Blok?'

'Well, one thing was uniquely reinforcing the truth of what I've just said. And hang on, Tristram. Don't you – surely you hate the thought of little duffers reading a Russian classic in English and telling themselves they've done it, they've got it, they know it, when all they've got and know is a . . . A what? A pale – distorted – shrivelled ghost of the reality. Or perhaps they don't think they actually know it but they know *about* it. My God. I'm sorry, I had to say it even though I know you've . . .'

'Heard it all before, even if in a more temperate style. Yes.' This time, groaning to himself, Hallett writhed to and fro to more purpose than before and eventually succeeded in heaving himself upright. 'A small one before you depart. Yes, and I always tell you you're wasting words. Nobody, however learned, however wise, can stand in the way of regress. Or have I said that before too?'

'You mean I ought to just give up, do you?'

Hallett was in the middle of denying it when the door to the landing opened briskly and a small fair man in his late twenties came in, knocking on it in passing. This was the Jenkins mentioned earlier, the most junior teaching member of the department.

'Hallo, Neil,' said Hallett equably. 'We all thought you'd gone.'

'I very nearly have. Next stop Heathrow, stop after that good old Mockba. I just popped in for an early stiffener before the journey. And to say good-bye, of course.'

'You're lucky to have caught us,' said Richard.

'Yes, I am so sorry I missed the meeting.' Neil Jenkins spoke with a private-sector accent, and only his irreducible academic record had atoned for it sufficiently to let him in here. 'How did it go? I see you both escaped undamaged.'

'You'll get a copy of the minutes,' said Hallett.

'Oh, we still have those, do we? Anyway, there's no hurry as far as I'm concerned. I have six weeks of glorious freedom before me.'

'That's a funny way of talking about where you're going,' said Richard.

Before answering, Neil Jenkins put down on a low narrow table the drink he had been handed, then judged his distance to the nearest overweight chair and propelled himself through the air on to it. With this action went some of his rapid laughter, which he constantly gave vent to. More of it came as he looked from Richard to Hallett and back again, though in a manner hard to resent. 'Maybe,' he said. 'Maybe. I'm making careful preparations to be taken completely by surprise.'

'Are you staying in Moscow or moving about?' asked Hallett.

'Trip to Kiev, didn't I say? Yes, should be fun all round. The only fly in the ointment is that I'll miss the gorgeous Danilova.' After a short silence and a couple of syllables of his laughter, Jenkins went on, 'Anna Danilova, poetess, I mean of course poet. Surely you knew she was over here?'

'Oh, her,' said Hallett. 'That whizz-kid.'

'According to what I hear her whizzing days are over. She's respectable now. Solid body of achievement kind of thing.'

'Who says so?'

'I don't know, Richard,' said Jenkins, looking from one to the other again. 'People. Ones who aren't such sticklers for merit as you are, I imagine. Yes, but is she any *good*, is he any *good*. It's no business of mine, but don't you sometimes wonder if you're missing something?'

There was no reply. Hallett said, 'I shouldn't be surprised if we ask her to give a reading, since she's here,' and shortly after that Jenkins made his farewells and left.

'You must admit he's quite fun. And he does know rather a lot about Pushkin.'

'Gladly,' said Richard, 'but I'm still glad I'm not going to be responsible for him in Moscow.'

'Can't you remember being that age yourself? Everybody over forty seemed not so much old as unbelievably set in his ways. Which reminds me to go on at you about not caving in over your Russian texts but not being inflexible either. Start thinking about saving something from the wreck while it's still there to save. You must learn to roll with the punch, as I believe it's called.'

'That's appeasement. And it doesn't even work.'

'Maybe not. Well, the best of luck, Winston.' For some reason, Hallett's beard looked specially grotesque at that moment. 'The trouble is you haven't got the people behind you.'

'What people?'

'And you won't have me behind you, well, me not agreeing with you but not trying to stop you, for ever. I mean I'm not going to be where I am for ever. In fact, further from for ever than you know. Damn it. I'm sorry, Richard, I'm trying to tell you I'll probably be gone by the end of the year, certainly before the end of next.'

'Not health, I hope?'

'No. Well, only partly.'

'I'm sorry too, Tristram.' Richard was sorry. He had got used to Hallett in eleven years in the job and admired him for having stuck to his own set of principles.

'Thank you. I'll let you know more about dates, about reasons, when things are more settled. Anyway, as far as you're concerned, after that, when I'm gone, look out. It's very hard to imagine a new head of department who'll keep his hands off your Russian-writers-in-Russian arrangements.'

'Or her hands.'

'Her hands particularly. Oh, before I forget, there's a message for you to pick up at the data dissemination centre or whatever they call the porter's lodge these days.'

A few minutes later, after a downward lift-journey that gave mysterious views of academic life on other levels, Richard was moving across a narrow stone-paved court towards the front gate. His rather tall, rather dark, serious-looking figure, head lowered as usual, reached the entrance to the lodge under the clock-turret. Here he looked up to catch sight of two girls, evidently students, unknown to him, approaching from the street. One was no more than a blur, the other a blonde with long sleek hair and a tightly cut light-blue skirt. At that moment, a

6

lorry rattling past a dozen metres away let out a loud snort or whimper or other noise unusual for a lorry. Richard's attention was distracted from the blonde girl long enough for her to have walked past him before he could focus on her again. It was true that the light-blue skirt did most for her when viewed from the rear, but all the same he felt a premonitory chill of age. Only forty-six, and a tooting lorry was enough to get his eyes off something as obviously good as that. Ah, once a full-scale crash would not have caused a flicker. Or was it nothing but a sign of age to think so? Richard shook his head and turned into the lodge.

Inside, under another low ceiling, though this one was of more antiquity, he was faced by a middle-aged female hunk of death-camp-guard material in uniform, though mercifully without headdress.

'Met again, my lass,' he said, quoting Housman uncomprehended, unheard. The portress foul to see gave no immediate sign of noticing that he was there at all, but quite soon brought out from some recess a sheet of mini-stationery on which an unskilled hand had written a string of stuff about Meeting and was it Poetry and Russian and a telephone number that had enough assorted digits in it to be at least believable.

'What time did this come?' asked Richard.

The woman's eyes were busy on the shelves under the counter. 'Morning,' she seemed to say. 'About . . .'

'I was in my office most of the morning and there's always a secretary on call.'

'I haven't been on long,' said the portress, smiling triumphantly as she brought into view a piece of food whose wrapper she started tearing off into mid-air.

'But you still do relay calls to the departments, don't you, from here?'

With her mouth half-closed over a length of caramel and nuts she shook her head, not necessarily in denial, and waved her hand from side to side, indicating that the question should be considered closed. Very likely she was no longer even on.

Without further inquiry Richard crumpled up the piece of paper and tidily stowed it in a pocket for disposal later. He felt there were already more than enough Russian meetings and poetry in his life. 'Thank you,' he said nevertheless. Teaching

7

staff were advised to be co-operative with non-technical staff, which meant in practice always saying the minimum, or teaching staff might find no message at all next time. The member of non-technical staff at present behind the counter tidily brushed a few crumbs off it with her fingers and nodded sharply in dismissal.

It was June 1990, cold and damp, with dirty puddles drying reluctantly on the pavement. Soon Richard was walking down busy Caret Street, WC2, towards the horrible but almost convenient underground labyrinth where his Viotti TBD rested, and not so soon after that he was fitfully driving it up the same even busier street towards the smart end-of-terrace Regency house in W9 he lived in. He was going to sell the car at the start of the winter term to save money, postpone heart-attacks, etc., as he had intended every working day for several years now.

On arrival he put the TBD in what had been most of his front garden and let himself in at the front door. It was warm in the house, and the ceilings were higher than at the Institute, and there was none of the dejected, unfinished, comfortless feeling to be encountered there, and today as always he was grateful for that. None the less, all was not precisely as he would have had it.

To start with, the temperature, though indeed higher than that outside, was not that much higher. Because of the position of the month in the calendar, the central heating was not turned on. Richard made no move to go and turn it on, and any such attempt on his part would quite likely have sent the ambient temperature into the 30°s C, possibly caused an explosion. He had never been taught how to work it, or had never learnt, and even if he had he would no more have considered such interference than, say, trying to get the hot-water supply back when it had switched itself off between the hours of one and five, am and pm alike. No, Richard left everything in the least like that to his wife, from the various types of heating and of breakfast cereal right up to fixing the holiday and seeing the accountant.

The name of Richard's wife was Cordelia, and he went straight across the lofty hall and shouted it to announce his homecoming. Although he had never found it a particularly easy or natural name to shout, and to yell it would not have been right, he had his usual fair crack at it. The usual reply floated back down, faint, high-pitched, more like a forlorn cry than a greeting; it was known that Cordelia could not shout.

As usual at such times, Richard now went to his study on the ground floor. This was a small room with a small desk on which, apart from a typewriter and items associated with it, like typescripts, there stood short piles of books and other printed material in the Russian language or dealing with some aspect of it or the literature written in it. More such books, many larger, some in uniformly bound series, crowded the carpentered bookshelves round the walls, and there were more of them on further shelves in part of the hall and along the short passage beside the staircase. Nothing superfluous was to be seen, no pictures or photographs, no ornaments, not even a book jacket, however drab, for Richard always pulled these off at the first opportunity, just retaining the flap if it had information on it.

At the moment his attention was on a black-inked note on top of his typewriter, laid there as ever by Cordelia and written in her firm, distinctive, regular hand. It was a hand that from a distance resembled medieval script in a good state of preservation and, seen closer to, was about as easy to read. But it was clearly a telephone message. Other households had answering machines to save this kind of trouble, but Cordelia had never warmed to the idea.

Richard could make out enough of the present message to be reasonably sure that what he had before him was another version, corrupt in a different way, of the one handed him back at the Institute and soon afterwards consigned to a litter-bin in Caret Street. The text of this meant as little to him as that of the other, but the telephone digits, transnumerated out of Cordelia's figure-cipher, seemed confirmed. Richard listened for a moment, heard nothing but heavy traffic roaring and snarling past thirty metres from his study window, and reluctantly picked up the telephone.

Soon a grunt answered him.

'I got a message to ring this number.' Caution, innate and acquired, kept him from saying more.

'Who is it you are wanting to speak to, please?'

This was said haltingly and in a Russian accent, not a heavy one but helping to suggest perhaps that English was not often ventured into. Richard repeated in Russian what he had first said, and after hesitation a minimum about who he was.

'You are saying you're English?'

'Yes, of course I'm English.'

'One moment.'

The tone was sternly conspiratorial. There followed a minute or so of the underground-brawl effect of a conversation on the far side of a blocked telephone mouthpiece, making Richard feel now that he had enough trouble with the British without ever speaking to another Russian, especially when nothing continued to happen.

Then a young woman's voice spoke in good Russian, probably from Moscow, though he would not have claimed to be good on accents. 'I'm sorry, would you say your name again?'

Richard said it again.

'Ah, it is indeed you, Dr Vaisey, I wasn't sure. How wonderful, I've managed to find you at last. Allow me to introduce myself. My name – '

The dialling-tone sounded. Richard hung up and sat at his desk for a moment with several thoughts in his head, one of which was that he would leave till later any decision about trying later, another that he had rather fancied the girl's voice. Finally . . . The call had been cut off not by her but by another, no doubt the earlier speaker, anyway someone who had not wanted her to give her name. Why not? Well, that was the Russian character for you – secretive under the Czars and before, under Lenin and Stalin and their successors and no doubt for a lot of the future. So there it was. For the moment.

Richard sat on a moment longer at his desk, inertly hankering after a simpler world, until he heard Cordelia in the drawing-room, or realised that she would be there. Actually it was her drawing-room, not that there was another one elsewhere in the house belonging to him, nor that he was allowed in the existing one only on special occasions or never, but it was hers as regards its décor and contents, her choice from pink-washed walls covered with drawings and engravings of classical ruins to the multi-period furniture, heavy crimson curtains and trailing greenery. Paid for by her, too, like the house itself and its appurtenances and most of the other objects within it, whether permanent, like a bath, or transitory, like a bottle of burgundy. Richard paid for the TV and sound systems and ran the car.

He was unfeignedly glad of and grateful for his wife's money, and very seldom bothered to complain, even mutely, that it could have timed its arrival to accord with his moral repute better. Cordelia had inherited it from her mother before marrying him, true, and though it was no less true that the marriage had been fixed earlier, and that Mummy had been in the best of health at fifty-four when she went down with a few hundred others somewhere in the Rockies, these were considerations other people overlooked. But he could shrug off all that. What took rather more in the way of shrugging was the fact that his wife's ownership of this money led without a break, as they said of linked movements in concert works, into her control of what it was spent on, or not spent on as the case sometimes was.

One thing it was not spent on was Richard's preferred brand of China tea, which was said or assumed to be more expensive than other teas and was certainly not available at every shop that sold tea. In the first couple of years of the marriage, Richard would probably have offered to pick up a packet in the course of his daily round, or even have fetched one home without previous announcement. Not today. He could visualise very clearly how Cordelia would have been stricken by remorse and self-reproach at the extremity he had been driven to, and a little hurt as well. After that, she would have explained to her husband, as carefully as if the point had been a difficult one or quite new to him, that it made life so much simpler all round if just one person (herself) took care of and assumed the responsibility for everything to do with the running of the house, checking larder and store-cupboards, making up the orders, paying the bills. Especially that. But of course Cordelia would make a real effort to get hold of some of that tea – what was it called again? No, well, he said to himself, she had never had much of a head for names.

Some, even a fair amount, of her money had gone into her considerable wardrobe, not only of course the literal piece of supposedly William IV furniture in the marital bedroom, which was so considerable that it made his own clothes-cupboard (*c.* 1935) look rather paltry, but what she wore on her back and elsewhere. This afternoon the ensemble included a white polo-sweater, plain and thinnish but shiny and rich-looking, a skirt of

11

a rough suede-like material in turquoise, and Italian shoes with the manufacturer's initial attached in gold. The gold motif was picked up in the heavy bracelets Cordelia wore on her wrists or, more precisely, over the cuffs of her sweater. She was fond of gold bracelets and sometimes said they were her one extravagance.

As he opened the door to join her, she immediately looked up at him with a smile of pure greeting and affection. One of her strong points for Richard was that she was always glad to see him. Another, stronger yet, was her looks, most noticeable in substantial eyes of an almost royal blue and a glowing fair complexion, elements well supported by her bodily shape. Richard had thought her beautiful at first sight, long before he had considered whether she might have had a mother at all, let alone a rich one. He still thought so now she was forty-one and, what was something altogether different, now he had been married to her for nearly ten years.

She jumped up from her chair and, with a small click of bracelets, held out her arms to him while he still had some ground to cover. On his nearer approach she kissed and hugged him warmly, which he enjoyed and thought was good, too, but also made him wonder slightly, as sometimes before, how she would greet him on his return from being shipwrecked and adrift for a few days off Alaska, say. No more than a thought.

They sat down with the tea-tray on a low table between them and she poured him tea out of her pink-and-white, mostly white, teapot. It was China tea of the sort she liked and one he quite liked, and she filled his cup about two-thirds full. He would have preferred it about seven-eighths full and had said so a couple of times, but Cordelia had explained that that was how Chinese people served their tea, the way she served it, so that was that.

'How was your day?' she asked him, as he had strongly suspected she would.

'Oh, very little to report. Departmental meeting. Tristram Hallett gave me a drink afterwards and had one or two things to tell me about next year.'

Cordelia evidently thought she had heard a complete news item, for she went on without interval, 'That Greek or whatever he was who came last week was no good at all. The tank was boiling its head off just as I was finishing my lunch. It was nearly exploding when I managed to get to the switch.'

'Did that turn the central heating off as well?'

'Darling, surely you know they're not connected. The central heating was off already. Why, are you cold?'

'Well . . .'

'If you are then put on a *woolly*.' She pronounced it approximately whoo-lee in her curious accent, other points of which included giving unvoiced consonants a touch of voicing (Greeg, eggsbloding, nod gonnegded) and unstressed vowels some of their full value (hee, wozz, too thee switch/sweedge). Never having cared to ask her about it, Richard had had fantasies of an Andorran nanny, a childhood in a posh Albanian household that had left no other mark, before concluding that Cordelia just spoke Cordelian, a pronunciational idiolect. However derived, it had puzzled him pleasantly at first, then charmed him rather. After a time he had stopped noticing it at all more than a couple of times a day, and for years had given up speculating what speech-sounds she might make if, for example, he were to creep up behind her and fire a loaded revolver past her ear.

Now, holding her teacup not by the handle and looking up at him over it as she drank from it, she said, 'Did you manage to find somebody to have dinner with tonight? You know, so I won't have to bore you with Crumpy and my other old Newnham buddies?'

'Yes, I know. I'm going out with Crispin and Freddie.'

'Oh, of course, you told me, how silly [see-lee] of me, it completely slipped my poor old mind. But darling, do tell me, who's Freddie?'

'Crispin's wife. Short for Frederica. I honestly thought you knew that.'

'*Goodness* how posh. Of course I remember now. But you must forgive me, Richard, if I can't manage to keep myself up to absolutely one hundred per cent about everything to do with Crispin *all* the time.'

'I quite understand,' said Richard, again speaking what he took to be the truth.

Crispin Radetsky was the brother of the Godfrey of that surname, Cordelia's divorced husband. He, Godfrey, had been moving out of the picture before Richard came into it, but there had been enough overlap for the two to bump against each other

13

once or twice. Godfrey had not, could not have, appealed to Richard greatly, but his brother Crispin rather had, to start with as a fellow to play tennis with, soon in a more general range. Needless to say, Cordelia was closely aware of their friendship, and had done a wonderful job of conveying to Richard her feelings of pain, betrayal and suchlike at her present husband's association with the more than suspect brother of the swine who had gone off with a floozie, or trollop, or fortune-huntress and left her, Cordelia, high and dry. The wondrousness of the job had lain not just in its intensity and persistence but in its being effected partly by psychic osmosis, it must have been, or gamma radiation, not in words, though they had had and still had a fair look-in too. Today's quota, not yet fulfilled, was well up to standard.

It was Cordelia's habit to be bewilderingly deft and expert at things other people might find laborious in some way, like getting an ostensibly full foreign hotel to give her a room or opening a postal packet. With things other people found straightforward, or fancied to be straightforward, however, she often took a long time and full concentration, like pouring hot water from a jug into a teapot. It seemed the quantity added and the rate of pouring were highly critical. Another man might have laughed with some affection at such performances, while probably taking care to keep his laughter to himself, but not Richard, who after nearly ten years of it no longer noticed them. And perhaps only someone with a really great sense of humour could ever have found anything funny in the way she held her replenished cup in *both* hands, neither of them quite touching the handle, and went on holding it like that between sips. But Richard had stopped noticing that too.

'Of course you and Crispin have always got on so well, haven't you? Took to each other right away, I remember.'

'Yes, I suppose we did.'

'Darling, would you mind terribly if I asked you something?'

'No,' said Richard, breathing altogether normally.

'I mean I must have asked you it before, I know I have. It's just I would so like to ask you again.'

Some time went by, during which the windows rattled at the passage of some leviathan of the road and Cordelia, having put her cup down, reached out her hand to her husband across the

14

tea-table, wordlessly and with her eyes fixed on his. The gesture was made in such a way that a mere acquaintance of hers might have wondered if he was supposed to seize the hand and cover it with kisses, but Richard knew what was expected of him and placed his own empty cup in it. She had merely been stressing the importance of the coming question, which was delivered not long after his two-thirds-refilled cup.

'Awfully silly of me darling, but I'd hate to think of you and Crispin discussing me and things coming up that would go straight back to that ghastly Godfrey. There is nothing like that, is there?'

'Absolutely not,' began Richard firmly. 'Grizbin, I mean Crispin, he never mentions your name to me.' Very rarely, anyway, though he uses expressions like 'your good lady' and 'the old bag' quite a bit. 'I expect I refer to you now and then in passing, the way one does – still, we never *discuss* you,' he finished firmly, but lying his head off by now.

'Thank you, my darling,' said Cordelia with one of her best bright-blue gazes. 'I just wanted to hear you say it.' Then she suddenly went, 'Ooh!'

'What is it?' he said, trying to sound startled.

'Just, you did get that message I left on your typewriter?'

'Oh yes, thanks. It was some – '

'Most mysterious. A woman, or a girl, who wanted to know if I spoke *Russian*. She had a Russian I suppose it was accent herself you could have cut with a knife. Only a few words but I'm afraid I didn't get all of it.'

'Never mind, you got enough.'

Closing her eyes and raising the brows, Cordelia said, 'She sounded quite, well, you know, slinky.'

'How do you mean?'

'Well, sexy if you like. Just a sexy kind of voice.'

'Anyway, I shan't be meeting its owner. Mad as a hatter.'

Cordelia at once lost all interest in what just before had been most mysterious. Over the next few minutes Richard thought once or twice of how she had made the very idea of her speaking Russian seem a bizarre, outlandish one. She had not always found it so. Early in their association, at the impressionable age of thirty-one, she had said she would find out for herself what there was in these Russian writers that had cast such a terrific spell on him, and with his guidance had set about reading the works of Tolstoy, Dostoevsky (of course she had read them quite a bit before, though not properly), Turgenev and others, perforce reading them in translation, but that was understood as not much more than a helpful preliminary to learning to read them in the original. That end-product or project had been suddenly abandoned, removed, heard no more of, about the time of her marriage to Richard. The books from the London Library stood on the shelves while she was so terribly busy with the house, getting into it and being in it. In the end he had returned them himself and, finishing his tea now, remembered the odd sense of humiliation he had felt in doing so.

But now it was time to go, for him to go to his study for an hour or more, for her to go to hers, a rather larger, quieter room on the first floor facing the garden, for however long it might take her to wrap up that day's supply of work to do with the house. Before they went off they kissed again, but not in the same spirit as their earlier hug of greeting. He was totally reminded of how beautiful she was and how wonderful she was, as ever, in that far place where there were no turquoise skirts or half-filled white-and-pink teacups or voicing of unvoiced consonants.

TWO

'But he must have married her for her money,' said Freddie, otherwise Frederica Radetsky.

Her husband shook his head slowly. 'He didn't, though. That's the terrifying thing. But Sandy doesn't want to hear all this.'

'How do you know I don't?' asked Freddie's divorced sister Alexandra, similarly known as Sandy. 'I've never seen much of him, but I've always thought of him as rather an attractive man. Of course I want to hear about him.'

'He's the most frightful stick-in-the-mud,' said Freddie. 'Not a glimmer of a sense of humour.'

'He must have more than a glimmer, to stay married to Cordelia,' said Crispin.

'What's so attractive about Richard?' Freddie asked her sister.

'I didn't say he was *so* attractive. He's just very sexy.'

'Oh God,' said Freddie.

'No, I just mean he looks as if he's keen on sex. Some men are, you know. Just because he knows about verbs and things it doesn't mean he never fancies a nice piece of ass.'

'Oh Christ.'

'And as for stick-in-the-muds, I've got a bit of a special thing about them. They make such a lovely plopping noise when you winkle them out.'

'Sandy, you're disgusting.'

'I think that's quite funny,' said Crispin. 'Anyway, you'd have to be keen on sex to put up with Cordelia for ten minutes. To the threshold of satyromania.'

'I don't see how that would help,' said Freddie, refilling her glass.

'Oh come on, darling,' said Sandy – 'we all know she's

17

absolute murder but you must admit she is gorgeous. Can't you see it?'

'I won't see it. What a *name* for Christ's sake – Cordelia, or Nggornndeenlia as I suppose she calls it. What's wrong with Cordy? Or Deely? See you down the boozer, Cordy. She'd vanish in a puff of smoke.'

'Darling, you do realise you're going out to dinner later, don't you?' Sandy was two years older than her sister. 'Just . . .'

'And those *bracelets*.'

'I know, I've seen them.' Sandy turned to Crispin. 'What was that just now about Richard not marrying Cordelia for her cash?'

'Oh yes. Quite clear, all that, or it gets clear in due course. Brother Godfrey gets fed up with Cordelia because no offspring, at least he says that's the reason. Our Pop gets fed up too – well, he's an immigrant, isn't he? So when Godfrey finds Nancy, the sort of barmaid type who instantly starts limbering up to bear offspring, he's off straight away. But he's still so cross with Cordelia, you see, that he makes only a crappy little settlement on her and fixes it so it won't be worth her while to go to court for more. I gave him a hand there. These foreigners can be devilish cunning, you know. And nasty with it. So when Richard comes along, he finds her with not very much to eke out the not very much she gets from her Mum, who's another penny-pincher. Like her daughter, I mean.'

'But what was arty Godfrey so cross about?' asked Sandy, rather cross herself, or so it seemed. Normally she had a pleased but rather hungry expression, putting one in mind of a rather amorous, very good-looking rabbit or other little animal. Dissatisfaction, like curiosity, visited her rarely. 'I mean you can't blame a girl if she can't get pregnant. At least you couldn't when I was at school. Far from it. Thought to be jolly handy, in fact.'

Freddie, a size larger, less blonde and more human in appearance, or perhaps just less devotedly got up, managed to say, 'You can blame this bugger,' before choking slightly on a mouthful of vodka and tonic.

'Yes,' said Crispin, giving his wife a perfunctory pat or two on the back. 'I wondered about that. Godfrey talked about ovulation cycles and such but I always rather suspected he thought that sort of thing would go down better with our Pop than just saying he couldn't stand her any more. Taking it out on her financially could have been just habit.'

'What I couldn't see,' said Freddie, still swallowing and panting, 'was why it took him such an age to decide to pack her in. As you said, ten minutes – '

'Godfrey's a bit of a romantic,' said Crispin. 'Goes with him being an artist and all. I rather fancy he thought she was an aristocrat of some sort and you take your time about getting rid of one of those.'

'*Christ*. Cordelia an *arreezdongrrannd . . .*'

'I know it's a dreadful thing to say.'

'What do you suppose Richard thought he was marrying?' asked Sandy.

'No idea in the world. He won't say, not to me, but I reckon all he was thinking about was getting his – ' The front-door bell sounded. 'That'll be him now. You can ask him yourself.'

Crispin quite enjoyed hearing and seeing his wife and sister-in-law going on in the way they did, a way that might mislead a stranger into mistaking Freddie for unmarried or divorced, Sandy for a wife, he always thought – but a short rest from them was welcome too. A tall figure with an almost military bearing and short-cut light-brown hair, he recalled at first sight an Englishman of special distinction and long lineage, possibly sprung from one of the old landowning families of Northumberland, past the middle of a good career in the Diplomatic or, perhaps nearer the mark these days, an even better one in the City. He certainly looked and sounded like the kind of actor chosen to play that kind of part on the screen, as befitted the son of a Prague businessman of partly Austrian descent who had got out not in 1956 or 1948 or even 1938 but the patrician year of 1933. Crispin was occasionally thought to be Jewish, to which he would say that an enterprising Czech in England had no need to be Jewish. Then, or a little later, he would sometimes mention his great-uncle's commission in the Imperial lancers, but never his right to the title of count, a rather overpopulated distinction in his judgement, and hardly needed anyway by a fashionable QC with a dozen centimetres in *Who's Who*.

Crossing the austerely furnished hall of his enviable house

near the Boltons, Crispin opened its front door in person, as he often did to expected friends. The expected Richard proved to have on an unfamiliar and rather peculiar pair of thin-rimmed glasses. Crispin thought they gave him a defiant look.

'Did you drive here?'

'Like any sensible man about to dine with you I took a taxi.'

'So the shades were to help you to read the latest *Proceedings of the Slavonic Society*.'

'Precisely that,' said Richard gamely, whipping off the novelties and stowing them away.

'How are things at home?'

'More or less as usual.'

'Oh, I see.'

'You mean, "You poor bugger," don't you?'

'Well . . .'

At once Richard veered off to one side, not because he was affronted but in order to make for the downstairs loo. Crispin stood at the half-open door.

'I'm afraid we've got Freddie's sister Sandy with us.'

'So you said over the telephone. Is it so terrible? I've met her before, twice I think.'

'Some men seem to have found her quite attractive. Rather a large number of men as a matter of fact.'

'Nothing very terrible so far.'

'She's just been saying she thinks you're rather an attractive man. She said she thought you looked, er, rather attractive.'

'Better and better. I remember you telling me she was divorced, don't I? That's right, from a chap who used to dress up as a parlourmaid.'

'No no no, you're mixing him up with someone else. Sandy's husband used to dress up as a nursemaid. Her nursemaid, so to speak.' Crispin noticed that Richard, having urinated, was now rinsing his hands at the basin. 'I always wonder why you do that. Not that you're the only one by a long chalk. I tell people I keep mine so clean I ought by rights to wash my hands *before* I pee. It's an old – '

'Crispin, are we going to go on chattering here all night? If you want to borrow some money for God's sake come out and say so. I can let you have anything up to five quid without turning a hair.'

20

Crispin laughed carefully at this, enough, as he hoped, to encourage Richard to go on trying to be funny without making him think that his present effort was the kind of thing there ought to be more of. When he had finished laughing he said, 'Sandy said something about going on for drinks somewhere after dinner. Freddie and I don't want to go with her.'

'Drinks where?'

'No idea. Wouldn't be very far.'

'But you and Freddie don't want to go. I see.'

'Whether you do or not, I should imagine Sandy would be quite glad of your company. Doubly so in the circumstances. Of course if you've got a date with Anna Karenina or somebody we shall all quite understand.'

The last part of this came out a little huffily. Crispin seemed irritated at Richard's ungracious reception of his well-meant pimping efforts. Or mostly well-meant. If, as was rather unlikely, something happened between Richard and Sandy, her behaviour would be under improved surveillance and she might take to dropping in less often on her younger sister. Sandy tended to have a dodgy effect on Freddie, over-exciting her, disposing her to drink more, generally sapping her sense of discipline.

What with these cross-currents, together with Freddie's intermittent attempts to bring Cordelia up in conversation and give her a series of goings-over, Crispin had his work cut out keeping things in order, especially by the time they got to the restaurant. This place was one of the sort that appeared in numerous eating-out manuals embellished with crowns, stars and tiny pictures of cutlery, chef's hats, cheeses and coffee-pots. It was a small room furnished by the look of it with the odd wooden chairs and tables left over at the closure of some penurious school. In one corner, a doorless wardrobe that offered sight of a collapsed pile of lager tins and several large slivers of window-glass, carefully propped up for future use, heightened the academic atmosphere. A Labour MP recognisable from television and one or two progressive journalists were to be seen.

'Sorry about this,' said Crispin. 'I should have cottoned on when I read in the *Spectator* that somebody called Marc, who I took to be the chef, derives his philosophy of cuisine from the poetry of Dylan Thomas, in which, it will be remembered, many adjectives meet their nouns for the first time ever. What is it, my love?'

'That's just the trouble,' said Freddie, who had been chewing a mouthful for some time, pausing reflectively now and then – 'I can't make out what it is. If I could, it's on the cards I might be able to enjoy it.'

'You're not supposed to enjoy it. That's not the idea. You've put yourself in the path of a gastronomic experience.'

'The fellow, what's his name, Marc, well Marc sets out to challenge your palate, not flatter it,' said Richard. Saying it made him feel a bit ingratiating, but he wanted to stay in the conversation and go on being noticed by Sandy, who had been looking at him for a couple of minutes in silence and with what might have been an inviting expression. He was ready with more stuff attributable to Marc, about imaginativeness, innovativeness and the like, which he rather hoped he would not have to use.

'I suppose . . . you must have been here before,' she eventually said, getting or trying to put something into it he could not identify.

'I don't think so, but if I had I'm sure I should have – '

'Nggornndeenlia,' said Freddie, swallowing at last, 'would never consent to come to a bloody box-room like this. She likes marble halls with the menu in joined-up writing like, you know, on a, you know . . .'

'I know,' said Crispin. 'Like handwriting.'

'I thought that sort of thing had gone out with, I don't know. Black-and-white films,' said Richard. 'It just goes to show – '

He would have done better not to speak just then. 'If you ask me, there's far too much money around in this sodding world,' Freddie said to him, like her sister loading her words with a message not spelt out in them, though a different one. 'Would you agree with that?'

Richard hesitated. 'Well, not a hundred per cent,' he said.

'No, I should imagine not. Tell me, Richard,' said Freddie, perhaps beginning to spell out her message, 'do you ever take, er, your wife out to dinner? Or let me rephrase that – do the two of you go out to dinner in a restaurant together much?'

'No, not much, now you come to mention it.'

22

'When you do, do you pay by card or cheque? Or does Cordelia – '

'I came across some real money the other day,' said Crispin. 'Frightful swine I was defending for doing something unspeakable to his company's shares. He's got a disc-jockey-sized house down outside Lewes. Quite a decent place it must have been till he got his greasy fingers on it. You know the kind.' Crispin put on his 'not a pretty sight' expression. 'Anyway, much to my disgust and envy, there on the wall was a picture I'd actually seen in a gallery somewhere, probably in Paris.'

'What was it?' asked Richard.

Crispin stared at him for a second. Then he said, 'It was a Van Gogh, "Hyacinths in a Yellow Vase". I expect you know it too, don't you, from books and so on, the way I did?'

'Standing on a blue cloth by a window, is that the one?' Richard was quite good when first pointed in the right direction.

'That's the one.'

'I've never seen it,' said Freddie, looking from one to the other. 'In a book or on a postcard or anywhere.'

'No, well it's not one of the better-known ones, would you say, Crispin?'

'Yes. Yes, I would.'

Apart from Richard's need for a good listener on the subject of Cordelia and Crispin's fascination with what he heard, both enjoyed little conspiracies like the impromptu Van Gogh, blocking Freddie's debouchment into open tirade. To Richard it was not merely something to enjoy, a reassurance that the world had more in it than just Russian, him, Cordelia and other females. Especially just him and Cordelia. So might a lonely nationalist under even a tolerant and enlightened occupying administration be deeply comforted by running across another of his kind.

Sandy had abandoned the conversation by the time the Van Gogh first appeared. Now she said, 'Do you and Cordelia go on holidays together?'

'We used to, but not so much now. She tends to go and I stay at home.'

'Doing what?'

'Well . . . you know, working. What I always do.'

'Don't you ever feel like a change?'

'What for? I have been to quite a few other places in my time and they're never as convenient and interesting as London, and there's nothing to do in them from morning till night except try to enjoy yourself. It amazes me that people decide to live in one place and keep wanting to go somewhere else.'

'Oh well, if you're a workaholic . . .'

She said it not so much like 'eunuch' as like 'MS victim'. Richard saw that he had broken one of Crispin's rules, 'Never talk to a woman about anything that interests you,' and cunningly changed tack. 'I expect you go away quite a lot yourself, don't you?'

'You bet I do, and to the most expensive place available at the time, and if it's amazement you're after you ought to see how keen the people who go there are to go there. And as for enjoying themselves, my God. Especially the men. Well, especially the women too, I suppose.'

'I don't think it would suit me very well.'

'Have you tried it, Richard?'

She lowered her eyelids and when she raised them again it was as if a pair of tiny searchlights or even machine-guns were pointing straight at him. He knew there were plenty of wrong answers to her question as well as right ones, and was sorting through them under adverse conditions when Freddie, who had perhaps caught the last few remarks, butted in again.

'What does Cordelia imagine you're up to this evening?'

'Well, naturally I told her I was coming out with you and Crispin. I didn't know then that Sandy was going to be with us.'

'Do you always tell her where you're going?'

Again Richard hesitated. 'When she's around to be told. Don't most people?' He had never thought about it.

'Anyway, you do. Of course.'

'Have some coffee, darling,' said Crispin.

This revealed what Richard took as a temporary failure of invention. But was it? The thought struck him that he really had no idea, beyond the largest, crudest outlines, of the kind of life Crispin and Freddie led when he was not around. And, a more uncomfortable thought, it had never occurred to him to bother to wonder. So perhaps Crispin was playing two games with him, one in which the pair of them were in some sort of husbands' league, another in which a happily married Crispin entertained himself, and perhaps enjoyed giving some comfort to a poor bugger of a Richard, by the double fiction of the first. Christ, as Freddie would say, that was a notion that could only occur to a man who had read too much Russian literature and watched too little television, gone to too few soccer matches – what was he talking about, *too few* soccer matches? *None*, or none since school, was the fact. And, well, he had listened to too much classical music and too little . . . too little . . . At this point his mind gave up its feeble struggle and he drained his glass of voguish dessert wine and played with dim but fierce thoughts of Armagnac.

Freddie had watched her husband fill her coffee-cup and at once pushed it aside. Now she said, 'I've nothing against you, Richard, please don't get that idea, I think you're sweet and terribly put upon, you poor little thing, it's that bitch Cordelia with her bracelets and all her . . .' A spasm crossed her rather widely separated features and she turned to Crispin and said, 'You're hurting me.'

'What? Hurting you? What would I be thinking of, hurting you?' He spread his hands in what Richard suspected was a Jewish imitation.

'Sod off, you're treading on my foot.'

'Oh my God, I thought it was part of the table-leg. I swear to you – '

'You're still doing it, you bastard. You know perfectly well.'

'Honestly . . .'

Over these minutes Sandy had kept quiet, though she had several times seemed on the brink of some momentous utterance, catching and losing Richard's eye every few seconds. While Crispin called for the bill, a process rather than a single action, Freddie stared round the room with a downcast expression, perhaps at realising she had been finally headed off from her Cordelia theme, perhaps just at her surroundings or the thought of the dinner she had eaten. When Sandy spoke it was in a matter-of-fact tone pitched as if by chance below her sister's hearing.

'I suppose you'll be going back to Crispin's after this?'

'Yes,' said Richard. 'I don't know.'

'What? Early night?'

'No. I don't know.'

25

'Not pissed, are you, darling?'

'No. I wish I was,' he added without thinking. It was not a state he normally favoured, not these days.

'Well, you'll be able to get it where I'm going all right. Drink, that is. Or pissed too if you still feel like it.'

In the middle of another stoppage, Richard caught a glance from Crispin that implied a better appreciation than his own of what was going on – a pathetic bugger of a Russian expert on the point of turning down an excursion with a presumptively available female in it and deciding instead that he had better be getting home to a sort of Mum: unfair, untrue, irresponsible, but deadly. Even then he might have opted for ignominious return to the world of unactivated central heating and shiny white polo-sweaters, if Crispin had not tightened the screw by a peep at his watch, a calculating blink or two and a horrible nod of acceptance and resignation.

It was too much even for Richard. 'Fine then, whenever you're ready,' he told Sandy, and wished too late there had been the chance of working in a fuck or shit or so to lend a touch of earnestness to his affirmation. Ten minutes later, most of them disagreeable ones standing on the crowded, littered pavement, he and she were in a taxi heading for one of the many corners of London he knew nothing much of. Crispin had been impassive at the last, nodding briefly when thanked, eyes averted, but Freddie had earnt a second glance, her expression divided between chagrin at her sister's scooping-up of a man and satisfaction at the vague prospect of damage to Cordelia. Or so Richard had thought. More certainly, Freddie had looked a bit drunk – pissed, rather. Never mind why.

The light inside the taxi was fitful, but there was quite enough of it for him to see that Sandy was looking at him not so fitfully, perhaps with expectation, even the expectation of being grabbed in some way there and then, or any moment. He tried to sort out in his mind their exchange about holidays. Well, in any case, he decided, there would be no sort of grab from him. Like getting pissed, grabs in taxis were to be avoided as having unpredictable consequences.

'I must apologise for Freddie's behaviour,' Sandy suddenly said.

'Oh, that's all right, I mean, you mean . . .'

'She's never actually let on, but I think she wanted to marry arty Godfrey. Did you ever meet him?'

'Of course I did, more than once. Thanks.'

'I'm not sure I care for Godfrey myself.'

'Cordelia hates him, naturally.'

'He's probably not so bad. I hardly know him.'

'Tell me, er, Sandy, that second wife of his, Nancy isn't it, was she supposed to have been on the look-out at all for a fellow with a bit of cash? If you've heard.'

'No, painfully respectable, though apparently you might not think so to look at her. Well-off folks and all that. Why?'

'I just wondered.'

'They've got three children now.'

'Oh, really?'

A silence fell in the taxi while Richard waited to find out whether Sandy was going to ask him about Cordelia's continuing failure to produce a child and, if so, what form her question would take. There was a swishing, slithering noise as the cab-driver slid aside his communicating window, to ask for further directions, possibly, or to try to find out whether there was an interesting reason why the silence had fallen. If the former he thought better of it, but left the window where it was.

'Crispin said he thinks Godfrey married Cordelia because he thought she was an aristocrat,' said Sandy.

'I see.'

'Oh . . . Do you think she's an aristocrat?'

'I've no idea. I don't know about things like that.'

'What? You're missing a terrific lot in life if you don't know about things like that, *any* things like that.'

'I dare say I am.'

'Do you mind if I ask you something, Richard?'

'No,' he lied. By now he would have minded being asked almost anything he could think of. He was also disconcerted by this filching of Cordelia's style of interrogation.

'It's frightful cheek, but what was it that made you *marry* Cordelia? I can see why a lot of men might – '

By now, too, Richard had begun to regret quite keenly his surrender to the whole idea of going off with Sandy. 'I married her because she was and is the best fuck I've ever had,' he said, and in no confidential tone either.

27

Sandy appeared startled. 'Really,' she said, 'I don't think there's any need to put it like that.'

'Don't you? I do. In fact I'm quite certain of it.'

'I thought you were supposed to be a professor or something.'

'I am a professor or something. But not an absent-minded one, not about everything all the time anyway. It might help you to know I don't come from anywhere round here, but from a place some way up the map on the left-hand side. That's the way they tend to – '

'There's no need to boast about it.'

'I've never thought it was anything to boast about. I was also going to say I thought you were, well, if not an aristocrat then an old married woman, not a . . . not somebody's maiden aunt.'

As he said it he realised that she had probably never heard of a maiden aunt, but left the reference unclarified. Turning his head, he set about looking vigorously out of the window. He knew he was not young or drunk enough to evade forethought by telling himself he was just being carried along by events and *she* would do nicely if it came to it and never mind if not. He knew too he had been a bit like that at one stage and it had come to it once or twice in a blue moon. Then he had met Cordelia and found himself still being carried along by events, only much, much more slowly than before, and with more complications. In other words, what he had just revealed about her charms was true enough but only half the story, the more straightforward half. Early in their marriage, more out of habit than anything else, he had reverted to the old mode another once or twice or even more, though not for a long time now. All the same, he liked to think his eye for a pretty face and allied areas was unimpaired, even if he had to admit that the discomfort he felt at such sights, while still keen, had become transient, short-lived, as the former cigarette-smoker finds his periods of nicotine-hunger have grown briefer with the passing years.

Sandy had a pretty face in a kind of small way. He remembered noticing it particularly when they first met. It had very good cheekbones and teeth, on the numerous side as the latter were. And, if Crispin was to be believed, she found him, Richard, attractive, or at least rather attractive. Did she really? Was he? It was one of those questions that, like the ultimate standing of the works of Nekrasov, he had confidently expected

28

to have established for all practical purposes about the time he graduated from Oxford, but which still popped up now and again as fresh and unsettled as ever. Of course *Cordelia* thought he was attractive, or said she did. One thing about her saying so was the way she threw in an 'I think' or an 'according to me' along with it, and another, or part of the same, was the slight emphasis she would give the personal pronoun. So, left to themselves, how would other women react? Scream the place down, or want to? Burst out laughing? Richard had never seen matters quite like that before, but by the time he swung round on Sandy again all he did was say eagerly, 'What sort of party is it we're going to?'

'Oh, got over your grump, have you?'

'Grump? I wasn't aware of being in any grump, as you call it.'

'Oh, *aware*, it was coming off you in waves.'

'Which I gather have now stopped coming off me.'

'Look, it's not me you're married to, you know,' said Sandy.

The next moment both of them rose into the air for a moment when the taxi went over an unusually large bump in the roadway. When they were down again Richard said, 'That wasn't a very nice thing to say, was it?' But he said it gently.

'Do you mind if I tell you something?'

'Yes I do,' he said at once but, by some feat of self-mastery, still gently, 'I mind very much. I don't want you or anybody else to tell me anything for the rest of my life. Sorry.'

'That's all right, I was only going to say I shouldn't have asked you why you married Cordelia.'

'That's all right.' His voice sounded odd to him. 'I mean never mind.'

'That's better.' Her voice sounded odd to him too. 'Richard . . .'

'Yes?'

'Would you ask the driver to shut his window?'

In the first second or two after this had been accomplished, Richard found time to be amazed at how fast and totally he had abandoned his firm decision not to grab Sandy before he grabbed her.

The grabbing was rather a success as far as it went, so much so that after no great lapse of time he found himself voluntarily slowing down.

29

'Shall we go somewhere?' he asked in a muffled sort of way. Sandy might not have heard him.

A little later he said, in the same sort of way, 'I could take us somewhere, or have you got somewhere?'

There was another interval before Sandy spoke. 'Later,' she seemed to say.

'What? Oh. Why? Why not now? Why can't it be now?'

'We're nearly there.'

'How do you mean?'

'Just another couple of minutes.'

Through a process unrecollectable by him, they disengaged. By common consent they sat in silence for yet one more limited period. The cab-driver swam back into Richard's notice like somebody he had encountered in some quite different capacity. Then Sandy asked if it would be all right if she explained.

Having no firearm ready to hand, and still being very much interested in what he thought they were going to get up to, he said it probably would.

'This party round the corner – '

'What?'

' – I'm afraid I am a bit set on turning up.'

'Oh, I see.'

'I honestly don't think you can altogether. I'm not disinviting you or trying to get rid of you or anything like that, I promise you. I was told to bring a chap, anyone I liked they said.'

'You can't seriously mean they won't admit you unless you're accompanied by a man, and even if – '

'Of course not, but I wouldn't like just not to appear at all. It would be very awkward for me if it got back to Crispin.'

'What the hell's it to him where you go or don't go? You must be – '

'He's got this crappy Central European thing about being head of the family now poor old Pop's more or less gaga. But you'll come, won't you, Richard? We needn't stay long. Bags of booze and all that. Come on.'

Caution had had time to extinguish lust in Richard, for the time being at any rate. He could not tell Sandy that, nor could he have explained to anyone how he had come to have such a detailed mental picture (with sound-track) of the prospective party. 'Sorry,' he said. 'Not my kind of thing. Can I ring you tomorrow?'

'Suit yourself. So you are a bloody professor after all. Sorry, I shouldn't have said that, I don't know why I did. Sorry, Richard, I do say all sorts of silly things, I know. Ring me before ten. Second house on the left along here, driver.'

THREE

After rapidly establishing that he would not change his mind, Sandy left Richard in the taxi. As he turned through his diary in semi-darkness he came across an engagement written in for that very evening, to wine at Mrs Benda's at an address not far away. Mrs Benda was one of the more persistent of the Russian-speaking London exiles he had half-willingly come to know over the past years. Not exceptionally, he had made a note of her party without any real intention of turning up at it, but to go straight home from here was unappealing and he felt he could do with a hard-earned good mark or two, so off he went.

The house was a tall narrow one situated, not to the great advantage of its occupants, close to Lord's cricket ground. Old man Benda, dead since before Richard's time, the child of a St Petersburg museum curator, must have bought the place for a couple of hundred pounds between the wars, and nobody could have spent much more on it afterwards than was needed to keep it almost clean. The door was tardily opened by the kind of semi-servant common in such households, elderly, silent, gruffly conferring a favour by the act of admission. This person led Richard a couple of metres into a drawing-room and halted him there while she conferred, it seemed in dumb show, with some other elderly people grouped round the empty fireplace. Like the passage outside, the room was poorly lit. Nevertheless, its style of decoration and furnishing could be seen clearly enough as heavy, old and old-fashioned, but also foreign in a way he would not have defined, though in spirit at least it came from more than half a continent away. He could make out large screens, stone figures, uncomplicated pictures of some obvious age and authenticity unless, as he had thought to himself on previous visits, run up by children or in the course of some parlour game. There was a smell of mothballs, in itself evocative of a long-vanished era, and what he rather hoped was wax polish of an unfamiliar form. On a tray in the middle distance stood a wine-bottle and a dozen assorted glasses, but no one he could see was holding a drink.

After some peering in his direction, Mrs Benda, small and of Tatar or Uzbek rather than Great Russian appearance, recog-nised him and gave a brilliant smile. As usual they shook hands formally with an ample up-and-down movement.

'It's most kind of you to come, Dr Vizey,' she said, in Russian naturally, since she could hardly have got as far in English after half a century in this country.

'Not at all – I'm afraid I can only stay a short time.'

'Time enough to meet my other guests. Some of them you will no doubt have had the pleasure of meeting before. So – Mrs Stephenson-King . . . Professor Radek . . . Mr Stephenson-King . . . Dr Vizey . . . Dr Nachna-Kuthara . . . Miss Střbny . . . Mrs Polinski . . . Mr Klien . . . Mrs Radek . . . Mr Nollidge . . . Professor Stumpf . . .'

Rotating slowly, once or twice nearly recognising someone, Richard took in and let go of much baldness, facial hair, dental work and optician's glass. He told himself it would be no use trying to remember why he had turned up here instead of going off with Sandy. The introductions were soon over and the little swirl of energy that had gone with them vanished at once, though he thought he recognised a sense of expectation. It was sadly difficult to imagine anything worth expecting here. His mind was touched by confused memories of settings he had come across in novels or photographs, of Edwardian Leicester or Birmingham, Moscow of the same period, unstylish Weimar Berlin, touched too by platitudes about finding it hard to believe London was just the other side of the wall that had most of the pictures on it.

'We have met before, I think,' said Professor Radek or Mr Klien or even perhaps Miss Střbny.

'Yes, of course. You're looking well.'

'Not for some months, perhaps. When were you last in Russia? Where did you go?'

Richard set to work to answer these questions with a conscientious precision even he found boring, but when the remoteness of the date had sunk in he found that details of place were not required of him.

'It has been very difficult to discover what is actually taking place there. That's to say in Russia.'

'It has indeed,' confirmed Richard.

'Until tonight, I think.'

Just then a large man in his sixties strode across the threshold where Richard had made his own more tentative entrance twenty-four hours or so earlier, a man as full of detail as the other figures had been hard up for it, what with such things as plenty of red face and tricoloured hair and beard, ultramarine velvet jacket garnished with pink silk revers and sash and turquoise frogging on patch pockets and cuffs. At the sight of this fellow, the company from Mrs Stephenson-King to Professor Stumpf collectively said, 'Ah!' and closed in on him, assuring each other that they had not heard the doorbell. 'There you are!' they said. 'Here you are. Ah!'

'Excuse me, I'm not sure I've – '

'He is Julius Hoffman,' one of the women told Richard, frowning a little.

'Oh yes, and what exactly – '

'He is . . . Julius *Hoffman*.' Nervously revolving her belly-length rope of pearls, whoever-she-was blinked at him now and backed off a pace. 'With news,' she added.

'Please. Please,' said Hoffman, his unnaturally large hands raised. 'Please. If you wish, I will tell you first of all what is the state of Russia today in broad general terms. Having done that, if you permit me I propose to descend to particulars, of which I have a great many to offer. Is that agreeable to you?

'So,' he went on into a remarkably complete silence, 'the hateful Russia of Lenin and Stalin and their heirs is collapsing and will gradually disappear beyond recall. But what is replacing it is no better, no less violent, no less tyrannical, no less ugly, dirty, barbaric, illiterate, boorish, no less complete and irremediable a cultural desert. No less a foreign country. Our country, the one so few of us remember, known only from the memories of our parents and their parents, is gone for good. We must abandon all thought of ever having anything to do with the place where it used to be, with what the maps and reference-books still call Russia. We will vow to keep *what was* in our hearts and minds and never think of *what is*.'

34

After some seconds an old man in a belted jacket asked, 'You are certain it's as bad as you say, Julius?'

Hoffman shut his eyes and reopened them. 'Everybody I have spoken to over the past months tells the same tale – the son of an old friend after a year in Moscow, a party from Kharkov, two British engineers back after six months in Uzbekistan, a Byelorussian writer arrived here to teach at a northern university, a teacher who speaks the language well . . .'

Nobody in that company thought Hoffman should have gone and seen for himself, any more than the least surprise or disappointment or sorrow was shown at what he had said. The common response was satisfaction at being told what was congenial to hear, heartfelt relief at not having to think again or to contemplate the upheaval of inquiring about the children and grandchildren of friends or cousins or classmates, let alone of inviting a Russian visitor, still less dreaming of a Russian visit. When Hoffman had descended to his particulars Richard moved closer, and saw with some distress that the pink silk was splotched with recent gravy stains, the velvet jacket showing the bare fabric where the pile had worn away. Time to be off, but not before a call at the far end of the passage.

Richard remembered there was something special about the lavatory there without remembering what it was. Unfamiliar stenches as of crop-spray or nerve gas drifted about from unstoppered containers, he soon found, one of them standing on a convenient shelf next to catalogues of works by forgotten artists and superseded books of travel. No, more than that. He lifted the ancient wooden lid of the w.c. and there it was. The pan had a similar archaic structure with an extensive level area at the rear and a kind of trench at the front down which deposits were carried away. All over the flat part and the sides of the bowl there was a carefully executed colour picture, sunk into the material by some fusing or baking process, of a fox-hunt in the England of a century ago, complete with horses, riders, hounds, followers, fields, hedges, distant steeples, even the fox itself about to vanish into a covert in the low foreground. The tints were a little faded with age and repeated cleansings but had proved remarkably persistent, a paramount feature of what must have been easily the most valuable object in the house. Richard ran his eyes over the spectacle. To have come across it here at Mrs Benda's thoroughly daunted and depressed him, he could not tell whether by its incongruity or some hidden aptness. When he gave the length of chain a gingerly pull, the cistern voided itself with remarkable speed and violence and then was in a second inert. A long decelerating series of throaty noises, not quite fit to be called a chuckle, came from the lower recesses of the washbasin.

On his return up the passage, Richard checked his stride to look up a long dark stair. At the same moment he heard a woman's voice from behind the open door of a room on the other side, a young woman's he knew he had heard recently. Looking through the doorway, he saw facing him a middle-aged man with prominent hair and beard, but built on a smaller scale than the celebrated unknown in the next room, in talk with a tallish female in black. Just then the man was saying something harmless about buses in hesitant Russian with a thick English or Dutch accent. At Richard's movement towards them the woman took a quick half-look at him over her shoulder, but only for a second, as if mistaking him for somebody she knew or had met earlier. The man gazed wonderingly through his spectacles.

Richard thought he had earned the chance of a little joke. In his best Russian, diversified with a ring of officialdom, he said loudly, 'Now, if you please, may I know exactly what is going on here?'

He was sorry before he had quite finished speaking. The girl – as he now saw her to be, hardly more than thirty – had turned towards him again in a curious movement, much faster than before, half simply startled, half fearful. With his mind in overdrive after much idling, he remembered what he well knew, that long and deep conditioning was not to be effaced in a few uncertain months, and at the same time that this was the girl whose voice had spoken to him on the telephone earlier that day. It seemed a lot to take in.

When he had enough breath he said in English, 'It's all right – everything's all right, I'm English, I'm a teacher,' and dully repeated most of it in Russian. Meanwhile a fragment of folk-tale drifted into his mind and out again, something about the boy who won the goose or the sorcerer's ring by giving the wrong answer to the vital question, whatever it had been.

Anyway, the girl in black smiled and said in the good western

Russian he had heard, 'Do please forgive me for being so stupid, but I've just come from Moscow and things are different there, which means they're the same as they used to be except for the things that are worse. But how is it you speak such marvellous Russian? You must have lived over here, of course I mean over there. You see I'm still confused. Oh, my name is Anna Danilova.'

What else? That was a third thing Richard had known, though this one was less readily accountable. The hairy man, edging forward, told him emphatically in the same unattractive accent, 'I am Andreas Binks. Miss Danilova is an important Russian poet on her first visit to this country. May we hear your name, sir?'

Miss Danilova had been looking at Richard and now promptly said, 'I know you. We talked on the telephone. You're Dr Vaisey. I'm sorry we were cut off.' Her look made it clear she wanted no questions on that. 'It was unfortunate. But now you're here in the flesh.'

'So are you, I'm glad to see. Thank you for praising my ability in Russian. Yes, I spent a year mostly in Leningrad.'

'When was that?'

'Are you familiar with what Miss Danilova has produced?' Andreas Binks asked.

Faulty choice of words imparted a sexual insinuation to this inquiry, but Richard was able to ignore that because a phrase suggested itself. He grabbed at it and said, '*Skulls and Flowers*, at any rate, yes. It made a great impression.'

As regards himself the last words were untrue, though he saw he had got the title right. Not that Anna Danilova's answering snuffle seemed one of pleasure. Abruptly, she folded her arms high on her chest, a movement that made her look older.

'But it is an early work, representing Miss Danilova's early phase. Her later development shows a far freer use of – '

'Andreas, I am not yet an old woman, so please don't talk about *later* like that, it gives me shivers. And in any case this about the early work is too boring and embarrassing.'

'But I'm sure Dr Vaisey would be interested to hear – '

'Too boring for *me*, Andreas. What are you doing here, Dr Vaisey? I'll tell you what I'm doing here, or rather not doing. Andreas brought me to meet somebody called Julius Hoffman,

37

but Julius Hoffman was not to be found, so I made Andreas take me in here and out of that room with all those old people who were at school with Chekhov and had an affair with Tolstoy. All still there. Did you come to meet Julius Hoffman, Dr Vaisey?'

'No, I can't say I did. Anyway, he's here. Arrived just now.'

'You must meet him, then, Anna,' said Andreas, trying now to edge her away.

'Before you do,' said Richard, 'could you give me your telephone number? I doubt if we'll get a chance to talk here.'

With impressive speed and practicality, she brought a shiny notebook out of a pocket in her skirt, followed by a ballpoint pen too primitive in appearance not to have been Russian-made. Very likely the skirt was too, but he could not have done much better with it than see it was black and not shiny and not all that long and clean and a skirt, with a black pullover above it. In the short time before she had passed him the torn-out sheet and he had put it away he sorted through other bits of her appearance – rather dark hair worn rather long, not fat, not thin, not beautiful, not ugly, not striking, not at all Neil Jenkins's gorgeous Danilova. It was odd that he had recognised her voice, which heard direct had turned out to be no more than clear and middle-register, not at all, again, sexy or slinky as Cordelia had said she found it. Nothing positive, then? Yes, like many Russians he had met she was *too Russian*, too conscious of it or herself with all those words and gestures and expressions. And anyway she had come to this oddly unpleasant house for some reason involving the voluble Hoffman.

Andreas led the way back to the drawing-room. Anna Danilova said to Richard, 'Who is this Hoffman person?'

'Didn't Andreas tell you?'

'He was sure I must know. When I protested I didn't, he thought I was being Russian, or making a joke, or making a Russian joke. But Dr Vaisey, didn't the lady, the hostess tell you?'

'No. Neither did anybody else.'

'[O Lord], it's getting to be a strange evening.'

They had halted for a moment in the passage a few paces to the rear of Andreas, who turned towards them impatiently from outside the drawing-room door.

'Courage, comrade, and forward,' said Anna Danilova, again to Richard. 'It'll all be over in a moment, I promise you.'

And it was, perhaps sooner than she expected. Richard took her by the upper arm and escorted her fast towards the front door, which he succeeded in opening.

'Come on,' he said.

She hesitated, but not for long. 'Wait for me outside.'

Looking back through the doorway he saw her say something to Andreas that sent him hurrying back the way they had come. Without delay the girl joined Richard and he shut the door gently behind them. It was a fine night, at least not raining.

'What do we do now?' she asked.

'We walk till we see a taxi.' They began to walk quite briskly, down the empty side-street and towards the larger street at its end where traffic moved to and fro. Richard felt not merely pleased with himself but elated at his capture and at having managed to leave Mrs Benda's without ever establishing who Julius Hoffman was. He turned towards Anna Danilova, who he thought now looked rather better than he had thought earlier, perhaps because he could see her less well.

'You're not cold, are you?' he asked.

'A Russian, cold? You would be the cold one. Oh no, of course you have your English woollies.'

Oh Jesus, he thought. Aloud he said, 'Of course. Where's Andreas?'

'I sent him to that back room to fetch my scarf.'

'Don't you want your scarf?'

'I didn't bring a scarf. To be honest I wish I had now.'

'I feel rather bad about just walking out on him like that. Yes, and who is he? Or what is he?'

'I'll tell you later. Don't feel bad about him. Or do you mean you liked him?'

'Of course I didn't. I mean not specially. Why should I?'

'That's all right, then.'

She slipped her arm through his. He tried to remember what sort of girl, if any, it had been who would take the arm of a nearly strange man in Leningrad in 1966, and what it would have meant, if anything. They went on walking down towards the street where the traffic was. More than half of the houses they were passing were in darkness and several looked empty.

'Have you got a wife?' asked Anna.

'Yes, and I live with her too. Have you got a husband?'

'Isn't that a taxi? Ah, but it has people in it. No, no husband, but I've nearly had one twice.'

'I suppose somebody came to England with you.'

'No, I came alone. I'd been planning a trip for some time but when I got the chance to go it was sudden.'

'Where are you staying? I apologise for all the questions.'

'There'll be some for you in a minute,' she said, then gave a house number and the name of a street he failed to recognise before mentioning SW1.

'Oh, very superior.'

'Not where I am, I think.'

'Well, it's quite a distance.'

They had reached the corner and all at once there was movement, noise and a great many lights. When no vacant taxi was to be seen Anna looked at Richard in an exaggeratedly pleading way.

'May I have some coffee before I start my journey?'

He knew that what was required of him was warm agreement followed at once by implementing action, but only got as far as the warm agreement. 'We'll look for a suitable place,' he said, feeling horribly bourgeois and class-ridden.

'Wouldn't that place be suitable?' she asked him, nodding towards the spaghetti joint behind him. 'Or don't your restaurants serve coffee?'

'Yes of course they do. Let's try it.'

He realised that he had been rather depending on her as a woman to explain their wants, and it was not till they had moved into an interior like a station buffet hung with empty wine-bottles that he also realised that the staff here might well not understand Russian. When one of them approached, he put their request, adding in extenuation that the lady was Russian and recently arrived in this country. The footballer-like waiter glanced at Anna rather as if she had been described as a cannibal or a thought-reader instead, but made no other demur, and remarkably soon she and Richard were sitting in a shallow artificial alcove being served with coffee accompanied by brandy – his suggestion which she instantly fell in with. She told him at length about her doctor father and the rest of her family. He told

40

her more briefly about his railway-employee father and some others before breaking off to pursue the matter of Andreas.

'Ah, now *his* father is a schoolteacher, now retired, and his mother is a daughter or niece or something of one of those old people back there who somehow found out about me and where I was. Aren't they a terrible crowd?'

'Are they? How?'

'What do you mean? They're terrible – boring and stupid and living in the past. They had to be pretty bad for me to talk to Andreas on his own.'

'They're indeed old and must be expected to be boring and to live in the past because the past is all they've got. Especially these old people. I suppose some of them must be stupid.'

'Oh I see.' Anna looked at him with some impatience over her brandy-glass. 'Let me remind you it was your idea to leave without saying good-night.'

'Yes, that was bad, I'll ring Mrs Benda in the morning. So no doubt you prefer young people?'

'Certainly not, that's why I'm staying where I am, with a classmate of my father's, away from everyone. Young people are greedy and noisy and uncultured.'

'If you mean Russian young people then I say good luck to them, let them be as noisy as they like after years of oppression.'

'*After* such years? But please don't let's start a political argument.'

'Agreed. Then who do you want to see in this country, if anybody?'

'The powerful people.'

Richard had started to be unpalatably reminded of talking to one or other of his students. Now he was disconcerted. 'What sort of powerful people? I'm afraid I can't introduce you to the Prime – '

'People powerful in poetry, who else, not your Queen or the Archbishop of Canterbury, surely, my dear man.'

'Well, I suppose there's the Poet – '

'People who give prizes and degrees. Not necessarily poets. Also people in newspapers and journals. As many as possible of the people who can make my poetry famous in England.'

'I see,' said Richard. 'As I say, I'm afraid I'm not quite the – '

'No, Richard, please, you couldn't see. It's not for me, it's for

41

someone else. Someone I'm trying to help. I told you there are things in Russia that are no better.'

'You mean you're trying to get someone out?'

'I'm . . . Well, yes, in a way I am.'

'Wait a minute – you're saying if your poetry becomes famous in England it will help to get someone out of Russia? I must say it doesn't sound very – '

'I can explain, but I don't want to do it now. When we meet again.'

The last phrase held a question. He said, 'Yes, I want to hear. I have your telephone number,' and tried to send her the right facial signals to show he meant what he said. In fact he thought it might be a good time to show more than that, as it might be by seizing her hand. But two British versions of the kind of young people Anna had briefly described just earlier, sitting across the aisle, had heard the sound of Russian and were watching with very uncultured interest, and he wanted to find out a little more about Anna's project now so as to be able to put together his excuses for not actually, when it came to it, *doing* anything to help. He went on, 'But you must have realised there are other chaps who could do more for you than I possibly could.'

'I expect there are, Richard, no doubt there are, but I don't know them, I don't know England, my Moscow friends don't know anyone of that sort, but I know you, your book was translated, and now I've done something better, something luckier, I've found you and I can ask you to help me as a personal favour from you to me.' Without waiting for this to sink in she added, 'There was a photograph of you on the back of your book which I liked very much.'

She said this without looking at him and in a tone that would have fitted in perfectly well with having liked the photograph in question for its depth of focus or the way it rendered the contrast in the stripes of his tie. Though so far she had not touched him anywhere, having merely got near tapping him on the chest or arm a couple of times for emphasis, he could not throw off the feeling that Anna Danilova had been trying to use her sexuality on him in some way. But then she went on again, 'I thought it, that's the photograph, I thought it made you look exceptionally kind and trustworthy.'

'That's nice, but I'm afraid I've forgotten which photograph that was. Probably an old one, before 1980 anyway.'

'Yes, I thought so when I saw you.' This time she continued without interval, 'You haven't read any of my poetry, have you?'

'No.'

'It's not very interesting. I'm sure you wouldn't like it. Some of it has recently been translated into English by a Canadian called Anatoly McKinnon. He's quite good, my friends say.'

'Yes, he is. Why don't you get him to help you?'

'[Oh the Devil.] He lives in Germany. Other reasons too. He told me he was sending you a copy of the book, but it probably hasn't reached you. It's called *Reflections in a Russian Mirror*.' She said the last words in her very rough sort of English. 'The publisher's title, not mine or his.'

A memory stirred in Richard, wriggled in fact, rendering him more than half-sure a work called that had recently turned up in his office and now lay somewhere in it unopened. 'I'll find it,' he said. Formless uneasiness at the prospect lent authority to his tone.

'I think you'll wish you hadn't.'

'Oh, I shouldn't imagine so.'

'From your book it seems you have the highest regard for poetry.'

'Oh yes. I had strong ambitions to be a poet when I was a boy, in fact before I really understood anything about what it was to be a poet. As a young man I found I hadn't got the talent, but I still regard it as the supreme calling. Getting to know the work of some of the Russian poets has only confirmed me in that view.'

'I'm sorry to say this Russian poet's work won't give it much support. At least I'll be pleasantly surprised if it does.'

'We'll see.'

Richard's uneasiness, in being since the lady's actual poetry had first come up, had increased. He disliked the sound of what he seemed to have at least half undertaken to do without really knowing what it was. He had become aware that he was attracted to Anna Danilova at almost the precise moment that he had seen in her a threat to his ordered set of beliefs and secure life. Well, perhaps it was time to try one of those, a little further anyway.

'Have some more brandy,' he said experimentally.

She hesitated, then smiled and shook her head.

'Are you sure?'

'Thank you no. I might take a nightcap in my lodgings.'

He thought it might seem inquisitive of him if he asked the composition and size of the possible nightcap, so he called for the bill.

The street outside seemed just as crowded and as brightly and variously lit as before. Soon Richard saw a taxi approaching on the other side of the road and hailed it. He got a quick response, but there was an interval while the vehicle waited its chance to turn and cross over to them. He said to Anna,

'Er, can I ask you not to talk Russian in front of the cab-driver?'

'Why not? Why mustn't I?'

'He'll listen in to everything we say after that.'

'And understand it?'

'Of course not, that's not the point. He'll recognise it as Russian.'

'Is it illegal to speak Russian in this country? Will he report us to Scotland Yard?'

'*No*,' said Richard, conscious of a lack of logic somewhere. 'He'll chat to us the entire way, who are you, how long are you over for, all that.'

'In Russian?'

'In *English*. I'll have to talk to him in English.'

'You can tell him to be quiet, can't you? Anyway I thought London cab-drivers were very interesting fellows.'

'They're not, take it from me.' The taxi drew up by them and he thankfully seized its rear door-handle. 'Just get in, will you?'

'I beg your honour's pardon,' she said in her English. 'Okay?'

Richard, on the pavement within the driver's hearing, forgot his prohibition and said to her in Russian, 'Will you please shut up, Anna? Kindly shut up?'

She put one hand over her mouth and waved the other from side to side in the washout signal.

'Oh, for God's sake, why can't you be *normal*?' he asked her.

'What do you mean, I'm always normal,' she said from her seat. 'Or is it a special word in this country?'

The driver, who had been staring at Richard, now said to him, in a tone of weary accusation that left no room for the least hint of male solidarity, 'Look, sir, if you speak any English, would you be so good as to tell me where you wish to go? In that event, I'll consider taking you there. That's assuming you follow my drift.'

'All right,' said Richard in defeat. 'It's somewhere in SW1. I'll tell you the exact address in a minute.'

'When you're ready, sir.'

FOUR

Early the next morning Richard was in his study, not to study, still less to work, but in order to find something if it was there to be found, one or more poems by Anna Danilova. Before he had started to look seriously, he came out of the study again and went to the part of the hall where he kept his never-mind stuff, unsolicited books and pamphlets of negligible resale value and yet, because of content or provenance, he could not quite bring himself to chuck out altogether. There was official and unofficial stuff from Russia, Eastern Europe, Central Europe, going back years, émigré stuff from all over the rest of Europe and from North America.

Chance or buried memory led him almost at once to a thin paperback in Cyrillic characters that admitted to no place of origin, but he thought he recalled, had been posted in Vienna. A page near the front gave a list of poets that included Anna Danilova, but he could find no list of contents. Hardly knowing what it was he hoped or expected or feared, he turned through the text with anxious impatience. She was not there after all. Yes she was, with a short poem, just one, too short for him to be able to tell if it was good or be sure it was bad, a personal message to some man, so personal and so much of a message that nobody coming to it without prior information could have been expected to understand more than its general tendency. That was as much as Richard could understand or make of it. He reminded himself that this was one of the things people were likely to do under totalitarianism, using poems to send out private signals as well as . . . instead of . . . without necessarily . . .

He knew he was making an excuse he saw little value in and trying not to admit to himself he was afraid Anna would turn out to be no good as a poet, no good beyond any argument. After all,

46

that was what most poets were. With stiff movements he put the small volume back where he had found it, and brought out and looked through and likewise replaced a number of others. He was still standing at the shelf when the telephone rang round the corner in his study.

'Richard, this is Anna, I hope I haven't disturbed you, but I thought you might be leaving early to go to your college.' He missed the next few words in the hollow clatter of the extension being unhandily picked up in Cordelia's study on the floor above. '. . . woken your wife, do apologise to her . . .'

'No, don't worry about that. As a matter of fact she's . . .' Richard stopped himself from adding, 'listening on the other phone,' and instead went on, 'up and about.' Only then did it occur to him that he and Anna were talking in Russian, of which language Cordelia notoriously understood not a word. Nevertheless, it was still a little creepy to hear Anna go on,

'I was wondering if you still want to meet me after last night,' at which point the instrument upstairs disconnected. 'To hear more of my project for getting someone out of Russia.'

'Oh yes, of course I do. Can I ring you back in an hour?'

'I have to go out shortly.'

His mind was a blank. After some time a fact came lurching into his consciousness. It said, it was that he would be finished soon after twelve. After that he had planned to read and make notes on an article by two Australians on Lermontov, the subject of his own great or at least long work which he hoped to complete and publish in 1992. But now he found himself asking Anna where she was going to be at twelve-thirty.

'At eleven-thirty I must be in a place called – the *Trafalgar Square*.'

Richard tried to remember what there was in Trafalgar Square besides stone lions and real pigeons. Then quite suddenly he was going to meet her at the National Gallery. Fear had set his thoughts going, fear of embarrassment, fear of what she might get up to. Well, she would not be able to get up to much at the National even if she felt like it there.

Out in the kitchen Cordelia was making coffee. This involved a machine deemed too complicated for her husband to understand and a process so critical that now, for instance, she had to keep all her attention on it for fully five seconds after he had appeared. Then she looked up at him with a little gasp and said, 'That was a wee bit early for your Russian girl-friend to be calling you up on the telephone, wasn't it?'

Some ancient reflex had given him a moment's warning, the same that might once have advised a remote forebear of an approaching crossbow bolt. 'Fancy your recognising her voice in a flash like that, darling! Oh, she said she had to catch me before I left for work. *Had* to. Quite sensible from her point of view,' he grinned.

'And what did she want from you so urgently?'

'Oh, a . . . an introduction, I don't know. She was pretty vague. These Russian visitors, they think you only have to wave your magic wand. But what can one do? I'll have to see the woman.'

'She didn't sound vague when she was talking to you on the telephone.'

'Really? That's just in the language.'

'It seemed to me she was saying something over and above the words she was actually using.'

'I don't think you can feel that unless you understand the words,' he said, still trying to grin.

'Oh I could, darling. Coffee?'

Only Cordelia and people on the screen said, 'Coffee?' like that when everybody else said, 'Would you like some coffee?' straight off. So Richard thought, anyway. He said, 'Oh, lovely, yes, thanks, I'd love a cup of coffee. Good party was it, last night?'

'I couldn't help thinking that . . . what's she called darling?'

'What? Oh . . . Anna something.'

'Thinking that *Anna* was certainly saying something *extra*, you know, something almost sexy. Silly of me of course.'

And you've come up from Zummerzet, where the zider apples grow, Richard was thinking now, after all those heavily voiced Ss of Cordelia's. Or was getting somewhere near thinking of it, thinking along comparable lines. This time he said, 'You must be imagining things. After just those few words.'

'All right, darling, no need to be so literal-minded. You say you will see her?'

'Get her in somehow at the end of my morning.'

'Such energy, Richard.'

This, and the slightly fluttering look that went with it from under her emerald-green silk head-scarf, the slight wriggle inside her powder-blue house-coat and, for specialists, the minor display of added thigh as she sat on her tall stool – all this referred to their lovemaking the previous night, later than usual, rather more prolonged and energetic than usual, too. But he could find no way of referring to it himself, and reached for the semiskimmed milk to pour over his cornflakes, a cereal recently restored to legitimacy by something she had read in one of her monthly magazines.

After a moment, Cordelia said, 'Oh yes, how was your evening? You didn't give me much time to ask you when you came in.'

Before she could have gone on to be chummy or roguish about the hurry he had seemed to be in at that stage, he said, 'Oh – very dull, really, well, not too bad, I suppose,' and talked about the restaurant, then about Mrs Benda's as a very curious house where there were a lot of foreigners, old ones mostly.

'Poor you. I suppose you had to talk Russian to them.'

'Quite a bit. That was the, well, the least bad part.'

'Yes, I can imagine. I suppose your friend Anna didn't happen to be among those present?'

Richard, severely broken down as he was by the unfamiliar exertion of having to tell somebody something without telling them anything, almost panicked at this. He remembered all at once bits of what Cordelia had overheard on the telephone just now, enough to see that they might be suggestive. To a Russian-speaker. Had she secretly learnt Russian for use in just such a contingency? No. Had she psychic powers? No – at least without more evidence. But her last question was more than a shot in the dark.

After a subjective hour or two of silence he somehow said, 'Oh – no such luck, alas!'

Even before he spoke, Cordelia had seemed satisfied, or dissatisfied with another thing. She looked vigilantly round the kitchen.

'What about you?' he asked her.

'Me? Oh yes, you mean my evening. Oh, it was as boring as you've made yours sound' – she paused as if listening for the rumble of his guts – 'except for *one* rather nice thing, well, it

49

might be and it might be sheer hell. You remember Lettice Hare.' When she paused again he nodded his head. 'She's very big and powerful now. She's on horners these days.' This time he simply bowed his head instead of nodding it and trusted in God. '*Horner's and Princess*, the magazine. Lettice thought this kitchen might be all right for a feature they're doing. I said yes, jolly good idea last night but now I'm not so sure. What do you think?'

Quite soon he established what it was that she wanted to know what he thought about, and proceeded to tell her what he thought about it to the best of his ability, wondering once or twice whether other men – Tristram Hallett, for instance – had half as much fun talking to their wives as he had talking to his. He made allowance for the fact that the kitchen meant something special to Cordelia because she had built it herself. It was with much wonder that he had once heard a schoolmate's landowning father profess to have ripped up a patch of woodland several acres in extent, shifted a road to the other side of a hill and stuck a bridge for two lines of traffic over the river at the bottom. Later study of language had suggested to him the name of rich person's installative for this verbal category, but his eventual familiarity with it had not stopped him visualising, at times like the present, Cordelia in dungarees lathing her kitchen ceiling or levelling its floor with a paviour's rammer. Somehow, for all its dungarees, her imagined form still wore a full set of bracelets.

These reflections sustained him while, with a speed he hoped went unnoticed, he got himself together, into the driver's seat of the TBD and away. Traffic hold-ups on his way down to Caret Street brought him all the time in the world for uninvited self-examination on what the hell he thought he was up to, lying to his wife about his relations with Anna Danilova. On the rare and distant occasions in the past when he had found himself nearly in such a position, he had always managed to evade it, like any other husband, by prodigality with the truth and nothing but the truth and being tight as a drum with the whole truth. And there would have been something not to tell the truth about in those days. This time round, incompetence and funk, perhaps from lack of practice, had jostled him into two major distortions, one flat lie *and* the prospect of no end of more in the pipeline, all for what? To cover up a small mountain of bugger-all in the matter of a woman he had never seriously contemplated laying a finger on, even when, as less than twelve hours ago, sitting close up to her in a taxi. Dr Vaisey had put his cake in some danger without so much as having nibbled at it. Why? Never mind for now – the whole thing was enough to make a fellow . . .

Having billeted the TBD he hurried back up Caret Street, across the front court of the Institute and into the waiting lift, where there already stood the bearded figure of Tristram Hallett. He looked rather pale, also in some indefinable way more disreputable than on the previous afternoon. Richard remembered hearing his head of department say he always put any new outer garment on his wife's clothes-line for a few weeks before venturing to wear it in any academic circumstance. Seeing Richard now, he said,

'My poor fellow, what do you think you're doing, hurrying to work? You must be' – his accent changed as his eye fell on a couple of probable students who had followed Richard into the lift – 'you muss be out of your tiny little mind, squire.'

'Just want to look for some stuff before my lecture.'

'Oh God, look for. I don't mind losing things any more, you know, it's looking for them I can't stand. One might say it's a philosophical question whether . . .' Hallett's glance shifted to the floor-indicator and he seemed to lose interest in philosophical questions.

'Where are you off to?'

'Board of Studies. Still called that, funnily enough.' The professor hitched his sky desert pants up under the band of his octo jacket as he waited for the doors to reopen. 'Next door to the Court of the Star Chamber.' He pushed his way forward. 'I mean the Star bleeding Chamber, of course.'

Hallett was gone without having left any space for a question about how much fun he had talking to his wife. He left Richard possessed by the urgency of laying his hands on *Reflections in a Russian Mirror* and by what felt like real fear of being unable to. Only a translation, he reminded himself for the dozenth time – no real guide. She would have copies. If he had seen it, why could he remember nothing about its looks? He bustled out of the lift and across the bridge between the old stuffy building and the new stuffy one that had started looking battered without having stopped looking temporary. There was nobody about, no secretary as yet in the departmental office, no sound but the generic term-time burble of distant shouting and movement broken by small surges as passage doors swung to and fro, the trill of telephones and faint unexplained crashes, quieter in sum without the typewriters of earlier years. From further away Richard caught a rising din as the Caret Street traffic lights changed.

In his own room, he faced the greyish-painted metal shelves with none of the sense of expectation he had felt in front of the ones at home. *Reflections* . . . was he even sure of that? He sauntered from left to right with his head oscillating irritably to cope with titles running opposite ways. In eight minutes he must go to his seminar. Nothing on the top, nothing on the next two down. Abandoning the search, he glanced back up for a token check and immediately spotted the very book in full view, even protruding a little, the title easily read. He snatched it from its place. A fanciful man might have thought that if the paperback from Vienna had been trying to be found, this thing had done its best to stay hidden. But Richard was not cut out for that sort of fancy.

But then perhaps he was after all, because when he saw he must go at once and put *Reflections in a Russian Mirror* on his table for later, he picked it up again and took it back with him over the bridge and down to the sort of cellar under the audio-visual centre where the seminar was held. Not that he even looked at it till he had come back whence he came and shut himself in with it. He had half an hour before the next stage of his gradually losing battle with the sub-librarian in charge of foreign publications.

Richard had not had to tell the secretary to hold messages and turn away callers. She did the one as a matter of routine, and there would not be any of the others. Apart from the elderly Reader in Old Bohemian, who came in once a term to give a lecture and pick up her post, colleagues never voluntarily darkened Richard's door. They suspected with good reason that he despised them just a little, which was harder on them than inordinately, for being rather in favour of looking through this old foreign book or that from time to time, provided of course some geezer had done it up into proper TV English, and for thinking they ought to be paid for it. And no students of any kind, not the destitute or by now even the drunk and destitute, came dropping in on old Dr Death. As soon expect one of them to tool off to the British Library to look something up there.

Anyway, behind his closed door Richard sat and looked at the still-inviolate *Reflections in a Russian Mirror*, feeling rather like a man with his head in a turned-on gas oven contemplating his first sniff. Then he thought this was overdoing things and pulled the covers smartly open, nevertheless keeping his eyes half-shut as he riffled through the prefatory matter to arrive at a page of what must be verse.

The title was 'me in lingerie' or at least a line on its own at the top said that. Further down, more lines said, or went,

> seductive is what you wanna be said the other girls,
> hows that i asked oh cmon chrissake in only wanna know.
> well says the crosseyed one supposed to blow like a grampus
> what ever the fuck a grampus is, well she says
> seductive thats kinda fuckish see like madonna
> of samantha fox and if you wanna make fuckish
> get your ass into some lingerie & smell good.

There was more, more of the same or near enough, down to the bottom of the page, and further for all he knew, but he had stopped, never to go on, or so he hoped. He had read what he had read attentively enough to be sure in the first place that the 'in' following 'chrissake' in line 2 must be a misprint for 'i' standing for 'I' and that in line 6 the word 'of' should have been 'or', and in the second place that no amount of talk about translation being not what got poetry to you but what stopped poetry getting to you was *any use at all* when it came to preventing him from seeing that *anything at all* that a qualified translator had turned into 'me in lingerie' could not be *any good at all*. Unless, against many odds, it had been written in a spirit of ferocious parody or satire, in which case there would surely be an indication of that somewhere in the book. He soon established there was none in the text. No notes. The introduction gave no clue. He turned down as too unlikely the idea that a satiric purpose could be extracted from the material as it stood. What looked so much like rubbish could hardly help being rubbish.

So where did that leave him? Grabbing the outside telephone on his filing table and punching Crispin's number, not his private line but the general, directory one. A voice he recognised as that of the Filipino butler soon answered.

'May I speak to Mrs Radetsky's sister, please?'

'Please? To whom?'

'I'm afraid I don't know her surname. Er, people call her Sandy.'

'Ah, Sandy, yes.' The voice laughed richly. 'Who's speaking?'

'Dr Vaisey.'

'Oh yes, doctor. She's not here but she's all right, I think. She's staying with friends.'

'Friends?'

'Well, you see, doctor, she went out last night and she hasn't come back. That's called staying with friends.'

'I see.'

'But she's all right, doctor. You like to leave a message?'

'No thank you.'

Sandy had entered Richard's head for the first time that day only a few seconds before he made the call. She was on the point of leaving it again when the replaced telephone rang, or rather warbled affectedly in the new way it had. That happened not very often, because Richard was wary about divulging its number. No one belonging to the Russian side of his life, in particular, a large, inconstant but generally growing portion, could be allowed to know it, obviously. Some day it would leak, and all he could do then would be to keep out of the way while they changed his number. Anna could not possibly have been the first intruder, and of course it was not she who had called.

'How are you today, doctor?' – Crispin.

Both timing and content shook Richard slightly. 'You've just caught me as a matter of fact.' He wanted to talk to Crispin, but not then. 'Oh yes, I'm fine.'

'You don't sound very fine. I hope you haven't been getting ticked off for – '

'No, she's fine too.'

'Nothing to tell you, really. Sandy's been being indignant about the way you ditched her last night.'

'Oh yes?'

'She rang Freddie from wherever she was at crack of dawn and could talk of nothing else, it seems. What a pity, I thought the two of you were getting on like a house on fire before you went off together. I could have sworn that before the night was out you'd have been taking advantage of her, or she of you. Well, there it is. Or will you be returning to the charge?'

A quality in Crispin's unremarkable words or his unemphatic tone showed Richard, quite clearly enough, how far he was from the other man in outlook and temperament and how impossible it was that he would ever be able to discuss anything of real importance and intimacy with him. And how even so Crispin was about the nearest thing to a close friend he had. Nowadays. 'I haven't thought about it,' he said in answer to his question.

'No rush. Sandy's always around, if you see what I mean.'

'Oh yes.'

'Richard – have you got somebody with you, by any chance?'

'Me? Good God, no.'

'Well, I won't keep you now. If there's anything you want to tell me you can tell it at Rocky's about six tomorrow. We might squeeze in a couple of sets.'

'You book the court.'

When Crispin had gone, Richard wished he was still there. Ten minutes or more to sub-librarian time, and he could not read any more of *Reflections in a Russian Mirror*, not even the biographical facts in the front or on the jacket, not now. He stood for a moment by the telephone, frowning, telling himself that most good poets had written rubbish from time to time. Most? How many poets born since 1945 had he read? Looked at? Heard of? Even ones who wrote in English?

A knock at his door cut off this decelerating spiral. The secretary, not old, not young, so much an ordinary human being that in this setting she looked and sounded like somebody's next-door neighbour in a twenty-year-old television play, put her neat dark head in.

'I'm sorry, Dr Vaisey, but I seem to have an urgent call for you.'

'Impossible, Mrs Pearson.'

'A Russian accent, I thought. Very gentlemanly, though. He asked for your private number earlier on and hung up when I wouldn't give it him. Now he's come through again. Important, he says. Well . . .'

'It can't be, but thanks.'

When Richard got to him, the man with a Russian accent turned out to have an American one as well, but his English was excellent. After some expertly compressed apologies, including a good one for telephoning out of the blue, he said, 'My name is Arkady Ippolitov. I'm a cultural bureaucrat, not your ideal kind of person, I'm sure, Dr Vaisey, but to speak as a blunt plain man I can actually be quite useful. Not so much to you, I'm afraid, as to others. But you can be useful to me, in just half an hour of your time. Can I buy you a drink in a bar somewhere? Wherever you say.'

'What is the name of your organisation, Mr Ippolitov?' Richard asked in Russian.

'I doubt very much if you'll have heard of it,' the other replied in the same language. 'You know how we love inventing new organisations and changing the names of old ones. I'm with the Ad Hoc Committee for Cultural Relations. We've only been going in our present form for a couple of months. Used to be part of the KZhM.'

Richard had heard of that, a so-called cultural section of the Soviet bureaucracy. 'I suppose you work pretty closely with the KMPCh,' he said, putting three random initials after the K for Committee. 'I hear they're still going.'

'Do you?' Ippolitov's tone immediately sharpened. 'Well, you hear more than I do, Dr Vaisey. I know of no such body. And would it bother you if we switched back to English?' he asked, doing so himself. 'I need every ounce of practice.'

'Really. All right. Would you mind if I checked on you at your embassy?'

'Yes I would,' said Ippolitov with a different sort of sharpness. 'I'd mind very much. I'd hate that. Please don't do that. If you do that – '

'Why, have you got an enemy there?'

'I don't know what on earth I have there, Dr Vaisey, and I don't think anyone else knows what they have, not even among themselves. Not these days. But I'm taking up your time. Do say you'll meet me for a drink, just to take a look at me. I can't kidnap you and spirit you away, much as I might like to have that power to use on one or two of my countrymen.'

A time and place were soon agreed on. There was no point in

doing anything about Arkady Ippolitov until he had been duly looked at, not even much in thinking about him. The only suspicious detail of his approach had been the absence of flattery from it. But come that surely must, reserved no doubt for more spacious circumstances. Richard remembered a Bulgarian poet (or so he had described himself) who had inexplicably managed to get hold of him at home and subjected him there to a good ten minutes of assurances of his world standing as a scholar and its ample justification, delivered in a fluent and unfortunately just-comprehensible mélange of Bulgarian and bad Russian. In it, he had then asked to be lent £500. Richard's instant refusal of this or any other sum had seemed neither to surprise nor disappoint him much. Obtaining permission to visit the bathroom before he left, he had used his orientational flair to get to Cordelia. Her too he had asked for money, and then for another favour on the spot, with no better luck.

The brief exchange with Ippolitov had filled in the required interval. Richard thanked Mrs Pearson and left her in her office, whose perpetual static riot of disorder went so oddly with her own neat appearance. On his way he further remembered getting back to his front door after vainly chasing the Balkan versifier some hundreds of metres down the high road towards central London. Cordelia had been waiting for his return.

'One must do one's best not to be too hard on a poor fellow like that. Coming from wherever it is he comes from he must have been completely bowled over by the experience of being inside this house. Quite deranged by the grandeur of all those things you and I take for granted darling.'

On being told the story, Crispin had laughed nastily and said something, never properly recalled by Richard, about a chap of course having to be off his head to have a go at Cordelia. Well anyway, Arkady Ippolitov would not be coming to the house.

But in the meantime, what was all this about helping Anna?

FIVE

'So you see it's quite simple,' said Anna.

'Simple to describe,' said Richard.

'Oh, you mean it's not simple to understand?'

'It's . . . Look, it's simple to *understand* that the, the earth goes round the moon, I mean the sun, to understand what that means, but that's not the same as – '

'Oh, professor-doctor, please. Again, then – I become famous, as a famous poet I get a message sent to Moscow telling them to let my brother out of gaol, they let him out. Or they don't. If they don't I think of something else to try. Hard to understand?'

'Yes. Now. Why didn't you come over before, when things were more settled?'

'You weren't listening. The illegal detention of my brother after the expiry of his sentence has gone on for less than a year. I came at the earliest opportunity.'

'They have plenty of other things to think about in Moscow at the moment if half of what I read and hear is true.'

'They'll have even more things to think about before long if a tenth of what I see and hear is true. Next year may be too late.'

'Why should anybody in Moscow take the slightest notice of a message from England about – excuse me – about an unknown person found guilty of a currency offence? Even if it attracted the least attention it would be dumped and forgotten.'

'Maybe. You know that Sakharov said it was opinion in the West that kept him out of gaol for so long, but yes, he wasn't an unknown person. The men I want to get to are more sensitive to opinion in the West than they ever were before. Not as a concerted thing, but there are many individuals who would give a great deal to have friends here. And as you say it's a small matter. That's to our advantage. Such a man would have a lot to gain for a little.'

'You mean,' said Richard, and stopped for a moment. 'You mean we send a letter to *Pravda* saying – '

'We put an announcement in the English and perhaps the American Press saying.'

'You should have gone to America in the first place, Anna. Much more weight.'

'No no, you're wrong, not in cultural matters – England sets the style there, or we wish it could, in literature, gardens, furniture, clothes, of course not riff-raff clothes – serious clothes. And with this announcement America will probably come along.'

'And the announcement will say, "The famous and honoured, internationally honoured poet Anna Danilova has a brother unjustly imprisoned in the USSR. This is a terrible disgrace to – everything, and we call for his immediate release. Signed, the Poet Laureate, the Minister for the Arts, Sir Stephen – " '

'Don't make it sound so foolish, Richard.'

'At least one part of it is to my certain knowledge. You seem to me to be asking me to make you famous, or to help you to become famous. How do you expect me to set about that?'

'Only famous in England, and of course I don't mean *really* famous, I only mean famous in the way people use the word to impress other people, ignorant people.'

'Even that would be beyond me. I'm sorry, Anna, I can't do it, I wouldn't know how to set about it. I don't move in those worlds.'

'Perhaps you mean you don't want to help me. I know something about you, Dr Vaisey, but one thing I haven't got clear yet. Are you perhaps in some way friendly to the kind of government we've had in my country and still have ninety per cent of in some parts and at least a hundred per cent of in others?'

Intentionally or not, Anna had raised her voice with her last sentence, and the other two men in the room looked up. The men had been introduced to Richard as Professor Léon, an elderly Russian with a short-cut white beard concentrated chiefly round his mouth, and a fat clean-shaven perhaps younger man called approximately Hamparzoumian, though his looks had nothing Armenian about them. Two ladies of Léon's age had been present earlier, his sister-in-law and her cousin or perhaps his cousin and her sister-in-law, but both had soon vanished silently.

The room, on the ground floor of the house in Pimlico, was evidently a general sitting-room last redecorated in the 1950s, by the look of things, and apart from some framed photographs of similar date showing scenes and persons that were at any rate not English, and vaguely martial pottery figures of which the same could have been said, there was nothing visible to suggest that the present occupants had brought anything with them, even their taste, from their original home. Every so often the pieces of pottery rattled and the whole room shuddered at the headlong passage of some giant of the road, one that triumphantly discovered this new clear route through what, until the other day, had been a peaceful refuse-littered backwater.

It was into this not very private place that Anna had led Richard for what she had called their real talk. Their unreal talk over lunch in a McDonald's (at her insistence) had largely comprised his reluctant answers to her questions about his life, which had led to a certain amount of unsolicited material about his wife. At the start of the real talk Dr Léon had been supposedly engrossed in some learned work, certainly one that was not new, and anyway was sitting a couple of metres further off than the man with the Armenian name, who had shown no sign of being a Russian speaker when introduced and since then had been intermittently looking through a copy of *The Times*. Both now dropped any attempt to seem inattentive or indifferent to what Anna and Richard were saying.

What Richard said next was, 'No,' and he would have liked to leave it at that, but saw he could not. 'I learnt the Russian language not out of any feeling about modern Russia but because I was attracted by classical Russian literature, I don't really know why, I don't even know how. Of course I had to master the language completely in order to read the literature.'

'You had no reason to learn the spoken language so well,' put in the professor mildly. 'You speak it like a Russian. Oh, you have a slight accent, but only an expert could be sure it was not Polish, say, or Siberian. Very few Englishmen can have done so much.'

'In order to hear properly how the words ran I found I had to be able to make the sounds myself.'

'And those few will have had some non-literary motive for acquiring such ability. Are you saying you're unique, Dr Vaisey?'

Anna stirred in her seat, a tall armchair that must once have seemed marvellously strange to look at, and Richard said, 'Quite possibly. To speak Russian well enough to pass as a Russian was a way out of speaking English either like a provincial Englishman or like a kind of Englishman I'm not and can never be.'

He had thought of that only as he said it. No doubt Léon found it obscure, as it probably would have been to anyone born outside the kingdom. 'It might be best if you were to tell us at once which department of your Foreign Office was successful in securing your services.'

Léon said more, but his gentle voice was lost under the swelling uproar of some quite uncommonly gigantic vehicle in full career past the house. By the time it no longer seemed likely to enter the room or at least bring the place to the ground in a sonic shock, the professor had subsided under the disgusted glares and fiercely snatching, chopping gestures of Anna and Hamparzoumian – so the fellow understood Russian at any rate, or perhaps took his orders from Anna.

'In Russia we have a saying, "Old habits go on till we die," ' she said to Richard when she could be heard. Then she blushed, more on the forehead than the cheeks, he noticed. 'But of course you know we have.'

'Oh, but I wouldn't if I didn't speak Russian, would I?'

'What?'

'I was merely about to tell you that to have learnt the Russian language, and thereby to have been enabled to understand what Russians have written, was enough to display in front of me beyond mistake the one achievement of the Soviet system that nobody will ever be able to deny or undo, and that is the destruction of Russian literature. That's an impoverishment not only of Russia but of the world, and that's why I answered no to your question just now about whether I liked that system, and I hope you think it's a good enough reason, because it's the only one I can swear to personally.'

'In giving that reason you have answered another question.' The professor was apologetic. 'We know now why you learnt

61

our language so exactly,' and he and Hamparzoumian beamed at each other.

'It was love,' said Anna, smiling fondly.

'If you have to put it like that,' said Richard, but he wished very much that she had not put it like that, and thought to himself it was all very well to talk in such a strain, but if all sorts of things were going to be deemed to be love, then there would be less of the actual thing left to go round. He wished too now that he had expressed himself more temperately in this company on his feelings about Russian literature. It was always happening with Russians – they made you take them on their own terms and then you were trapped in intimacy, or in more of it than you had bargained for. He heard Professor Léon calling for tea, and supposed morosely he should think himself lucky it was not vodka with little bits of stale bread heaped with decaying lumpfish roe.

When it arrived it was not tea either, not proper tea, not Russian tea but, as often in such households, something they thought must be better, English tea, Western tea, parliamentary-democracy tea with milk and sugar and accompanied by elaborately patterned sweet biscuits. Richard avoided these and the sugar, but the milk was sloshed in before he could prevent it. Fussing over this helped him not to have his eye caught by Léon, who as well as doing the sloshing and everything else was obviously about to say something important and deeply felt and awful.

In the end it had to come. 'So . . . Dr Vaisey . . . respected sir . . . you have heard our plea, Anna's plea . . . and you are to lend us your help.'

Richard had already started to gear himself up to saying that, as to that, nothing had changed in the last ten minutes and that he was as incapable now as then of doing what he still only dimly saw as required of him. Then he noticed that Anna in her turn had a message for him. This one asked him to say yes to the professor, but not with a routine wide-eyed stare of desperate appeal. Instead, frowning, wrinkling up nose and mouth, nearly winking, she was like an indulgent aunt silently begging a small indulgence for a deserving nephew. Like a fool, as he told himself, Richard gave in.

'Very well, I'll do anything I can . . .'

Dealing the tea-tray a severe buffet with the side of his leg, Léon sprang up and pressed forward and shook his hand, a form of action he had apparently never quite mastered. 'Ah, my dear sir, you will never regret that decision, never.'

Telling himself something more, Richard went on, '. . . but I must tell you I consider it most unlikely that I can do anything effective . . .'

'To have tried is all that can be required of any man, and is noble.'

'. . . and moreover I can think of nobody who could, nobody in this country.'

'Still, to have tried, Dr Vaisey.'

'Tell me, Professor Léon, assuming for a moment that something could or can be done along the lines Anna and I were discussing, do you really think it's likely that it would have the effect we hope for in Moscow?'

'No, I don't. Not very likely. But possible.' The professor spoke faster and in a sharper tone than before. 'I have known likelier efforts fail, it's true. But then I've known less likely ones succeed. And that was then, before. Now, it's hard even to guess. But don't you want a crack at the bastards, my friend?' he asked, dropping aural quotation marks round the main phrase.

'Of course,' said Richard. 'But isn't there a risk of damaging the very person we're supposed to be trying to help?'

'Oh yes,' said Anna, who had also got up. 'But Sergei and I talked the whole thing over and he wants us to go ahead no matter what.'

'A man must try,' said Léon, dropping back into his earlier manner.

'Yes, of course, darling.' Anna was gently driving him from the room. 'Now Dr Vaisey and I must be left in peace to discuss our plans and make our lists.'

'Of course, my love, but first a brief word with you in private.'

Richard welcomed the prospect of a few minutes alone. He had been finding it a small effort to concentrate his attention on what he and Anna had said to each other since a few moments after their meeting in the National Gallery. She had glanced up with an unimportant expression at a large picture hanging in the vestibule there, something with the Virgin and Child and angels, as far from her world as could be, he had thought. Since then he had found it hard to take his eyes off her. He had put her down as not attractive at first sight, he remembered. Now, he was not sure, he must go on looking. A little voice in his mind, more than one, murmured to him with questions, allegations, accusations, but to no avail – theoretical, conditional.

Intent on movement for its own sake he stopped looking out of the window, where the temporarily motionless scene encouraged only a trance of depression, and turned towards the bookshelves. They were just that and no more, the work of a long-vanished amateur and never finely planed, irregularly covered with grey enamel. On them were some English paper-backs, mostly unknown novels, left by another departed hand, and several dozen books in Russian – what else? History, political theory, history, political history, flora and fauna of the Caucasus, history, and selected poems 1980–88 by Anna Danilova, inscribed on the title-page to respected and beloved Alexander Léon. What else?

But three times in one day, three selections, was more than anybody should have been expected to cope with. After no more than five minutes Richard had seen all he needed to see, all he would ever need to see. What appeared most defeating for the moment was the uncanny fidelity with which the two exhibits seen earlier had rendered the qualities of the poet whose work he had just seen close to, so to speak. And when almost at once Anna came back into the room it was in the person of that poet that he saw her for the first few seconds.

She smiled at him, no doubt apologetically, but it seemed to him false, a grimace. 'Alyushka is a very old friend. He sees so few people nowadays, I had to have him in here just now and let him join in the conversation.'

'I quite see that.' He thought he spoke rather stiffly. 'And what he said at the end was good. Useful.'

'He's having me to stay for nothing and he knew my father well.'

'And your brother,' said Richard more easily. 'No, very natural, I understand.'

'Good. Do you want some more of this tea? I think it's horrible.'

'So do I. No more for me.'

'But English tea, it's supposed to be a national drink.'

'I'll explain another time.' There was a great deal he wanted to avoid discussing with Anna, but he could not start going on about tea now. He said without wanting to know, 'Has the professor a wife?'

'No. In fact that was the chief reason why he had to get out of Russia, if you see what I mean.'

'I think so.'

'He was very lucky. He was lucky to get Hamparzoumian out. Hamparzoumian is his friend.'

'I see. That's an Armenian name, isn't it, but he doesn't look Armenian to me.'

'Nor is he, he's Russian, Hamparzoumian isn't his real name. More a nickname. It's complicated.'

'He doesn't seem to speak much Russian.'

'He doesn't speak much of anything. It was he who answered the telephone when you called yesterday because no one else was near. And he who cut it off.'

'Yes.'

'He used to speak like you and me. And he sang beautifully and was beginning to be quite famous for it. Not any more. There's not a great deal to see on him, but they took care of the whole thing in the place where he was. He's mostly all right otherwise but sometimes he gets very tired.'

'Oh.' Richard shut his eyes. 'I'm sorry I mentioned it.'

'Don't be, my love. It might remind you what sort of gentlemen they are, which could help. It could help a lot of people who don't know that the place where Hamparzoumian was is still there, and the man in charge when Hamparzoumian was in it was still in charge of it when we last heard. Why shouldn't he be?'

Richard hoped that Anna would never think of him as to any degree one of the lot of people whom it would do no harm to be reminded of such things. Then he put that thought away as selfish and unprofitable. Sooner or later in any discussion of such matters there came the point where the Westerner had to say nothing more, and he and Anna had reached it. Unfortunately this left the way open for the discussion of a different if not unrelated matter.

'You're worried,' said Anna. From time to time in the last

minute or two he must have allowed his attention to drift back to the indefensible, unalterable poem he had just read.

'Well . . .' He could not deny it or contemplate inventing something else to be worried about, gloomily fearful that she had already guessed the true cause. He lowered himself into or on to an armchair that matched hers with its high curving back, designed possibly by a physiotherapist to promote sciatica. They faced each other under a patchily coloured drawing of anti-quated blazered and boatered toffs and their long-skirted lady friends cavorting along a spray-swept promenade. But in jugs and vases here and there, quite a good show of freshly cut lilac, tulips, irises and daffodils could be seen.

'You've been reading my poetry, haven't you?' asked Anna, and glanced over at the bookshelves, as he perhaps had a moment before.

So here it was. The suggestion of an accusing parent or school head might have amused him another time, but not now. 'Just one or two bits,' he said, failing to keep a placatory note, not quite a whine, out of his voice.

When she had asked and been told what bits, she said, 'And you didn't care for what you saw,' like a statement.

He had several not very sincere palliatives and extenuations ready, like insufficient sample, only a translation, hasty look, but could do no more than get started on any of them, even though he got up from the armchair again for emphasis.

She got up too, held her hand out towards him and frowned heavily. 'I told you you wouldn't like it, I didn't expect anything else, I don't put it very high myself, what I've done already, especially the pieces McKinnon translated, he liked them because they're sort of American, they're my American phase, I've got out of that now, and please try not to be so worried about it, Richard, what does it really matter if you don't like the poems I've written, what difference does it make?'

He managed to cut in there. 'Anna, please, surely you must see it makes a very great deal of difference.'

'Are you going to tell me it makes a difference to the amount of help you give me, or the kind of help, or are you even going to turn round and say you won't help me at all?'

'No, of course not,' he said robustly. He said it like that because the only alternative he could think of was, 'Yes, I'm afraid so,' for which almost any tone would have done as well as another, and his thinking had not had time to get that far.

'Then what's the trouble?' she asked in a huffy sort of way. 'Naturally I'd be pleased, I'd prefer it if you liked what you've seen of my poems, but it's obviously not essential, and I'd be silly to expect it. Conceited, too. After all, why should two people as different as you and me have the same taste in poetry, any more than we have the same taste in food?'

'But Anna, that's not the same thing, that's not the same kind of thing, food and poetry.'

'Who says they are, any fool can see they're not. Food's much more important, without food you die. Poetry is a side-issue. The human race survived for millions of years without it.'

'I don't think we know that. We certainly don't know how long it'll survive in the future without poetry. Now just tell me something plainly, if you will.'

'Certainly, professor.'

'It doesn't help to call me that, Anna. All I want is you to tell me how important poetry is to you – your poetry.'

'Ah, but these are two more things that are not the same, Richard, surely. Poetry to me is the world, everything I think is wonderful, whatever you like to say about it. But my own poetry, that's a very small thing, a very tiny thing in comparison, if it compares at all.'

'Yes, yes, I see that, and of course it's right, but it has to be the case, it simply must be the case, that you believe in your poetry . . . that you think it's good, it has *merit*.' It seemed intolerable to him then that she should share or should ever come to share his view of her poetic abilities.

'It pleases me, it amuses me.'

'More than just that, surely, for the love of God.'

'Yes, more than just that!' she said, with irritation again. 'It fascinates me, it delights me, it takes up all my interest, all my mind and soul, all of me, what would you? It makes me feel the greatest person in the world while I'm writing it, but when I've finished I start to get my sense of proportion back. Oh yes, I'm good, I'm brilliant, I'm a genius, I feel I am. But then compared with Pushkin, Lermontov, Soloviev, Alexander Blok, what am I? Compared with many others too, I assure you. What I meant just now when I called you professor was not intended as hostile, what I should have said was that for a very learned man like you, who knows far more about literature than I ever will, and no, Richard, I'm not being sarcastic, I swear to you, I'm just saying things are always more difficult and complicated than they are for me, ever. For me, it's simple – I write poetry, I enjoy doing it, some people may enjoy reading it, some people may even think it has merit, some people who don't think that now may come to think it of what I shall write in the future, I don't know. Again, what difference does it make?'

Richard had been following this as closely as he could, straining his ears and attention once or twice as another multi-wheeled monster shook the building. 'It's bound to make some difference if you go round saying you don't think much of your own poetry, whatever you may or may not feel about it, and never mind Pushkin. People won't want to support someone who doesn't believe in what she's doing. Or doesn't seem to.'

She stared at him furiously for a moment, then softened, seeming to understand. 'I take your point. The bureaucrats must be conciliated. You may rely on me for all demonstrations of that kind. I've schooled myself in the part, as any Russian poet has to do.'

'The part may call for something a little different here.'

'Then you can help me with it. Anyway, that's bureaucrats. There can be no difficulty with the performance.' Anna spread her hands and raised her head, evoking already Niobe or Volumnia. 'It'll be sure to produce great dramatic effect. You'll have seen our Russian actors in the theatre, so you must know.'

'Yes, and poets too. Reading or giving recitations or declamations. We have readings at the Institute here. I could probably arrange for you to give one.'

For the past half-minute Richard had been concentrating less closely than before. He was dimly but firmly aware that some time in the couple of minutes prior to that he had lost an argument. Or rather he had found it constantly getting away from him, no longer there when he reached each bit of it in turn. The experience had been not so much like taking half a second too long over every tennis stroke as playing chess with a conjuror, one who was not doing it for a joke but was not necessarily determined to win either.

'You're worried again,' said Anna. 'What is it?'

'It's just that I can see such difficulties ahead.' Now they were back, he saw them as impossibilities again.

'Oh, don't think of them. And are you sure there's nothing else? It's such a shame, you and I were getting on so beautifully together and these difficulties, these worries, this trouble keeps coming up between us. I know we're not at all the same kind of person . . .'

'Not between us. The trouble isn't between us, it's ahead of us.'

He had said the last few words before he had known what they were going to be, and at once felt them tainted by what he hoped was nothing worse than gross affectation, though she gave no sign that she minded them at all. Then for the first time since she had come back into the room he looked at her otherwise than as somebody who had written poems, and saw for instance that she was really quite a good general size and shape, the right sort of distance across the shoulders and hips and with the look of being able to do necessary things, a serious girl in the way one talked about a serious consideration, a serious effort, a serious person but without any limiting sense of serious-mindedness. And her facial bone-structure was finer than he had taken in before, quite different from the squareish, flattish eastern European look he had grown familiar with over the years. He had noticed those grey eyes of hers before, but now because of them and the rest of her face all his questions about her attractiveness were answered immediately, suddenly, in full, despite the unpropitious moment, perhaps, really perhaps once in a lifetime, because of it. But he thought of the last part later.

Then and there, he would have found it hard to say what the grey eyes were expressing. She kept them on him a little longer before half turning away, a movement in which he found it quite easy to see disappointment. 'You must have some more of my poetry to read for longer. I don't hope you'll come to like it but I think you should know more about the sort of thing it is, the things I write about, what I say in my poetry, when I say something.' It was hard to believe now that she had ever spoken of the delight and enjoyment that writing 'her poetry' had brought her. As if to stress this gloomy view she hugged her elbows in to her sides and clasped one hand round the palm of the other, like an old woman in head-scarf and long shabby coat

69

waiting outside a Russian prison with, for preference, snow starting to fall.

This kind of female behaviour was not wholly unfamiliar to Richard. 'Yes,' he said, nodding his head critically, 'After all, I must be able to speak with a certain amount of knowledge.'

'Speak? To whom? I don't understand.'

'When I set about enlisting support for you and your poetry. To bring about your brother's release.' With the words a conviction of the absurdity of the whole enterprise possessed him. He must have been deranged to agree to help. And had he really heard her say last night that she must be back in Moscow in three weeks?

'You won't still be wanting to go ahead with that.'

'Why not?' He spoke mechanically. 'Because I dislike your poetry? You said twice over you don't think that makes any difference.'

'But you do. But that's not what I mean.' In a moment her dejection seemed to fall from her and she gave a kind of smile, 'You must have thought I was cross with you or sorry for myself perhaps. Well, I am sorry for myself but that's not the point. I've something to tell you which will relieve you of any responsibility you may feel for me. You're a good man and you must feel some. In fact you're such a good man that I must tell you this now. That brother of mine in the gaol in Moscow, he's not at all a good man. Did I tell you he was guilty of what they charged him with? Well, he was. And other things. All this, this adventure of mine, the petition, was my mother's idea. I think she overestimates me. She overestimates my brother too but in a different way. He's a, well, he's quite irresponsible, Richard, I'm sorry, not fit to receive your help, I shouldn't have asked you. If I were as correct and conscientious as you are I should be advising you to withdraw at this point.'

Richard had been half-expecting to hear that Anna's brother was a serial killer, Gorbachev's boy-friend, really her husband. 'I see,' he said.

'You say that too easily, you know. Remember the Russian proverb you must have come across — where there is one serpent you must expect to find more.'

'No doubt. How many people in this country know that part of the story?'

'I think Professor Léon has guessed. Or he knows something is not right. But I'm sure nobody else.'

'Your brother's . . . crime doesn't seem to have weakened your own resolve.'

'No. I'm not trying to get him a retrial or a pardon or anything like that, just released now he's served his sentence according to the law.'

'And is the whole of that part of the case as you stated it? Nothing more to come? Nothing different?'

'No, all of it is true and correct as I stated it, as I told you.'

'I see,' said Richard again. 'You mentioned to Professor Léon something about making lists, I suppose of possible contacts. Well?'

Anna gave him a serious, grateful look and took a folded sheet of paper from an upper pocket of the dark-brown tunic affair she was wearing. 'I started one with the advice of Andreas. Some of the writing is his. The man from the Russian society this morning was helpful.'

The list proved to contain vague titles of offices like Head of BBC and names of individuals he had never heard of. While he thought of it he added the British Convention (Donald Ross). But the general prospect still daunted him.

While he was still pondering, she said, 'Before you go I'll give you a book of my poems. Not because you want to read them but because I want you to have them. I want you to have something of mine.' She looked at him now for a very short time, but still long enough to let him know that she had seen what he had seen in her just earlier. 'And I think you'd like to have something of mine.'

'Yes, I'd like that very much.'

She smiled. 'You know how not to say things, don't you? I don't imagine they actually teach you that here, do they? Perhaps they do.'

SIX

In Cordelia's drawing-room, near the tall narrow window by the door, there stood an antique table, which is to say it was a table that had at some time suffered some minor battering and was now of a dark colour and highly polished. Cordelia herself usually said it was a William IV piece, once or twice varying this to William and Mary in reference, perhaps, to some hardly-known morganatic connection of the Sailor King. Anyway, she, Cordelia, simply adored little pieces of pretty furniture whenever they happened to have been made. She sometimes said they were her one extravagance.

Much of the top of this table was covered by a large jigsaw puzzle, half completed. When fully completed or at length abandoned it would be broken down, returned to its box and put aside for the daily woman to give away to somebody, while a fresh puzzle would be laid out in its place. Not for nothing was that place situated by the door of the room, in that a selection of those entering were likely to find themselves detained there, jocularly prevented or at least discouraged from going any further till they had added a minimum of one piece to the finished part. This could take a minute or two, because Cordelia was obviously going to have done the more interesting, busier bits herself and left her helpers the sky and stretches of water.

Alongside the jigsaw, chessmen were laid out on a board apparently in mid-game. Having been machined out of some common wood *c.* 1960, they were not on a social par with their surroundings, but they would do for purposes of suggestion. Richard's old set was no longer used for play, though until quite recently Cordelia had been known to set up a chess problem with it, one out of the *Evening Standard* or a book of them kept at hand for the purpose. The solution rate had been poor or non-existent but the pieces stayed on. The nearby copy of *The Times* for that day, folded to show the crossword, hinted likewise at intellectual activity, and arriving guests sometimes picked it up, though the sight of a fourteen-letter anagram with only a couple of vowels in place was usually enough to make them put it down again. But after all the bloody paper had to be somewhere, as Richard had once put it to himself.

Cordelia spent a large part of the day not in her drawing-room at all but in her study on the first floor. She sat facing the window at her desk, or rather her specified-reign work-table in a named wood. Through the window, the only one in the house it was really easy to shift up and down, she could see a stretch of parkland scattered with human figures. Sometimes she seemed to be following closely the movements of one or another of these, even to smile, but from the speed with which this look faded she might just as well have been watching a tank of fish. She was given to muttering under her breath when alone or preoccupied, mostly in running commentary on what she was doing or short-term predictions of what she was going to be doing.

In front of her were ranged an engagement diary, a manuscript book of telephone numbers, a telephone fitted with most extant devices and a millboard with all manner of stuff clipped to it in the way of postcards, leaflets, letters, pages torn from pads. Nothing else, as always. In his time Godfrey had mentioned this relative bareness to Crispin, noting that active types of people liked to keep their desks clear, and Crispin had said it was curious how the same principle seemed to apply at the other end of the scale, and Godfrey had seemed not to understand, not much unlike Richard, who when his turn came along had pretended not to have heard.

Muttering now, frowning too, Cordelia found a number in her personal telephone book, peered at it in a triste fashion and pressed the buttons with the top of a partly transparent pen, more troublesome than a fingertip but more professional-looking, more officey. When the ringing tone had sounded six or seven times without raising the person she wanted just then, she cut off, a famous proceeding of hers. She rang two more numbers with the same result, leaving a total of two people checked in midstride as they reached out from a couple of metres short of their abruptly silent instruments. One, a man who had rushed from the lavatory tugging his braces up over his shoulders, roared, 'Bleeding Cordelia again! Why can't the bitch die!', another, a woman in her forties who had run from her kitchen and the making of a cheese sauce, merely smiled, glanced to heaven and said, 'Well, there's only one Cordelia,' to which her husband retorted, 'Do you really think so?' But he retorted it from behind *The Daily Telegraph*.

On a fourth try, the distant handset was lifted as promptly as if the subscriber had been waiting within arm's length, a contingency not to be ruled out. 'Hallo darling,' said Cordelia vivaciously. 'Listen, er . . .' After some seconds she went on, 'You are coming this afternoon? What? But you must. Darling don't be silly darling, of course you can. You might have got someone dying. Yih . . . oob . . . gh . . . tuh . . . unh . . .' These syllabic fragments fired at intervals into what the distant person was struggling to say finally seemed to overpower it. '*Good.* Four o'clock – no – *no* – four-fifteen. Oh, and darling, on your way I was wondering if there was the slightest possibility of your picking something up for me from that good fishmonger in Bolitho Street. Well, it's very nearly on your way darling. You only have to . . . Well, start a little earlier then, for goodness' sake. That's better. Er . . . he'll have skate today, so two skate, medium size, say about a pound each. What? No I'm afraid I don't but it's about the only fishmonger in that street. Three or four doors up from that restaurant or coffee place or whatever it is. That's right. See you this – Darling! Oh, dash and *blow*,' said Cordelia, and restored her own handset.

She had ticked an item in a list on her millboard when the telephone rang.

'Hallo yes?'

After some hesitation a man's voice said, 'Oh, door-to-door delivery, please.' It was an unreconstructed plebeian voice.

'I'm sorry, there's nothing that would answer that description here.'

'Oh, well then.' There was another pause. 'Excuse me, do you mind if I ask you a question?'

'Not at all if you're quick.' Cordelia was busy again with her millboard.

'Paki, are you, love?'

'I beg your pardon?'

'Well, I beg yours and all, madam, I just thought, the way you talk, ennit. Was it Europe, then? I said was it Europe?'

'Vug of, uzzhaul,' she said in an eerily unchanged voice, cut him off and punched another number. When a woman answered, Cordelia asked her if there was any chance of her picking up some stamps at the post office on the corner – well, nearly on the corner, and surely she would be coming by taxi – and carefully specified the denominations and numbers required. Before the millboard had been dealt with for the day, representative selections from a six-weeks-old theatre programme had been read over the telephone to an elderly man in Finchley, never more than a lukewarm admirer of hers, who had last seen a play performed in 1979, and extracts from a St James's wine-merchant's list, with particular stress laid on those little-known first-growth clarets, to a Cambridge contemporary in Cheltenham whose husband had always bought all his wine locally. A point of interest about this second and further-reaching call was that it was really two calls, a short outgoing one in which Cordelia asked to be called back and rang off without giving a reason, and then an incoming one that went on for much longer. This was standard procedure, but slightly prolonged today because the pal's husband had been in the room to start with, and he might easily have kicked up a fuss if he had realised that he was going to have to pay for twenty minutes or so of having Cordelia talking to his wife at peak rates. The husbands of Cordelia's pals formed a vast national and indeed international brotherhood, unknown to one another except in a few local cases, but united in mind and heart on that subject at least.

Still muttering and frowning, the afternoon sun through the window picking out highlights on her bracelets and glinting here and there among the faint down on her upper lip, she ringed a couple of presumably unclinched items on her agenda and slashingly crossed off the rest. To round off her day's work she made another of her coitus-interruptus telephone calls. This last one fetched an old woman grunting up her garden path at the double carrying two plastic bags that bulged with groceries. She had time to drop these on her doorstep and grope frantically for her latchkey before the sound of the bell inside the house broke off in mid-ring.

Cordelia looked at her wristwatch, a feat of modest legerde-main with all those bracelets to cope with. She was standing at her dressing-table mirror with an expression of faint dissatisfaction when the front-door bell rang. At that she opened a very small round box and carefully put hardly any pinkish stuff on her right cheekbone, taking a good half-minute over the job. Then, with measured tread, she made her way downstairs, singing fairly quietly in time with her progress,

'Hosh . . . hosh . . . hosh . . . hirr calms tha bawgie-munn . . .'

She had learnt the song off an old 78 record which went back to her nursery days. It had been a bad moment for Crispin when his researches had established beyond doubt that Cordelia really had spent part of her childhood in what could conscientiously be described as a nursery, and in the charge of somebody it would not have been overdoing matters to call a nanny, too.

'Jost . . . prittand . . . thut yah're a croc-o-dile . . .'

The lyric had been designed, rather touchingly perhaps, to reassure young children about the bogeyman by outlining strata-gems that would frighten him off, but it would have taken a funny sort of little kiddie to be much heartened by Cordelia's rendering.

'Tal him yah've . . . got sawldyahs *een* yahr bad;
Bawgie-munn wheel navver gnaw they're awnlee mide of lad.'

The song lasted Cordelia till she had reached the front door, by which stage its bell had sounded a second time and given her the chance to do her best to bawl 'Coming!' with her face three or four decimetres from the latch while at the same instant hurling the door wide open. Unfortunately from some points of view, the youngish and rather pretty woman on the doorstep was attending not to any of this but to two well-dressed black men some metres down the street who had seemed about to fight each other. When this prospect evidently lapsed she turned to Cordelia. She held a plastic carrier several sizes smaller than either of the two full-blown bags mentioned just now.

'Oh hallo darling,' said Cordelia in what for her was a monotone and without further greeting began walking away across the hall.

Darling, also known as Pat Dobbs, called after her, 'I'm afraid I couldn't get any skate.'

That brought Cordelia up short. 'What? I'm terribly sorry darling, I just can't seem to understand. What did you say?'

'The fishmonger hadn't got any skate in his shop today, it only comes in on Wednesdays, he said, so I got two nice-looking lemon sole instead.'

'They're not very similar, darling.'

'No, I suppose a couple of sting-ray would have been nearer the mark from that point of view.'

'Why, had he some in stock? How unusual.'

'No. At least I don't think he had. I didn't ask him.'

'Well,' said Cordelia, 'perhaps you could put those . . . fish away in the refrigerator for me if you would.' She spoke without animation.

'Right.'

'Not in the freezer, of course.'

Pat Dobbs too was muttering to herself while she stowed the lemon sole as bidden, but more connectedly than Cordelia. The two women had once been neighbours, until Pat and Harry had found the district too expensive for them, and had also found that it had Cordelia in it. But for all that the two had kept in fairly frequent touch, Cordelia so as to send Pat on errands and to have her round to bully and to say things to, and Pat out of morbid curiosity. Or so Harry called it when he was not calling it masochism, bloody female martyrdom and the rest. Actually his second set of suggestions was wide of the mark, unless masochism etc. were deemed to include entertainment. So Pat had been altogether free that afternoon, had even been thinking it was time to find out what old Cordybags was up to, and her plea of inconvenience had just been a way of inciting awful old C. to fresh mini-enormities. For instance, she had known perfectly well where the fish-shop was, well enough to have herself introduced Cordelia to it a couple of years before. That evening she would be able to give Harry a treat, punctuated by a few bursts of incredulous rage, with a replay of selected highlights.

A destined one of these, though far from a novelty, was now awaiting Pat in the drawing-room. But first she had to endure the sight, always forgotten between visits, of the display there of jigsaw puzzle, chess game and *Times* crossword. At one time it had irked her that Cordelia had never invited her contribution to any of the three, and even now it tickled her slightly to notice that only two crossword solutions had been filled in, and these short and in a bottom corner. Cordelia, braceleted and blue-eyed, annoyingly handsome and youthful in appearance, sat as though absorbed in a book with a lot of photographs in it.

'That's £4.50 you owe me,' said Pat. 'For the fish.'

'For the . . . Oh of course. Would you put it in writing for me darling?'

'It is in writing, as you can see.'

Anybody who looked at the proffered bill could have seen, but Cordelia only said, 'You know, it's so much easier for me if everybody sends in their bills at the end of the month and I pay the whole lot in one go.'

Yes, I do know, said Pat to herself, or I can guess. Come on, now – it's not all beer and skittles, it's no joke. . . ?

'It's no picnic, honestly, running a house this size single-handed, I can tell you, Patricia. Listen, er . . . Do you know this?' Cordelia lifted the book on her lap, but too short a distance and too briefly to do any good.

'What is it?' asked Pat, sitting unwarily down on a sofa equipped with a kind of engulfing upholstery that lifted her knees up to her chin in a single decisive movement.

'He's a marvellous writer. Are you all right there darling? He knows Athens backwards. The Parthenon. The Erechtheum,' said Cordelia with an accentuation of her own. 'M'm?'

'If you're asking me if I know them, I've never been to Athens.'

'He writes so beautifully and the photographs are so marvellous. It's just your sort of thing.'

'Cordelia, at the risk of shocking you, I'm not in the least interested.'

'I know you'll absolutely adore this. You take it with you when you go.'

'No really, wasted on me, thanks all the same.'

'You won't be able to put it down. Can you stay for a bit?'

Well, Pat certainly could, indeed it was her understanding that she had been invited to tea. Now, already, there was a clear case for leaving, but to do so would reduce her to the status of a mere fish-fetcher, dismissed after a couple of minutes without so much as a cup of char. That was where, or whereabouts, Cordelia always had you. But there was no need for any decision because the thought of tea had already crossed the ether, and Pat was left alone with the intimation that at least she must stay and say hallo to Richard.

Hallo was getting on for all she generally felt like saying to Cordelia's husband. If she had ever known him to show some sign of what anyone short of a raving lunatic or a creature carved out of stone must assuredly feel about that woman – and he was *married* to her, so to speak – Pat would have been ready to say a good deal more. She was not asking for any proportionate demonstration, like hurrying over to burn Cordelia alive, nor any hint of connivance, just a quick twitch of the mouth now and again, a faint wince, something showing. But zero. Was that the point of him for Cordelia? Thinking it was somehow all right for her to be as she was, the only man who did? Of course he was quite attractive in a sedate, buttoned-up sort of way. Perhaps he and she . . . Rather than contemplate sex and Cordelia as parts of the same universe, Pat jumped up and hurried across to the table where the jigsaw was and turned through the loose pieces, at first with some interest, very soon listlessly and even with a vague sense of humiliation. That was the trouble about having anything to do with Cordelia – you turned up afire with curiosity, on the alert for the reappearance of familiar themes and extensions of the repertoire too, and in what seemed like no time you were sliding into apathy and wondering why you had come, when you had really known all along what it was going to be like when you got here.

The phase of depression was soon over. Pat heard broadcast music start up in the kitchen as suddenly as a gun being fired, in mid-career and hard at it, some piece of instant grandeur from the present century, probably American. Getting the tea was one of the things Cordelia was handy at, and the outburst of music indicated that she had successfully completed the main body of the operation yet once more. She probably rather disliked music but thought she should have it on now and again, so now she would leave some of it to blare and clash away where it could do comparatively little harm.

All genuine Cordelia scholars knew that, while quick as a flash at the preparation of tea, she normally gave pouring and handing out an ample measure of time. But today the little sloping-sided cup reached Pat not far from full and in short order, plus a plate of rococo biscuits that obviously came from some shop in particular. Perhaps Cordelia had something to say, though she opened routinely with a command to listen and an indefinite period of frowning silence. At last she said, 'Before he gets in . . . Richard's found himself a girl.'

'Surely not.'

The tone of simple and total disbelief went down less than well. 'Darling are you saying it's not possible, because if so I can assure you you're much mistaken.' Any hint of eye-rolling with this would have been most unwelcome, but for some reason Cordelia never went near that one, even on tiptoe. At least as far as Pat knew.

'Oh I see. Who is she?'

'I bet you can tell when Harry's taking an interest in somebody else whether he says anything to you or not.'

'The question doesn't seem to arise,' said Pat rather coldly.

'What, darling? Oh, she's a Russian girl he met through his college thing. It seems she's a poet, and he thinks she's a good one. Well, he'd know, I *suppose*. The story on her, or on *them* . . . is that he's meant to be getting a lot of poets and people together to get somebody out of prison somewhere in Russia. Er . . . does that sound likely to you?'

'No, and I can't understand it, either. How do you mean, get some poets together to get someone out of a Russian gaol? Are they going in by parachute? In which case why poets? They're about the last – '

'Well it doesn't sound likely to *me*, darling,' said Cordelia. People often assumed that when not speaking she was listening. 'He's doing his best to prevent me from meeting this . . . Anna female. He says we'd have nothing to talk about.'

'Something in that, perhaps. Mind you, there'd always be him to compare notes on, which would be fun I shouldn't wonder. But anyway, what would the two of you talk to each other in? What language?'

'I expect you've forgotten I studied Russian pretty seriously for a while some years ago. And she's more than likely to have picked up a bit of English on her own account. A lot of Russians do these days, you know. I simply can't wait to find out what she looks like. Richard says she's not at all attractive. Well . . .'

'Oh, so you'll be meeting her anyway. Of course.'

'Dowdy, too, he says. Well, one takes that for granted in such cases. I must say I'm on fire with curiosity to see what she'll make of Harrods, wouldn't you be, darling?'

'I don't quite see . . .' said Pat, and stopped. There was a lot she did not quite see, or see at all, as often when Cordelia was proceeding with her own type of selective exposition, skipping the bits that bored her. 'Yes, of course I would. Well, not on fire exactly. But how long – '

'We can't have poor Anna turning up in front of all these big important people dressed as if she's jumped straight off her tractor on the collective farm.'

'No, of course we can't. But a Russian girl wouldn't be able to afford more than a packet of pins at Harrods. I hardly could myself. Surely.'

Cordelia smiled at Pat over her refilled teacup, which she held in both hands though not at all by the handle. 'Oh but *I* can darling. And I think I can say I'm not precisely renowned for my meanness when it comes to questions of simple cash.'

'First of all,' Pat heard Harry's voice saying from somewhere close up, like just over her shoulder, 'it's not just a matter of thinking you can say anything, it's saying it *without fear of contradiction* darling. Secondly, if you really think you can say *that*, with or without contradiction, then I see I have to tell you you could hardly be more gravely mistaken. Because thirdly, what if anything you are renowned for is for being one of the meanest, greediest *bleeders* north of the Park. You have some smaller claims on our notice. None of them nice ones, just to put your mind at rest on that darling.'

Audible only in its distant plane of the continuum, this went on before, during and after Pat attended to what for her was a far more interesting and immediate matter. 'How seriously are you taking this?' she asked in ordinary human tones. 'I mean is Richard serious about it? How long's it been going on?'

'I don't know darling,' said Cordelia, leaving it open which question or questions she might have been answering. But the small vertical lines that had appeared along her slightly fluffy upper lip perhaps suggested that she was taking part of it seriously enough. 'Of course he's very self-contained, Richard, always has been. Sometimes I'm not even absolutely sure what he's thinking at any given moment. But I do know he hasn't been interested in any other woman for a long long time. Years darling. But now he's behaving so oddly, not wanting me to set

81

eyes on whoever she is. A bundle of nerves. You have met that lecturer's wife, haven't you? You remember the one.'

'Who's that?'

'Have another biscuit. Wasn't she here the last time you were here?'

'I don't know who you're talking about, Cordelia.'

'*Yes,* he lectures in agriculture, surely, or not quite that, one of the ones like that, would it be agronomy, *I* don't know.' This was said with a mutinous dowse-and-flash of the blue eyes, as if precision had been unreasonably demanded. 'Swept-up hair and earrings and . . . No, no, *she's* the one with the . . . Barbara whatever it is, that's right.'

Even for Cordelia, this was switchback stuff. Anybody who knew her less well than Pat might have thought she was worried or upset about something. 'Yes, of course,' said Pat almost soothingly.

'She promised faithfully to pick up some stamps for me on her way. It's rather a bore for me to have to go traipsing down to the post office in Carmarthen Road there, you know, Asian gentlemen running it and there's always a queue. Do have another biscuit darling. Hang on – hang on, this is her now.'

A human shape had passed the window and a sound was heard at the front door, soon identifiable as that of a key being inserted into its lock. Cordelia sat upright and went into a fast pantomime of eyes first dilated then close-shut, shaken head, brandished forefinger, shoulders raised to ear level, though anything less than a bellow would have been quite secure and perhaps more informative. Pat watched, vainly striving for detachment, for close observation only, as always at one of these shows. There came a final wrap-up gesture from Cordelia and her husband entered the room with a kind of skirmisher's gait, quite unlike his familiar rather irritatingly resolute stride and suggesting that he was indeed in some sort of rare condition. His smile at Pat, whom he had met here two or three times, always in her present chair and of course her present role, was free of contempt but also of liking. That at any rate was usual.

'You remember Pat Dobbs, Richard,' said Cordelia. She left it open whether she was putting him into some category of amnesic dementia or reprimanding him for being insufficiently cordial to an old and valued friend, ruefully in either case.

Still moving and standing unnaturally, Richard had to wait while Cordelia did her standard precision job on refilling the teapot and then hesitated over which cup should be his out of a choice of one. While this was going on he spoke of having had to drop his car in at the repair place on account of a tracking fault, but not in a tone that carried much conviction. In the end he was passed something under a gill of fluid the colour of very dry sherry, as Pat saw when he came and sat near her.

After giving him a second or so to settle down, Cordelia said, 'I've been telling Pat about this Russian girl of yours darling,' and Pat saw something else — what she was here for over and above the fetching of fish.

'I can't think that that would interest, well, anybody at all.'

'Oh but you're so wrong, isn't he darling,' meaning this time Pat, who was saved having to take any sort of decision before she could have got her mouth open when Cordelia went on, 'I mean it's most intriguing, the way Anna Pavlova and I are being kept apart, and I can't help thinking a teeny bit hilarious too.'

'You no doubt find it intriguing, as you phrase it,' said Richard steadily, 'and more besides, I dare say, but it doesn't seem to me to be suitable for public discussion.'

'Seem to you! Suitable! Public discussion! Darling, aren't we being just a weeny bit pompous?'

'Quite possibly. Nevertheless, if you'll pardon the expression, we shouldn't be talking about this sort of thing in front of someone else, whoever they may be and however much we may like and trust them. I'm sorry, Pat, I know you didn't ask to be here.'

Pat had been wanting not to be there for some time, since not long after arriving in fact, and actively intending to leave for nearly a minute, but still not actively enough to get her out of the horrible reproduction-Georgian chair she now occupied. Her sense that these two had seldom or never talked like this before kept her in place while she went into a bit of muttering about time getting on, examined her watch, etc. Not that she expected to enjoy going over the scene with Harry any more whole-heartedly than usual.

'I'm afraid,' Cordelia was saying, 'I'm not quite crystal-clear about what sort of *thing* it is we're talking about, my darling.'

'Oh yes you are, Cordelia,' said Richard as steadily as ever.

'That's on one view of the matter. But in fact we're talking about nothing. Nothing at all.'

'*Well*, if it's nothing, that's to say *zeeing as how* it's nothing, give me the girl's telephone number and I'll arrange to take her to Harrods and give her a lovely treat.'

'She doesn't speak English. As I told you.'

'Oh, I bet she'll understand if I say to her, Here heap big rich shop sell rich pretty things to wear, you choose which, you take and me give money.'

This latest in a famous series – jewels of Cordelian taste and intellect – might not have been so noteworthy without the accompaniment of dilated Apache-type eyes and the gruff staccato bass-baritone delivery, together with the strong likelihood that it was being presented *as a joke* to the man of all others on earth least likely to appreciate it. As things were, Pat felt the back of her neck going hot.

She wondered why, unless he was gathering resolve to kill his wife then and there, Richard did not simply leave the room at least. But, after swallowing more loudly than she would have believed possible without practice, he said, no less steadily,

'Anna Danilova is an educated Russian, not a savage. Like many Russians she's not well off, and even if she were she wouldn't have been able to bring much money out with her, and out of what she has got there'd be very little to spare on clothes. She's fiercely independent and she doesn't want charity. It wouldn't be a kindness to dangle a lot of stuff she could never afford in front of her. In fact it would be a . . .' He stopped before saying what manner of thing it would be.

Having waited courteously until she was sure Richard had finished for the moment, Cordelia said, 'What a lot you seem to have found out about this girl, darling, after only knowing her for what is it, a couple of days? But then you're such a tremendous expert on Russians, aren't you, how silly of me to have forgotten that.'

'I have run into a few human beings too in my time.'

'I say, have you really? My word, what a luggy vellow you are. I never seem to come across any myself. But with all respect, my darling, perhaps you don't know such a frightful lot about lady human beings. You can't, or you'd know that any woman whether she's Russian or Siamese or Eskimo would be absolutely thrilled to bits just to have the chance of strolling through a place like that and simply casting an eye over what's there without the least thought of actually possessing any of it.'

'I can't help that,' said Richard. 'I don't know about any of that. It's just a bad idea. Not right for somebody like that.'

'Goodness, there we go again. Not right for her to be shown the scrumptious goodies that wicked old capitalism can produce. Would it be hurtful or offensive to her poor little communist soul?'

'People like Anna don't think like that any more, if they ever did.'

'Well, honestly, Richard,' said Cordelia, sounding as much like an ordinary human being as she ever did, 'I can't see anything to get excited about at the thought of a young Russian woman being taken round a large London department store by another woman who's been there before, who may not speak her language but with good will et cetera et cetera. And she's got eyes in her head, hasn't she? Why all the fuss, for heaven's sake?'

'But it isn't just another woman, any other woman.'

Richard stopped again and Pat continued for him, needless to say without letting her lips move, 'it's you darling, and you can't be trusted, or rather you can be bloody trusted to get every last drop out of a situation like that in the way of patronising and humiliating someone who's completely out of their sodding element darling.' Then, still subvocalising but on her own behalf, 'And by the way weren't you supposed to be able to speak Russian before Richard came in?'

'You mean it's a rich woman,' said Cordelia in something close to her usual tone.

'Well yes, but – '

'Well, I'm afraid there's absolutely nothing I can do about that at this stage, you'll simply have to get used to the idea. I should have thought you'd have managed that already, you've had plenty of time, haven't you? And I'd also have expected you to have noticed by now that I'm not the sort of rich woman who embarrasses people by going round flinging her money about for the sake of it. If you think I'm going to load your little Russian peasant girl up with mink and diamonds then you've got another think coming, my darling. In any case, I'm sure she's got far too much of a sense of sturdy independence to sponge off a rich capitalist like that. And of course she's a poet as well, and you say she's a good one, so she'd tend to be above that kind of thing anyway.'

This time it was Richard who hung on to make sure the last bit was over. Then he sent Pat a glance of desperation, of appeal, possibly of reproach. She saw, as she put it later to Harry, that an additional trouble about having anything to do with Cordelia was that from being a mere observer you could find yourself turning into an accomplice.

'I'll come with you,' she told Cordelia.

'Oh, there's no need for you to go to that trouble darling.'

'No trouble at all, I assure you, it'll be a pleasure. I haven't been to Harrods for ages, if that's where you were really thinking of taking – what is she called?'

'Oh, but you must have so much else going on in your life, you can't just – '

'I'm in a series in the autumn but I haven't even had the scripts yet, so for instance I was able to come here today without any trouble at all. As you saw. No, really, I'll be glad to join the party.'

'I've got her telephone number here,' said Richard as smartly as if they had been rehearsing together all morning. 'And she's called Anna Danilova. Got a pen?'

Thwarted on that one, Cordelia struck back on Pat's departure by forcing on her the book about Athens (Ganymede Press, 1937), not perhaps much of a reverse in itself but carrying with it the penalty of being several times rung up to report how she was getting on with it, the first time at half-past eleven that night or at first light the next morning, and after a couple of days being urgently and repeatedly asked for it back. To eke that out, and just to show there was no ill-feeling, nor ever had been, Pat was given a note to deliver to an earl's divorced daughter-in-law who lived only a couple of minutes off her way home, and surely she would be going by taxi. Harry, whose family had come from Dumfries, had been known to say that that Cordelia was a bonny wee fighter, admittedly less often than he said other things about her.

On her way out, Pat thought to herself that it was not really odd that Cordelia went on about being rich the whole time, considering the way people with titles went on about titles and people with grand houses about grand houses. She wondered too whether it was Cordelia that Richard wanted to keep away from Anna or the other way round, but saw that more time must pass and more must happen before that could be answered. Then she forgot all that on encountering a woman of her own general age and sort coming without alacrity up the garden path. It was no great feat to spot her as the agronomist's wife.

'Hallo, Barbara,' said Pat suddenly, rather unkindly too no doubt, but that was what a session with Cordelia was liable to do to you. 'Got the stamps all right, I hope?'

'Got the – '

'Because Cordelia's in a bit of a state about missing the post, you know. Oh, and by the way . . .'

'What? What?'

'Eleven Across is CUNTS NEVER LEARN.'

'Who are you?'

'Not that you're the only one, love.'

SEVEN

'What I can't understand is how you get on in bed,' said Crispin.

'Believe it or not, we get on quite adequately, thank you. Do you want details?'

'No, thank you too. But I didn't mean that. I knew that, at least you've told it me before. What I really meant was, how you, singular, manage to get on, scilicet at least quite adequately, in bed, with somebody like Cordelia, correction, with Cordelia, correction, with somebody who talks and behaves in the way Cordelia is heard and seen to do when out of bed, if you can piece together what I'm driving at.'

Richard had already assured himself more than once that no one in the tennis-club bar was paying them any attention, but now he did so again before replying. 'Haven't we reached this stage rather soon? And what has Godfrey to say on the point?'

'By the way there's no need for anyone to run through again how extra splendid she looks when she's not out of bed, all that. Godfrey's always been reticent in this area. You'd think he'd find it easier to talk to his own brother about that type of stuff, but it seems to make it harder. I rather suspect things never went very well for him and Cordelia in that sphere, but that's just brotherly feeling on my part. And if we have reached this stage rather soon, you and I, it was you who brought us to it. Not that I'm complaining, but you were going on like a tobacco auctioneer about how terrible she was while you were still coming into earshot. If I didn't know you better I'd have thought you'd been drinking.'

'I'm sorry, Crispin.'

'I said I wasn't complaining. Quite the contrary. I've never heard you talk like that about her before. Like an exhilarating breath of foul air. Something must have happened. But let's go into what it might be after we've done a bit of what we're supposed to have come here for. I think we're on.'

They went, but were back in just over the hour. Or Crispin was, still in his tennis gear while Richard showered and changed in the club as always, in furtherance, presumably, of vague feelings of independence, the same sort of thing that made him never be the one to book the court, though he paid for it in scrupulous alternation. Taking up a copy of yesterday's *Times* business section, Crispin looked at it with feigned closeness, as notional deterrent to the cruising bores who were now and then to be found at Rocky's and whom Richard was so bad at detecting beyond a couple of metres. Crispin spent a short time trying to imagine what it was like to make love to Cordelia, and then a rather longer time trying to back-track.

Along came Richard, his dark hair still damp, his expression grave, in fact with his familiar air of incomplete recovery from some recent spiritual crisis. 'That wasn't very good, I'm afraid,' he said in a heavy tone.

'Oh, come, 3–6 against me is about your mark. And where did we get to after that? You got a couple, didn't you?'

'It was 3–1 in your favour. My service wasn't too bad, I didn't make any actual mistakes but I could feel myself hitting them too hard. I wonder why.'

'Don't start talking in that tone of voice or you'll suddenly find you're dead. Would you like a drink? I'm going to have one.'

'No. No thanks. Oh, a Coke would be nice.'

'Well, anyway.'

They sat down by the window that gave a view of the show court. This held a small boy in his twenties and a middle-aged coach with a gouty nose. Just then the coach was not actually coaching but engaged with a machine that resembled a small supermarket trolley. It evidently had the property of sucking up inert tennis-balls into itself. Watching him at work brought a feeling of lassitude.

'It's this Russian poetess I met the other night,' said Richard.

'Of course it is. Are you going to tell me about her?'

Richard was and did. 'It's not just that she's attractive,' he finished. 'She's very nice as well, if you know what I mean.'

'Better than you do, perhaps. That's the time to look out, my lad, when you start thinking one of them's nice. Especially . . .'

'When you're married to somebody like Cordelia. Just so. Anyway, it must be meeting her that accounts for the new way I've started feeling about Cordelia.'

'All right, what way's that? I'll prod you this once but not again.'

'I've started to hate her. I think I'll have that drink after all. My turn.' As soon as this was done he went straight on, 'I don't hate her all the time, I may even go back to not hating her at all, but she was threatening to take Anna to Harrods and that got me. And just you shut up, Crispin. No, you were going to say something clever about that sounding a very modest form of persecution compared with some others in Cordelia's repertoire, weren't you? Eh?'

'I –'

'People like you seem to think I've never noticed the way she talks and makes people do things and keeps the central heating turned off, but I notice it better than anybody. It doesn't make any difference as a rule. But when she started threatening to take Anna to Harrods I couldn't stand it. And if it wasn't Harrods she'd find something else. Inexhaustibly. I can't let, I simply can't have those two meeting under any circumstances.'

'Don't you, old top. But can we get back to this Russian poetess? How far has it gone, whatever it is?'

'Nothing's been done or said. Well, I've only known her a couple of days and she's got people to see.'

'Is that to do with this scheme of hers about a petition or whatever it is?'

'Partly, or it will be. She's got relatives to see, too. In places like Watford.'

'You said something about a statement to the effect that she's one of the great poets of our time. Should I have heard of her? Is she that good? What do you say?'

Richard was not quite unprepared for a question along these lines. 'Well, it's not my kind of thing in a sense. There've been a lot of developments over there in the last twenty years and especially the last five that I just haven't kept up with. But she's pretty well known for her age, highly regarded by colleagues, gets translated, coming on in America, beginning to be known here, all that.'

'I think I see,' said Crispin after a pause. 'And you find her attractive.' He spoke as if Richard's feelings in such matters were notoriously eccentric.

Richard retorted stoutly, 'Yes. Whether anyone else agrees with me or not.'

'And you want to give her a hand with her petition and scheme and what-not.'

'Yes.'

'But you don't think that you yourself can do anything very effective to help her with it or them.'

'No, I don't.'

Ever since first hearing of the scheme/petition Crispin had looked slightly low-spirited. Now he looked very low-spirited. 'So you're asking me to have a crack.'

'I suppose I am. I mean yes, with all your contacts and connections and what-not. Yes.'

'Oh dear. I'll have to hear more about it, but not at this very moment. I want to get home. Come back and have a drink. In fact get moving right away, there's that horrible golfing bugger, I can't bear, quick, no, oh Christ, keep going, had it, shit. Well hallo there.'

One of Crispin's contacts or connections, a man of about his age but with white hair, barred their path near the door. Ignoring Richard, he seized Crispin's hand in both of his and stood for a short time, mutely smiling with current blessedness and the contemplation of more to follow. Instead of imparting wisdom from on high, however, he eventually said in a South London accent, 'You are coming to Harpenden, aren't you?'

'Am I? I mean when is it?'

'The 17th. It would mean, such a lot, such a tremendous, amount, to everybody, not only the boys, but the Harpenden crowd, too, if you, could possibly be, on the team, my dear fellow.'

'Well, thank you, very much, I mean thank you very much, I'll let you know.'

'I'm sorry, I'm sorry, but it has to be settled today. Now. And you promised you would. Actually.'

'Oh. Did I. In that case I'd love to come.'

With no sign of pleasure or relief, the white-haired man immediately went on, 'Assemble here three pm on the 17th.' Pause. 'Write it down, eh?'

91

With this there came a little wink and a half-cocking of the head that, for a fleeting instant, made Richard feel like one of those conscientious maniacs who at certain times ask their keepers to lock them up before they cause damage to property or loss of life. Nevertheless it had not escaped him that the golfing bugger had by now released Crispin's hand and so allowed writing-down as a physical possibility. Yielding this point would have been a clear acknowledgement of defeat. But at the last moment Crispin roused himself, pushed his way forward, said in a high voice and twice over that he would remember when and where, called good-bye without turning his head as he moved. Richard was relieved to see his champion emerge shaken but not shattered, never before having seen him as much as shaken. But he knew he could never mention any of this.

On the way to the outdoors, Crispin said reprovingly to him, 'You see? That's what it's like.' Then he went straight on, 'During that most unfortunate encounter I seem to have come to a sort of conclusion. Without needing to hear any more I feel strongly that all this talk of petitions and schemes is quite absurd, impractical, the purest bookish fantasy. I'm slightly surprised that you should have listened to it for five minutes. You, a man with some knowledge of the world even if it's less than you imagine, and beyond argument a real knowledge of Russia, in most respects superior to mine and certainly more recent. You must indeed have found the young lady attractive. Richard. Pull yourself together, please, and reconsider your position.'

Coming from a dishevelled fellow in a sort of dressing-gown approaching a busy set of lifts, this might have seemed incongruous language. Not so to Richard. He paid no attention to the clink and rumble of nearby machinery but said, 'I hope at least you'll agree to see her, Crispin.'

'What purpose would that serve?'

'Well, for one thing you'd be obliging an old friend. And don't you want to see what she looks like? You need be under no obligation, but I think you should hear what she has to say for herself.'

'Possibly. You mustn't forget she's a Russian.'

'I can assure you that having met her I'm in no danger of doing that.'

'Or that I'm a Czech. Let me remind you that from our point of view the Nazis came and went, the Russians came and stayed for forty years.'

'They did so without consulting Anna.'

'No doubt. But the thought somewhat abates my naturally generous impulses.'

They left the building. When Crispin's dark-blue BMW with its Ugandan chauffeur had drawn up at the kerb, they got into it and were driven away. After a moment Crispin said without much apparent interest in the answer,

'Anna Danilova. Is that a Jewish name?'

Richard moved round as he sat on the dark-blue corduroy. 'It might be. Why?'

'Surely it's a point of some significance. As they'll tell you themselves, Jews aren't like other people. I've always found it helpful to remember that.'

'Oh really?'

'Yes really, Richard. Even if you think that any and every remark a gentile makes about Jews must be anti-semitic. There are plenty of people who think so.'

'Now you mention it I seem to remember her saying something about an uncle of hers who's a priest, or tried to be.'

'A firm negative, then. Now. Richard. Reference Anna. My desire to have a look at her is sharpening with every moment that passes. So farewell to caution – I'll see her. For once I've got a lever to winkle you out of your secretiveness. How would it be if we went and picked her up from her hotel or safe-house or whatever it is?'

'Well, it would embarrass her, the car and everything, and she's probably not in anyway. And surely you don't mean now, do you, this minute?'

'Why not? It might make a bit of a distraction for Freddie, and she could do with something in that line. You may have noticed the old girl's been rather knocking it back recently, I don't really know why. She was quite extraordinary this morning, as alert as she ever gets and yet paying even less attention than usual to what was going on. Quite worrying if one thinks about it. A Russian poetess would be just the thing to take her out of herself. If little Anna's not available you could tell Freddie about her at any length you fancy. All right, we won't insist on calling in person at where she may well not be. You ring her from home, eh?'

The Radetsky residence, known as the Dom, was on a corner and stood back a few metres from both roads, from which it was partly hidden by trees of unfamiliar genus, with dull greyish leaves. The chauffeur took the BMW briskly up to it, then, when the door of an intramural garage flew up, moved it forward in a single bound, at the end of which some external agency like the arrestor gear on an aircraft-carrier seemed to come into play. Richard was used to this, and to the abruptness with which the house door slid into the wall, and to the cylindrical glass-enclosed lift from which an apparatus-infested exercise area could be briefly seen. But as usual he was not quite fully reconciled to the part of the house they now stepped into, whose Axminster-type carpets, dark panelling and paintings of spaniels, dead salmon and pheasants and stuff to do with fox-hunting reminded the newcomer of the kind of Mayfair hotel favoured by Americans. 'It's not meant to put you at your ease or be in good taste,' Crispin had explained on an early visit, as they hurried past a lifelike stag's head, 'just to make you feel either superior or poor, both healthy frames of mind. As you can imagine I do quite a lot of entertaining here. Some business too.'

'Don't you actually like any of it?' Richard had asked then or later.

'Actually I don't care for things much at all, not ones to look at, but there are a few bits and pieces down in Wiltshire I can't help having a sort of soft spot for. I don't go in for all that much entertaining there, do you see.'

Although Richard had yet to see those bits and pieces, his experience told him that they would not be scattered over the entire county of Wiltshire, as Crispin's words undoubtedly implied, but concentrated in some dwelling there, one he owned and had several times referred to in other contexts. At such times he seemed to Richard to have an immense life, in comparison with which his own was bloodless and underpopulated, even though it would still never have occurred to him to want to swap.

Now Crispin showed him into a small room he had probably not seen before and left him, saying that here was a telephone. It was a moment before he noticed it lurking among other items of hardware. It had a lot of buttons and lights on it or attached to it and he drew from it a variety of noises, including a husky organic-sounding howl, before he got Anna. In reply to his explanation and summons she was very brief, almost military, as if fearful of tapping, and was gone before he could pass her any of the encouraging phrases he had had ready. Beset by undirected anxiety, he glanced out of the window at some of the grey greenery while noises louder than the telephone ones began to be audible outside the room – muffled shouts, running feet, more running feet, running water, a slithering thump against the other side of the wall as if some animal about the size of an ox had blundered against it. Then Freddie came in.

'What the hell do you think you're doing, you silly bugger, hiding yourself away in here?' she asked. By the time she reached 'bugger' her tone had shifted from instinctive impatience to a more calculated geniality.

'Crispin parked me in here to telephone.'

'What? Crispin's changing. I mean he's changing his clothes. He said something about some Russian poet girl coming round.'

'So she is.' Now that Richard remembered Freddie had been said to be drunk he could see and hear that she was, though no more so than usual, he would have said. 'She should be here quite soon.'

'What? Hey, how's me oh pow git-non then?'

'Pow?'

'Nggornn . . . I'm sorry, Richard, how's Cordelia?'

'Very well. Thank you.'

With a fresh dose of geniality, Freddie said, 'Come on, come and have a drink in the . . .' She got no further, less from the assault of alcohol than because the rooms in the Dom tended not to have definite names.

'Good idea.'

'How much does she know about Olga, meaning your Russian friend?'

'Anna. I'm afraid there's not much *to* know, at least nothing *interesting*.'

'I'm sorry to hear that,' said Freddie, loudly and distinctly.

'Yes, well, suppose we go and have that drink right away.'

'Of course, how frightfully silly and rude of me, let's go now. It's early days yet, after all.'

In the room where they were to have their drink, a man with a glass already in his hand was peering at a bookshelf, a slim dark man with hair of the texture that most often goes with early baldness, though he had kept most of his. When he heard the door open he said in a high, discontented voice, 'Does Crispin actually *read* about all these castles and country seats?' Then he looked round and said, 'Oh, I'm sorry, Richard, I didn't see you.'

Not quite at once, Richard recognised him as Crispin's brother, Godfrey Radetsky. On their rare meetings Richard had found him polite but wary, as if uncertain of where the talk might lead him. No powers of penetration were needed to indicate that the topic of Cordelia was not one he would relish. About her general state he would sometimes blurt out a short question, calculated less to elicit facts than to assure Richard he bore him no ill-will in this regard. Today as always he wore clothes of surpassing neatness.

Saying it had been a long time and that he expected Richard had been as busy as he had (successfully designing stage sets, though he left this unsaid), Godfrey joined the other two at a butler's table where a tray of drinks stood. At Freddie's invitation Richard poured himself a whisky and soda, making it a stiff one on his own initiative. He had no objection to Godfrey either as individual or as marital predecessor, but found him an unequalled conveyor of embarrassment. Russian scholar had just managed to form the wish that man of the theatre would painlessly disappear in a cloud of smoke when, looking from one man to the other, Freddie said emphatically,

'Oh Godfrey, Richard was telling me Cordelia's much, much better.'

Godfrey took it like a real pro, hardly dilating his eyes at all and spilling almost nothing of his glass of Perrier. Richard spoke up quite quickly for him and asked him how (yes) Nancy and the children were. Like Cordelia, they were doing fine and that was that. Like everybody else.

The consensus that all was well made Freddie uneasy. She stepped up her rate of looking from one man to the other, which at least had the effect of making them talk faster. Finally her rather long face showed that she had something in particular on the way, and she suddenly said, 'It is wonderful seeing you two blokes getting on so well together. You run into each other about twice in ten years to my knowledge and here you are chattering away in no time like a pair of bloody magpies. Wonderful.'

The two blokes showed the depth of their concord by simultaneous total silence.

'Absolutely marvellous, especially considering what totally opposite types of human being you are. One all heart and emotion and the other all intellect and power of the will.'

Richard felt like asking her what she had been reading lately, but still said nothing. Godfrey said with unexpected impatience, 'Which of those two am I supposed to be?'

'What do you mean, obviously you're the artist, aren't you?'

'In any case I'm afraid I don't see the point.'

'But you must have more in common than meets the eye because after all you have both been married to the same woman.'

Godfrey parted his jaws and blinked.

'It must be rather eerie in a way,' Freddie went on intelligently, 'but then I expect it all happened so many years ago that the two of you have more or less forgotten all about it or at least take it for granted. But then sometimes – '

'If I can just break in there,' said Godfrey, giving a brisk nod and doing something emphatic with his glasses like taking them off or putting them on. As he continued, his voice seemed to tremble once or twice, and Richard wondered what Freddie might have been saying to him earlier. He wondered too what convulsion of nature would reconcile her to Cordelia's existence, evident character and marital and other history, short of her own death.

'For your information,' Godfrey was saying without acrimony, 'and I'm pretty sure this is no news to Richard, I have neither more or less forgotten being married to Cordelia nor do I take it for granted any more than I have more or less forgotten he is now married to her nor take that for granted. What I'm quite positive about, and here I think I can speak for Richard too . . . is that I don't want any of that, any of it, brought up in conversation for any reason or for no reason, anything to do with any of it, in any connection . . . whatever. At any time. Now have you got that, Freddie?' he finished gently.

She had got the general drift and responded with some huffy apology-simulation and saying of things like had no intention and had no idea and really. But Richard took the message as also aimed at him for good measure. He let Freddie finish and said, 'Where are you and Nancy living now?'

Godfrey smiled. 'Near Parsons Green. You must come out and see our new house, my dear fellow. When we can persuade the builders they've done enough for us.'

And the warmth in that was genuine, but Richard knew no such visit would take place, just as when Freddie had muttered something about putting potatoes on and left the room there was no exchange between him and Godfrey of even a mild glance of triumph or comradeship. Little indeed was said in the luckily brief time before Crispin reappeared. He was wearing a sort of après-polo outfit of such blatant cheapness to Richard's eye that it must have been surpassingly expensive, or else blatantly cheap. Crispin walked through a beam of late sunshine that made his face look momentarily younger and also more careworn. He glanced distantly at Richard and said to his brother, 'What did you think?'

'I'll ring you later. Nothing shattering. Well and truly drunk, though.'

'Oh yes. I do wish she had a pal, one of her own sex. It's bad when a woman hasn't got one of those.'

'Also when a man hasn't,' said Godfrey, polishing his glasses.

'No doubt. Sandy's worse than useless. Well, Richard, are we going to see this Russian girl of yours?'

'I can't pretend I don't know who you mean. Yes, she's on her way.'

'How's she coming?'

'Tube from where she's staying. It's only a couple of stations. Anna likes the Tube. Well, it gives her a chance to tell me how much better the Moscow one is.'

Crispin said to Godfrey, 'Anna's a Russian poetess Richard picked up the other evening whom he wants me to get presented at court and given an Oxford doctorate and a few other things like that. I'll tell you more about it later.'

'If you must,' said Godfrey. 'As far as I'm concerned, poetry packed up in 1928 when Hardy dropped off the twig.'

'Anna writes in Russian,' said Richard.

'No really? All right, Blok went about the same time, didn't he?'

'Good God, I didn't know you knew anything about him.'

'I don't, really.'

'And you're not to start telling him about him,' said Crispin, and to Godfrey, 'You will stay and meet this girl, will you?'

'If I'm not going to be in the way.'

Richard had been hoping slightly for the departure of the man of the theatre before Anna turned up, just to help her to feel less outnumbered, but now he saw that a little harmless dilution of the company would have its points too. Without much of a struggle he accepted another drink. Drinks and Anna seemed to have some sort of natural affinity.

When, not much later, the doorbell rang, Crispin hurried off to answer it without stopping talking to the other two, over his shoulder to start with, then on his return facing the way he was coming with Anna driven before him. He might have been playing up to what he took to be an untravelled Russian's expectation of a well-to-do-Englishman – friendly, self-assured, decent, not taking much notice of anything anyone else had to say, stupid.

Anna held her own by talking to Richard in Russian. She was wearing a long-sleeved orange-yellow garment with a loose belt of the same material and all told of no general description or certain provenance. If what Richard had once read in a fashion magazine of Cordelia's, a rather intellectual one, was to be believed, and every garment made a statement about its wearer, then what this one was stating must run something like, 'I know this isn't very nice but I don't mind. The people here will think it's because I'm Russian that I've got it on at all, and then when I've got it home I can clean the kitchen with it.' But he thought she looked nice in it too.

After some detailed introducing, a conversation of a sort started up. Hardly any of it seemed to be in Russian or Czech. Even if the two languages were more closely allied in practice than Richard's understanding told him, not every Czech was going to admit to an acquaintance with Russian and almost no Russian would have any with Czech. Nevertheless something was interchanged on the ever-serviceable and dependably boring topic of changes in the USSR, their significance, unreality, etc. Richard did a little interpreting for Anna. Though speaking hardly any herself she evidently understood quite a bit of Godfrey's English. She and Crispin managed some German, which left Richard following at a distance. Anna talked of the difficulties of being a poet in Russia without mentioning any special difficulties encountered by a lousy poet in Russia. After some of this Godfrey said he must be going and left. He went without delay or fuss, but Richard thought he glanced at his brother last of all and sent him some kind of affirmative message.

'Good,' said Crispin absently. He had seemed preoccupied for some minutes and had hardly opened his mouth. Now he recovered and went on, 'Let's all have another drink to fortify us for the short serious bit to follow. That bit will mean more interpreting for you, Richard, if that's all right.'

Richard was spared finding himself saying it was what he was there for when, in defiance of any instructions Crispin might have issued earlier, Freddie came back into the room. For a wonder she seemed genuinely anxious not to interfere with what was in progress. She even looked a couple of sizes smaller as she sidled along by the wall making don't-mind-me faces and gestures. Managing not to fall down flat on his face with relief, Crispin waited while Richard explained to Anna who Freddie was and Freddie almost looked uncomfortable at being the centre of attention for a moment. Then Crispin broke in.

'Miss Danilova knows I'm a Czech by parentage and that I'm rich and powerful?'

Richard answered a little distantly. 'I described your family history earlier. The rest she's probably managed to pick up for herself.'

'No doubt she has. Ask her this, please. What is her attitude towards the Czech wish to escape from subjection by Russian power?'

In due time Richard said, 'Miss Danilova says her attitude is favourable. She will do all she can to further the Czech cause as soon as she and her family and friends have themselves escaped from subjection by Russian power.'

'Convey my thanks. Now if you would, ask her, what would be her attitude towards receiving Czech help in an enterprise that has aspects of opposition to Russian power?'

'She says she would accept any kind of help that didn't come from German fascists or Uzbekistanis.'

'My thanks again.'

When he had conveyed them, Richard said to Crispin, 'Then you're going to help her after all.'

'Yes. You might as well tell her so.'

But Anna needed no telling. She went over and shook Crispin's hand and thanked him in English. Freddie too seemed to have an inkling of what had been at stake and approached her in turn.

'She's all right even if she is a Russian. And however ridiculous it'll make a change from what I normally get up to.' Crispin moved aside. 'Whatever my better judgement tells me. It'll fail, of course, but what of that?'

'Nobly spoken,' said Richard, shaking his hand in a different style from Anna's and clapping him on the back. The slight theatricality of words and actions was uncharacteristic of Richard, in whom a different voice was saying, 'After that fine display of worldly wisdom, patriotism, prudence, scruple, all those, you can't wait to do the lovable thing. Czech or Russian or sub-Carpatho-Ukrainian, when it comes down to it you're all the bloody same.'

Perhaps Crispin sensed part of this. Anyway, he said quickly, 'It's what you wanted me to do, isn't it?'

EIGHT

Crispin at once set to work to define and build up Anna's project. He scorned the notion of any sort of committee, saying no such body ever accomplished anything but getting through time and money, and declared he could do most of what was necessary over the telephone and by chatting to a few mates here and there.

Three of those mates, close or distant, were somebody in the Foreign Office, a popular novelist and a public-relations consultant, who together drafted the text of the public announcement or citation that would in time set forth Anna's claims and also issued interim Press handouts. Crispin sent her with an introduction to this individual, accompanied her on a visit to that official, went on his own to the other governing body. He rigorously filtered her public appearances, impressing on everybody the need to damp down any kind of newsy, flashy image and to promote one of sober, almost scholarly distinction. This view of her was helped by her shortage of English and her uncommunicativeness to interpreters, not least about the contemporary state of Russia. For the same reasons she was poor value at drinks parties, one late-night TV interview, on which she even managed to look not very good, turned out to be enough, and they of the media got tired of hanging round the stuffy Pimlico retreat which she seemed to like and nobody wanted her to leave.

Except perhaps Richard. As the days went by he saw comparatively little of her, less than Crispin did, he calculated, for instance at the couple of dinner-parties, hearteningly described as 'stuffy' and 'just diplomatically useful', that they had evidently attended together. In one way this suited Richard, because it lessened the danger that her horrible poetry might come up in conversation. Without any abatement of its horribleness in memory it was more easily borne there, becoming at that distance the almost funny phenomenon it very much was not when seen from closer to. But, on the other hand, every time he did see her he found himself wanting her to take her clothes off more and more and finding it harder and harder to believe that there seemed to be no other bugger round the place similarly energised.

Richard's feelings in both aspects of the matter sharpened when in due course Anna came to the Institute to give the reading from her works that he had helped to arrange. Seeing without difficulty that he would have to go to it relieved him of the need to decide whether he could bear to or not. Crispin threw an early dinner before the occasion, inviting Tristram Hallett and his wife and a couple of pundits and their wives as well as Dr Vaisey and his wife. It was no more difficult to judge that the attendance of the last-named wife at any such encounter was, if not epistemologically unthinkable, as close to it as most things get. So last-named husband stayed away too to be on the safe side. The reading itself, represented as the latest of the ordeals coming the way of that omnipresent Russian expert, was a different matter.

With as little to-do as workmen putting up scaffolding, Cordelia had prepared herself for giving Richard a cheerful send-off to this event. She was standing in the hall with her hands clasped behind her as he prepared to leave.

'The things you do in the cause of international culture,' she said.

'Oh, it shouldn't be too bad. As these things go. Anyway.'

'Might even be fun, conceivably. Now I remember, you did say her poetry had its points.' It was possible to infer that if Cordelia's phonetic system had been normal she would have stood revealed as one of those who talk of poytry.

'Well, it has a certain crude vigour I suppose you could call it.'

'I imagine there'll be some sort of get-together afterwards.'

'I'll have to hang about for a few minutes but then I'll be slipping away.'

Not quite swinging her shoulders to and fro and not putting her head on one side exactly, just sort of round the corner, she said, 'Is it possible that Anna and I might meet some day?'

'As soon as I can arrange it. Crispin keeps her pretty busy these days – I hardly catch a glimpse of her myself. You could have come tonight of course but it really would be ridiculous for anyone to go who doesn't have to.'

'Of *course* darling, you run along.'

Seven out of ten, he thought to himself as he drove to the Institute. That last stroke had really been the best for his side. He could have afforded to push it harder, betting that contrariness, realistic fear of boredom, desire to hold out for a more advantageous first encounter with Anna, would have combined to keep Cordelia away tonight. Going over their exchange just now, mercifully short but as rich as ever in silent parentheses and unuttered footnotes, he came to Anna's poetry. Position held: while never falsely praising it he was not going to let the old – let Cordelia have his true opinion. Then Anna herself and the threatened meeting. Position under growing stress – well, anybody could see, if there was nothing in it, and there was nothing, why not? Just to start with, Anna was to any eye much better-looking than he had rashly said at first. He had done his best to dismiss what had since been seen of her in the newspapers by talking about showbiz camera techniques, people who happened to be photogenic and so on. Fragile stuff. And more important, when and if the dread confrontation took place, then if he was present, which he would unquestionably have to be, whatever he said or did or failed to do or say, Cordelia would only have to see him looking or not looking at Anna and something awful but unforeseeable, but still awful and un-controllable, would happen and oh God. Cordelia's peculiar version of a send-off had economically blunted his expectation.

What it was he expected he had no very straightforward idea of. He was bound to get a good and a fresh look at Anna, and he was quite excited about that even after Cordelia's parting shots. On the other hand, he doubted whether her nervous, high-pressure style of talk and behaviour would go down in front of an audience, whatever they might turn out to be like. Well, perhaps to suit Crispin's views the advance publicity for this do had been low-key, chiefly round the Institute and the university, a few small ads, a diary paragraph or two but no general Press coverage. Yet previous experience told how a great deal less notice than that would reach the most unclassifiable and dramatic bores and haul them in from all over the Home Counties, together with droves of silent faceless lumps who might have been making for a talk on new ways of looking at something or other. At least Anna's looks would appeal to anyone who saw her. She had a good voice too. It would go down all right. It might even be a success. He hoped it would. Did he, did he really? He felt a shit for letting the thought even enter his head, but such a success would, in a sense beyond all personal considerations, be a victory for something hostile to what he thought was valuable. It would encourage the notion that there could be a sphere of meaning beyond language.

Richard forgot all such tenuous concerns on entering the not very cheerful public hall, scene of many a bewildering inaugural lecture and well-received keynote speech at a conference in the vacation, where the reading was to take place. He went in at the back and moved forward a couple of rows at a time to the front row of chairs. Representatives of numerous callings, from literature down to modes of communication, with assorted academics and art-loving industrialists somewhere in between, were all about him. Crispin, Freddie, first and second pundits and wives, came in at the front and sat down in the body of the hall. As earlier new arrivals had done, they picked up and glanced at the printed folders awaiting them on their seats. These contained English prose summaries of the poems to be read. Richard had put his aside after no more than a glance, to leave his mind unencumbered for Anna's performance. He was briefly in almost breathtaking suspense till the accumulated memory of a hundred similar gatherings made his eyelids start to droop. But they came fully apart at the sight of Tristram Hallett leading Anna on to the platform. At least it would have had to be Anna. Well of course it was Anna, but Richard had noticed her rig-out first, from dark-green beret or tam to half-boots of the same general colour in a non-shiny material.

Hallett was less adventurously got up, in an actual suit and tie, but had laid off somewhat by brushing his hair villainously forward over his brow. After some thin handclapping he spoke a couple of dozen unambitious words of introduction and welcome in English and then rather more in Russian, his good correct almost accentless Muscovite Russian that lurched once or twice from educated convention into outmoded slang, recalling his style in meetings with Duncan and his crew. When he closed there was further applause, louder but more scattered, recognisable to a blind man as issuing from people who were there to hear their language spoken.

Anna's appearance, to be fully taken in now as she stood at the front of the platform, caused first a hush, then a stir. There was no doubt that she had intended to look extraordinary and had succeeded, perhaps more thoroughly than she knew. Her beret was in fact a round brimless cap of the type to be seen in different forms in Scotland and parts of Spain, her middle garments were a smock and a gathered skirt, both in subdued green and plain but for a decorated dark-yellow border to the skirt, and her boots seemed to be of soft canvas. Under the beret her hair was tightly swept back and her face was artificially pale and uncoloured. Without prolonging the pause she began to speak in a strong, level voice, the voice Richard knew, but slower and more clearly enunciated to suit the occasion.

'Good evening, ladies and gentlemen,' she said in well-rehearsed English, repeated the sense in Russian and continued in that language. 'Tonight I have for you some poems of mine about Russia. By Russia I mean the country, the land itself and the people who live there. I have nothing to tell you of politics, nor of history as considered in any way from which a political meaning could be taken. As a citizen and as a person I believe politics is most important, but in these poems I am silent on the subject. So now, with your permission, ladies and gentlemen, my first poem, the title "Winter".'

She stood for a moment, looking taller than Richard had thought, also straighter, her hands clasped in front of her, her head lifted, taking a slow breath like a singer waiting for her cue. But if her demeanour recalled the opera-house or the concert-hall, as soon as she began to speak her poem the association was with the theatre, the old-fashioned heroic Russian theatre of the late nineteenth century and earlier twentieth. Richard had found recognisable offshoots of that tradition in verse recitals by Yevgeny Yevtushenko and other Soviet poets, but Anna's style reminded him more directly and vividly of an actress he had seen in Kiev playing Portia in a State production of *The Merchant of Venice*. As hers had done, Anna's delivery moved from a sombre directness to impassioned resonance and her use of gesture was broad and plain. More than any of this, she gained and held attention with her certainty, her conviction that what she was saying was true and important. By the end of the first minute her voice was the only perceptible sound in the hall.

Richard was almost as soon absorbed in the voice and in the way it produced the lines of the verse. Each poem had been so thoroughly rehearsed that full value and appropriate emphasis was given every phrase, and Anna's diction was so good that not a word was ever in doubt, nor was a single syllable fluffed. As she had promised she spoke of Russia, setting forth in simple language the large simple themes of the changes of season, the lakes and forests, the unending treeless plains, the farms and villages and the people who lived and worked there. All this was treated in a style he had not found in her work before, one purged of modernism, almost a style of the last century, almost no style at all, no treatment, only statement. The emotional subject-matter was likewise simple – fortitude, hope, grief, pain, love of home and of family, the transience of human life and the perpetuity of the land.

Well before the end Richard was in tears, but not the sort of tears that might have been intended or allowed for. He wept that all that honesty of feeling, which he could not doubt it was, all that seriousness of purpose, all that sincerity that had found expression through such outstanding dramatic gifts, as again they undoubtedly were, should have come to nothing. To worse than nothing, to cheapness, shallowness, dullness, vulgarity, to a number of sequences of words in which there was no vestige of poetic talent or feeling for literature. Different from other work of hers – yes! Bad in a new way! Worse than before! Hopeless! Useless! What on earth was to be done? What could mortals do when the golden goddess stirred and spoke, and hark! her words were made of lead?

The recital was over and it had been a success, not a wild success but enough. For the moment Richard took in little more than that, being occupied in keeping his head down where he sat at the end of his row and pulling himself together. By the time he was breathing normally again there was a chattering group on the platform, not large but close-packed. At one edge was Tristram Hallett, who at once caught sight of him. Hallett made a tiny movement of head and hand that was enough to show most of what he felt about the proceedings just concluded.

Richard went over to him and the two men found themselves shaking hands.

'I thought that went down rather well, didn't you?' muttered Hallett. 'Considering, I mean.'

'I suppose so. Who were all those people? I didn't get much of a look at them, I'm afraid.'

'No, you were giving all your attention to the speaker, weren't you?' Hallett smiled slightly. 'Very understandable. There weren't many of our students, as you must have noticed.'

'No, well, there's the language barrier there, isn't there?'

'A number of rave-up freaks, if I may so express myself, who melted away when they saw Miss Danilova was unsuitable material. Then . . . some miscellaneous artistic persons. Some who looked like Russian friends of hers. Some what you might call professional Russians from old St Petersburg. This lot' – those on the platform – 'seems to be mostly drawn from them.'

'Oh God, poor little Anna, we'd better mount a rescue operation.'

'You mount it. I've done all I'm going to do, thank you very much, up to and including the offering of congratulations. Home and the telly for me now.'

'You look a bit washed out, Tristram. Are you all right?'

'You'd look washed out if you'd had to keep pointing this way all the time that was going on, preventing your face from expressing your opinion of the material being so ably performed. Successfully performed too, it must be said. I was pleased with the response. Just warm enough without being embarrassingly fervent.'

They said good-night and Richard approached the circle on the platform. Before he could go over to Anna, who had her back to him, Crispin interposed himself. In a suit of very dark mustard-colour, one of the type with the first-day-on look, he had an eager, almost excited air that Richard had seen before and put down to enjoyment of a specially selected kind of power. Any fool could force others to do what they disliked while pretending they liked it – it took real application to arrange matters so that they really thought themselves lucky. Now he confronted Richard with one of his concomitant pundits, a long-faced fellow in his sixties, while adroitly blocking off his much younger wife, who just might really have wanted to meet him.

Crispin introduced the two men. Without any sense of loss, Richard failed to gather the pundit's name, which was available in several sections, and of what he worked at or did gathered only that he was the head of something, something large and spread-out like a publishing consortium or fast-food chain. But he switched everything on again when Crispin gave him a look and said, 'I'd particularly wanted you to meet,' then the first part of what he had said before, 'Richard.'

'You're a professor then . . . professor,' said the pundit thickly. Despite his undeniably long face he had no obvious neck.

'Well, actually a – '

'In Russian. You must meet a lot of Russians in your work. Meet them. Talk to them. Find out what they're thinking. That one tonight. What was she talking about? I couldn't make head or tail of that thing on that piece of paper they had there for us.'

'No,' said Richard. He was experiencing serious difficulty in remembering that he had come to find Anna and should persevere in it. He tried to rouse himself. 'Er, about Russia itself, really, the land, the . . .'

'Saying it was pretty poor, I expect, wasn't she? You know. No money. Everybody poor.'

'Yes, of course that's always been one of the great – '

'I knew it. I thought as much. If they're as poor as they say they are, and I've no reason to doubt it, don't mind taking their word for it, who's fault's that, that's what I'd like to know.'

'Well, there's never been a – '

'Money, money, money, that's what they call the name of the game, you know. All that lot have ever wanted is our money. For years and years they were going to come and take it from us, and now they're unfitted for such behaviour they're coming and asking us to give 'em some of it. Simple as that.'

Those last three words were too much for Richard, who had found what preceded them no more than the sort of thing to be expected from anyone at a get-together like tonight's. He had started to say he would have loved to discuss the matter further when he saw that nothing would be lost if he just slipped away, so he just slipped away. Not far enough, though – just out of the frying-pan into another frying-pan, a more crowded and retentive one occupied by Mrs Benda, Professor Radek, Mrs Polinski, Miss Strbny, Mr Klien and countless others, all of whom he seemed to have seen before and all of whom seemed to have far too good an idea of who he was. They all addressed him with questions in Russian – had it not been a truly wonderful experience, did he not admire the way the young lady, had not the old true Russia been brought, was she not surely, was it not uplifting. Yes it had, agreed Richard, he did, it had, she was, it was. When he tried to move on a few paces he found himself physically blocked by an echelon of representatives of the old true Russia with Mrs Benda herself at their head.

'You sneaked out of my house without saying good-night,' she said, fluttering her eyelids to show she was not seriously reprehending him.

'I'm sorry, I telephoned and left a message, but it can't have reached you.'

'And you took with you the young lady whose poetry we have just been enjoying and admiring so much.'

'They certainly breathe the authentic spirit of Russia as she has been over the centuries.' Richard permitted himself a small inner smirk at this stylish piece of deflection.

'So it's no wonder we find you here again this evening, you wicked fellow, and we all thought of you as a respectable married man content with his library. Shame on you, Dr Vizey,' etc.

Near the start of this fearful roguishness Richard saw Anna look round everywhere but in his direction and then turn away, and he drew in his breath. But he would have to stay and help Mrs Benda to get everything possible out of the very short and exceptional stretch of time she was out of her house and in some sort of pallid, shrivelled version of the real world. So he smiled sheepishly at her and hung his head in pretended contrition and let her call him a naughty man, and then suddenly, amazingly, it was all right, she said she must not keep him, they would be meeting again soon, and he caught up with Anna just as she was leaving in company with Crispin and a straggle of assorted punditry. And then again, as soon as Richard appeared Crispin said, 'Good-night, Anna, see you in the morning,' and drove his group irresistibly off ahead of him. It was as if somebody or other . . . Richard lost the thought.

'Congratulations,' he said.

'Was it all right?'

'You were lovely.'

They kissed with great enthusiasm, but neither of them was the type to forget where they were, which by this time was the start of a kind of sloping tunnel between the lecture-hall and the outdoors, with a treacherously wrinkled drugget carpet under-foot, some puckered club and other notices and a few fading graffiti on its walls, and near its further end a cubby-hole containing the hunched-up figure of a porter, unknown to Richard and distinguished by no badge or item of dress, but radiating the unmistakable malignity of his calling. Just inside and outside the entrance four or five children with autograph-books and a couple of middle-aged women with cameras stood waiting unhopefully. Nor was there much spring in their step when they closed on Anna.

'Who?' a small girl asked Richard as the more human-looking of his party.

Feeling it was jolly clever of him to have thought of it, and so fast too, Richard spelt out Anna's names. He had to do so letter by letter because syllable by syllable was too fast. Then he nodded as impressively as he could. Anna presumably wrote her names on the proffered pages. They had hardly glanced at each other while, jostled from time to time by others more urgently set on leaving, they cleared the corridor without falling down. Now they were left alone in the open, with people passing but not looking, it dawned on Richard that she was no longer wearing her beret. When he mentioned this she agreed with him.

'What a terrific outfit,' he went on with feeling. 'It must have cost you a packet. Or did you bring it with you?'

'I bought everything at a market near Professor Léon's house for nine pounds. Very cheap. I didn't know there were cheap markets in England. In my country the markets are very expensive.' She spoke nervously. 'Or perhaps you knew that.'

'Yes, I think so.'

'I wanted to look like what people would expect a Russian girl poet to look like. What did you think of the poems, Richard? Did you think they were good?'

111

'I was . . . bowled over by them,' he said, trying to show he had trouble finding the words, which was quite easy for him because he really had. 'Quite different from anything of yours I've come across before. A new style. So honest and direct. I was completely – '

'Yes, good, thank you, I'm delighted, it's very kind of you to say that, but you must tell me, did you think they were good?'

'What can I say? Before it was over I was in floods of tears. Not much poetry makes me cry. I tried not to let you see me. I felt . . .'

At the memory of what he had felt, how much he had felt, the tears came back to his eyes. He made no attempt to hold them in check, and doubted then and later whether he could have done so even if he had tried. But it made no difference either way, because Anna had believed what he had said, had taken it for the truth, which it was, and what he could certainly not have said was that it was not the truth she took it for. They kissed for some time and went on holding each other for longer. Eventually she said,

'Richard, darling, please take me home.'

'But don't you want to – '

'Please, darling, nothing more tonight. Let me go where I can think.'

She was not the only one with some thinking to do, he said to himself grimly when, having done as he had been asked, he set off for home himself. He was committed, involved, pledged, in it, one of those, and what it was he was committed, etc. to was only the nearest of a rank of questions that stretched away out of his view. Before he came to any of them, there was one about why he had not earlier insisted on making himself absolutely clear – nothing less would have done – that in his opinion the poems he had heard that evening were just as bad as any of Anna Danilova's he had previously encountered, and whatever the differences between these and those such differences were strictly immaterial. Richard made up his mind that a man who could have done that, said that, would have been a much more unselfish man than he was, but that he would not have been able to get very friendly with such a man, assuming he wanted to.

No, he, Richard Vaisey, was not well fitted by nature or training for this kind of thing, whether you defined it broadly or narrowly or any other way. Perhaps very few people were, but they all seemed to keep needing to be. Well, that put everyone in the same boat. Thinking that was rather like trying to cheer up about dying by thinking that everyone had to get it done sooner or later.

NINE

'Hallo darling. Listen, er . . . what did you think of the book about Rome? About *Rome* darling. Yes of *course* Athens. Well when will you do you think? Surely you must have *some* idea. Well you see I need it *back*. No no, I just need it back. All right darling all right darling, good-bye.'

Cordelia replaced her telephone, which perhaps recalled a model of 1950 where Crispin's domestic instrument was of 2000, and with a flourish of her partly transparent pen cancelled an entry on her millboard. That done, she went on sitting at her work-table for a minute or two frowning and moving her lips. Then, after raising and lowering her head several times as if to stretch her neck, she got up and went downstairs.

Richard was just putting his things together to go to the Institute, indeed she was perhaps lucky to have caught him. He looked up at her and smiled, not in a totally artless or unpremeditated way, some would have said.

'Hallo my darling.'

'Hallo . . . love.'

'Er . . . you know that Anna somebody, that Russian girl, well, she rang up just a few minutes ago wanting to speak to you . . .'

'Oh, that must have been before I'd – '

'. . . but then you see somebody else rang up and I'm most terribly sorry but I wasn't able to come down and tell you absolutely straight away but she does seem to do an awful *lot* of ringing up, the Russian girl, so I thought perhaps . . .'

'I'd better just go and see what she wants,' said Richard, this time with a careless, devil-may-care intonation, and walked off not too briskly into his study. Since he had introduced Anna to Crispin several changes had taken place here at home, one of which had affected Cordelia's official attitude to her. Thus she was no longer Richard's Russian girl, firmly destined to be taken

114

on an educational-cum-sightseeing tour of Harrods as a first stage towards being morally engulfed or at least flattened, but just the or even that Russian girl, tiresome perhaps but irrelevant, a figure that had passed from the scene without ever having occupied it. When he told Cordelia at no great length of taking Anna to see some person who might advance her cause, of giving her a 'quick' or 'snack' lunch somewhere inconsiderable, Cordelia listened silently with an almost truly blank expression. She had had the same look just now announcing that girl's telephone-call. Richard was uneasy. Once or twice he had caught his wife wearing a doubtful, troubled expression which in anybody less continuously self-assured might have indicated uncertainty about what to do next. And another once or twice he had caught her sending his way a look of what he took for unprecedented displeasure. About as often he had had it in mind to make love to his wife and then found he was thinking about something else. It had occurred to him then or later that at times of such intimacy couples were supposed to tell each other important things, quite likely not in so many words. He was not sure but he could not remember that happening between himself and Cordelia. In fact what he could remember quite clearly at the moment was reading of a wartime Resistance chief in German-occupied France and the local Gestapo commandant who, finding they shared a love of Mozart's operas, had met periodically to play the gramophone records under a mutual guarantee of safe conduct that was never broken. Richard had before now seen something in that story that reminded him of his relations with Cordelia. Besides, although he no longer hated her as much or for so long at a time as he had when he spoke to Crispin on the point, he still did a certain amount.

Over his telephone he heard the voice he now knew to be Professor Léon's and then Anna's. She sounded vague and out of humour, which aggrieved him after Cordelia, so to speak. What could she do for him, she asked him in pretty formal style.

'I was told you had requested me to ring,' he said back.

'What? That was some time ago, were you out? And I'm sorry, Richard, I didn't recognise your voice at first. Perhaps you have a cold.'

He answered quickly in case she started trying to tell him that she among others knew for a fact that Englishmen were peculiarly susceptible to colds. 'No, I'm fine, what about you?'

'Very well. Thank you.' More hanging about. '[Mmm], I know you're always very busy . . .'

While he waited, Richard heard from the kitchen a great, prolonged, booming chord of music, full orchestra with tubas and massed timpani, submerged after some moments in a roar of applause with stray shouts. For a moment the din swelled as Cordelia turned the volume-on-off the wrong way on her obsolescent radio, then was abruptly lost.

'. . . in about half an hour,' Anna was saying. 'But I should very much like you to come too if possible.'

'Come where? I'm afraid I didn't – '

'You seem to have extremely bad telephone lines in London, Richard. I was saying that Mr Crispin Radetsky is taking me to see an extremely important man whose name I can't understand this morning, and he's sending his car for me in about half an hour, that is Mr Crispin Radetsky is sending his car, and he and I are going to see the important man, which of course I understand is very kind of Mr Crispin Radetsky, but I don't – '

'Anna, I think you can call him just Crispin by now.'

'By now? Then to you I will. But would you please come with him and me to see the important man? Crispin . . . is very kind but somehow he doesn't seem to me the easiest person to talk to that I have ever set eyes on. Sometimes I want to ask him a question and then I find I'm too nervous to speak or I think it would sound silly. [Mmm] Crispin, he knows so much more than I do about so many things.'

'For God's sake, Anna, he's bound to know a lot about England after living here all these years.'

'Oh?' The tone of her voice grew sharper. 'How long has he been in England?'

'He may even have been born here,' said Richard, and went on fatuously, 'He goes abroad several times a year.'

'Oh.' Anna's voice went dull again. 'Then no wonder he knows a lot.'

'You must try to understand . . . that's a great English thing, knowing a lot. Not saying so or showing off, perish the thought, but leaving it in no doubt.' He instantly abandoned as profitless

116

any notion of explaining to Anna that Crispin had a special attitude to the English and Englishness and being English. 'Americans don't do it,' he said instead.

'So will you come, please, Richard?'

He started to ask if it was far, but realised after a few words that it could not be very far with Crispin making the trip, and at a pinch he had a free morning but for a single conference with a Hong Kong Chinese. This young man, having got off opium and on to rum, could be relied on not to appear, so Richard agreed to be ready when Anna called to pick him up. He was about to end the call when a thought struck him, the more forcefully for being belated.

'Anna – before you go, there's no special reason, is there, why you want me on the party today?'

'*Special* reason?' Her voice was full of wariness in a moment. 'What sort of special reason were you thinking of?'

'Well . . . do you want me to be there in case Crispin starts misbehaving?'

'I can't imagine a gentleman like Mr Radetsky being anything but correct in any circumstances.' Now she sounded honestly puzzled.

Not for the first time in conversation with Anna, it occurred to Richard that his grasp of Russian colloquialism and slang was less than perfect. On instinct he took refuge in pomposity. 'I wondered if you were afraid that Crispin might try to force his attentions on you if circumstances were such that . . .'

A noisy laugh came down the line. 'Oh, you're ridiculous.' More laughter. 'It's no trouble for a girl to let a man like Crispin know she's not available. Surely you knew that.'

'I'm sorry, I wasn't thinking.'

After that little bit he explained to Cordelia about the imminent pick-up. She listened closely with a slight fixed smile, watched him closely too, with her eyes shooting out to the sides every now and again, as if he had been telling her how he was going to be collected presently by a flying saucer (with a Russian poetess already on it). He filled in most of the intervening time without any exertion by telephoning the Institute and talking somebody into finding somebody else who might well induce some third party to tell the drunken Chinese he need not even think about being conferred with that morning.

When an expensive hoot sounded above the clamour from the roadway, Richard hurried out of the house with some sense of expectation. He told himself he was off on a voyage, however short, into the unknown, and had no need to tell himself that what he usually voyaged into was quite sufficiently the known. The black chauffeur came out of and round the car to get him on board. Anna watched the two of them from the back seat with an intentness not much different in appearance from Cordelia's just earlier. But then, before he knew it, this female suddenly kissed him, though not very personally, it had to be admitted, her intentness gone.

Very soon after they had moved off, she said, 'Can I ask you a question about English social attitudes? In what I suppose would be called the upper classes?'

'I'll do my best to answer. You understand I don't belong there myself.'

'Yes of course.' She assented a little more readily than perhaps she needed to have done. 'The important man I was telling you about, he's called Sir something, and Mr, and Crispin says his wife is Lady something similar. That doesn't make them members of the upper classes, does it?'

'Well, not by itself, probably. They might be that already, of course. Upper-class, I mean.'

'I don't think so. I think he looks down on them.'

'There are several reasons why Crispin might do that.'

'I think he looks down on me.'

'I doubt if he does. Please don't mind my saying I think you'll miss a lot in England if you go on about class and the upper classes and what-not. People here move up and down and to and fro without noticing much or trying much or minding if they stay where they were, not like joining the Party in Russia from all I hear. If you're looking for a country with a real class system, apart from your own, try the USA, though it's not called it there. Or France. Here, someone's class is about as interesting to think about as him training his hair across his head when he's nearly bald. Less. Much less than if he goes in for model trains in his attic. Now foreigners, they're interesting. The English go on about them all the time.'

Anna nodded uncertainly. 'Does that mean you like them?'

'I do, I suppose. In the plural, well, I'm not so sure. But

anyway I'm not aware of any barriers between Crispin and me. At least not that sort.'

Richard was conscious that the pleasant feeling of anticipation he had recognised in himself on leaving the house had quite died away. He looked furtively over at Anna. She was wearing a purple skirt of exotic cut, if of any, a part-worn approximately matching jumper and a pair of sort of tart's shoes, not old but not far from falling apart, in a distantly related hue. The ensemble made her look foreign all right, but without drawing much in the way of interest, let alone sympathy. As well as these visual non-appeals she gave off a perfume that, while clearly a perfume and nothing else, enlarged his experience of such fragrances in a direction he was not fervent about going – Nuits d'Ulan Bator, he guessed without much will to precision. Sitting rather perched forward on the dark-blue cushions she seemed restless, even defiant, as though not at all convinced she wanted to go where she was being taken. When she spoke it was without turning her head.

'Is Crispin one of your closest friends?'

'Yes, in so far as I have closest friends.'

After perhaps waiting for more, she said, 'You know his wife drinks like an old-fashioned Russian, every day too.'

'An old-fashioned Russian?' he repeated to gain time.

'Until she can hardly speak.'

'Is that old-fashioned?'

'These days it's not always easy for people to get hold of as much drink as they want when they want it, I mean in Russia. Not even hooch. In former times they could have swum in it, or so my father says.'

'Does he, I mean is he fond of a drink now and then, your father?'

'Now and then, yes. His two older brothers died of liver ailments before they were forty. If you go back further you find that a typical Russian social evening ended with the entire company falling down insensible, old and young, clergy and laity, man and woman – even then there was some equality in the social system.' She had spoken with more animation than just now and he began to wonder if she had perhaps taken a quick nip or so herself to brace her for the journey, but then she went straight on, 'That's rather the sort of way Crispin's wife, he calls her Freddie, she drinks like that.'

'Oh, surely not,' said Richard instinctively, not at once remembering that the chauffeur was probably weak on fast conversational Russian.

'Perhaps you haven't seen her late at night.'

'No, not that I recall.'

'But she's very nice to me. Why does she drink so much, do you know?'

'Seeing as how she's not a Russian. I haven't thought about it.'

Anna frowned. 'But surely Crispin must have discussed it with you.'

'He's never mentioned it. We don't discuss things like that, not in that way. You know, I don't think people have to have a reason for drinking a lot. They just do it. That doesn't mean to say you won't find some sort of reason if you start looking for it, even in your old-fashioned Russians.'

'I think no reason would be good enough for you to drink so much.'

This sounded enough like a compliment, or a boss shot at one, to make Richard instinctively set about fending it off. 'I've never had the taste for it. Not so far, but you never know. What about you?'

'Only sometimes but then yes – but have I offended you?'

'Good God, certainly not. Why do you ask?'

'You seem to refuse to tell me anything.'

'That's just me being English. But English people do sometimes tell people things, even important things. Like this one. The important thing now is that you and I are here together.'

Her response told him beyond doubt there was something that interested her more than anything to do with class systems or drink, for the moment at any rate. Within quite a short time their embraces were entering on a stage at which the chauffeur might well start to take an informed interest. Unlike others Richard could have named, she evidently sensed this or something of the kind.

'You don't mind me being Russian?'

'What? I think it's marvellous. Especially for me.'

'I mean you don't mind all our conversation going to be in Russian?'

'Well, you don't know any English yet, do you?'

'Buckingham Palace, Royal Navy, stiff upper lip, not cricket,' said Anna in raucous and terrible English. 'But what I did want to say to you in Russian,' she went on more agreeably in that language, 'was I'm sorry I was awkward with you before. I was nervous.'

'I didn't notice anything.'

'Over the telephone as well. I was afraid you might have changed your mind about me or about you and me. You understand that? Please forget. But don't forget everything. Poor Freddie is still very drunk and it's not just that she likes it.'

'I'm not likely to forget. That she's very drunk. Well, I'll forget it for now.'

They sat hand in hand, not a usual posture for Richard. Among his feelings there was room for pleasure at the fact that Cordelia was not among those present. This was fully for the obvious reasons but also because she was quite capable of making just the kind of specially selected remark, in this case something about desiccated academic responding to inarticulate appeal of earth-goddess, that was annoying because of its annoyingness rather than any possible relevance. Her friends' husbands, not so much the friends themselves (Harry Dobbs, not Pat), might have found this section surprising until they remembered that after all Cordelia was Richard's wife.

A final brief survey of the chauffeur's top rear was re-assuringly negative, although it was true that the back of the man's neck, often held to speak volumes in the case of a chauffeur, could hardly have done so much as change colour. Crispin, or more probably some agent of his, knew how to pick them. With Anna at his side Richard felt he was probably radiating complacency. This seldom got the chance of happening with him, so he let it go on.

When the time arrived, no beckoning toot, perhaps some ultrasonic or astral trigger, brought the great man from his abode, but anyway out he came. Crispin Radetsky, CBE, QC, FRSA, was wearing an almost inaudibly wonderful greyish suit with an unexpected dark shirt and a lighter tie embellished with science-fiction flora. Richard worked out that the suit was intended to impress the important man with Crispin's own importance, respectability, money, etc., while shirt and tie were saying how terrifically cultural and artistic he was at the same time. In the service of this latter theme his very hair seemed to have grown a centimetre or so since Richard had last seen him. Then he, Richard, discarded this analysis, feeling humbly that anything obvious enough in that line to be intelligible to him could not be right. He realised that he and Anna were still holding hands and they withdrew them together.

'Morning, morning,' said Crispin in his incisive paramilitary fashion, getting briskly into the passenger's seat, though not so briskly as to hinder those in the back from taking in his generally upright carriage if they had felt like doing so. 'Good morning, Anna,' he amplified when all doors were shut, turning quite a long way round in his seat to do so. 'I hope you slept well,' he went on rather loudly and slowly, nodding his head and smiling as if to reassure her that there was nothing disdainful or anti-Russian in what he was saying.

'Thank you,' she said.

'Not at all.' He nodded in obvious approval and after a short pause said to Richard, who was placed directly behind him, 'I'm afraid this trip will take us a few minutes.'

'Where are we off to exactly?'

'Oh, just up to old Stephen's.'

'Would that be Stephen – '

'Fellow like that would never consider for a moment living anywhere in the world but Hampstead. Anybody would think his family had been hanging out in a castle there since the Tudors, you know, with a moat and cannons and things. Well, I wouldn't fancy living anywhere but down here or hereabouts, I admit. Yes, the more I see of London, the more I'm *convinced* there are two distinct types of humanity among its citizens, those who belong north of the Park and those who belong south of it, and that never the twain shall meet. Talking of which,' went on Crispin in his same headquarter-mess style, 'I see that you and our visitor have started to get on together like a house on fire. I'm sure I can trust you to proceed with reasonable caution, not that it's any business of mine.'

'Oh yes,' said Richard whole-heartedly. 'Oh, very much so.' He was aware that Anna had been paying attention to all that had passed, though she would have been able to make little of the actual discourse beyond an occasional nugget like 'London' or 'Park' (Russ. *Park*). In the same rather decent-chap tone, he said to Crispin, 'I hope it wasn't as obvious as you made it sound.'

'No no. Not really. Only to Hanni here.' Crispin indicated the chauffeur, then looked sportingly at his watch and out at the traffic. 'I admit to some vulgar curiosity.'

'Isn't it a little more than that?'

'Very possibly. If so I apologise. But I thought we came up with a very useful slogan a few moments ago: never the twain shall meet. Well, never's a bit harsh, admittedly, and meet, of course, that's a relative term, one wouldn't want to be too literal-minded about it. Anyway, it's a bit late for any such thing, what?'

'On the contrary, I should have thought it was a bit early for warnings-off.'

'Oh, would you? Better early than never, dear boy.'

'Is what you always say. I'm afraid I'm getting a bit out of my depth in this conversation.'

'So am I, perhaps. But while we're on what I always say, another thing of that general description is look after number one but in a highly sagacious and attentive fashion. If it's a little early in the morning for that kind of talk I'm truly sorry.'

Richard had started to feel stupid, or irritated with Crispin, or both. He gave it a moment and said, 'But it is Stephen – '

'I take it you do know old Whatsisname, you know, the famous chap?'

'Who?'

'You know, the *famous* chap, novelist mainly, living over here now after America, wrote a great saga, supposed to have turned down the Nobel Prize some years ago, crusty old bugger, *you* know, er, oh, Kotolynov.'

Crispin had mispronounced or mis-stressed this indeed famous name well beyond Anna's powers of recognition even had she still been listening. 'Of course,' said Richard. 'Well, I say I know him, I've met him but I doubt if he remembers me.'

'Do you feel you know him well enough to take our little flower of the steppe out to Berkshire to call on him?'

'What, to drum up his support? Surely he won't see her, will he? I mean, he's never gone near – '

'Oh, he'll see her. It's all arranged. Friday morning. All right?'

'It depends. Why can't you go?'

'Because I'm *doing something else*. I have got other things to do than the job flower-of-steppe asked you to do and you're incompetent to do.'

'Oh, have you really?' asked Richard, making quite a fair fist at it considering. 'I have other things to do as well, you know.'

'No doubt you have, my dear Dr Vaisey. The difference is that if for any reason you leave any of your things undone, the result is merely an irreparable cultural loss, whereas if I do anything like that it can have consequences that really matter. And you think I'm joking but I'm not joking. Anyway on Friday I see a man about a horse, and not to put a fiver on it either.'

'Have you told her she's going, I mean asked her if she wants to go?'

'No, I thought that would come better from you. Leave you a bit more room for manoeuvre. You'd better give him a ring to confirm.'

Any other questions could wait. It occurred to Richard that since his nursery-style greeting Crispin had not looked towards Anna even when referring to her, and that he himself had barely glanced at her. He turned to her now and said at top speed, as if with some notion of restoring the balance,

'I'm sorry I was so ridiculous over the telephone about what did I call it, misbehaviour?'

This time there was no comprehension problem. 'Oh, don't be sorry. It was natural and quite flattering too. If we'd had more time I'd have told you that the good gentleman made it clear he found me attractive but had no intentions.'

'What? What did he say?'

'Say, he said nothing in words. You don't need words to say, surely you know. He saw to it that I understood.'

At Richard's original school up there on the left-hand side of the map, there had been a noise you made by puffing between your teeth and lips that meant you gave somebody best for showing you up as a stupid or ignorant prat. Richard felt like making that noise now, but in the circumstances contented himself with looking crestfallen and muttering unintelligibly.

Anna seemed to understand. 'He's got enough to worry about at home.'

'Oh, you mean the drink – '

'I'm quite happy looking out of the window at your great city.'

Richard allowed the matter to drop from his mind as the car reached the upland approaches to Hampstead. Then another ascended back into it. He waited till Crispin was turning over what looked like the galleys of next year's *Good Food Guide* before suddenly saying, 'Oh, of course it must be old Stephen – '

'I had a rather mysterious telephone-call from a fellow yesterday I think it was,' said Crispin, encircling in red something on the sheet before him. 'A compatriot of er, little rose from the snows here, but he knew about you. Apparently you'd made an arrangement to meet him for a drink but hadn't turned up.'

'Oh my God I forgot all about it. I forgot to write it down.'

'Not like you. The fellow asked if you were ill or anything and I said not as far as I knew, and he said he'd be in touch with you. He talked about telephone numbers a fair amount but rang off without leaving his own. As I say, not like you to stand a fellow up.'

'I just forgot.'

'Not a bad idea with compatriots of little rose from the snows. I dare say old Sigmund would have a relevant note somewhere about the repression of unwelcome thoughts. Talking of which, this fellow did give a name but I couldn't make it out. But there was something I made a note of. Can't remember now. I'll ring you.'

And he turned over a page rather decisively, so Richard broke into a voluble account in Russian of the historical and especially the literary associations of Hampstead. He spent a few moments on Keats before perceiving that Anna had never heard of him. This he found disappointing until he reflected on the odds against running across an English person who had heard of that poet. And at least he was spared any temptation to go on now to Sir Walter Besant or Rabindranath Tagore.

The chauffeur, doubtless thoroughly briefed, took them in silence over the crossroads and up Holly Hill into the maze of little squares and lanes, infested with pretty houses, round the inconsiderable summit. They pulled up close by one of the most remorselessly pretty of all before Richard was any the wiser about whether they were or were not going to see the old Stephen he had rather assumed they were going to see. He knew, as certainly as if he had heard him speak the words, that Crispin would have thought him less than grown up for not having found an irresistible way of extracting the information in the first minute, nor was it too late even now. But he glanced at Anna and instead told her about Kenwood House. He had reason to believe she knew what pictures were and thought she might well have heard of Rembrandt.

TEN

Enlightenment as to the old-Stephen question did not arrive at once. On previous form, or rather on that of Richard's preferred candidate, a very large photograph of somebody like Lenin or Hitler might have been expected to be prominently on view, but such a thing would hardly have pinned down the occupant of a pretty house in these parts, and perhaps it was a little late for that anyway. Works of art, some of them in three or so dimensions, and most of them distressing or puzzling in tendency, were much to be seen, but again this was Hampstead.

A cheerful lad got up like a labourer had opened the door to them. 'Come to see Sir Stephen, have you?' He spoke like a labourer too, which was unexpected. Without taking his eyes off Anna he got in first with her name and Crispin's, or with close approximations to them. Richard gave his own name when it seemed safe to do so. In his pocket there were a number of visiting-cards Cordelia had designed and now made him take about with him. They carried much detail about him and his attainments in a dark purple script that seemed to him to lean over a great deal, and he was too shy to use them, but he still carried some and replaced them when they got too dirty and battered.

When approached more nearly, the lad turned out to smell like a labourer into the bargain, with a background of rather expensive soap and a plentiful foreground of aftershave. He took them into a room like one in an art gallery or a museum, with an uncarpeted woodblock floor, nowhere to sit down and a great deal of stuff displayed on small tables and hung up as photographs on the walls. The nature of the stuff and the sight of the tall elderly man hurrying towards them, his head leaning so far to one side with good will that it practically rested on his shoulder, made his identity clear. This was controversial famous-architect old Stephen or Sir Stephen, not the slightly more obvious famous-novelist-cum-famous-knower-about-Tibet-*and-Bhutan* Sir Stephen whom Richard had more or less settled on in his mind. This second Sir Stephen had sunk to being only slightly more obvious than the first one when the first one had moved up, from restricted noteworthiness as the leading post-deconstructivist in his chosen field to wider eminence as the man who had given the world discrete voidance. In a rich, client-reassuring voice he apologised to the visitors for having had to lug them into his bloody showroom, the rest of the house being upside-down because of the fucking decorators not having finished yet. He invited the three to find themselves somewhere to sit if they could, even at the cost of chucking some of the shit on to the floor should they consider it necessary. His manner was welcoming but timid. With him, or near him, were two closely similar women of about fifty, dressed and with their hair arranged in styles that would only have suited much younger and better-looking women than these. Sir Stephen introduced them, jerking his thumb at one after the other, as his wife and as a great friend of theirs whom they must have come across somewhere before. Then he sat himself down at one end of a lightly padded bench and addressed himself to Crispin.

'Now what can I do for you?' he asked, his head now almost upright on its neck.

'Well first of all,' said Crispin, 'let me say unequivocally that none of us wants any of your money.'

At this, the illustrious architect went off into roars of laughter that lasted throughout his introduction to Anna and Richard. 'Bloody hell!' and 'Christ!' he said vaguely from time to time, then, more collectedly but still humorously, 'Well, that does clear the air in no uncertain bleeding fashion,' and finally, 'In that case what do you bloody want?'

'I can probably explain that best by telling you who Anna is and what she's doing in this country.'

Before Crispin had got very far with doing so, Sir Stephen had started smiling and crinkling his face in a way that obviously meant he had something rather special of his own to contribute, and not much later this had to be allowed out. But first his demeanour turned abruptly and totally grim, as if at an intimation of a death in the family, for as long as it took to satisfy himself that nobody needed any refreshment. This established, he turned jovial again and, fixing his attention on Anna, said to her in a sort of Polish,

'My mother's father came to this country from Poland. A city called Lublin.'

Anna responded at once. She answered in slow Russian, 'That is most fortunate. What was your grandfather's profession? A teacher, perhaps?'

A Polish speaker from east of the Vistula ought to have got the drift of that, thought Richard, but rather to his satisfaction the answer came in plain English, 'I'm sorry, I'm afraid I don't understand.' So he interpreted and in due course told Anna, 'The gentleman says his grandfather was a poor peasant.'

'In the city. I see. Please thank him and tell him that is most interesting.'

When Richard had done that, Sir Stephen tried something else in near-Polish but less successfully.

'Thank you,' said Anna in English, and looked away to her left. In that direction there stood what looked like a model of a large machine that had some resemblance to a block of buildings, so after a moment she looked away to her right instead.

'Well,' said Crispin cheerfully, 'we all know you're a busy man, so let me tell you a little more very quickly about what Anna hopes to do in England.'

But a little more was indeed all he had time to tell before one or other of the women spoke.

'Er, excuse me,' she sort of called as if accosting a stranger in some public place, 'do you mind if I ask you a question, please?'

Rather daringly, Crispin took his time before finally deciding that the request was in order.

'I've no wish to appear rude, but I'm sorry, I don't know who you are. I mean I've been told your name and I've been advised of the public positions you occupy, but I haven't been informed of in what capacity you've come here to ask for Stephen's help on behalf of is it Anna whom you present as a young poet from Russia on an unofficial visit to the UK.'

'I don't think it's necessary to have things quite as cut and dried as that at this stage,' said Sir Stephen. 'Darling,' he added after a pause, making it more likely than not that it was his wife and not their great friend who had spoken. Whichever the other one was laid her hand on the speaker's arm and made a silencing face. Anyhow Crispin was allowed to go on from where he had left off.

Again not for long. Sir Stephen broke in, 'You did say you weren't going to ask me for any money.' There was just a hint of desire for reassurance in the distinguished edificer's tone.

'I did and we're not.'

'Ah. Well now, that being so, what exactly do you require of me?'

'Just your signature to a commendation of Anna Danilova as a leading poet of her generation, or at this stage your verbal undertaking to sign.' And Crispin passed a paper across.

Holding it at a fearsome distance from his eyes, Sir Stephen said, 'But why are you asking me? I'm no expert on bloody poetry, I don't see any from one year's end to another, I never seem to get time.'

'You wouldn't say people had to be experts on architecture to appreciate your buildings, would you, Sir Stephen?'

'Christ Almighty, no! I bloody well hope not, anyway! But I still don't see why you want me to sign your thing.'

'It's quite straightforward.' Crispin spoke in the inexpressive tone he had used from the beginning. 'You're a leading architect of your generation, just as – '

'Have you got a list of who else you're asking?' As this was being handed to him, Sir Stephen started to put on a pair of spectacles. He did this in a furtive, shoulder-hunching way, like a man putting in or taking out false teeth. Then, like a stage actor now, he read through the list reacting visibly in one way or another to every name on it. Once he looked up to say, 'I'm not quite sure, it isn't my field, but I rather doubt whether young Chris Bouffler has the sort of weight you seem to be looking for, or am I wrong?'

'Well, I gather he has been invited to give a series of concerts in Padua as part of the Tartini tercentenary.'

'The what? Oh, has he now! Really! Well, fuck me!'

'Absolutely.'

'Oh well.' Sir Stephen read on for a little, moving his face and shoulders about as before, then took off his glasses. 'And when you've collected your signatures or promises to sign, what then? An illuminated scroll? A medal? A cash award?'

'The signatories agree on a second statement, or a second part to their statement, calling on the Soviet government to show their recognition of an internationally acclaimed artist by releasing from custody her brother Sergei, who is detained under a section of an emergency decree of last year punishing certain economic crimes, for a minor offence that consisted of what would be colloquially described in this country as selling electric fittings on the black market. That was over eight months ago. As an act of clemency, therefore, designed to do no more than rectify a minor administrative error – '

'You have chapter and verse for all this, Mr . . .'

'Radetsky,' supplied the woman who had not spoken before, throwing in a mispronunciation. Near one nostril she had a large mole that looked black enough to have been improved with boot-polish. Once or twice she nodded to herself but kept her eyes, of less definite colour, on Crispin.

'Certainly,' he said in his impassive way. 'I have certified copies of all records connected with the legal process and the committal to prison, what amounts to a public or Press report and other corroborating documents. I have a copy here for you which you may inspect at your leisure.'

'Certified copies,' said 2nd woman, the one with the mole. 'Certified by whom?'

'By two experts on Soviet law and penology and an international authority on the domestic situation in the USSR, past and present.'

'Have you had them double-checked?'

'Nobody will be asked to sign anything on which I and the others mentioned would not be prepared to stake our professional and personal reputations as far as they may be at risk.'

Anna knew well enough where matters stood. Her gaze was on 2nd woman, not on Sir Stephen, who seemed quite satisfied with what he had heard, indeed to be looking forward to receiving the mark of distinction conferred by the batch of documents unintelligible to him. After a moment 2nd woman interlaced her fingers pointing downwards, in the manner of somebody about to give another a leg-up on to a tree or high wall.

'This is a political move,' she said.

'Yes,' said Crispin.

131

'It's a move to interfere in the internal affairs of the Soviet Union.'

'With any luck. I mean it has that aspect. Though as a matter of simple equity it surely calls for – '

'Nothing's ever that simple between sovereign nations, dear, but you can't do this one. They need our support and our forbearance there as never before. So forget it, sorry.'

'Oh, damnation,' said Sir Stephen, quite failing to sink to the occasion with the fuck or two or shit or so that might have been expected of him. 'Well, there it is, it seems.'

At once Crispin began preparing to leave. 'I'm sorry to have taken up your time. Our loss, of course. I'm afraid it rather looks as if we shall have to fall back on young Brian.'

The architect nodded belatedly but fast in recognition of the other and substantially younger architect who had crowned some years of achievement by developing the concept of the disjoined evictator. 'Yes *indeed*, a most powerfully imaginative and ground-breakingly innovative little bugger, incontestably. But surely it's a bit soon to credit him with the kind of lasting authority and international significance needed for an enterprise of this dimension. I have to say I feel this puts a slightly different – '

'Stephen dear,' said 2nd woman, 'we've agreed in several discussions that the present balance of internal forces in the Soviet Union makes it absolutely imperative that nothing should be initiated that might weaken the power of the central authority and thus endanger the continuance of the survival of the entire great socialist experiment.'

'Which means – '

'Nothing whatsoever.'

'And . . . and . . .'

'This might look bad.'

'In that case,' said Sir Stephen to the visitors with real regret, 'I'm very much afraid I can't see my way to – '

'Thank you for seeing us,' said Crispin.

The labourer-like lad saw them out. Richard thought perhaps his function was to give what to some who came here was a grateful hint of nonconformity before the unrelieved grimness of a heterosexual household closed round them. Then he thought that that would be just the sort of flippant idea he might have picked up from Crispin, and discarded it at once. In any case the lad had gone on looking at Anna as if she had been a hamburger done just the way he liked it.

On the pavement, Anna said in English, 'So no good.'

'That's right, Anna,' said Crispin. 'No good. Now if neither of you two mind, I propose taking a short walk along this rather awful elegant and refined street before we resume our journey by automobile, because I want to stretch my legs.'

'Can we come too?' asked Richard.

'Please do. I've never been much of a one for talking to myself, and people tend to think you're off your head if you start shouting to yourself.'

'What do you want to start shouting about?'

'What? That fellow in there. The sewage-creation expert with a knighthood. You don't run into a fellow as contemptible as that every day.'

'I should have thought that that was just about what a fellow in your line of work would be running into every day,' said Richard.

'Well, in a sense of course that's true. But most of them seem able to keep it covered up better, however contemptible they may be in the sight of . . . There. And I'd have said I was hardly shouting at all, wouldn't you?'

'There? Where?'

'Those two.'

Past them down what Crispin had quite properly called an elegant and refined street, a little disfigured by a skip full of rotting armchairs, two young girls were strolling with arms folded, looking over their shoulders and laughing in a snooty way that managed to include a blockish puzzlement. Pieces of chocolate-wrapper fell to the ground as they moved.

'You see? Off my head.'

'I remember reading somewhere that laughter is a sign of sexual attraction.'

'Only when seen in civilised peoples. Among savages it denotes suspicion and hostility.'

'Please tell Mr Crispin,' said Anna, looking at him politely as she spoke, 'that I'm grateful to him for all his efforts. Also that the gentleman's two ladies are just like the ones in the security committee and the Party in my country.'

'I expect she can see I gladly take her word for it, but you'd better tell her so too. What swine they are. What *swine*. No need to tell her that.'

'How much does it matter that that man won't help us?' asked Anna as, having reached a coffee-shop outside which hatted and scarved patrons defiantly sat, they turned back towards the car. 'And what are those things on the tables in his house? Are they pieces of art?'

Richard took it upon himself to explain about the things on the tables, which turned out a longer job than he had expected, but passed the first bit to Crispin.

'Nothing at all as God sees it, and not much even as man sees it,' was the answer, setting Richard a problem or two in translation. 'Tell her that over there they surely won't know any different, and over here putting that young fiddler fellow in the list of signatories may even seem excitingly venturesome.'

'I'll do my best.'

'Of course I don't know,' said Anna, after nodding slowly a few times at what Richard had told her, 'but I don't think that anybody back there mentioned my poetry more than to say I'm a poet and some people have heard of me because of that, and that's what our manifesto will say. I suppose that's how it'll be and, well, it doesn't matter, does it?'

'I'm sorry,' said Richard, but could think of nothing more. Crispin said, 'Tell her I'm afraid we think quite highly of our poets in theory without caring what they write or even being at all clear about who they are.'

'Say that's much nicer than in Russia, where the idea of poets makes them unhappy and suspicious, though they know poets are people to boast about at conferences. They'll say, here in the Kharkov area we now have twenty-three poets, which is two more than last year. On the other hand they care a great deal about what poets write, or seem to have written, as many a man and woman in prison or in a camp or in internal exile could tell you.'

Richard said as they climbed back into the car, 'Things must have eased up a good deal, surely. After all, you're here, and you're not exactly – '

'In many places the ice is growing thin and here and there it has melted altogether. But just one breath of winter will be enough to freeze it again all over.'

134

They moved off down the hill. Richard remembered being told by a contemporary during his time in Leningrad that the recurrent heavy pauses in Russian conversation had grown up along with the periodic need to refill vodka glasses. Actually now he came to think of it he could have done with one of those glasses right now, or rather its contents.

Crispin leaned round from the front seat. 'I was telling you about that fellow who rang me up about you in a mysterious fashion. Did I say what good English he spoke? Anyway I thought there was something a little odd about what he had to say, or rather didn't say. What he didn't say was how he knew I might know why you'd failed to turn up at the rendezvous you'd arranged with him. I asked him how he knew but then I found we'd moved on from there. I didn't notice at the time but afterwards it stuck out like a sore thumb. Do they, by the way, in your view?'

'Do what do what?'

'Sore thumbs. Stick out.'

Richard had noticed that when Crispin talked like that it was a sign he was thinking hard about something else, so for his own part he kept quiet. After a minute Crispin spoke again while still facing his front.

'I'm sorry, I can't hear you.'

'I'm sorry, Richard, I was starting to say another thing that stuck out like a sore thumb was the way that poncing little brick-shifter told us his grandfather had been a poor peasant.'

'I didn't see anything wrong with that.'

'Because you're a nice chap with insufficient experience of the great world of shits. Perhaps there are poor peasants in the middle of that sort of industrial city, I wouldn't know. But what Sir Stephen was doing was laying claim to an impeccably proletarian and disadvantaged family history.'

'That's not so terrible, is it?' Richard was aware that Crispin had quite suddenly turned a good deal angrier than he had been when Sir Stephen was mentioned a couple of minutes earlier. 'A piece of sentimental romanticism?'

'Oh yes. Oh, quite possibly. I expect something like that comes into it. I may be indulging in sentimental romanticism myself, of a different order. But Richard, bear with me now if I jump a stage or two in the argument, but those three dreadful people in what may be different ways have been defending everything that vile tyranny in Moscow has done over the years, which is bad enough in all conscience, but at least the past is past. But wretched creatures like that will never change. They'll simply look round for some other evil thing to promote. That would be an enemy worth challenging if you like. Unfortunately none of us can match their dedication and their staying-power. They and their descendants will still be there when all of us are dead and forgotten.' Instantly reverting to his ordinary mode of speaking, Crispin said, 'I'm afraid it might tax your interpretative skills to convey that speech in an appropriate form.'

'I wasn't going to try,' said Richard.

'Tell her that as a Czech I can't forgive Sir Stephen for being one-quarter Polish. I'm sorry I let the Czech side of me take over just now.'

'I'm not sorry. And I don't think you are either, much.'

'No, you're quite right, I'm not. The *swine*.'

When Anna spoke a moment later it was to ask Richard not about what Crispin had said but about prices in the boutique-type shops they were passing.

ELEVEN

While what happened about half an hour later was still happening, Richard managed comparatively little in the way of actual thinking. But one of the things he did think was roughly that his own volition, his will, was not involved in it at all, and that his actions were automatic down to the last detail in a way that was completely new to him. Then as soon as it was over he thought it had really been the other way round. What had been new was how single-mindedly and totally he had acted as he wanted, and not out of habit or memory or with some indefinable but largish part of him otherwise engaged.

The car had driven its three passengers to a spot just outside the front door of the Dom, where Crispin got out. Before departing he handed Richard a sheet of his unexpectedly austere notepaper on which, in his even more unexpectedly childish handwriting, he had jotted down an address in Berkshire, no doubt Kotolynov's, and some information about how to get to it. By the time Richard had made it out and put the folded sheet in his pocket, the car had just about taken them to Professor Léon's house. Afterwards Richard could not remember telling the chauffeur he could or must go, though obviously something of the kind must have occurred, nor was he at all sure where he had got the idea of telling him that, though he felt he knew he would never have done so without some sign coming or not coming from Anna. That sign must also have hinted that the house was empty, or at any rate that there was nothing to stop them going up to its top floor and into a small room that was clearly her bedroom. It had very little in it that could strictly be called furniture, but there were a great many objects of various sizes spread over the floor, though not so many as to impede their path to the bed itself.

After some minutes he began talking to Anna in Russian.

Almost at once Anna stiffened in his arms. 'Talk English,' she said, also in Russian.

'But you won't understand.'

'Talk English.' She had her back to him.

'You're absolutely beautiful and that was really lovely,' he said experimentally in English, and stopped. For some reason a picture came into his mind, the first to appear there for quite a while – of Crispin looking uninterestedly at him while he divulged Anna's present requirement and perhaps also the fact that until just now neither he nor she had spoken a word in either language, as if for a bet or a dare. So perhaps on the whole not. At the time, he realised, he had thought like one with brain damage that she would not be able to understand anything he said because he was English and she was not.

Even after all this had groped its way through his consciousness she still said nothing, but her outer eye was just visible to him and was open.

He had another go. 'Isn't it incredible how this kind of thing can just sort of take hold of you and you just find yourself, you find it's all happening as though it had all been decided on beforehand in some funny way.'

The eye shut and reopened after a longer interval than that of a simple blink.

'All right, I agree I'm not that marvellous when it comes to talking about it, and I'm sorry about that, but I do think you're sweet, but surely you know that.'

Anna turned her head slightly on the pillow so that her whole face was hidden from him. He seemed to remember catching an expression on the back of a girl's neck before now but there was none at all on this one's.

Okay, he thought to himself a little fractiously, you have a bloody go yourself, and of course what I was saying sounded about average, in other words fairly crappy, and just you see how you sound under these conditions, and who said anything about being supposed to be on oath at a time like this, and even if you had a bit of Slovak or Slovene from somewhere that would still not be a fair parallel, and what the hell do I say now? 'I'm sorry, I just can't think of anything else to say, any other kind of thing, and I thought on this sort of do it was supposed to be what

138

you did and how you did it that counted, not what you said, or is everything different in Russian?'

If he had expected this speech to send her twirling round to face him, on the basis of its superior honesty, realism, whatever, he was disappointed. Anna pointing towards him and talking was his official objective and to be conscientiously striven towards, but the prospect allured him less than he considered it should, no, bugger it, *knew* it should. Sure as fate she would go Russian, or Russian woman, on him, not the same thing, he acknowledged, but not in practice easy to separate. He had not spent long enough in Leningrad, or had not considered either aspect of the problem closely enough while there. And it occurred to him now that he had never managed to find Anna Karenina as interesting or believable as Vronsky, let alone as Karenin, and that none of the three's doings had appealed to him as strongly as those of Levin. 'All right, what do you want to do, stay on here for a bit or have a drink or what?'

After another pause while she considered what could hardly have been more than the sound of this, or perhaps drifted back into unconsciousness, she turned over in bed towards him. She did this and followed it with small settling movements in a way that gave a tremendous air of her just happening to have done that then. Her eyes were nearly shut. But she put her foot on his and told him, 'Say that in Russian, please.'

He did his best, conscientiously matching equivalents.

'I'd like a drink. But not tea if you don't mind.'

'Why should it be tea?'

'I read an English novel once in which the man got up and prepared tea for the woman and himself after they had made love. Regularly, I think. We've talked before about the English and their tea.'

To throw off the disagreeable feeling of unreality these remarks gave him, Richard swung his legs off the bed. 'What drink would you like, then?'

'There's a bottle of champagne in the refrigerator in the kitchen.'

He started to get half dressed. 'What are all these things on the floor?'

'Some of them are things I brought to sell here. Some of them are to give to friends here and to send home and some are for me.

They're not very expensive, I haven't been extravagant. We have half an hour till Professor Léon comes back from taking Hamparzoumian to the park. They go every day.'

'I'll be quick.'

He looked over at her sitting up in the bed with her arms round some of the front of herself. Without his glasses as he was he realised he could not see her face at all well, but was sure she was smiling and nearly sure she was blinking her eyes rather fast too, and in any case he felt he could see her well enough for his present purposes.

What he took in of the house on his trip to the kitchen, the narrow passages, steep stairs and heavy old dark wallpaper, recalled to him Mrs Benda's where he had first met Anna, not directly but in that both put him in mind of places he had seen in Russia. He thought it must have been that the first immigrants from eastern Europe had sought out such familiar surroundings, like the early Spanish and English colonists of the New World who had settled in parts of it that resembled the native country. Probably someone else had already spotted the parallel. Not his field. The smell, waxy, not unpleasant, was similar.

The refrigerator, in which he had been expecting to find eatables going back some years, turned out to hold almost nothing but a couple of dozen small cubical cartons of milk and a half-bottle of champagne. This felt cold to the touch but not very, just about as cold, he thought, as such a bottle would naturally be after sitting in an appliance of *c.* 1960 for the interval between Anna's departure and now. He had always been one for noticing things like that, and immediately did so this time despite still feeling slightly confused, with only half his attention on what he was doing and the rest nowhere in particular.

She was sitting up in bed wearing a woolly garment that was probably a bed-jacket. Richard remembered from somewhere about as far off as his childhood that when Cordelia put on a bed-jacket, nobody within pistol-shot was left in any doubt that it was indeed a bed-jacket in a very real sense that she had on. Then he said to Anna, 'When did you put this in the refrigerator?'

'Oh, some time yesterday as far as I remember.'

'I'd have expected it to be a bit colder after that time.'

'I wasn't going to and then I popped it in this morning just before I came out and got in the car.'

'So you knew this would happen,' he said gently.

'No, but it did, didn't it? I just thought it might. Nothing unreasonable about that, the bottle wouldn't have burst. Anyway, I hoped you'd be pleased.'

Showing her that her hope had been justified actually spilt some of the champagne out of both of their glasses, and by the time they had poured the last of it Anna said it was time to start getting up. When he experienced a feeling of relief at seeing her take off for the bathroom, Richard asked himself savagely if he had been expecting the poor little thing to give herself a rub-down with birch twigs or pumice stones before climbing into her badger-pelt. Again he seemed to sense Crispin's glance, going along with a nasty grin this time. Mechanically he swallowed the last drops of champagne and was mildly amazed that such a consistently horrible drink should have seemed all right just now.

'I didn't understand the part about me speaking English,' he said when they were both in the bedroom again.

'I'm sorry, that was rather bad of me. I thought that you'd feel you could say what you liked in English without being afraid of sounding ridiculous or anything like that, and I could tell what you really thought about me and about us making love and so on.'

'You must understand more English than you've said, in that case.'

She opened a drawer and looked closely at him over her shoulder. 'No, but I've heard enough English to be able to recognise the sound of *bullshit* in it,' she said, using the English word. 'And you didn't make that sound.'

'What did I say?'

'I don't know, I don't understand English. But I could tell you didn't want to say anything and what you did say sounded awkward. Oh my love, you don't know how much I like that awkwardness and what a high value I put on it.'

'That's good, then,' he said.

'I was nervous too,' said Anna, looking away from him now. She had put on a different jumper, one in rather better repair than the last. 'I suppose . . . I'm afraid I've been behaving rather in the way you expected me to behave. And before you ask me what that is, I'll tell you – it's like a Russian. Of course like a Russian girl, but especially like a Russian. Now you can tell me I'm right. Dickie,' she added.

'Oh yes, you're absolutely right, Anyushka, how extraordinary. But it means I've got to ask you how you know that's what it is and what it looks like, expecting you to behave like a Russian.'

'You do speak the most marvellous Russian, you know. How I know, well, like with *bullshit*, which isn't at all the same, I've been long enough in England already to recognise the look. Not just interest or curiosity, as if you heard somebody was a, I don't know, a Turk or an Afghan or an American. More a matter of being on the watch for strange behaviour and then finding everything understandable in the circumstances, even if it's me yawning or blowing my nose. I can see you thinking, oh yes, they're just like anyone else in their way. When you get to know them.'

'How stupid. How awful.'

'It's not stupid or awful when you do it. And don't forget I keep thinking, well then, he's English, but I mean it as a compliment.'

'You're still nervous. Are you wondering whether this is going to happen again?'

'Yes.' She stood in a round-shouldered attitude, head down, arms hanging, that he determined to find womanly, human, universal, not special at all.

'Yes, well as far as I'm concerned it is.'

They put their arms round each other and hung on. There was something there this time that had not been there before – relief probably. Something else too. Cheerfulness.

'Darling,' said Anna.

'Darling. Even though I've got a wife.'

'We must hurry now or Professor Léon and Hamparzoumian will be back. You go on downstairs. I'll follow you in a minute.'

He stood for a space in the murky hall in a state of wonderment, not at or about anything, just wonderment. When Anna joined him she brought a thin book. At once, even before she handed it to him, he knew what it was or what sort of thing it was, and his spirits sank with astonishing speed and thoroughness.

'I want to give you this,' she said. 'Don't look at it now. But please do look at it later, I mean not just what I've written in it for you.' She smiled as if at a slightly improper thought, and then said in a matter-of-fact way, 'Perhaps after what's happened you'll like my poetry better than you used to.'

Unable to think of any words, he put his arms round her again, and it felt different from before and quite wrong, but apparently she noticed nothing, though he did think he noticed a bigger proportion of sheer amiability, chumminess, something like that. How much bigger? Twenty per cent? Fifteen per cent? To hell with it. 'Ah well,' he said. 'Well, I suppose . . .' The book was small enough to put in his side pocket.

'You'd better go now.'

'I'll telephone you.'

She nodded fiercely – she believed him. They gripped hands very hard for a moment, and then he stepped into the street under the immense clamour of a helicopter that was waddling importantly through the air no more than fifty metres above his head.

To begin with, Richard thought he would wait till he was safely immured in his study before he looked at all at the book of Anna's poems. Then he thought he would wait till he was sitting in the taxi he expected to be able to hail in the larger street round the corner. Then, full of dread and of a sense of things getting out of control, more acute than anything he had experienced up to that point, he stopped on the pavement where he was and pulled out the book and opened it. The traffic was less heavy than on his previous visit to these parts, as if drivers of juggernauts had found a preferable route. Pedestrians were few.

He saw but did not stay to read a scatter of Cyrillic handwriting on one early leaf and went to the text. Before he started reading there, it seemed to him perfectly possible, in theory at least, that at this stage he would find the poems, some of them, parts of them, all right or even quite good in some unlooked-for way. Immediately after that, he considered it more likely that they would seem to him just or just about as free of merit as ever, but that he would somehow not mind that, would pick up bits of charm, say, or notice compensating points of historical, cultural, etc., interest. And of course personal interest.

At the end of three or four minutes while he stood in the lee of a receptacle for used bottles, he had read enough to be going on with. He put the book back in his pocket and started walking again towards the corner. A middle-aged and then a youngish woman went past. Neither of them so much as glanced at him, let alone accosted him to inquire whether he knew he was mauve or chalk-white in the face or was making his hands tremble like that on purpose. What he had seen on those pages was worse than he remembered, no less emptily pretentious but with a note of unearned impressiveness not noticed before, quite as unoriginal in diction but also slackly expressed. Needlessly obscure – he knew he could trust his grasp of informal Russian to take in most expressions even remotely suitable for serious poetry. Technically incompetent. All that.

Soon he got a taxi and without thinking gave his home address. When he did think he let the destination stand. He would shut himself in his study, pleading if necessary a sudden violent attack of work, and not come out. Not come out until when, until what? All the way home he gave himself a voluble and severe lecture about what on earth was the matter with him, what difference were a few poems supposed to make to his feelings about the whole of the rest of Anna, what was so grand about him, what if she had been a rotten seamstress or household manager or performer on the balalaika, and what on earth was the matter with him? None of this made the least impression. He was still upset, and no nearer being clear about why, when he paid off the taxi outside his house and met Pat Dobbs coming down past the parked TBD.

'Hallo, Richard,' she said. 'Do you happen to know where Cordelia is?'

'Isn't she in there?'

'Not unless she's locked herself up and thrown the key away. Which I agree could be the case.'

'You mean she asked you round and when you came round you found she wasn't there to let you in?'

'That's about it, yes.' Pat peered at Richard. 'Are you all right?'

'No,' he said.

'What is it? Nothing awful?'

'Not death, no. Or illness. Accident, nothing like that.'

They went on standing there for a moment. Then Pat said, shouting a little to beat the noise of the traffic, 'Would you like me to come in with you?' When he made no reply, she added, 'I wouldn't mind a cup of tea.'

Quite efficiently he took out his latchkey and let them into the house. It would not have been altogether true to say that he had forgotten who Pat was, but he realised he was not at all clear how well he was supposed to know her. He also thought he might have seemed rude if he wordlessly made straight for his study and stayed there, as he remembered intending earlier. So he stood looking round the hall rather as if he had come to view the house in the role of a prospective buyer.

Pat had been hoping very much that Cordelia would not turn up all of a sudden and get in the way of whatever it was Richard clearly wanted to tell, or could soon be prodded into telling. The odds were pretty long that it was something about this Russian girl of his, whom he had presumably been to bed with and/or had perhaps strangled. But she felt she could not very well start showing him she was ready and willing to listen on the spot. 'Can I get you some tea, Richard?'

'Oh yes. Thank you.'

'You go and sit down and I'll bring it into the drawing-room.'

'No,' he said strongly – 'I'll come out to the kitchen with you.'

'What a nice idea.'

They were still crossing the hall when Richard spoke again. 'Perhaps you remember,' he said, having just remembered it himself, 'er, was it the last time you were here, Pat, there was some talk about somebody called Anna Danilova, a Russian girl over here on a visit. She's a, she writes poetry.'

'Oh yes, of course. Rather good poetry, you said.'

'What? I never said that. Who said that?'

Pat had turned on the cold tap at the kitchen sink and was waiting for the milky liquid that came out of it to change to something nearer water. 'It must have been Cordelia, then, but she would have had to get it from you, wouldn't she?'

'Well, I never said it. Anyway, erm . . .'

'There was also some talk of a trip to Harrods. Is that still on?'

'No. I don't know. Anyway, the thing is . . . Pat . . . this Anna Danilova . . . She and I seem to have, seem to be . . .'

'You have . . .'

'Yes. This afternoon. Just now, really. It's all right, you needn't say anything about that.'

'I wasn't going to say anything about it. But don't you want to say something?'

'Well yes, er, it was wonderful, no question about that, for both of us, absolutely wonderful, and there we are,' said Richard with a confidence and at a speed that would have surprised anyone who knew him. He gave no hint either of the extreme diffidence he would normally have shown in making the least claim to knowledge of a woman's feelings in such matters. At the same time he failed to impart much sense of lively enthusiasm.

Pat had seen enough of him before to notice most of that. 'So there's no problem there,' she said in an encouraging voice, and settled herself as comfortably as she could on one of Cordelia's kitchen chairs, one whose seat had been moulded in high relief to fit a backside a couple of sizes larger than Pat's at any rate was.

'No, very much not.' Richard was leaning against the sink. 'Except that in a way it is the problem, or half the problem. If this Anna thing weren't so important it wouldn't be so important.'

'Nor would it. So the other half's Cordelia, presumably.'

'No. I haven't got to her yet.'

'You'd better get to her soon, hadn't you, because any moment she'll come – '

'It's Anna's poetry. Far from being rather good, it's very bad. I don't know Russian as well as I know English, how could I, but I do know it well. Quite well enough to be quite sure whether more than a few lines of poetry in it are good or bad. And hers is bad. Bad through and through. Bad to a degree that means something unimaginable would have to happen before the same person could ever write anything good. No question. Which raises a profoundly serious problem. It wouldn't be one if I didn't . . . if I weren't . . .' He was losing his fluency again. 'I suppose all this sounds very silly.'

'Not to me,' said Pat.

Richard had been hoping against hope that it would sound at least rather silly to him, but no such luck. In fact it sounded more ironclad and inescapable than before. 'Of course it's only my opinion,' he said desperately.

'That doesn't help, does it? There isn't anything but opinions in things like poetry. Bridges and buildings fall down and no argument, and even then I wouldn't know what to do if it was my boyfriend who'd put them up. What have you said to her? Does she know how you feel about her ghastly poetry?'

'I told her I didn't like it before . . . things had got as far as they have.' He felt a little resentment at Pat's adjective and realised he had thought the right to belittle that poetry was somehow exclusive to him. 'She treated it as just an unfortunate matter of difference in taste. And . . . now she thinks I might find I feel different.'

'M'm.'

'But it's not a question of taste or how people feel, it's to do with truth.'

The duly filled kettle at the end of its flex, from beginning to mutter and grumble satisfactorily as its contents warmed up, seemed to have lost heart and had fallen silent. Now, at some imperceptible stimulus, it started itself off again. Pat got up and went over. She thought of the tale she would be telling Harry later and asked Richard, 'When are you seeing this girl again? I mean you have arranged to?'

'No, but I will.'

'Mind you do. How important is her poetry to her?'

'Oh, quite important. Very important.'

'Pity, that. You must see if you can't find some way of turning it into just a hobby of hers.'

Pat reached out for the teapot, but went rigid as a limited uproar broke out some metres away round the front door of the house – the crunch of a latchkey, the clicking to and fro of the lock, the wheeze of hinges and a noisy juddering as the door itself was thrust wide, the clash and jingle of a chain, a final reverberating boom as the door shut.

'That sounds like Cordelia,' said Richard.

And indeed it was she, carrying in a couple of smallish plastic bags that nevertheless seemed to be disproportionately heavy. She yielded them up with a tiny gasp of complaint as well as relief, blew at the strands of blonde hair that had fallen over her face, blinked her eyes a good deal, and in no time had bundled

Pat off to fetch stuff like toothpaste, chocolate and an evening paper, rallying further to complete the making of tea. In not much more than no time she and Richard were sitting opposite each other in the drawing-room.

'Hallo my darling,' she said as if she had recognised him only that moment. 'I imagine the Russian girl picked you up and took you off according to plan, whatever your plan was.'

'Oh yes,' he said, trying to remember not only what he had disclosed about the imagined plan for the last few hours but also what had actually happened in rough sequence.

'Good, very good. I thought you and Pat seemed a little confused or upset when I came in just now.'

'Oh, really? Well, I suppose she had rather been expecting you to be here when she turned up.'

'No doubt she had been, darling, I really couldn't say. Anyway I had the feeling I'd barged in in the middle of something.'

Coming as it did from his wife, this insight surprised Richard and also disconcerted him a little. 'What are you talking about, Cordelia?' he asked.

'Well, darling, what I'm obviously *not* talking about,' she said, giving all the Ts a double dose of voicing, 'is interrupting anything, you know, *going on* between you and Pat.'

'Well, so I should have – '

'What more natural after all than that she should arrive some minutes early and you should appear and let her in and *Bob's your uncle*,' she finished on a solidly informative note, passing him a cup two-thirds full of tea.

Richard nodded his head slightly. He had never quite got used to the way Cordelia was unalterably on time for her appointments, perforce leaving any unpunctuality to others. But now she turned and looked at him and he quailed, internally only as he hoped.

'All the same, *darling*,' she said, 'you and Pat were deeply involved in I don't know what. Something had come up, something serious and important. Like a death.'

'There's been no death affecting any of us as far as I know. I'm afraid I – '

'Something serious, though,' said Cordelia, still looking.

'All I can think of, I had been going on a bit about the rather ghastly time I'd been having with this trendy architect fellow. He was an absolute – '

'You told me that was where you were taking the Russian girl.'

'Yes, and old Crispin was of the party too, which didn't exactly – '

'Richard, why can I still not meet her? What's happening? Please tell me what's happening darling. Are you having an affair with this Anna? Or intending to? Or wanting to?'

'None of those.' Richard hoped he looked and sounded as all right as he could in the saying of this and what followed, and felt like a helpless shit for hoping so. 'I suppose one of the best ways to convince you would be if you could just see her for a moment,' he went boldly on, which made him feel like a shit on two fronts, so to speak. Although this part of the problem had got nowhere near coming up in his conversation with Pat Dobbs just now, he knew that he would not have been able to equip himself so fast with such a thundering denial without that conversation, without a little mental video of Pat telling him with great authority that no good ever came of admitting anything – ten seconds' glow of righteousness and decency and love, he could imagine her saying, and worse all round ever after. Worse for both of them, he could have added off his own bat, but especially worse for him. So he went on with some more troubled but unbudging innocence. Looking on the bright side, he realised that for as long as he had a stretch like this in front of him with Cordelia he could at least not be trying to cope with the Anna awfulness, which lay irremovably in a corner of his mind, unregarded but there, quiet but unsleeping, like a monster in the dreams of some unenlivening character in *The Possessed* or *The Brothers Karamazov*.

First clicking her tongue or sucking her teeth with a noise like a car door shutting, Cordelia turned herself a few degrees in her chair so as to face her husband as squarely as possible. It was as if she wanted to spread out in front of him everything she was and had, not only heavy moss-green shirt, very pale pink polo-sweater, one or other pair of Italian shoes, twisty, thinner-than-usual gold bracelets, but deep blue eyes that for the moment seemed not to be doing much blinking. 'You probably think I don't notice very much of what's going on round me,' she said in

149

her usual tones. 'That's partly my own fault, or at any rate of my own doing. Until I was sixteen I had a sort of speech defect, or two really. One was a sort of stutter, well, more of a hesitation, I suppose. Anyway, it meant that people soon got terribly tired of trying to follow what I was saying, you see. And my voice itself . . .' Now she did blink her eyes, and opened them wide too. 'It was so thin and sort of *scratchy*, nobody could hear me properly, and so nobody paid me any attention. I decided I was going to do something about that. Are you following what I'm saying, Richard?'

'Yes,' he said, 'of course,' and he was, but he had kept being nearly distracted by not being able to see the chessmen and chessboard from where he sat, and wondering if they had been moved, and if so to what effect. 'Do go on.'

'Thank you darling. So I made myself a new voice and a new . . . manner to go with it. A new way of behaving. And did it so completely that I can't do the old ones any more. I know, because not so very long ago I tried twice to do them and I just couldn't either time. Like that English actor, you remember, what was he called, went to Hollywood and stayed there for years and years and then when he had to play the part of an Englishman he found he just couldn't do it and just sounded like an American imitating an Englishman. So if I sometimes sound a bit funny to you in the way I talk,' Cordelia swept unhesitatingly on, 'that's why it is, nothing more than that, and it doesn't mean I'm not taking in what's going on and it certainly doesn't mean I don't know what a man looks like and sounds like and doesn't do and doesn't say when he's fed up with me. The last time that happened was with Godfrey and you're not so very different from Godfrey my darling. He came and talked to me when he was ready and no doubt you'll do the same if and when. And now if you'll excuse me I have a few telephone calls to make.'

Richard refilled his teacup to the brim from the pot, then set it down untouched. He went on sitting where he had been until he recognised the figure of Pat approaching the front door, hurrying towards it as if to miss as little as possible of what might have been taking place inside. With no alacrity in his own step he went and opened to her and, as she stepped over the threshold, saw inquisitiveness gathering in her face. But then they heard a high-pitched but unignorable summons to her from upstairs, so for the moment he was spared any more discussion of anything, and now he did dive for the shelter of his study and the revision of the first part of his notes on Lermontov.

TWELVE

For the rest of that day and for the whole of the next, Richard saw nothing of his wife. None of the individual bits of seeing nothing of her meant anything much in itself, from the sleeping in the smaller bedroom across the landing, her recourse half a dozen times a year after a couple of bad nights in the old twin bed, to the entire absence from an early hour of the following evening, presumably on one of her monthly dinner-and-night visits to an old Cambridge chum in Maidenhead.

Richard himself spent all day at the Institute going over what had purported to be a new text, lately unearthed in a Leningrad archive, of Blok's drama *The Fair Booth*, but that turned out on investigation to be a garbled and mutilated old text with two unauthentic passages inserted. After several false starts he telephoned Anna and told her his feelings were the same as ever, but he could not see her that day because of difficulties over his wife. Even if his really difficult difficulties were over Anna herself and her poetry, what he told her was a bloody distillate of truth on his present form. Just before leaving for home he happened to pick up the new number of an American journal of Russian studies and found his conclusions about the Blok text duplicated, indeed anticipated, with the addition of a third, shorter interpolation he had missed.

The next morning was sunny and warm. Like a man who wakes up with a clear head after a boozy evening, Richard lay in bed waiting for hangover to strike from one side or the other – Anna-plus-her-poetry or unvarnished Cordelia. Neither did while he got up and went into the bathroom. Here the bath itself, the shower and one or two of the cupboards were panelled in a streaky dark-grey material resembling marble but said to be both cheaper and also somehow better than it. Here too a gold chair, one at any rate smothered with gold paint and quite a lot of gold leaf, faced a gold table, a gold-bound one at least with a gold-framed adjustable mirror on it. The table-top also bore dozens of bottles, jars, pots, vials, phials, including a selection of nine or ten shampoos, some of which went by higher-flown names than that. Richard's own hairwash reached him in a pale plastic container unfailingly loaded with inducements like 6p Off and 15% More Free. At the moment he was unstocked and yet intended to wash his hair, so he took a shampoo at random from the line on the table. He took it at random because, whichever it was, it was certain to embody an amazingly rare and complicated blending of virtually extinct materials produced only in Paraguay and flown over specially for Cordelia. She would sometimes say that buying this sort of stuff was her only extravagance.

And the reason Richard intended to wash his hair, not a daily habit of his, was that in an hour he would be off to pick up Anna and take her down to Berkshire to call on the venerable Kotolynov in the hope of enlisting his support for her cause. In the shower, which was rather less expensive-seeming on the inside than its outside would have been to a visiting eye, Richard contemplated this trip with pleasant anticipation, with no interference from the troublesome feelings the thought of Anna had earlier brought him. Why so? There must have been a hundred old Russian proverbs advising against asking such questions. Without trying to think of one he concentrated on admiring the sunshine and getting through the successive tasks in hand. One of the less predictable of these took him into his study a few minutes before he should have been on his way out of the house.

'Isn't this Richard?' asked Freddie's voice on the telephone. She sounded too controlled to be altogether sober.

'Yes, is Crispin there? Or here, or whatever one's supposed to say now? Anyway, may I, can I, could I speak to him?'

'What, of course, but how's my old friend, what's she called, too early in the bloody morning, for Christ's sake, er, Richard, how's, how's my old buddy-girl *Nggornndelia* this morning as ever was? Er . . .'

'She's all right, thank you,' said Richard, feeling there might be something to be said for Cordelia after all, or perhaps merely that after all one had to be married to some woman or other. 'Is

Crispin there?' The private line was not for light conversation like this.

There was a sound like a great quietus being dealt and soon Crispin's voice spoke, a little breathily, as if between press-ups, and also with special cordiality, as if after a silent interval of some months. Oh good, he said, so today's outing was on, and no, nothing special to bear in mind, except of course never to trust a Russian, especially a famous or distinguished one.

Richard said into an expectant silence, 'Well, there's one Russian I seem to have got myself into the position of having to trust. Not such a famous one.'

'Oh.'

'I just thought you'd better know that.'

'Yes. Has this affected local conditions at all?'

'Local . . .'

'*Christ*, does Cordelia know, are you going to – '

'I haven't said a word, I've denied everything, but she seems to–'

'But when she came in unexpectedly and found you on top of little Otchi-Tchornya she didn't believe you were teaching her Cumberland wrestling.'

'I think I'd better be off. It's Friday and there'll be traffic heading out to the west.'

'I'm sorry, Richard. Anyway, she knows.'

'As good as. I can't think how. Honestly, I thought she only saw what she wanted to see and as little as possible of that.'

'Some egotists wouldn't notice a bomb going off in the same room unless it happened to blow their leg off. Others, you can't breathe on a daisy in their garden and get away with it. And there are ones that switch. You ought to have a chat with Godfrey.'

'Don't laugh, but Cordelia said she thought he and I were rather similar.'

Crispin ignored the interdiction. After a minute he said, 'Some of what he has to say about her isn't funny at all. You ought to hear it for your own safety.'

'I will some day. Well . . .'

'You're pretty new to all this, aren't you? I mean *all* this?'

'I suppose I am. Yes, I am.'

'How are you making out on the guilt front? Remorse, self-reproach. Contrition.'

'It's at arm's length at the moment.'

'See you keep it there or push it further off. If you want any help, send for me. But perhaps Godfrey would be more useful. And of course for the instant version there's always Freddie.'

'Yes, of course. I'll let you know how we get on with Kotolynov.'

Apart from an emphatically shut bedroom door in the middle of the night, and a twenty-minute chunk of roaring choir with full orchestra, suddenly there in mid-bar and chopped off again as abruptly, from the kitchen at breakfast-time, Richard had not heard a sound from Cordelia, and had seen nothing of her at all, for nearly twenty-four hours. On the point of departure, he thought of leaving her a note with the information that he expected not to be gone for ever, but was dissuaded by a mixture of motives, of which the most immediate was boredom with the task. But he left his study door conspicuously open and significant stuff on the desk, like open notebooks and a half-finished letter to Hallett in the typewriter. Enough for anybody really wanting to know, and anybody not really wanting to know could . . . Could go and fuck themselves, he thought, completing the phrase with a rare audacity.

He had filled up the TBD the previous evening and slid straight out into the southbound traffic, with the added satisfaction of causing a moustached learner-driver under instruction to screech to a halt a couple of dozen metres upstream of him. You too, he thought. It was a beautiful day and he was going to drive to the country with a girl, or a person of the feminine gender. Did anyone *say* that? he wondered briefly? Well, anybody who did could certainly go and . . .

When he drew up outside the Pimlico house, the girl or person of the feminine gender who emerged on to the pavement did so with such instantaneity that she must have been watching from within. Richard knew who she was, and only a distinctly less hard-headed man than he would have pretended he had a moment's trouble recognising her. But even he had to say to himself that she looked like a younger version of herself, even a healthier one. There was a soft warmth in her cheeks that he was nearly sure had not been there before. A more conceited man would at least have wondered if he had put it there. Richard never quite did. He got quickly out of the car and smiled at Anna. 'How lovely you look,' he said.

'Will you teach me English?' she asked, kissing him.

'If you like, but of course you realise it would take time.'

'This is for you.' She handed him a small package loosely wrapped in tissue paper.

'Thank you. Depending how thoroughly you wanted to learn it,' he said, unwrapping the package and revealing and unfolding a handsome red-and-blue handkerchief.

'Oh, I'd never expect to speak it as beautifully as you speak Russian.'

'They're my favourite colours. How did you know?'

'I guessed.' Anna grinned at him and nodded her head.

'I'm afraid I haven't got anything for you, darling.'

'That's all right, it doesn't matter.'

'How old did you say you were?'

'I didn't say, but thank you.'

'Who do they think they are, that's what I'd like to know,' said a voice in English from near by. 'All over the pavement nattering away in their horrible language just as if they was at home. What is it, Polish, Hungarian?' The voice stayed audible because its owner, a long-haired middle-aged man dressed like a youth on holiday, was moving past only very slowly. 'One of those, I don't care which, do you?'

'They spend their money in our shops, anyway,' said a younger, closer-cropped man.

'You can tell the fellow's suit wasn't made here.'

'Please, please, English friend,' called Richard, stretching out a hand. 'Where is House of Parliament and Prime Minister and Mr Speaker?'

'Well, they're a long way from here, mate,' said the older man without trying to speak any slower or more clearly. 'I'd get a taxi if I was you. Well, or a bus. You know. Bus?'

'Also Big Ban and Tan Dovnink Street?'

'You stay exactly where you are and a bus'll be along in a minute. You know, one . . . minute?'

'English friend,' cried Richard, advancing with spread arms, 'Russian friend thanks you.'

'I should never have imagined you behaving like that,' said Anna when the space about them was suddenly clear. 'In Moscow perhaps not so surprising.'

'And spare me the lovable-simple-peasant crap,' he snarled at her. 'Don't you forget I've been there.'

'Richard, where does this come from?'

'I've never done it before, you know. Well, not for a long time, anyway. I must have got it from my father. He was always embarrassing my sister and me by pretending to be drunk or deaf-and-dumb. Once he nearly got into a fight by imitating a drunken American in front of a real American. He couldn't manage the accent. None of his generation could.'

'What did he do for a living, your father?' Anna had got into the TBD's passenger seat and was efficiently fastening the seatbelt over herself. 'Is he still alive?'

'No, he died eight years ago,' said Richard, staring at her a little, but not in surprise. 'What? Oh, he sold brushes, or helped to.'

'Hairbrushes?'

'Well, not so much them. More industrial brushes. Not very exciting.'

'Did he encourage you to learn Russian?'

'Good Lord no, what an idea. That was because of me reading a story by Chekhov when I was at school, in English of course. I can never remember which one it was now. Dad always thought I was a bit odd and that proved I was past saving.'

Richard hoped that by going so far but no further he would encourage Anna to talk of her own family, perhaps especially her brother, but she did not. In fact as always she said little directly about her life, though there was enough about places in Moscow, getting about Moscow, shopping in Moscow to justify his looking at her a lot. More than once he was looking at her when he would have done better to be looking at the traffic, and the driver of a cement lorry provided an excellent impromptu example of the colourful London vernacular Anna had heard about.

The sun was still shining when they went through a horrible series of bunchings and delays and halts on the motorway. Of course they did. Richard was rather glad of it because the irritation seemed to be helping him not to worry about the fact that the lovely and desirable girl in the seat next to him was in the second place an absolutely bloody awful poet. Anyway, something was evidently seeing to it that this unpleasantness remained at a distance, like a tax demand sure to come but yet to be presented, or what guilty memories were supposed to be like. Perhaps he was in the process of reducing that poetry in his mind to – what had Pat said? – a hobby. But to venture any nearer the question was not to be thought of.

After much too long a time they left the motorway by a road that led among such things as fields rather than distantly past them. Anna stopped explaining how no one in Moscow had anything to give street robbers any more, except the worn-out clothes they were wearing which were the same as the worn-out clothes everybody else was wearing, and looked round to her left and right.

'I suppose in such a small country you have to put something in all the places,' she said sympathetically. 'But I expect you're used to hearing visitors from Russia saying things like that. But it doesn't bother you that I'm not original, does it?'

'Aren't you? I thought you were.' Richard had spoken unironically but was quite quick to switch his expression. 'Yes. But I don't see all that many visitors from Russia, you know.'

'What? I thought you knew all sorts of Russians in London.'

'Not so many. I keep well away from anybody official or with official connections, with the embassy for instance . . .'

'Quite right – if they're not dangerous they're unpleasant.'

'. . . and the ones I do know seem to be mostly one sort, people who've settled here, older people. And their children, of course, though occasionally – '

'Ah, you mean people like those poor ghastly creatures at Mrs Benda's. I keep thinking of them and whenever I do for more than a couple of seconds I want to kill myself. And I've seen others too. I suppose Professor Léon and Hamparzoumian and the old ladies are like that really, but I know them. Those people are like characters in fairy tales, cursed with growing older and dying but inside staying the same age with the same ideas and thoughts and memories and everything as they had when they came out of their lives and into the enchanter's garden. Richard, you must know some people, some Russians who aren't like that, some younger ones.'

'I do, yes, a few, but I don't find I get on with them so well.'

'What, with no language problem?'

'They don't want to speak Russian here, Anna, they want to

speak English, American even more. That's what they want to be, that's why they came. Can you blame them?'

'I certainly can.' She had turned fierce at the thought of them. 'How can they think of leaving their country? Would they leave their family? – I don't just mean to work or get married, I mean never see them, forget them, behave as if they didn't exist for you? Would you ever do that?'

'Suppose my father beat me? For things I hadn't done?'

'Suppose he did! The more reason to stay! Who's to protect your mother? And your sisters and your little brother? See, I am one young Russian in England who doesn't mind speaking Russian at all and with no disrespect doesn't want to be English or American – oh, I know I asked you if you'd teach me English but of course that's because of you. It's always been bad in Russia, everybody knows it's getting worse, it will most likely never be better and it will certainly not be all right until long after I'm dead, but it's my place, I live there, my home is there. Which is sad in one very serious way because I love you and your home is here, and you won't leave England, will you, to go anywhere for any reason? Will you?'

The last words had no hope in them. Richard was glad he had stopped the car a couple of minutes before and had taken it a metre or so off the road. 'I haven't thought about it,' he said. 'But I love you.' He noticed now for the first time that she was wearing a dark-red dress that looked fine on her and just right. It looked to him as rare and remarkable as any of Cordelia's array, and he almost wished she had been there for him to explain that that was not actually the case. No. Not even almost.

'Anybody would know you'd never leave England after talking to you for five minutes. You couldn't even think about it without being a completely different person.' Anna sat and smiled at him with her hands loose on her lap. 'I heard what you said, my love. Now you might as well start the car and take us where we have to go. I imagine it isn't very far from the highway to London.'

'A few miles. You don't mind if I . . .'

'What is it?'

'I suppose you must have met Kotolynov?'

'Never. Richard, he's been in the West for nearly twenty years.'

'My God, is it really that long? Yes, of course, he was at Harvard for a time, wasn't he? I've always rather wondered he didn't stay on in the States.'

'Too many other Russian writers in America. Solzhenitsyn to begin with.'

'Oh. You mean he doesn't like competition?'

'That's among the troubles of these people who come abroad to live. Each of them is treated as the true voice of Russia and it's not easy to be one of a dozen of those. Naturally Kotolynov has said England is a nicer country. Very likely it is.'

'That's a little harsh, Anna. He did his eight years in Vorkuta, after all, and then there was that trouble over, what was she called . . .'

'Oh, I wouldn't blame him for leaving, I wouldn't presume to. Nobody would who knows what it's like. No Russian. We all have our pressures. And please, I know I've been very lucky.'

'I've no right to say anything. I'm sorry.'

'Nevertheless you feel I disapprove and you disapprove of my disapproval.'

'Well, since you'll be meeting him in a few minutes . . .'

'You're thinking of something. Go on.'

'Well . . . you perhaps know the story about Akhmatova and her son. Another Anna.'

'She died when I was a child. Once her work was banned but not now and for many years. What happened about her son?'

'I don't really know at all, but he was in trouble with the régime. Or he was going to be if he carried on with what he was doing, whatever that was. So . . . his mother gritted her teeth and wrote an Ode to Stalin and . . . it didn't happen. She sacrificed her integrity to protect her son.'

'Of course she did,' said Anna without hesitation. 'What else could she have done? It was wonderful that she did it, but for the love of God she had no choice.'

'It's easy for anyone who isn't there to see it so quickly and so clearly. Like you. Like me, but also like you. And that's not the point of the story. Which is that when it was known what had happened, nobody said anything to her. No rebuke, no commiseration, no triumph, no sympathy, no regret, no word of support or of blame. Nothing at all, including no silence and no turning away. On anybody's part – friend, admirer, enemy,

rival, bureaucrat, régime writer, man, woman. Because everybody understood. I'm sorry, Anna.'

'Are you stopping the car again?'

'No, I'm looking for a minor road leading off to the right.
Wait a minute, I think this must be it now. Yes, here we go.'

'It's not quite that with Kotolynov,' said Anna after a
moment. 'Well, it's not just that he left, it's the way he talked
about it. As if everybody who hadn't left was a hack or a cynic or
an accomplice.'

'That's what they'd say he said whether he said it or not.'

'Oh yes. And I take your point.'

'I think we're almost there.'

They were almost in Upper Ramsbury, the village that was
stated to contain Kotolynov, and were soon almost out of it
again without finding any trace of Rose Cottage, advertised as
his actual habitation. Then a middle-aged man dressed like a
poacher out of an old movie gave directions in a nanny-goat
clubland voice, while at his side some connection of his, a tall girl
in formal riding clothes, stood mutely inspecting Anna and
Richard. A poster in a nearby health-shop window advertised a
current exhibition of objects, so described.

Anna began as they drove off, 'Was that man one of the – '

'No he wasn't. Nobody is now, not in England. Southern
England anyway. I'm sorry, I can't help being a bit bothered by
this Rose Cottage thing. I didn't say anything, but Rose Cottage,
it can't be right.'

'Why not? A simple name, a pretty name . . .'

'That's just it, it's exactly the sort of name cottages people
actually live in don't have. Unless they're trying to be funny. I
suppose that might be it.'

'I don't understand, Richard.'

'First left past the bus-shelter. In which case it probably
wouldn't be a cottage at all but a waste-disposal facility. A
helicopter barn.'

'And I thought Russia was the place where nothing's what it
seems.'

'I'm sorry, my love, I think I must be a little nervous at the
prospect of meeting Kotolynov.'

'I thought you were supposed to know him.'

'No, I just met him a couple of times for a couple of minutes at a time, years ago when he was over from America. Here we are. Here we incontrovertibly are, by God, as Crispin would say.'

A finger-post pointed across the lane to Rose Cottage, where a gateway clearly marked Rose Cottage offered a view of a small dwelling built or totally rebuilt about 1980 with a nameboard saying Rose Cottage on it. There were quite a number of plants in the space between hedge and house, and all the ones Richard could see were roses. A few were even trying to climb up the wall near the porch. He could tell that Anna was thinking how English everything was.

A ring at the surprisingly unremarkable doorbell quickly brought a clean-shaven man of about sixty in old grey flannels and a woolly shirt. 'Hallo there,' he said heartily in an American accent. 'Would you be Dr Vaisey and Miss Danilova?'

'That's correct. We've come to see Mr Kotolynov.'

'Very good, that's exactly what you're doing as long as you're pointed this way. I'm Kotolynov. Come on in.'

The inside of the cottage was got up in what Richard assumed to be some comparatively restrained American style, or at any rate in no obvious English or east European one, but this suggested itself to him only in spaced-out bits, when air-conditioning stirred a brief chill, for instance. To start with he stared a little at Kotolynov, who in return was laughing a good deal at them both, principally at him.

'I know it's awful of me, but I just can't resist it. And you know I kind of don't see why I should try, because I'm this way all the time when I'm here.' He paused. 'Or nearly all the time.' As he turned now to Anna he underwent the thorough transformation shown by any master of two languages in switching from one to the other, and more than that besides. 'My sincere apologies, Miss Danilova, for not at once addressing you in your own language. It's the living outside Russia.'

'Of course,' said Anna, smiling. 'I recognised you anyway.'

'Not from my photographs with all that hair? Not please God from my accent?'

'No, you look Russian.'

'Holy shit,' said Kotolynov, relapsing momentarily into English. 'Please God again, only a Russian would see it. Do you speak English?'

'Not to talk,' said Anna.

'That's a pity. I'm more at home in English now.'

He looked at Richard, who said what had been in his mind almost since their arrival, 'You've made great strides in the last few years. I saw you in a TV discussion programme some time in the mid-Eighties and you were, well, pretty Russian then.'

Kotolynov's demeanour changed again and he broke again into English of a kind. 'Of course, then I was being still the exiled Russian writer, you understand, *gospodin*, full of the problems of transplantation into another culture, you see, with the best beard I could grow at two weeks' notice.' He went on in his full American English, 'That really was awful of me, and I made up my mind it would have to be positively my last appearance in that role. Now before we settle down . . .'

Anna, who showed signs of having taken in the drift of the foregoing, was told she must need to go to the bathroom and in effect sent upstairs. Kotolynov sat Richard down in front of a picture window through which further roses and a piece of off-the-peg garden statuary were to be seen.

'Like some coffee, Dr Vaisey? Drink?'

'Neither, thank you.'

'I guess it's still a little early, but I sometimes find a middle-sized Black Jack on the rocks comforting at this time of day.' Kotolynov crossed to a sort of sideboard.

'You've made a very complete transformation.'

'In the village here they call me the American. No point in going halfway.'

'Why did you leave America?'

'In England I found I could still be different without being a Russian. But there's another reason that'll probably come up later. Meantime, tell me, Richard, what do you think of this girl's poetry? All right, I'll tell you what I think of it. I think it's shit.'

'So you won't be putting your name down in her support.'

'I didn't say that. What about your name, will that be going down?'

'I haven't been asked.' Richard hesitated briefly. 'I think it's shit too, that poetry of hers.'

'Good for you, doctor,' said Kotolynov, raising his glass. 'Quite a looker, isn't she, though, our little Anna?' He paused and gave Richard a quick glance. 'Yeah, I can understand that might put you in kind of an awkward spot. However.'

Richard could not have said what he had seen round the place that encouraged him to ask, 'You've got a wife, haven't you, Mr Kotolynov?'

'Andy. Short for Andrei. Yes, I do. She's American. I sent her out for the day.'

'You sent an American woman out for the day?'

'Sure. That's another thing about England. Are you still sure you won't be needing that drink? And I don't quite understand what this thing is all about, but should somebody like you be mixed up in it?'

'Half of what you've given yourself. And probably not, but . . .'

'All right, coming up. And I know.'

When Anna reappeared she did so by degrees, as if to allow for anything in the way of male regrouping. Kotolynov was well on with it, shifting chairs, reflecting and shifting them again, fetching biscuits, regretting the blameworthy absence of tea, asking Anna rather less than inquisitively how she found England. He seemed to be putting not quite as much into being a Russian host as he had into his aspect as American émigré. Then after a few minutes he said,

'Tell me this. I have heard something from friends in London, but what do you know of Mr Crispin Radetsky and why is he taking the trouble to organise an appeal to the Soviet central government to put right what the world will see, if it sees anything at all, as a rather regrettable blunder in some local court or prison over there? Why?'

'Mr Radetsky is a Czech lawyer and businessman,' said Anna readily enough, 'who by means of his great influence in English affairs is organising this to make a demonstration against the arbitrary and barbaric so-called system of justice still prevailing in the Soviet Union and to hold it up to international rebuke and force the Soviet state to admit its failure to respect its own constitution. And a local blunder is what it may seem to – '

'No, I'm sorry, of course I shouldn't have put it like that. Anyway, are you quoting Mr Radetsky, Anna, is that the sort of thing he says about it? And the sort of way he says it?'

'No, I agree. I'm summarising, I'm saying what he would say.'

'If he talked like that. What would you say yourself, [little pigeon], about why he's doing all this?'

'Well, naturally I'm very grateful to him, but some of it is not so troublesome. It's looking up a name in a book or a list and making a telephone call. And I think he must get some satisfaction and enjoyment out of using – '

'Yes yes, I too think he must,' said Kotolynov, bringing out a nearly fresh packet of Camels and absently lighting one without offering them. 'Although I haven't met him I believe it of him. Anything else? About why?'

'I mentioned the fact that he's a Czech.'

'So you did. And that means what? That he's been given a chance of helping to do something to embarrass the descendants of the people who took over his country years ago and who continue to hold it in subjection. What we used to call *nationalism*.' He gave Richard a kind of acknowledging nod. 'Is that true, Anna, of Mr Radetsky's motives?'

'He wants to punish the Russians, or if not that to show he is their enemy. Our enemy.'

'Your enemy. I am an American citizen.'

'Our enemy in historical fact. I think you were a Russian citizen in 1948 and for some years afterwards.'

'Very well, Anna. Our . . . enemy. What a lot you know for a Russian of your age. Now have you anything to add? About Mr Radetsky, that is to say.'

'For the moment, just that from what he's told me this is the first time he's done anything that could be construed as in any way a demonstration against Russia and he may have felt it was time he was seen to be doing something.'

Kotolynov blew out smoke in a long sigh. 'Before it's too late.'

'It may be worth recalling that Crispin is no more a Czech than Mr Kotolynov here is a Russian,' said Richard. 'Far less so, in fact. He, Crispin, was born a British citizen of naturalised British parents. He – '

'Of course,' interrupted Anna, 'he has another reason and a very powerful one for being an enemy of the Soviet Union which I have so far refrained from mentioning.'

'Oh, please continue to refrain, [little dear].' Kotolynov had got in quicker still. 'With all your good feeling and politeness and gratitude to Mr Radetsky it's been clear from the start that you don't approve of him. He is rich, he is bourgeois, he is what you were about to call him, a capitalist. Disapproving of him for

165

that is not a luxury you can afford in your present situation. Whatever you say you're playing politics and even those in a strong political position, which you're not, know they can't be delicate over picking up allies. Even a Marxist knows that.'

Richard said heatedly, 'Crispin's real objections to Communism are libertarian a long time before they're anything else, though it's true that a Marxist might be too stupid to see that.'

'I'm not a Marxist,' said Anna, though without quite enough indignation to suit Richard, and Kotolynov looked furious for a moment.

'I know about people who aren't Marxists,' he said, 'they're like people who aren't Christians. Except I have a soft spot for the first lot because I used to be one myself. A Marxist. God. Think of it.'

'I see both you men are drinking,' said Anna. 'May I join you?'

'Surely, my little non-Marxist. I mean of course [little soul] – you must forgive me. What can I offer you? Bourbon, Scotch, gin? Water if you prefer.'

'I imagine you have no vodka?'

Kotolynov laughed even more wholeheartedly at this than when he had first revealed his identity. 'If any further proof was needed that you were harmless,' he said, still chuckling, 'you've now revealed it. A harmful person sitting where you are would have asked for cognac. Yes, I have vodka. But I fear it is not much like the authentic distillation of sawdust and chimpanzee food the Moscow connoisseurs prized in my day. This is Smorodin Vodka,' he announced, and read sonorously from the label, 'Prepared according to the processes of Petr Smorodin Sons, as purveyed to the Imperial Russian Court, 1888–1917. But I'm sure the Americans have improved it a good deal since then. How will you take it, Anna? With ice? Or perhaps a vodkatini?'

'Neat,' she said, smiling, and not staunchly or gamely either, and Richard liked her even more than he had before.

'Perhaps a tiny freshener for you, Richard . . . You did know Stalin was supposed to have liked cayenne pepper in his vodka? Always that great sense of humour. Now, I think we know where we stand. Politics. This is all politics. One sort, or a couple of sorts, for Crispin Radetsky. Other sorts for each of us. Correct, [little friend]? You agree you wouldn't be satisfied if they released your brother in a sudden fit of clemency. Delighted and relieved of course but not satisfied. You're not only being forced to make a political demonstration, you want to. Like Mr Radetsky. Correct, yes?'

After a glance at Richard, and a thought within herself, Anna nodded her head.

'Good. Splendid. You have my support. In fact you have more of my support than of your own, if that doesn't sound too foolish. My father was an enemy of the people. Well, you can argue about that, say something about it. Twelve years. My mother was the wife of an enemy of the people. Not much you can say about that. Eight years. I slandered an official of the Soviet state. Guilty. Eight years. Then there was somebody I was fond of. She was given eight years too, for licentious behaviour, but she never finished serving them. And I had friends besides.

'I tell you this,' went on Kotolynov without a pause, 'to suggest to you as strongly as I can that it is not out of inadequate belief in your cause or less than full devotion to it, insufficient *commitment*,' – he used the English word with a glance at Richard – 'that I refuse to sign your document. That decision cannot be shaken. I have my reasons for it but you may not wish to hear them. If you do, you're welcome to stay. If not . . .'

Richard went over and sat next to Anna on the suede-covered long seat where she was, and took hold of her hand. 'We'll stay,' he said.

'The trouble with your document and your demonstration,' began Kotolynov, then leant over and put his unfinished drink on a shelf where it was not easily to be reached. 'Excuse me. The objection to them from my point of view is their involvement with a form of literature. Anna's position, her status, her simply being a writer are being used for politics. This I will not countenance. Everywhere in the world literature is in retreat from politics and unless resisted the one will crush the other. You don't crush literature from outside by killing writers or intimidating them or not letting them publish, though as we've all seen you can make a big fuss and have a lot of fun trying. You do better to induce them to destroy it themselves by inducing them to subordinate it to political purposes, as you propose to do.

'I said this was happening everywhere in the world. Which may well be an exaggeration, not applying to Iceland or

167

Switzerland or Uganda or Singapore. But no, I think it must apply to Uganda, don't you? And Singapore too? It's applied in Russia for a long time, not just since 1931 or whenever you fancy or 1917. If we confine ourselves to my subject, the novel, it lived and died in Russia in less than a hundred years. The form of fiction continued, but ever since it has been all about politics. Even the work, the novels, of Solzhenitsyn, a great writer, or one who could and should have been a great writer, all gravely damaged by a fault he has acknowledged, crudity, bad construction, diffuseness, the result of being cooped up in Soviet literature. Also gravely damaged, fatally damaged, ruined, by something he doesn't acknowledge, that every word he writes is politics. As for *Dr Zhivago* – well, it was much admired in the West. His poetry, Pasternak's poetry, that escaped, that remains untainted. Poetry will probably survive longer. Though you must allow me to say the signs aren't good.

'I mean to say as little as possible about myself, but I must say something. Having nobody left, nobody who could be punished instead of me, I was able to escape to America. There I would be able to write my novels, or rather to complete and publish my, my large trilogy of Russian life, which I suppose is ultimately what brings the two of you here today. And I did. The title I wanted was *Late Spring*, because I thought it was about a man who had failed to find love when he was young but who found it later. But it was published as *Exile in the Snows*, because the publisher thought it was about the camps and the régime and the KGB, or so he said. But anyway when I read the printed book I saw that he was right. It was all politics. What else could it have been? No, please don't contradict me or say anything, either of you.

'So what did I do then? I had enough to live on, I wrote nothing, I learnt English, I taught, I lectured. I began to think about an American novel. Just one as a start, the first of several or many – I was still only forty-seven. But then after a time I realised I was living in a country and among a bunch of very bright, very nice fellows that didn't like novels. They preferred books – books about America, of course – that didn't even call themselves novels. But if for some weird reason a book had to be a novel, then let it contain as little fiction as possible. Maybe it's that Americans are a nervous lot and the idea of somebody inventing people and events out of imagination, out of nothing, makes them feel uneasy. Anyhow, *if* there has to be a novel, please nothing about the life and death of individuals, or growing up and falling in love and getting married and being bereaved, or loss and grief and pain and remorse and courage and any of that old embarrassing stuff. No fiction, no art, just statements. And statements are good in general – have you noticed they're starting to get made by buildings and sweatshirts and dishes in restaurants as well as by people? The statements in novels are special, because they're about guess what? That's right – politics. Hiroshima and Watergate and Vietnam and Wounded Knee, not forgetting Cambodia, and fascism and racism and male chauvinism and homosexuality, not just one or two or three of them at a time but all of them at once, and Hollywood and consumerism and whatever they call it now and [Lord have mercy]. Can you see that for me it was like being in Russia again?

'So where to go? To Australia and novels about Ayers Rock and Port Jackson and Gallipoli, or New Zealand and novels about, I don't know, the Maori and the nuclear umbrella, and South Africa and novels about South Africa? If there's a novelist in Gibraltar he's writing about British sovereignty or Spanish claims or both when he could be writing about the apes. So here I am in England, where admittedly a lot of fellows would like the novelist to be writing autobiography or social history or gossip rather than fiction, but what's left will last a little while yet. Or perhaps I just feel I've come far enough.'

After a moment, Anna said, 'Is it so far to Moscow now?'

'To Moscow!' said Kotolynov, as if she had mentioned Lhasa or Cape Horn. 'Where nothing even called a novel is written any more. The one place in the world where literature has died by its own hand. You can't blame the writers, they've seventy years of reality to tell about. And some . . . philosophy to try out on paper. Or am I misinformed?'

'No. But some poetry is still written.'

'Ah yes, poetry. Anna, I'm sorry I must confine my own demonstration to not signing your document. On its scale, that is a demonstration every bit as important as yours. It says that literature matters more than politics. We all have our notions of what is entailed in our calling, and to me being a writer is much more important to the person, to the writer, than being anything else is to the person being it, if you understand what I mean. More than being a painter is to the painter or being a composer of music is to the composer, more than being anything else except maybe being a priest. And if it doesn't seem like that to the person, I think they should drive a truck instead a little, you know. Yes. Well, that's all, that's the end of my story.' But the glance he sent Richard, furtive and humorous, suggested that his last statement, at least, was not quite true.

Anna had slid her hand out of Richard's. 'You believe that literature is more important than politics. I accept the fact that you have earned the right to do so. But aren't you saying literature is more important than people?'

'No. Literature has to do with people at least as much as any politics has.'

'Nobody ever starved to death for lack of words.'

'I seem to remember hearing that proposition contradicted at a very high level. But please, [little sunbeam], if we go on in this strain we shall begin to make poor Richard wish he had never begun to learn Russian. Instead, Anna, I beg you, I've said I'll never go to Moscow again and I never will, but I'll never stop wanting to know what things are like there, from trivial stuff like the state of the Writers' Union all the way up to where you go for electric-light bulbs. In my day there was a good man at the radio station. I long to hear. Meanwhile you can have another drink or you can still have coffee or you can have a glass of the lemonade my wife makes so well. She learnt how to do it when she was a little girl in Georgia. That's Georgia USA of course. Not so very different from Georgia USSR. There is fruit in both places.'

Like Anna, Richard chose the lemonade, which was slightly undersweetened in a refined way. After about twenty minutes he heard a distant door open and very soon shut. At once Kotolynov went out and returned carrying a large plain blue bowl full of cut roses of various sizes and shapes, yellow, crimson, fawn-coloured, several shades of pink, terracotta, white. With quick deft movements he popped them into white vases and smaller bowls that had stood unregarded here and there. Water was added from some special container.

'The air's good for us around here,' he said to Richard in

English, 'but there's a touch of gravel in the soil we don't like too well.'

'Rose Cottage,' said Anna, also in English, with a smile at Richard.

Kotolynov plunged contritely back into Russian. 'Do please forgive me, I suppose it's just that English seems the proper language for the subject. Yes, all out of our garden. I do a certain amount there, on my knees some of it, kindly note, but I have a lady who comes in to cut them for me. Now . . . look just for a moment, at this fellow here, isn't he fine? Almost golden. Not a great deal to say, is there?' He ground out his cigarette half smoked. 'You know, whenever I see something as wonderful as that, I think of a chap I used to know in Vorkuta. One of the — supervisors, he was. He used to like supervising dinner very much. He would stroll round and with great deliberation take one piece of food out of your bowl, or perhaps not your bowl that day, perhaps the bowl of the man next to you, and never more than one piece, but always a good piece, like a lump of potato. That was all he did, or all I ever saw him do. But I remember him very well. So well that when I look at one of my roses for a moment, I always think how much that chap would hate the sight of it. If you take my meaning.

'Now, another drink before you go? Oh, come on, please, you must, just a token. Please, both of you.'

When the roses were introduced, Richard had been pretty certain it was they that would provide the something-extra he had been waiting for, but by the time he and Anna had accepted fattish token drinks he sensed it had yet to come. She seemed to be expecting something too.

Kotolynov caught her look. With a flick of his eyes he said, 'I'm afraid the only toasts permitted under this roof, should anything so archaic be contemplated, are those drunk to the Queen and to the President of the United States of America. So in the circumstances . . . good luck to the three of us and to others we think of.' He drained his glass, set it down and looked at his watch. 'Twelve thirty-five. Very good. Turn left in the village and on your right you'll come to the Cor Anglais, which despite its name does a passable set lunch. I've booked you in for one o'clock. Avoid the house claret, but the red burgundy is really

171

quite good.' He escorted them to the front door and left them. 'Excuse me a moment.'

Anna touched Richard briefly on the arm and walked on down to where the car was. Laughing a little to himself, Kotolynov reappeared with a couple of brightly bound paperback books which he handed over. The top one was called *The Beast of Lake Baikal*. Then and later, but mostly later, Richard read:

> Andrew Cottle is an American who speaks Russian like a native. He was educated partly in Moscow and has a close personal knowledge of other parts of the USSR where his father was employed by the government department of forestry. *The Beast of Lake Baikal* is the fourth in the successful series of Colonel Tomski novels of the Russian 'Wild East' in the time of the Czars. *Washington Post*: 'Cottle has evolved his own brand of pacy gutsy action story without the schoolboy heroics of Fleming.' *Observer* (London): 'Spy-larking in old Russia, versts away from the banalities of the Cold War.'

Still grinning, Kotolynov watched Richard run his eye over this. 'Just to reassure you,' he said in English, 'all the Kirghiz and Turkoman et cetera characters are absolute bastards and nobody takes any stock at all in whatever fucking "cause" they might have had. As against that, in a way, the beast of Lake Baikal turns out late on to be a species of freshwater seal found only in that remarkable Siberian deep, as you very likely knew, but they didn't. Well, it's been great meeting you, Richard. Have a nice day.'

They shook hands. Richard said, also in English, what he would never have said to another Englishman, 'Do you think everything will come right in the end?'

'In the end? What end?' Kotolynov flashed his furious expression again. 'She's a good girl, that. Bright enough to show tact. A Russian dissident in a modest way, one of the last we'll ever hear about, I would guess. Take care of her, even though she is a lousy poet. At least she's a poet. And . . .'

He hesitated but said no more, raised his hand in farewell, and turned back into his cottage.

Anna was looking at some rather shapeless darkish-yellow

roses on a shrub round the corner, looking with a certain attention, as if she half expected enlightenment from them. When she saw Richard approaching she turned towards the car and the two met by it. Without bothering to consider why or wherefore he had expected a cool reception of whatever grade, but her smile was quite open. They kissed lightly and got into their seats. Before they had started to move off, she said, 'What a remarkable man. And so vivacious. I was suspicious of him before we met, but he completely won me round. I respect him now.'

Richard turned and kissed her with much more conviction than before.

THIRTEEN

The set lunch at the Cor Anglais turned out to be rather better than passable. Anna and Richard spent a disproportionate amount of time discussing it and the merits and likely motives of Kotolynov's having sent them out to eat instead of inviting them to share a crust or so with him. Fighting shy of producing *The Beast of Lake Baikal* and its companion volume, Richard gave Anna a shade more information about British catering than she needed and he wanted to offer. Every so often he found himself powerfully wanting to be playing tennis with Crispin and was immediately and just as powerfully glad and grateful he was with Anna and destined to go on being so for the next few decades. It was like being a young man again.

The red burgundy was as good as predicted. Richard drank a couple of glasses of it, no more, just enough to combine with what he had had earlier and be deemed a serious hindrance to purposeful thought. What were he and Anna going to do when they had finished here? Before that, anteriorly to that as some known to him would doubtless have said, what did he want to do?

Well, one thing he unquestionably could do was take Anna along to the Moran Arms, already marked down on a nearby corner, and book Mr and Mrs Raskolnikov in for the night, a night destined to have the peculiarity of coming to an abrupt unadvertised end well before the darkness of it actually fell. Anna, after all, was unlikely to be opposed to the general idea.

Or was she? While nothing seemed to be 'wrong', let alone wrong, she was showing no keener an interest in the average percentage of mark-up on restaurant wines than he was. It crossed his mind that thoughts of a session with the old balalaika were playing the same intermittent role in her consciousness as thoughts of tennis were in his. Rather more likely her thoughts were on her poetry and its status in other people's estimation. Yapping on now about the price of champagne, Richard switched his internal attention back to the Raskolnikov project. He had just begun to wonder how many acts of sex were the result of disinclination to talk when Anna made a decisive movement of her head and spoke up.

'Darling, I know you have things to worry and distract you and I suppose problems in your life it would be wrong of me even to mention. Let's go quietly back to London where I have people I must see. Now if you'll kindly offer me a small fruit brandy I shall be rather drunk and drowsy and quite ready to sleep for most of the journey back in your beautiful and very smooth car and we'll settle some very important questions later, perhaps in the morning.'

While she said this she gave him one of those looks of more than mere understanding, of having had a short tour inside his head, that he recognised as a great women's thing, unapproachable by any man. What she said sounded marvellous while she was saying it, very good indeed for the time it took them to finish up at the Cor Anglais and get into the car, not too bad at all in retrospect while they made their way back through the village and on to the motorway, and bloody awful thereafter. It was those very important questions that had done it. As he drove and Anna slept Richard saw there was really only one of them, one not to be effaced for long by the price of champagne, the hankering for tennis, the Raskolnikov project, Anna herself – the one that had to do with Cordelia. It was all over him as, having dropped Anna in Pimlico, he stepped on to his doorstep.

But five seconds later it was nowhere at all, because a man he had never seen before came up to him there, a little soon for his liking after the first appearance in his life of Kotolynov. This ensuing man looked so much like a Russian that it must be impossible for him to have been one in fact, but then again when he spoke his English carried an unmistakable though not strong Russian accent. Richard had heard his voice before.

'Dr Vaisey? My name is Arkady Ippolitov. I called you at your office the other day.' An immaculate visiting-card, its layout and typography betraying American influence, changed hands. Among other things it mentioned something called the Ad Hoc Committee for Cultural Relations, as also mentioned over the telephone. 'We arranged to meet for a drink, but some unexpected circumstance must have intervened and you were unable to let me know. No, please, of course I understand you're a very busy man and I'm kind of a professional nuisance, don't worry about it. I couldn't reach you earlier today, but as I happened to be passing . . .'

Whoever he was, Ippolitov obviously and rather reasonably expected to be invited into the house on whose doorstep its presumptive owner stood key in hand. And Richard was just going to stick it unthinkingly in the lock when he caught from the interior the enormous squealing, groaning and thumping of a hundred kilted and bonneted Scotsmen recorded or broadcast in performance. It brought Cordelia's image before him with remarkable clarity and force, and he went rigid with a couple of inches to go. 'I'm afraid my wife seems to be giving a concert,' he said with a careless man-to-man laugh.

'Ah yes,' said Ippolitov politely. 'And therefore . . .'

Remembering with an effort which wrist his watch was likely to be on, Richard looked at it or somewhere near it. 'Let's go out for a drink,' he said.

'Ah, to a *pub*,' said the Russian, nodding his head. 'Excellent. By all means.'

'Not necessarily. In fact I think not at all. On consideration.'

'The pubs hereabouts are perhaps not desirable?'

'Well, it's not so much that . . .'

'But this is surely a very desirable area, Dr Vaisey. Such beautiful houses and such elegant trees.'

'Even so . . .' Richard could not have explained what it was that he found unwelcome in the thought of that eager alertness being brought to bear on the Waterman's Rest or the Joseph Addison, neither of which he in fact much cared for or often used. 'I suggest I drive us to a bar,' he said, sounding slightly stage-Russian to his own ears.

'A *bar*. Good.'

While they travelled a mile or two, Richard put up a light pretence of concentrating on traffic and such while he tried to remember what the other man had said he wanted of him apart from a chance to talk. Nothing came to mind, and most likely nothing of significance was going to be the answer, but it was more than Mr Ippolitov's manner that was unappealing about him.

Not that this showed any sign of revealing itself for the moment. The guest, understandably enough, took the briefest of looks round the shabby-ungenteel lounge of the Cedar Court Hotel and evidently found nothing worthy of comment or comparison. Richard did not tell him that the place had most likely started its life as the visitors' lounge of a once-eminent block of flats, nor that the only people who came there now, apart from the residents or boarders and unhandy minor academics with unwanted Russian visitors, were solitary old men in suits and collars and ties who had walked there for their evening hour away from their one room.

Ippolitov bought drinks at the bar from one of the most incurious middle-aged women Richard had ever seen, and they carried them to a corner decorated by a fancy four-sided bucket that had once perhaps contained a potted palm. The ashtray advertised a defunct brand of peach bitters and if genuine might have fetched a few bob somewhere.

'The present sad state of my country,' said Ippolitov at once, 'not to speak of its possible future, could occupy us for hours, but as I said I know you're busy, so I'll come straight to the point. I'm an officer of our criminal police, with a rank corresponding to your superintendent. Not therefore of our political police, which is a separate organisation, or group of organisations. As you will have heard, Dr Vaisey, or at least can readily surmise,' – he stared briefly at Richard – 'ordinary civil crime, from murder and rape down to elementary thieving, doesn't go away from a society or fail to turn up there just because that society recognises other types of crime. In fact, there are those who see a positive correlation in the incidence of the two. Such people tend to think the Soviet citizen deserves fully as much protection against the one as against the other. I'm rather of that mind myself, to be perfectly open with you.'

The transformed English and the disappearance of the American accent left Richard disliking Ippolitov slightly more and feeling afraid of him distinctly more. 'Have you any credentials?' he asked, blushing slightly.

'Credentials!' said Ippolitov, not smiling. 'You're asking a lot, Dr Vaisey. Oh, certainly I have credentials. Not this – what is it . . .' He drew from his jacket pocket a card like the one he had produced earlier. 'Ad Hoc Committee for Cultural Relations. A lot of rubbish. In America it's called the Special Committee instead, because there they don't understand what ad hoc means. Here they don't either, but it impresses them.' Now he did smile for a moment. 'I'm sorry . . . Yes, rest assured I'm in this country officially, working in co-operation with the British authorities.'

'Working about what, about whom? All this seems quite – '

'About one Anna Danilova. Yes. I understand you and others are organising some sort of public petition to the Soviet government on her behalf. The petition is said to be in support of a certain person, her brother or half-brother, who goes under various names. What I have to emphasise to you most strongly, Dr Vaisey, as a Westerner, is that this person, Danilov or Rogachev by name, is a criminal, one who has broken laws that would be part of the code of any civilised state. He is a serious swindler who has cheated a number of small individuals out of something like eighty thousand pounds in your money. He is not a joker or a scapegoat or a so-called speculator or somebody who has offended the local potentate, though he may well have done that too. Many such people have. Do you understand so far?'

Richard looked at Ippolitov and saw a big man of about his own age with a big pale face bordered by a carefully trimmed beard, a man in a badly fitting brown suit and a none-too-clean blue shirt buttoned at the neck and protruding at the cuffs, not a prepossessing man in any way but one giving every evidence of believing what he said. It was hard to think of where to make a start on him. 'Have you any proof of what you've been telling me?'

'None whatever that would satisfy you I haven't for some reason invented the whole story. I suppose there might be such a reason.'

'Have you any proof that you're what you say you are?'

'None whatever. I have elsewhere in London my official card of office, which looks just like a forgery of an official card of office. Not a very good one, either. I've already explained to you that I won't go near my embassy. To be on the safe side, you know.'

'But you say you're working in co-operation with the authorities here.'

'I am, but it's a confidential visit. Scotland Yard and Special Branch would never admit to having heard of me.'

'Mr Ippolitov, are you really asking me to believe you've come all the way from Moscow to tell me this?'

'What! Come all this way to tell *you this*! We're not raving mad over there, I promise you!' Ippolitov snatched up his untasted drink, a large neat Scotch, and drained it without perceptible discomfort. 'Dr Vaisey,' he went on more quietly. 'Please. My main reason for visiting your country, accompanying incidentally a senior police colleague and a commissioner of our Ministry of Justice, is to assist your people in the preparation of prosecutions of persons now resident here but thought to be guilty of war crimes or crimes against humanity during the late war in our Baltic republics, including the People's Republic of Latvia, where I have served for the last eleven years. But like you, Dr Vaisey, I am a busy man, and my department at home is a busy department, and so while I'm here I'm doing what I can to clear up a number of minor cases, little cases, cases of which that of Rogachev or Danilov and the petition mounted in his support by Anna Danilova is one. Not a burdensome one, but it has taken up two hours of my time already, not counting the conversation I'm at present enjoying with you. And now, can I buy you another drink?' Ippolitov looked over at the bar and torpid barmaid and back at Richard and shook slightly, perhaps with laughter, though his face showed nothing. 'Or perhaps you'd prefer us to terminate our chat at this point?'

'I won't have a drink, thank you. I mean can I change my mind and have a large Scotch? Neat.'

'Certainly.' This time the other man gave no hint of a smile and withdrew at once.

Richard had reached a kind of steady state of indecision. Everything that happened seemed to make it harder to know what to do about anything. He got no further while two well-dressed young men and two comparable young women came through the gilt-handled double doors halfway into the room, glanced round it and went out again. That was all.

'I made up my mind to drink as much whisky as I could while I was over here.' In the last minute or so Ippolitov seemed to have relaxed somewhat. 'Within reason, of course. Also to drink as much beer and wine and gin as possible. Not forgetting vodka.

179

And to eat everything set in front of me from roast beef to cabbage, which as you may know is limits of desirable food in Russia. This, what we're drinking, is very good whisky, isn't it? They tell me the humidity of the Scottish climate has an important influence on the finished product.'

'What do you want me to do, Mr Ippolitov?'

'Superintendent, please,' said Ippolitov severely. Then he grinned, showing widely separated teeth. 'I'm sorry, I have this impulse to make jokes. Well, since you ask me, Dr Vaisey, obviously what I would like you to do is stop all this, see this project cancelled, see this petition withdrawn. Nothing more. Just dropped. Everybody go home. That would be no great sacrifice on your part, would it? In fact I find it odd that a person of your distinction should have become involved in such a matter in the first place. I assume you know Miss Danilova well, I mean her background, her friends, her what is it, her credibility.'

'No,' said Richard. 'No, I can't say I do.'

'But at least you will have met a number of her friends in London.'

'No. Only the people where she's staying.'

'That seems a little bit extraordinary. Hasn't she visited such friends?'

'Yes, but she hasn't taken me along. They'd be too boring for me, she said.'

'And you accepted that.'

'Yes. Am I under arrest, superintendent?'

Ippolitov grinned again. 'I'm sorry – force of habit. So, you put your trust in Miss Danilova because of her personal qualities to some extent, and you needn't answer that. You have the right to remain silent,' he added in his American accent. 'But please, do as I say, Dr Vaisey, and drop it.'

'I'm only a small part of the thing now.'

'Whether you know it or not, you are a large part. And the other parts may well disappear when you tell them what I've told you. If they believe you, that is, and that depends a certain amount on whether they think you believe me. Which as we've already agreed you have no particular reason to do. There.'

'You sound as if you don't much care whether I believe you or not.'

'I assure you that I do. I affirm that I disapprove strongly of Danilov-Rogachev and of his activities. Not only the inter-ference with little girls is revolting. Are you a religious man, Dr Vaisey?'

'No.'

'Perhaps that is your loss, sir. However, for various reasons Danilov should receive no support, especially of this influential kind. Other reasons . . .' Here Ippolitov paused for a moment to do up again an undone cuff-button of his blue shirt. 'Other reasons concern the undesirability of interference in what are often called the internal affairs of my country, especially during a troubled period such as the present.'

'I think I've come across that objection before,' said Richard, thinking of 2nd woman at Sir Stephen's.

'No doubt you have. Well, I think I've probably said as much as it's strictly necessary for me to say. Or profitable. I've carried out my orders, I can do no more. Now back to my hotel room, a couple of telephone calls and this day's work is over. But first – another whisky to go on my expense-sheet, yes?'

'Not for me this time. You have one, Mr Ippolitov.'

'I will.' He lifted a finger on high to the barmaid, and to his surprise Richard saw the creature snatch up a glass with extended arm and plunge with it towards the inverted Scotch bottle. When the drink came it was served from a small metal tray on to a paper coaster with another sweep of the arm. Ippolitov watched this performance with respectful attention, while heavy disinterest rather than uninterest seemed the necessary word for the female's manner. This warmed per-ceptibly but briefly when he thanked her, which he did with a heavier accent than any heard from him earlier. Richard started wondering, but soon stopped. He would leave this awful place when he could summon the energy.

'You haven't asked me anything about the crimes against humanity that are my main concern in coming to your country, Dr Vaisey.'

'Nor I have. But you wouldn't tell me anything about them if I did, would you?'

'I might. And the subject touches your curiosity?'

'Not really.'

'I see. In that case you and I may have very little more to say to each other. Just tell me, if you feel like doing so – will you use your influence, which as I say must be considerable, to dismantle the Danilov project?'

'I may well. At first I wasn't going to, but now I think perhaps I will.'

'I most earnestly hope you do, my friend. This thing . . . in the big picture, compared with those crimes against humanity that have so signally failed to capture your interest, Danilov's misbehaviours are very unimportant. But, how can I put it? – squashed up close together they're quite important. Now, perhaps on second thoughts I'll make my telephone calls from here and run over a few notes before I move on. So you and I could make our farewells now, but before we do that . . .' The superintendent paused again and smiled slightly. 'I expect like everybody else you see some television films from America of crime stories and police work and detection, yes?'

'What? Oh yes. Well, yes, sometimes.'

'They're very interesting to me in my own work, of course. Now I've noticed in such films what could be a convention, something almost expected at a certain point. At the moment when the detective, the principal policeman, is finishing a piece of his inquiries from the witnesses, you understand, he says good-bye and he turns to go, and then he turns back and he says in an apologetic way, "Oh, please excuse me, but there is just *one more thing* I'd like to bring up," and of course usually it's something quite important. Well, I have *one more thing* for you, Dr Vaisey. If you should see fit to tell your colleagues in this project, on this petition, what I've told you about this swine Rogachev, and you find they don't believe the story or don't believe it matters, then let me know and I'll come and talk to them myself, with yourself present if you wish. Not to all of them, naturally, just the most important.'

'Would Crispin Radetsky be suitable?' Speaking this line gave Richard the same stagey feeling as his earlier one about Ippolitov's credentials.

'Oh yes, he'd do splendidly. I've already had the pleasure of talking to Mr Radetsky on the telephone, as he might have mentioned to you.'

'How did you know he was a close friend of mine?'

'By the same means by which I learned of your close friendship with Miss Danilova. Curiosity and a telephone. Should you wish to get in touch with me, the telephone number on the card I gave you is the number of the Intravel office in Oxford Street, 071–580 something, and the number after my telephone number is so to speak my box number, at which you can leave telephone messages for me to pick up. Also by telephone. Well, Dr Vaisey, forgive me for saying that in one way I hope not to hear from you, because my time here is so limited, but a few words announcing your success would be welcome to me personally as well as most gratifying to my superiors.' Ippolitov stood up, seeming to have grown a size or so since last noticeably on his feet, and gave Richard a slight smile and a cold hand to shake. 'Good luck, sir. It's been most agreeable talking to you.'

'Good-bye, superintendent. I have just *one more thing* for you.'

'Oh? Yes?'

'The girl Anna Danilova, is she implicated in her brother's life of crime? Can you tell me anything at all about her?'

'I'm afraid not. Just the name and the relationship. She's your one more thing, not mine. What they call your problem. Good-bye, Dr Vaisey.'

As he left, Richard heard Ippolitov behind him crossing the room towards the bar. The fellow's last remarks had sounded distinctly impatient. Most likely he was irritated by having had his exit hindered. Incurable actors, these Russians. Kotolynov had been another. And come to that . . .

Outside the Cedar Court Hotel, Richard found that the parked TBD did not readily present itself to his attention. After what seemed like several more minutes he had still not managed to set his eyes on the vehicle. He was resigning himself to walking in ever-widening and increasingly inexact circles on the general look-out when he came across it in lo-and-behold style minding its business by a corner quite close by, though pointing in no certain direction. Then, for all he could tell, it was hardly any time at all before he was sitting in his room at the Institute hand in hand with Cordelia while Kotolynov, dressed like a butler in an archaic stage farce, handed them cups of China tea off a silver tray. Then again he soon realised he was sitting not there, but behind the wheel of the stationary TBD looking through the window into the remarkably ugly face of a boy of about twelve, who was smacking the glass with the heel of his hand and yelling indistinguishably at him. Over this one's shoulder there craned a larger but otherwise closely similar boy, also yelling. As soon as he had fully taken in the situation, Richard got out of the car, which he saw was where it should have been in his front garden, and with a howl of rage launched himself on the recoiling pair. Shouting curses in Russian that included instructions to the two juveniles to fuck their mothers and the like, he pursued them down the pavement as far as the entrance of the internationally celebrated abortion clinic, rather less far than he had once chased in that direction the offending Bulgarian poet, but a fair distance all the same.

The exertion set up a throbbing in his head that took up most of his attention while he retraced his steps. On his doorstep he halted and tried to consider. He also listened. No Scotsmen, nobody, nothing. After dropping his latchkey once or twice he used it to open the front door as quietly as he could, which was not very quietly at the best of times. Until recently, Richard had never felt any need to put in time wondering about houses, whether for instance one of them might or might not harbour somebody silently on watch, giving an uncanny soundless intimation of their presence. That might very well have been the case at the moment, with Cordelia's unseen, unheard identity making itself felt. On the other hand there might simply have been no bugger around. But then . . . Richard thought longingly for a moment of his study, of its telephone, and decided not to risk it. In half a minute he was restored to the driving-seat of the TBD, backing out into the traffic, reminding himself with incredulous self-admiration to go and fill up with petrol.

With his mind evidently gone into underdrive, he was well clear of most possible kinds of pursuit before being invaded by the image of Cordelia rushing at him and roaring just as loud as he had done five minutes earlier, and in English too, or a language nearer English than any other. Then a primitive flight-reflex banged his foot down on the accelerator and sent the car hurtling through a newish red light amid great unpopularity. His progress continued erratic. At first he made instinctively for the Institute, but then he turned off and made for Crispin's. Crispin might be out, even away, and was not alone in liking visits to be preannounced by telephone. Richard had no change and knew he could never face using his phone-card even if he should have turned out to have it on him. He would change a note somewhere and ring up from somewhere, but then saw he had reached the Radetsky house.

Something about the grandeur of the cars assembled outside it, at least one with lurking chauffeur, together with the sight of two successive couples in rich clothes being let into it, suggested to Richard that Crispin might be having one of his parties. So much the better, he thought vaguely, and set about finding a place to park. This took a little while, and when it was done he found himself in an equal and opposite difficulty to the one he had encountered near the Cedar Court Hotel. Then, he had had building but no car; now, he had car but no building. Where was it? Where was he? The great thing at this stage, he told himself, was not to get out and start looking, though he had to admit he had no better idea at the moment. Then his wandering eye fell on a street-sign that said ANGELUS CRESCENT, and he smiled faintly. All he had to do now was make a note of that somewhere and start walking and asking. He had been standing on the pavement for some time before he was quite certain that, most unusually for him, he carried no writing instrument of any kind.

The most practical option he had thought of after another minute or so was to inscribe ANGELUS CRESCENT in his own blood with a twig wrenched off the garden hedge nearest him. At that moment an additional grand car swept past him, not going very fast, slowing down in fact, with two expensive occupants to be glimpsed looking this way and that. Richard took off on foot in immediate pursuit, gaining ground as the vehicle slowed again at the corner, losing all of it and more on the straight, nearly coming up with the thing as it halted round the next corner for another look about and perhaps a glance at the A to Z, being left out of sight for a whole agonising half-minute. Every house he passed, every stretch of wall, every tree looked totally familiar and also as if he had never seen anything like it in his life before. He pounded on, of course overheating, of course gasping, beginning to be frightened too at the thought that among other things he might have been going seriously off his head, until he burst round the fourteenth corner and there, blessedly, the bleeder was, in the act of stopping to put down wife, who started to move in on the unmistakable stood-back front of the Dom Radetsky while husband drove off to park in northern Surrey.

Not that Richard imagined his troubles were over yet. He would be safe once indoors and Crispin would have his car found for him and brought to him wherever it might be, as long as he retained the solid fact that he had come by its means and not, say, on the back of a motor-bike. The task of getting indoors, however, gave him undefined misgivings, of which the least undefined rested on how he must look after his crack at the 800 metres in day clothes. To avoid a doorstep chinwag he hid by the gate till the antecedent wife had been let in, then counted sixty slowly like an SAS man waiting for the riot gas to take effect. Right. Now.

Nobody answered his ring while several busloads of nobs could have joined him at their leisure. Then when the door did open it revealed first nothing corporeal, then the bejewelled hand and part of the arm of a young or youngish female, then enough more to identify Mrs something he never could remember, better known to him as Sandy. The rest of her stayed out of Richard's view because she was continuing a conversation with someone further inside the building. Richard waited. He told himself that for all Sandy knew he was the Marchioness of Carabas, but at once told himself that any fool could have told he was not, because anybody who was would have rolled walking and talking across the threshold long ago. He gave a polite cough, which did the inside of his head no good.

About then Sandy happened to turn and see him. 'Hallo,' she said, then recognised him and gave a smile of what might have been pleasure, showing a fair selection of those rather numerous teeth. 'Hallo,' she said again, and at last shut the door after him. 'I didn't know you were coming.'

'I wasn't,' said Richard. Whoever Sandy had been talking to had either blended into one or other of the visible groups of dressy persons or become dematerialised. 'Look, I'm sorry I sort of ran out on you the other evening.'

'When was this?' She seemed puzzled.

'Forget it, then. Er, I seem to have to have a pee.'

'What? Are you pissed?'

'Well, you know, I don't really see how I can be anything else. I suppose it isn't my way but I've had rather a lot of drinks and I do feel most peculiar, so yes, I think that's probably it. But I still have to have that pee.'

'Over here . . . M'm. Have you got to do anything else?'

'No, I don't think so, not just at the moment.'

'Good. I'll wait for you.'

Before quitting the loo, he drank a lot of water out of an elaborate refining arrangement there. It made him immediately start to feel peculiar in a new way, as if a throttled-back flame-thrower were being played over him at extreme range. Or perhaps that would have happened to him in any event. Quite suddenly it passed and he felt better.

When he emerged Sandy was not only still there and by herself but looking at him in gratitude or wonder. She was wearing a yellow garment of some silken material which had the effect of encouraging him to glance from time to time in the general direction of her breasts. Nevertheless he felt he had to say, 'I had really come to see Crispin, you know, if that's all right.'

'Oh. Well, it may not be terribly, he has got rather a lot of people to see. The thing is, Paedophile came in.'

'Surely not here.'

'Pediatrician, I mean. Christ, it's a horse. His horse. One of his horses. It won some handicap at Gloucester at something called a hundred to eight, which is frightfully good apparently. Anyway he's dead chuffed and has got all sorts of boring owners and stewards and trainers and important bookie people in for champagne.' A distant roar that might have greeted a favourite's fall at the water-jump lent colour to this assertion. 'Is it important? It wouldn't be easy to prise him away from that bunch. Can't it wait?'

'I think I ought to have a shot just the same.'

'Oh you are a *bore* Richard. No you're not, you're very sweet. Wait a minute – I think we can . . .' She looked him over where before she had just looked at him. 'You're not quite got up for this sort of do, are you? M'm.'

She stepped suddenly forward with her hands held out and proceeded at a slower pace to take off his tie, which she rolled up and dropped into his side pocket. After that she undid the top button of his shirt and pulled its collar half outside his jacket collar but no further. While she did this she stood closer to him than necessary and put in a bit of extra fingerwork on the second part, with eyelids and mouth going too. Richard thought it was satisfactory of him that he saw he was not actually meant to do anything at this stage, just think about it, and even more that he kept quiet.

'I'm afraid we're stuck with the suit,' said Sandy. 'Still, you should get by.'

'Good. But what are you talking about?'

'Before, you looked like the sort of solicitor Crispin wouldn't be seen asking where his boss was. Now, you could pass as a spare second-unit director.'

'What an awful lot you do know, don't you, love? And cheers.'

'And don't answer back. This way.'

'What's in here?' asked Richard a few moments later as she led him into the small room with the bookshelves and the butler's table where he had not so long before exchanged remarks with Godfrey and introduced Anna to Crispin. The tray on the table contained bottles, mostly full ones, but they had a kind of non-current look about them.

'I thought you might fancy a little nap somewhere these horsy people can't get at you,' said Sandy.

'I don't see why they should want to get at me, in fact quite the – '

'What about a drink? Or I could fetch you a cup of tea.'

'No thanks. What you could do is tell Crispin I'm here and ask him if I could just have a quick word with him. There's something he ought to – '

Somehow Richard had imagined in some detail that the next thing would be Sandy telling him there was surely no need to be in such a terrific hurry, and the one after that him saying that that was actually why he had come round, to have a quick word with Crispin, but instead of any of that he and she instantly started grappling on a sofa or couch that was there. Within what seemed no more than a few seconds he was immeasurably far away, from Anna, from Cordelia, from everyone else, from every part of his life and everything he had done up to that moment of it, and yet was completely contained and hemmed in by the person and the body that was closer to him than anything else had ever been. But it could really have been no more than a comparatively few seconds, perhaps a minute, before he heard a series of noises from outside the room, not loud but distinctive, recognisable, approaching footsteps that stopped when somebody stumbled against the door, and now, as then, Freddie came into the room in an impatient way.

She said she might have known it, so this was where crafty buggers were hiding, and there was nothing for her to see, but her appearance there had had the effect of a soundless explosion, something that recalled for an instant to Richard the disintegration of a dream on sudden waking, and then he was just back where he had always been, looking round and drawing breath and having thoughts again, such as ones about that being a near one, only going to show, amazing how things could boil up or blow up with no warning at all. He caught sight of Sandy's face and clearly read there a look of bitter reproach, not for any inadequacy but for denying what he had felt a moment earlier, for purposely forgetting it, trivialising it, taking it away from her. It occurred to him that a dream suddenly woken up from was quite different from a dream as it was dreamt. Then he forgot all about the whole thing.

'I knew you'd sneak off if you got half a bloody chance,' Freddie was saying to her sister. 'Oh hallo Richard, you look a bit washed out.'

'He said he wanted a snooze which was why I brought him in here,' said Sandy. 'I mean honestly, if I can't even – '

'Look, the food's arrived in case you hadn't noticed. I can't do it all on my own, for Christ's sake, they're a new lot. You get your head down if you want to, Richard. Take no notice of us.'

'You mean you don't feel like doing it. How's Enrique propose to get through his evening?'

'Enrique's got more than enough on his plate as it is. He can't – '

'In his glass, you mean. There's no use expecting – '

'These people don't know where anything is, okay? You put your feet up if you feel like it, Richard.'

'What the bloody hell's,' said Crispin's voice approaching the threshold, 'going on here?' it finished inside the room. 'Why aren't you both out there? Godfrey's looking for a screwdriver to repair his favourite corkscrew. Sometimes I . . .'

The sight and sound of Crispin Radetsky, apparently three metres high and weighing some 150 kilograms, in full fig minus morning coat and displaying braces like an elephant's girths, and talking, made Richard feel drunk again, or perhaps more precisely for the first time. He lay on the sofa/couch with head and feet obediently down and up while the three argued across him. To find the point or points at issue between them seemed unrewarding and he never seriously attempted it. Anyway it was soon settled or abandoned and the party set about leaving. Richard was in the act of letting them go and good luck to them when he remembered.

'Hey, Crispin . . .'

'Hallo, dear boy. I saw you there. I thought you were having forty winks. Good lunch, I trust?'

'Could I just have a quick word? I know you've got all these –'

'Not now, Richard, there's an angel. It's a matter of keeping these fellows' hands off the silver, do you see. Never trust a horsy crowd, especially viscounts and above.'

'I'm sorry, but it is important.'

Crispin came back from the doorway and sat down next to Richard. 'All right, five minutes,' he said sharply, and shook with a silent gust of laughter.

Richard took no more than one of them to describe the advent of Ippolitov, summarise his story and mention the grounds for thinking him genuine.

Though he heard the tale out in silence, Crispin was very ready with questions. 'Did the fellow specify at all about not bringing in his embassy?'

'Just said he couldn't be too careful. Which I suppose need have meant no more than that he had reason to think there was one possible shit there. But I think that means we steer clear of it ourselves, don't you?'

'Yes, on the whole. And you say he wouldn't name any of our coppers either. Secretive little chap, isn't he? You don't mind if I mention Inspector Ippolitov to my friends in the filth, I hope?'

'Of course not.'

'And while I think of it I'll take that card off you. Do no harm to give Intravel a tinkle. Or do you feel you ought to be the one to do that?'

'No, no, you go ahead.'

'Obviously you'll want more time to think about it, but at the moment it would be fair to say, wouldn't it, that you're more inclined to believe this bugger's scenario than not?'

'Yes. Negative reasons chiefly, or entirely really. It takes some swallowing, the idea that a Russian phony or spy or agent of some kind came all the way here to spin me a yarn about a petty crook in Moscow.'

'Put like that it does sound unlikely, I agree. On the understanding that he came all the way from Moscow and not Chingford.'

'That would be checkable, wouldn't it? Also, he didn't ask for money.'

'Yes, I agree that seems to rule out his being any ordinary sort of con-man.'

'And then his offering to defend his story to anybody I pick, and saying where he can be found.'

'Not found, if I understood you correctly. Reached. But it'll be interesting to see if he can indeed be reached. As a first step.'

'What do you think yourself, Crispin?'

'Well, one thing I most certainly think, dear boy, is that you hope he's telling the truth. No no please, I mean no more than that, just hope, would rather it were so than not. As you showed to my satisfaction at three points at least during our conversation just now. That's no more than one thing I think, and it leads in among considerations which are no business of mine. As to what I *think*, about Assistant Commissioner Ippolitov and his most sportive and pleasant history, I think the facts he mentions are substantially true as they go, but their implications are not straightforward, not altogether. I think somebody over there wants our little initiative torpedoed and has told or asked Ippolitov, perhaps as a return of a favour, to do what he can while he's here to discourage our show of respect for Mr Danilov. Somebody wants Mr Danilov to stay in gaol. Probably somebody who wants a lot of things left as they are.'

'A political move, in fact.'

'Probably.' Crispin had been patting and pinching his garments, perhaps in search of a cigar-case, but he now abandoned the attempt. 'Which of course doesn't necessarily make Danilov a knight in shining armour.'

'I think I see that. But supposing he's as far from it as Ippolitov says? We can't be mixed up with a, with a petty criminal. It'll discredit the whole – '

'He was bound to get called that, alleged to be that, whatever he was. It won't cut any ice. Everybody expects a Soviet dissident to be smeared as a criminal by those chaps. Very often he *is* a criminal. In fact your girl-friend evidently hinted something about shady deals when she was talking to old Tony Salmon. We'll follow the Ippolitov thing up, of course, but I can't see it making much difference.'

'But surely it makes all the difference.'

'Really.' Crispin stood up, sighing and blinking. 'That's your problem.'

'These days a lot of things seem to be that. Here's another. Well, a question anyway. Why did Ippolitov seek me out when he could have come to see you or one of the other top names? He knows about you, as I told you.'

'Didn't he say why?'

'He said I had a lot of influence.'

'He was certainly telling the truth there. You're a top name all right, Richard. Literally so. In fact when we publish our illuminated scroll, your name will lead all the rest.'

'You're joking.'

'I am not joking. What's that PEN chap's name, anyway he insisted that they regarded you over there as the leading British authority on Russian literature since I don't know when, and the others agreed, those with an opinion. If you're not first on the list,' said Crispin, looking hard at Richard, 'it'll be bad for the cause.'

'Oh my God.'

'Yes, you have got quite a lot to sort out, haven't you, one way and another?' Crispin was still looking, but after a moment he switched his gaze to the open doorway and in doing so seemed to Richard to bring Sandy into the question. 'Well, you've earned a drink. Or you ought to have one. Or you need one.'

'I'm not sure about any of those, but I most assuredly want one.'

'Anything in particular?'

'Scotch. Neat.'

'Plenty of that in what's in front of you. Glasses in the tall cupboard. I'll leave you to it. Oh, well done – just under six minutes. How was Kotolynov?'

'Was that today? He was all right, but he – '

'Tell me in the morning.'

And with the air of a man who has settled something for any future worth foreseeing, Crispin went off, shutting the door behind him. In a short while Richard heard him returning to the party. Another, distant door shut.

The bottle of Scotch was new, unopened, and its cap was so tightly sealed that for some moments Richard was afraid he might be compelled not to forgo a drink out of it but to bash its neck against some article of furniture. But then it was all right, or rather he got the cap off and some whisky into a glass and some of the whisky down his throat. As a result either of its arrival in his stomach or of some coincident paroxysm he at once began to feel strange, doubly so, strange in a way altogether new to him. After sitting there taking this in for a time, he made his way to the smaller room near by where he had noticed a telephone on a previous visit. It showed none of the complications that had intimidated him before, and very soon his own number was ringing in his ear. He let it ring and ring away and at last hung up with a smirk of triumph, for his number was also inescapably Cordelia's number, and the world would end before her telephone rang and she failed to answer it. In other words she was *not there*.

And the sooner he got home the likelier it was that she would go on being not there. He hurried towards the exit, or entrance, distracted only when he passed a stray group of four or five presumably horsy people drinking what was surely champagne. They fell silent and lowered their eyes respectfully as he went by, like members of a colonial élite who come across a native inescapably engaged on one of his traditional observances. Then he was out, he was away, guided by some equally strange quality back to the TBD in whatever exotically named street it was. Then as soon as he had got home and shut the front door after him it suddenly stopped being at all funny.

Having had enough of intuitions, or of the thought of them, he went methodically into every room in the house and satisfied himself that Cordelia was not in any of them. Everything looked the same as it always had. There was nothing out of place, no used crockery in the kitchen, no book anywhere but on its shelf, no paper to be seen in her study that was not held in a clip. He looked through her clothes and her various accoutrements and realised he was impossibly far from being able to tell if any were missing. He could not even have said whether any piece of luggage had gone. From all visible evidence, his wife might merely have slipped out to post a letter, but he knew it was nothing like that.

In the drawing-room, her drawing-room, Richard looked over the uncompleted jigsaw puzzle and the arrayed chessmen without finding any significance in them, any more than in the absence of *The Times* – for all he knew that had become normal. In the kitchen he looked over some of the food without seeing it as stuff to be eaten. As he stood in the hall the thought of television crossed his mind without stopping. Then he went up to Cordelia's study again, looked up a number in her telephone-book and pressed the buttons. A man's voice answered.

'May I speak to Pat Dobbs, please?'

'Who's calling?'

'Richard Vaisey.' Quite why Richard Vaisey was calling seemed less clear to him.

'Oh.' The speaker got something besides recognition into the syllable. 'It's Harry Dobbs here, Pat's husband. I'm afraid she's out. Can I help?'

'Well . . . you don't happen to know if she's with Cordelia, do you, my wife?'

'I'm afraid not.' The extra something was still there. 'I don't think so. She didn't say she was.'

For whatever reason he had got on the line, Richard felt he could hardly get off it again then and there, so to speak, so he said, 'I don't know where she is, you see. I mean Cordelia.'

'Oh. Shall I get Pat to call you when she comes in?'

'Well, not unless she has been with Cordelia or knows where she is. Thanks.'

'Right.'

By now Richard had provisionally identified the extra something he had noticed. It was the tone of a man who thinks he may be dealing with a dangerous lunatic.

FOURTEEN

But the next morning Richard thought that what he had heard in Harry Dobbs's voice was someone pretty sure he was dealing with a bloody fool. This thought got in not long before nine o'clock, on coming to after what seemed a few minutes' genuine unconsciousness after some hours in a state that combined sleep and waking, none of the good parts of the one and most of the available bad parts of the other. He had at any rate passed them in a bed, his bed. To his profound relief he felt entirely normal apart from a burning thirst, severe nausea and a headache above the right eye like an emergent antler on the point of bursting through the skin. The thirst yielded to a couple of quarts of tap-water, which also reduced the nausea to a level at which he could hold it in check by swallowing every few seconds. And the headache stayed away while he remembered never to move his head relatively to his neck. That meant among other things that he had to lift his wrist to eye level to see the time and do a full about-turn whenever he felt the need to check on what was behind him. He could not laugh either, though that was not much in the way of a deprivation.

Moving like an African water-carrier of old, Richard made his way into his study, sat himself down at the desk and rang Professor Léon's number. It was engaged. Like any fool he tried it again in case he had got it wrong the first time, and had not. Then with a vague idea of preparing the next step he reached for his ignition key, but it was nowhere in his clothing. In the same carefully articulated style as before he went back through the hall, out of the front door and over to where he kept the TBD. The ignition key was not in its socket in the dashboard, which said something for his presence of mind under stress and so on but must mean the key was in some third place. The thought of looking for it, especially down on the ground, was not to be borne. He would return to the house and go straight to fetch his spare key from its special drawer. But he proved to have shut the front door behind him, and of course its key was on the same ring. So, having dressed and shaved at least, he had better pick up a taxi, no problem round here, and go somewhere in it. But, though equipped for the outside world in most other ways, he had not yet shifted his wallet from its place on his desk to his breast pocket, and found he was carrying in his trouser pocket no more than a pound coin and a selection of silver. At that moment he caught sight of a bus approaching the nearby stop. Its distance and speed looked like landing it there at just the moment when a man with his head on invisible gimbals would arrive there too from where Richard was standing, provided he started straight away. So he started straight away.

As he moved, he told himself that all buses going south past this spot had once also reached the main crossroads a couple of miles further down, and must surely do so still, even though it was a couple of years since he had travelled on one. From that lower point he could go east and south to the Institute, south and west to Léon's, elsewhere too. These thoughts, meagre as they might have been, took up all his time until he was actually getting on to the bus. It seemed very different from the buses he remembered, starting with the disgruntled black face turned in his direction from inside a kind of half-complete box near which a notice, presumably tampered with in some way, urged him to have exact fare ready. But, being an outstandingly clever and quick-witted man, Richard even in his present state saw exactly what he had to do at each stage – not very fast, true, but fast enough to save him from insult or assault. He got to a permitted and comfortable seat at the back and was starting to believe he might one day feel no worse than very unfit, when a voice spoke to him.

'Morning, Dr Vaisey,' it said, words not in themselves charged with any great menace, he would have had to admit, but they were enough to cause him to move his head suddenly and not quite scream. 'Didn't expect to see you here.'

'No,' Richard agreed. 'No,' he added on reflection. He saw by degrees that he had sat down next to the moustached, short-haired young man with the armful of bangles he had last encountered at the meeting in Tristram Hallett's room.

'Name of Duncan,' said the other helpfully. Although Richard had forgotten that, he did remember something about a wandering or lazy eye. The pair of eyes in the parsnip-coloured face in front of him, however, seemed to be operating binocularly today. 'Thought you ran one of these fancy foreign jobs.'

'What? Oh, I see what you mean, yes. Yes. But, er, it's off the road for the time being.'

'Oh yeah. Nothing what you'd call *untoward*, I trust?'

'Well, I don't know what you'd call untoward. I just couldn't get it to start.'

'M'm. You are all right, are you, er, Dick?'

What with the way he had caught his breath as the bus moved off, and just now given a sharp wince on clearing his throat, this was not an unreasonable question to ask Richard, who said a little testily, 'Of course I'm all right, why shouldn't I be?'

Duncan drew in his own breath gradually. 'Well, to kick off with, that's a nasty cut there down your jaw. It's started bleeding again – no no, don't touch it. Don't suppose you'd have anything to put on it, would you?'

Richard had also forgotten the slash he had dealt himself while shaving, and no, he had nothing to put on it.

'Allow me.' Duncan brought out from whatever sort of jacket he was wearing a freshly ironed, snow-white handkerchief. 'Here, press this against it. That's right.' He went on studying Richard with more curiosity than concern. 'You look considerably shaken up, Dick. I hope you haven't run into any kind of *trouble* or anything, have you, with anybody? Bashed your car or anything, you know, similar?'

'I just seem to have had rather a lot to do this morning.' Richard wished he had the kind of voice and manner that could end a conversation with a remark like that.

'I must say, I can't remember seeing you without a tie before.'

Instinctively Richard looked down and put his hand to his neck and did himself no good at all.

'I'd say you were in pain, Dick.'

'I tell you what, Duncan . . .'

Duncan sat as still as a stone, waiting to be told what.

'I . . . well, I ran into a few of the lads last night and, well, I'm afraid we put down a few.' Richard felt his face lurch shamefully into chumminess as he spoke. 'Aha, you know how it is.'

The other's face turned that approach down flat. After allowing plenty of time for this to sink in, he said, 'Is there any way I could be of assistance, Dick?'

Richard said nothing. His attention had been caught by a man of about fifty who was taking some time paying his fare. Up to then the interior of the bus had been like a tourist showpiece in an energetic totalitarian country, half full – no more – of typical contented inhabitants, middle-aged housewives with little tartan-covered shopping-trolleys, soberly suited old fellows on the pension, a couple of sedate blacks, one or two tractable children. Something about the newcomer called up a different image of contemporary behaviour on buses. It might have been his check-pattern bell-bottomed trousers or his platform shoes or the tall thin cylindrical can, handsomely designed in gold, carmine and white, that stuck up out of his jacket pocket. As if feeling Richard's eyes on him he turned his head and jerked it to one side in what might have been greeting. But as he came slowly down the aisle he jerked his head similarly a few more times, suggesting the movement was less purposeful. All the same he seemed to recognise Richard while settling himself down next to him on the other side from Duncan.

First puffing sharply a few times in match-damping style, the man said in a high, almost babyish voice, 'Have you heard anything good? Because I haven't.'

Turning towards Duncan, Richard found him already engrossed in whatever was taking place out of the window on that side. An elbow prodding him in the upper arm, not hard, brought him round the other way again, in time to witness the man with the tall can taking it out of his pocket, raising it to his lips and drinking from it, with some evident difficulty although the bus was moving quite slowly and steadily. Soon he had had enough for the moment, and there was mortification in the jerk of his head.

'Have you heard anything good?' he asked again.

Richard hesitated. 'No,' he said.

'Well, what do you expect? Do you expect anything better?' There was no bitterness in the man's tone, merely a sad resignation. 'Anywhere in these times?'

'I suppose not.'

'Will you give me a guinea, that's one pound and ten pee?'

'I'm afraid I haven't got it.'

'One pound fifty will do.'

'I'm sorry, I still haven't got it.'

'I think you'd better give it to him, Dick,' said Duncan, and went on to say, 'since after all the two of you are birds of a feather,' but he said the second part only with his face and the run of his voice, and in Richard's mind.

'I honestly haven't got it. I came out without any money.'

With only a short look at Richard and the other man and back, and hardly sighing at all, Duncan produced the coins and that was that.

When they were alone again on the rear seat, Richard said in the hope of lightening the tone, 'God, what a relief. What on earth was the point of the guinea? Some ancient law, could it be?'

'It's the exact price of a large can of Export Brew,' said Duncan, adding silently as before, 'which don't tell me you don't know.' He continued aloud, 'Have you really not got any money on you, Dick? Because I can easily – '

'Thank you, I've arranged to pick up some cash.' Well, he had better, and soon, the bus fare having reduced his working capital to the price of a newspaper. 'Down the road.'

'Oh yeah. That's good. Well, Dick, I think I can say I've seen another side to you in the last ten minutes. From the one I see as a rule, I mean.'

'I expect we've all got other sides to ourselves, don't you? I mean I don't suppose the person I see at those meetings at the Institute is the real you or the essential you or the complete you, any more than what you see is, er, the real me.'

'I'm sorry, I don't think I quite understand what you mean, not absolutely.'

Absolutely was far from being how well Richard understood what he had meant himself. In fits and starts the bus was approaching a stop and he was waiting for his moment to dash for the outdoors. 'Well, just when we're in that committee or whatever it is we're on opposite sides, sort of representing them, but now we've happened to meet like this, we turn out to be just a couple of . . .' The bus slowed to let somebody very insecure drive a hearse out of a side-street. 'Just a couple of, you know, one chap sort of giving another one a helping hand. Just that.'

'If what you're saying is that the *societal* differences between you and me are purely superficial and all that counts is our common humanity . . .'

'Well, perhaps I wouldn't go so far as to – '

'. . . then I'm afraid I must disagree with you, Dr Vaisey. Our mutual disparities are too deep-seated to be reconciled.'

'Oh. It was Dick before.'

'That was before.'

'Oh, I see.' Richard stood up and offered the handkerchief back. A final dab had shown the bleeding had stopped.

'Keep it.'

'No, you take it. Thank you. Duncan.'

Richard succeeded in parting with the handkerchief. He felt ridiculously relieved at having escaped the tiny humiliation of being forced into hanging on to the thing. Was he going to turn out to be wrong about everyone? Where had he learnt all the bloody silly bits of crap he had thought he knew? But he soon forgot such considerations on finding himself in the fresh – or at least the open – air in a place he would have said he knew well but had not actually been in for ten years or more, and very horrible it was too without a doubt. With surprising ease, in other words when he could still have walked a few yards without collapsing, he found a public telephone, a further phenomenon known to him almost entirely by sight alone, and rang Crispin's number, the only one he still knew apart from that of the emergency services. A foreign voice spoke, then Freddie's.

'I've locked myself out of the house and my car won't go and I haven't any money,' he said. 'Can I come round?'

'Won't – sorry, won't old Cordelia let you in?'

'She isn't there.'

'What? You mean she's gone away?'

'I don't know. I don't know where she is. But she isn't there.'

'What? Where was she before?'

'I don't know. Look, can I just come round?'

'Of course you can. Why shouldn't you?'

'I told you, I haven't any money.'

'Get a taxi and we'll pay him here, you daft sod.'

Thus encouraged, Richard got a taxi, going into the roadway to hail it at some risk to others as well as himself. A moment later the nearby traffic lights changed to red. The taxi-driver, a small elderly man, watched Richard in silence while he gave the Radetsky address and went on to say,

'Just take me there, right, and no solicitous inquiries about did you know you've got a nasty cut on your face, squire, you want to watch that, yeah, and no regretful observations about declining standards of dress, yeah, so just take me there, yeah?'

'Have I spoken? Have I uttered a single word?'

'Just drive, yeah?'

When they drew up at the Dom Radetsky the driver continued mute and facing his front.

Richard said, 'I haven't any money so I'll have to get some indoors so will you wait?'

'I'd better, hadn't I?'

As he had expected and done his best to allow for, it was Sandy who answered the bell. Although it was not yet half-past ten she seemed to be got up as if for a cocktail party, though without hat and gloves at this stage. There was no denying that, what with her breasts and teeth and look of herbivorous delinquency she was attractive, and not much more denying off the record that she found him so.

'Come in,' she said.

'I've got to pay this bloody taxi, I'm sorry.'

'So old Cordelia's locked you out at last, eh?'

Over Sandy's shoulder Richard caught a glimpse of Freddie lurking near the stairs, a wineglass in her hand even at this hour. He remembered Crispin remarking that she always tended to drink more when Sandy was about. He said, 'Actually not. To be fair, I must have left my key – '

'Oh bugger to be fair. Come on in.'

'I've still got to pay the, the bloody taxi, and I – '

Sandy produced a £20 note which she had had crumpled up in her hand. 'That be enough?'

'That'll be fine.'

'I can't change that,' said the taximan when he saw the note. 'I've only just come out.'

'You haven't got to change it yet,' said Richard, and gave the Léon address.

Before the taxi had moved away more than a few inches laterally from its place by the kerb, it was lengthily hooted at by the driver of a car passing it at speed. Richard saw for a moment a youngish furious face that cursed inaudibly. The owner of the face must have been experiencing with great vividness the exasperation he doubtless would have felt if the taxi had started off a couple of seconds later than it had. Very well, but what had impressed Richard more was that the car, now abruptly vanished, had been a Viotti TBD like his own, now sitting sadly outside his house while this other fellow was quartering London. It occurred to him that for the past hour he had had, was still getting, a reminder of what life without a car was like. And, thrown in, a foretaste, quite vivid enough to suit him, of more of the same going on for much longer. Because living on his salary with eight hundred or so quid coming in from books and articles in a good year ... Richard groggily envisaged an existence without comfort, without everything done for him or ready when he needed it, without anything that was not strictly necessary and a certain amount that was, all cafés, canteens, pubs, pavements, bus shelters, bus queues, buses. At the same time he saw his inner citadel of study, rows of books, shower, armchair, place in the kitchen, bed – the whole thing dissolving about him, dematerialising as at the wave of a sorcerer's wand.

When Cordelia took all her money away with her. Or did he mean if? For a moment he saw it as slightly splendid of him not to have thought of this before. Then very soon he saw that no, it was not splendid of him at all, because he had still not thought of what it would be like when or if Cordelia took herself away. Now that he had come this far in imagination he should be able to go further and imagine her absence, her non-presence, not seeing her, not talking to her, not having her there, within reach, only minutes away. But that would have meant being able to imagine her presence, to see her in his mind's eye, her face and expressions, her shape and movements, to hear her voice in the same way, and that he could not do. All he could have done was describe her. As soon as this idea had entered his mind, others followed at top speed, horrible generalisations, fantasies, accusations. If the taxi were to stop this moment right by Cordelia herself standing on a corner, he would not recognise her – nonsense. He had been unconsciously but systematically shutting her out of his memory in preparation for shutting her out of his life – double nonsense. He had never really perceived her, taken her in – no proof that he had, but not true. He could not visualise anybody, not merely Cordelia, never had been able to — utter nonsense, he could have produced on demand instantaneous mental snapshots of anybody from his grand-mother to that toothy little creature he had just . . .

In the next minutes Richard checked out the last rejoinder and found it fair, with a few odd blanks, though no girls of any note were missing, and some creditable pluses, like the portress at the Institute caught in a sharply defined still shot in the act of closing her jaws over her awful candy bar. He had settled down to convincing himself that he had not really forgotten what his wife looked like when the last and worst of the salvo hit him. He was a bloody professor, an academic, a PhD, a man of books and commentaries and capable of interest only in them, but he had gone all these years thinking he was not, could not have been, because he happened to be a randy bastard as well. His idea of a perfect day was a couple of lectures and a seminar in the morning, a fuck in the afternoon followed by a catching-up on linguistic studies, a solitary dinner with a learned journal by his plate and a quiet evening trying out a possible new line on Father Zosima's stuff in *The Brothers Karamazov*, with half an hour on Lermontov before retiring. Everything else was just filling in round that. Did he really care about tennis, China tea, Hallett, Crispin, that bloody marvellous TBD? In their different ways Kotolynov and Ippolitov had indeed impressed him, but only because they threw light on Russia, Russia in the way he saw it, as part of a subject of study. As for Anna . . . Was he just fooling himself again in seeing hope there?

Before he could even have said what he meant they had arrived. He ran to the front door, which opened in his face to reveal Anna. This saved him a certain amount of explanation. As at the Radetsky house he sighted a figure or figures in the near background and, having run past Anna, running now past a comparably startled sister-in-law/cousin and cousin/sister-in-law he said nothing except to wish them good morning. Across the threshold of the lavatory, Richard thought as hard as he could about dromedaries for the immeasurable time it took him to prepare himself for the act of peeing. Those glugged-down litres of water, which had seemed to disappear before even getting as far as his stomach, were not to be mocked. He had not noticed their presence until arriving outside. Their departure seemed to have taken with it his hangover and attachments. Something had, anyway, and he now felt hardly at all like his own ghostly double.

Anna was standing rather awkwardly at the open front door with a small man wearing a cap whom Richard recognised as the taxi-driver. Both turned to him with some relief when he reappeared.

'Ah, there you are, guv. That'll be – '

'Keep it all.' Richard handed over the £20 note.

'Well, that's extremely – '

'No, take 50p for yourself and give me the rest.' He told himself he had to start learning somewhere. When the door was shut he said to Anna, 'Sorry, were you going out?'

'Not now.' She looked at him carefully. 'Come and sit down.'

He put his arms tight round her, but not for long because he was afraid he might burst into tears, and there were several things to be said against that. Anna took him to the sitting-room with the pottery and tiles where he had first met Professor Léon and Hamparzoumian, and left him for a moment, presumably to keep them away. When she came back she settled herself next to him and took his hand.

'So those problems in your life are no better this morning,' she said.

'No, they aren't and there are a couple of fresh ones.'

'Having no necktie, is that one of them?'

'Oh God, so I haven't.'

'Leave it to me.'

He got through her second absence by concentrating on not thinking about Cordelia. When Anna returned this time she brought with her an ordinary brown-and-white slightly hairy tie from Léon's or Hamparzoumian's store. His spirits lifted a point or two when he saw that she could be trusted not to put it on him herself.

'I'm afraid it's not very good but it was the only one I could find without crossed pistols or food on it.'

He decided to let that one lie and told her what he thought was enough about his day so far, and she listened sympathetically but seemed to find it all quite unremarkable. Then he said he would go back to the previous evening. He added, sounding to himself

like a TV announcer as he did so, that she might find some parts
of it rather distressing.

Her hand jumped in his. She sat up straight and a lock of dark
hair swung forward in front of her ear. 'But you're all right, yes?
Nobody dead or hurt or ill?'

'Nothing like that. A man came up to me outside my house
and said he was a policeman from Moscow.'

Anna looked puzzled and also half-ready to be amused, as if
some English or other kind of exotic kind of joke might be
coming along, by no means a far-fetched possibility in the light
of his words and the ridiculously pompous way they had been
spoken. 'And was he?' she asked, wide-eyed.

'Yes, I think he was. He told me he was here to help us with
our trials of Nazi war criminals. But he also said he was from the
ordinary criminal police that investigated such crimes as fraud
committed in Moscow. Anna, this man wanted me to do what I
could to stop your petition because your brother is a real
criminal and deserves to be in gaol. That was what he told me.'

'And you obviously didn't throw him out or anything like
that. Quite right. It's true. You'll tell me more later but he was
speaking the truth about my brother. As the police see it he's
guilty.'

'Oh God.'

A feeling, a thought he had put aside earlier returned to
Richard, that at ordinary times he rather disliked prolonged
physical contacts with women, as now when holding hands or in
the past when walking arm in arm. And Anna had seemed upset
at his revelation but not enough, not as much as he considered
suitable.

In uncanny apparent response she took her hand away and
clasped it in her other one while she said, 'But I think perhaps it's
not so terrible, not as bad as you must think. From your point of
view, and that's not the only one, everybody in my country is a
criminal, more or less of a criminal. We have to be, to survive.
You must know that, darling. And surely you know too that
because everything everybody does in the Soviet Union is
political or can be made political, there's no real division
between the political police and the anything-and-everything
else police. Whenever anybody powerful wants to be nasty for
any reason to someone who isn't powerful, he can always have

that person charged with stealing or making a false entry on an official form or *something*, something illegal he's done. Wherever you go in Russia, in the other republics, in the satellite countries you hear the same old proverb. He who doesn't rob and cheat the state robs and cheats his own children. You must have heard that. Well, my brother has children. And a wife, who has a mother. Yes, it would be much nicer for everybody if he were being kept in prison for having done something like making a protest or speaking for democracy, but unfortunately it can't always be like that. Oh, I should have told you before, but it's not so much to tell.'

Apart from the last few words, Anna had said all this so gently that Richard had to force himself to say, 'According to that policeman, what your brother had done was swindle some, what did he call them, some small individuals out of quite a lot of money altogether.'

'Correct. The small individuals were officials of a trade union branch, and as you also know our trade unions aren't like trade unions in the West, they're just production committees, run like everything else by state bureaucrats. Sergei took money off some of them for a currency deal that was itself illegal, so they had a bit of trouble nailing him, and had to make up something about electric fittings. And as you see they're still cross with him.'

'Wouldn't it have been better to come out with all this at the start?'

'Yes it would. I see now it would. We underestimated their perseverance, their tenacity. Getting this policeman to you.'

'Who's we?'

'Sergei and me and a friend. It was Sergei's idea first, this scheme, but very soon mine as well. I had already arranged to come here.'

'You were lucky getting away, weren't you?'

'Sergei had some money left, and our friend helped.'

'I see,' said Richard. He supposed he did but had no sense of a cloud lifting.

'Are you going to tell Mr Radetsky this story?'

'I already have. He seemed to have been expecting something of the sort. Said he didn't think it would make much difference.'

'But you think it would, or will, or might, and yet you know so much about my country.'

'Maybe. I wanted to hear the facts from you. But one very important fact was confirmed by what the policeman said, or didn't say. He never referred to Sergei as anything but your brother.'

'And you'd been thinking he might be my husband or my lover or anything like that.'

'Yes, Anna, anything like that. Wasn't it possible? I never really thought of it but the possibility was always there. Wasn't it?'

Her disbelief and indignation faded as he watched. 'I suppose so, yes. Yes, of course you're right. So that's good.' She laid her hand on the back of his neck in a way he had no objection to. 'But you're worried about something else.'

'Yes, I am.'

'About your wife. Is it things happening or just thoughts? I know they can be bad too.'

'She's gone away without saying where or how long for or anything. She's never done that before. I don't know how to find her, but I feel I must.'

Anna waited before saying, 'That's all? Of course I don't mean that's nothing but it's not like burning the house down or shooting herself or you. In my . . .'

'Yes, I know, in your country they do things like that all the time when their boy-friend or whoever it is displeases them, or they say they have, make out they've taken poison just for a start, and it's bad form not to pretend to believe them, I know. And no doubt there are several sayings about it too.'

'I'm sorry.'

'That's all right.'

'So you don't know when she'll be back.'

'Can I use the telephone?'

This time he got Pat Dobbs, who knew nothing to the purpose and was heroically uninquisitive. Out of a hazy feeling it might have its uses, he filled her in some of the way. Then, no more purposefully, he tried Godfrey and got his answering-machine, which he told merely that he had called, but did that much in the hope of somehow reducing the shock if by any chance he had to call again. Then he sat and thought for a time without avail. Then he got hold of the garage in W6 he sometimes used and successfully petitioned them to send somebody to meet him at his car with keys.

When Richard returned to the sitting-room Anna was reading of all things a copy of *Pravda*, presumably Léon's. To help her do so she wore a pair of rather heavy bourgeois-style glasses, which he thought gave her something of the look of a film actress impersonating a female tycoon or professor. When she saw him she snatched them off.

'Any news?'

'Nothing at all.'

'Come and sit down, darling.' She gave him a cordial-handshake kind of kiss. 'Before I started reading I was thinking. And what I was thinking was, Do you think . . . Cordelia . . . you don't mind if I use her name?'

'Good God no. I mean that's all right. Go on.'

'Do you think Cordelia will be coming back today?'

'No.'

'Do you . . . this is harder . . . do you want her to come back today?'

'It's not harder for me. Again no.'

'Then . . .'

They stared at each other for a couple of seconds, after which he gave a single blare of laughter.

It was no great matter to rearrange Anna's meeting at the BBC, where she had been about to go. While he did that she made preparations. Very soon Richard was regaining the use of his car with the assistance of a rather surprisingly old but not remarkably surly man from the garage. All he had to offer him in the way of a tip was what was left of Sandy's £20, and just at first it looked as if the old fellow would turn it down as too paltry, but almost at once he changed his mind and accepted it after all. There remained the problem of getting into the house.

'Are you sure he can't help us?' asked Anna. The mere uncouth sound of an earlier version had been nearly enough to make the garageman call off the whole deal.

'I'm afraid so. I'll have to break in.'

'Go on, then,' she said when he made no move – '*nobody* will see you,' making it clear who in particular would not see him, and being slightly impatient too.

'Well, people will, you know. It's . . .'

She gave him a look of less slight impatience, modified it to one of speculation about what an Englishman's code might lay down about breaking or not breaking into one's own house, then went decisive. 'Give me a hand up here.'

'Hey, hold on a minute.'

'Darling, please, you breaking into a house is a man breaking into a house. Me climbing up a house is just a girl climbing up a house. Now.'

Richard would not have said there was much of anything that could be called a handhold or a foothold on that Regency façade, but in a few seconds Anna was outside the landing window. A sound followed, half clunk, half crack, that was nothing like the jangling crash he had been looking forward to. In another few seconds she had opened the front door and was dropping some small object by the wall.

'What's that?' he asked.

'A stone to break the window with. From the ground here, from the earth. It's back there now.'

'I didn't see you pick it up.'

'You don't know very much about me, do you?'

'I'm learning.'

They stood in the hall. The place seemed to Richard just the same, as it clearly ought, and yet to have grown months older. Both he and Anna were suddenly constrained in behaviour, as if a third person had intruded upon them. Each sent the other a brief smile.

'I don't suppose you want to be shown round the house,' he said with some confidence.

'No. Show me where I can wait while you get ready.'

'Do you want coffee?'

'No, nothing at all. A drink, but somewhere else.'

'M'm.' He was shy of letting her see his study. 'Perhaps you'd like to go in here.'

He took her into the drawing-room. On catching sight of the table with the jigsaw puzzle on it, Anna gave a low cry of delight like somebody greeting a favourite pet animal.

'This takes me back to when I was a little girl,' she said, bending down.

'Will you be all right in here for ten minutes?'

'What? Yes of course.'

Richard used the ten minutes on unsurprising things. The only special one was bathing and powdering the cut on his cheek. He also replaced the hairy Pimlico tie with a smoother, more boring one of his own.

When he went to fetch Anna she was still, or again, at the table, frowning now at an upper corner with what looked like a piece of tree in her fingers. This she put down at once on his return and straightened herself up, but held her ground. There was an odd pause. Then, with a momentary apologetic grin and hunch of the shoulders she reached over to the chessboard and firmly moved a piece on it, a white bishop, he saw.

'Mate next move,' she said.

'Whatever he does?'

'Of course. It's always whatever he does.'

Richard looked at the board. 'Can't he cover with his rook?' he asked, showing an appreciation of the game somewhat above his usual level.

'Not without discovering check from the queen. Have you got all your stuff?' She was in a hurry now.

'Yes. Tie. Right.'

'I'm sorry about that,' she said as they moved off. 'Well, that exhibition, I know it was awful of me but I just couldn't resist it.'

'I don't understand.'

'The really awful thing was, I wasn't going to tell you but I started looking at the chessboard as soon as you'd left me on my own in there, and I got the solution straight away, in fact I knew it, but I wanted to show off to you. That was terrible. Terrible.'

'Oh, I don't know that I'd go that far. After all, any Russian might – '

'That's just it, Richard. It was so revoltingly Russian, just what Russians do in films and books and plays and when they talk about themselves, which they do all the time as you know. I could feel it pressing in on me and I couldn't do a thing to stop it.'

'Now you are being Russian.'

'Oh, I probably am. But I've just thought of something in the last few seconds. Perhaps there are times when it's good to be like that, whatever it's called.'

'I don't quite see what – '

'Stay not seeing.'

They had been on their way for some minutes before Richard noticed in retrospect that not counting the jigsaw and the chess, Anna had paid no visible attention to the house or any of the things in it, large or small. And he himself had thought of nothing beyond his immediate actions and concerns. But he very clearly remembered shutting the front door after them and the two of them turning away.

FIFTEEN

'I greatly dislike having to tell you this, Richard,' said Godfrey's voice on the telephone, 'but I think you'd better come back.'

'You mean straight away? But I've only just – '

'As soon as you not too uncomfortably can. I'm pretty confident that when you see her you'll be glad you, well, you'll appreciate the point of coming back. I've never known her to be like this before. Not that it's particularly alarming. Not as such.'

'What happened exactly?'

'She rang me about an hour ago. Just caught me. She said she'd got back after a night with friends in the country and you'd vanished and left no note or anything but you'd taken clothes and stuff for an indefinite stay and somebody had broken into the place but nothing seemed to have been taken but you'd had a woman in the house with you. That was how she put it herself. Especially the last point.'

'My God,' said Richard, turning pale. There was no mirror in the hotel lobby near enough to tell him so but he knew it. He went on into a non-committal silence. 'For about five minutes. Well, possibly ten . . .'

'I imagine it was the one I . . .'

'Yes.'

'And wherever you are now she's . . .'

'Yes. Having breakfast in the dining-room as a matter of fact.'

'Well, I hope it was worth it.'

'Thank you for that kind thought, Godfrey. I don't know yet whether it's been worth it, do I, but in a way it was worth anything.'

'I'm glad to hear it.' There was neither obvious sincerity nor obvious sarcasm in Godfrey's tone. 'Well, I'll stay with Cordelia until you arrive. About midday? Do tell me, how soon did you let Crispin know where you were?'

'Oh, five minutes after we checked in.'

'You must have felt something was on the way to have dropped me that non-message like that.'

'Something's always on the way.'

Godfrey surprised Richard by saying, 'No doubt in Russia they have a proverb that says so.'

'No doubt. I'd better get moving. Thank you.'

Not many men perhaps would have passed up the chance of surprising Richard a second time by saying, 'You'll do the same for me some day,' but Godfrey did. He just grunted and hung up.

Richard and Anna had talked about a great deal in the preceding twenty-two hours or so, but not about everything under the sun, not even about what touched them closely. In particular, they had tiptoed round the periphery of Cordelia and got it over quite fast too. It could have been said that she had been a non-brooding absence from their escapade. Richard considered that Anna had shown herself impeccably under-standing in the matter. In other words she had said as little of Cordelia as simply humanity allowed. This must have been helped, he thought, by his clever policy of keeping the two apart.

'We'd have had to go back eventually anyway,' said Richard as they drove. He had told Anna that that sudden telephone-call had compelled his return to London to deal with official business there. Some such tale had seemed to him preferable both to any recognisable version of the truth and to saying nothing at all, which might have implied, or so he felt, a sudden ungallant distaste for the lady's company. Anyway, Russians were used to the notion of having to be in places to deal with official business. Most, if not all, of these thoughts made him feel a bit of a shit, but he had had so many others of that general type in his head already that a few more were not going to collapse him.

If Anna had had a better idea of the situation than she was supposed to, she was not letting on. In highly opportune fashion a thoroughgoing thunderstorm started up before they had been moving for more than ten minutes, and simple observation of its effects took up some of her time. But it left her plenty for a few stiff doses of aggressive withdrawal, in that mode which even Richard's limited experience had made him familiar with, if she had felt like administering them. He registered their failure to appear and hoped to be able to feel grateful one day.

When they parted she said, 'You go off now and decide what you want to do. What you think you ought to do must come into it, because you are what you are, but be quite sure that that comes second. Whatever you decide, I won't object.' So what had all that ever been about his having to deal with official business?

Having parked the TBD in its spot, Richard underwent physical difficulty in getting himself out of it and walking up to the front door, as in a dream. Having got there he stood for some seconds hoping he might fall down dead or at least permanently incapacitated. Nothing like that happened and, carrying his overnight case, he let himself in.

He had barely shut the front door when the one to the drawing-room opened and a man he had never seen before came out. Richard considered he had had more than his fair share recently of being confronted by men he had never seen before. Not that this one had never seen him before, or so it seemed, for he looked him in the eye and said, 'Hallo, Richard,' this in a voice Richard would have had to admit he might have heard before, and that recently. He still thought so when the man went on to say, 'You'd better come in here.' He saw that he was quite a pleasant-looking man of about forty dressed, conceivably for some costume piece, in dark suit, collared shirt and tie.

The first thing Richard noticed in the drawing-room was that the jigsaw puzzle had disappeared, doubtless inside the garish cardboard box that now stood in its place, and that the chessmen were likewise put away and their board folded shut. The next moment he caught sight of Pat Dobbs and had already begun to smile at this friendly presence when he noticed that the presence's expression was not as undilutedly friendly as it might have been. Her new swept-back hair-style might have contributed.

'Well,' she said. 'You remember Harry, don't you?'

'Oh yes of course.' Richard now fully did, remembering well enough too that after their recent telephone conversation he had been uncertain whether Harry regarded him as a loony or a chump. As neither for the moment, to judge by his downcast eyes and uncomfortable stance, rather as a fellow male known to be in difficulties.

What those difficulties might have amounted to in the present case sharpened up when Pat said, 'Aren't you wondering where Cordelia is?'

'Well, if I'd been given half a – '

'She's *upstairs*,' said Pat solemnly, as if naming some barely conceivable location. 'She's terribly upset.'

'How do you know?' was among the more urgent of the questions Richard wanted to ask then, but the one he did ask, rather ponderously as he saw in mid-utterance, was, 'Do you mind if I sit down for a moment?'

'Christ, it's your . . .' Pat stopped.

'No, it isn't actually my bloody house, is it? More to the point, what have you got me in here for if I'm supposed to be upstairs myself or should be or should want to be or . . .'

'Don't look at me,' said Harry. 'I just brought you the message. You two carry on and I'll bugger off along to the pub. I seem to remember one up the hill unless it's an Abu Dhabian restaurant these days. Round here you never know, do you?'

'Shouldn't you be getting back to your office?' While she talked to her husband Pat kept her eye on Richard in case he should try to sneak off before she had finished with him. 'It took a hell of a lot of getting away from earlier on.'

'That was earlier on. It's been my lunch-hour for nearly ten minutes now.'

'You stay where you are.' Then, relenting, Pat added, 'You can take me out to lunch later.'

With another apologetic movement of his head in Richard's direction, Harry slouched over to the table and began to study the lid of the box that held the jigsaw.

Pat drove Richard to a chair. 'Can we get on?'

'Get on? Before we get on anywhere, let me remind you that the last time we talked, you told me I ought to go further with my thing with Anna. So why, or what about, all the disapproval? – and don't try to tell me I'm imagining it.'

'Oh I see.' Pat was wearing a kind of updated forester's outfit, suitable for a hilarious television spoof of Robin Hood. 'I think you probably are imagining some of it. Not all of it, though. And perhaps you also remember telling me you were seriously worried about little Anna's poetry and how no-good you thought it was. So much so it amounted to some sort of obstacle, I don't know what or how or anything. But the stuff's got better

215

in the last few days, has it? Or don't you mind it so much? Or has the world just moved on since then?'

'I think perhaps I ought to – '

'I seem to remember something about truth as well. Anyway, of course you can do as you like with little Anna or anybody else, it's a free country, but you're supposed to let other people know when you propose vanishing off the face of the earth. Leave a message. Back Friday or whatever. Otherwise you *upset* people. All kinds of people.'

Richard had seen this point for himself and not liked the look of it, but was disconcerted at having it brought up now. And he had not bargained for having to face an extra morsel of horribleness, however well earned, before even getting in sight of the main one. 'Look, Pat,' he said, 'thank you for rallying round and all that, but why don't you get lost a bit? Cordelia exploits you in the most monstrous way all the time, I can't make out why you keep coming back for more, I know what you think of her, I've seen it in your face, everything, you think she's intolerable, you thought it would be *a bloody treat* if she got a spoke or two shoved in her wheel or her nose put out of joint, anything, yes you did, so why are you so not just cross when it happens but righteously indignant? Come off it, you can't be really annoyed at the way it was done, well yes you are a bit and fair enough, but what's got you fed up is that it was . . . actually . . . done. After she'd vanished without trace herself, really without trace, so that I couldn't have known or found out where she was or if she was alive or dead, but perhaps nobody's told you that, eh?'

Without uttering a sound, Harry had done an extensive and continuous job as chorus to this speech of Richard's, kicking off with invisible steam gushing from the top of his head to express the intensity of his agreement, moderating by degrees round about the righteously-indignant stage and winding up with small sedative motions as he foresaw the bad time he would have at lunch with his wife for being the same sex as the speaker of the last couple of sentences. He even frowned briefly at Richard but no longer as at a loony/chump.

Pat for her part seemed to have heard a little more than she had expected. 'Richard, I only meant . . . All I wanted to get across was that whatever you, whatever anybody thinks of Cordelia she really is in a state. Not putting it on. She – I don't know how much she behaves in a funny way on purpose, or how much you think she does, but not this time. Do you see? I'm afraid I haven't put it very well.'

There were one or two things Richard thought of saying, starting with their previous conversation about Anna's poetry, but all he did say was, 'No, I see.' He never even thought of saying that he had hoped to ask her advice some time about the very question of the importance of Anna's poetry, but saw now that that could not happen.

Upstairs, where he had been perfectly ready to believe Cordelia was to be found, Richard came across not only her, sitting on a monarchically designated chair in 'her' bedroom, the smaller one across the landing from the main one, and Godfrey, on his feet beside her like a husband in a nineteenth-century painting, but also another man, one he, Richard, had never seen before. The advent of this supernumerary man, who was so neutral in appearance as to be hard to distinguish except in outline, was almost too much for him. He could foresee wanting to surrender himself and all his goods unconditionally to anyone who would have him, them.

'Ah, there you are, Richard,' said Godfrey.

'That's right, Godfrey,' said Richard. 'Here I am.' He kept his eyes off the stranger in the far from confident hope that he might lose heart and go away if taken no notice of, and off Cordelia just to postpone that a little longer.

Godfrey watched through his glasses, his habitual wary look intensified. 'I don't think you've met Seymour Fairbrother,' he said.

Richard agreed he had not, nor was any guidance forthcoming about who or what Fairbrother was — medical, psychiatrical, legal, other — though something of all the first three seemed to radiate from him, plus disfavour, though that might have been circumstantial.

'Hallo, Richard,' said Cordelia. 'You've come up to see me.'

'Well, I just thought I'd . . .'

'I knew you would darling. I think I'll probably be able to manage all right, you see. Godfrey very sweetly came over as soon as I asked him, just dropped everything and came. It's always been on my mind how I let him down about the children. I've been afraid of a lot of things in my life but children was one

217

of the worst, having children. So small, but there, and going on being there and growing. I see now I shouldn't have let myself just not face it the way I did, not just straight away like that. The doctor said he'd make sure it would be all right and he was a very good man, everybody said. So was the other man I went to, terribly good, they all said. You didn't mind, anyway you didn't seem to, you didn't say you did. I told you, it can't be long ago, I remember telling you how I had to sort of make myself a new way of talking on purpose, oh, back when I was a girl. I think I must have spent too much time making it consistent, because that doesn't really matter does it? Anyway I've known for some time that I got it wrong. Now and then I seem to hear myself talking, just for a moment, and it sounds ridiculous, it sounds as if I can't mean a word I say. I see strangers looking at each other and grinning and rolling their eyes. But just because I sound ridiculous it doesn't mean I'm not taking in what's going on and I don't take things to heart or feel lonely and scared when my husband disappears or jealous and terrified of losing him, or feel like killing myself, although of course I'd never do anything like that in a thousand years. I sometimes think if I'd had the children I could have learnt to speak again with them. But I can't go back.'

Cordelia had kept her eyes fixed on Richard while she spoke. They were as blue and bright as ever, but now and then a tear oozed out of one or other of them and ran unchecked down her face. She was also dribbling slightly, though this she did limit with a rolled-up handkerchief. The general sickroom feel of things was intensified by the rough-textured white gown she wore, the loose sleeve of which showed a solitary bangle on her arm. Her hair was combed but not otherwise arranged.

After a silence Richard spoke a double truth. 'All I can say is I'm sorry.'

'If that's really and truly all you can say darling,' said Cordelia in a slightly stronger voice than before, 'then there doesn't seem to be much point . . .'

'For the time being.'

'. . . in my saying anything more myself. I didn't get a lot of sleep last night so I think I might as well get into bed for a little while. Godfrey, would you be a perfect angel and draw the curtain? There's a sort of thing at the side. No darling the other side.'

Richard stood there for a moment and then wandered out. Once clear of the bedroom he moved more purposefully along to Cordelia's study, but having arrived there he again turned irresolute. He heard somebody going briskly down the stairs. The various papers and pamphlets on the work-table were still as neatly squared up and clipped together as they had been two days before. He started to call Crispin's number but thought better of it. At the bottom of the house the front door shut. Then Godfrey showed himself.

'Oh, I was looking for a telephone.'

'There,' said Richard. 'That was absolutely terrible, wasn't it? I had no idea it was going to be as terrible as that. I quite see why you felt you had to get hold of me.'

'I realise I should have left the two of you alone together.'

'Thank God or whatever it was told you not to.'

'You expected her to be cross, I imagine.'

'I don't know what I expected. I suppose I thought she'd have found a way of dealing with the situation without going outside her character as I'd seen it before. But you probably think that's just bloody stupid and arrogant. I'm sorry.'

'It was more or less what I'd thought myself.'

Richard started trying to edge to the door of the study round an empty legless cabinet of uncertain provenance and a never-occupied padded chair. 'I'll get out and leave you to the phone. Sorry.'

'Don't be in too much of a hurry for me,' said Godfrey, not moving. 'I consider I owe you an apology of a sort. I got that Fairbrother chap along just to dilute the party. He's gone now.'

'Who was he? What is he?'

'He's a lighting layout man I was going over some sketches with when Cordelia rang earlier. I just told her his name, like you. Good, isn't he? Be interesting to know who she thought he was. Well, it might be. Look, Richard, without going into any rights and wrongs you and I have both been married to that poor creature oblique stroke unusual person back there. Where are you off to now? Do you want to make a call?'

'I was going to ring Crispin but then I thought I'd probably get – '

'No, Freddie's out. It's been arranged.'

'How do you know?'

'I'm on my way there now, it was fixed up.' Godfrey paused. 'Do you want to come along?'

'Oh God,' said Richard, and touched him on the sleeve for a second. 'I'd give anything to come along. But wait a minute, what about – '

'Sandy won't be there either. She's having lunch with the Master of Balliol.'

'You're not serious.'

'Perfectly, I assure you. She plays a wide field, as Crispin would say. Now I'll just give him a quick ring if that's all right, and then I want about twenty seconds' chitchat with a person described as an artist and we'll be off. See you downstairs.'

Downstairs in the hall Richard found the Dobbses on the point of leaving, or hoping to be honourably discharged. At least Pat might have been hoping, Harry just wanting his lunch.

'She's asleep now,' said Richard in what he hoped was a reassuring voice, and so Cordelia had been, or had seemed to be, when he looked in on her a moment before. 'We'll have a talk later.'

'Yes, good,' said Pat, then, hesitantly, 'You must admit she was upset.'

'Oh, no question about it. No question about it. Good job for all of us that chap Fairbrother was on the spot.'

'Yes indeed. Well, we'll be off now, Richard. Let me know if there's anything I can do.'

'Of course I will.' He narrowed his eyes to show how seriously he took this commission. 'Marvellous of you to come along. Both of you.'

As Richard stood on the step waiting to shut the door, Harry turned round and hurried the half-dozen paces back to him.

'Oh, tell me, what's the address,' he began, then as he moved out of Pat's hearing went on, 'of rhubarb rhubarb, never mind. Just wanted to say, she likes her, you see, if you can believe it.'

'At the moment I can believe anything.'

'Right, thanks very much,' said Harry loudly, turning away and waving his hand. 'Ring you in the morning,' he called.

In no time Godfrey had reappeared. 'Right,' he said. 'Shall we get a taxi?'

'We could go in my car.' Opening its door, Richard said, 'I suppose it is all right to leave Cordelia?'

Godfrey looked at his watch. 'If you think it would ease your mind to go up and sit with her, I'm sure you know that would be perfectly acceptable to me. No, I'm sorry, I think a taxi in case we want to talk. Thank you all the same.'

Richard had no desire for conversation, but it seemed that Godfrey had. For instance, they had not gone very far in their taxi when he said, 'I still feel slightly apologetic about that scene just now. There are times in one's life when the mere circumstances seem to make it positively incumbent upon one to take a certain line. It's, it's as if one's own inclination or experience doesn't enter into it.'

'I think I see.'

'In this case, now, there was no way I could have avoided taking a superior moral attitude towards you, like a reflex. When a predator sees a weaker animal in retreat it has no alternative but to set off in pursuit. Not a willed thing.'

'No.'

'I mean I don't *feel* the slightest moral superiority. After all I did leave Cordelia, walk right out on her. You haven't done that.'

'No, not so far.'

'And that makes certain moral assumptions at the start. You know, when she was going on about how pathetic she was and how frightful you'd made her feel and were still making her feel, it brought it all back, what it had been like being right in the middle of being married to her. Never knowing whether she meant a word she said and then gradually realising she doesn't know what meaning what you say means. Everything's just saying what you say. Now Nancy's quite different there. She knows about that. I wouldn't try to tell you she always means what she says, and certainly not that I can get her to admit she hasn't meant what she's said more than once in every few years, but . . . she knows. Whereas telling Cordelia about truth would be like trying to describe the colour red to a blind man. And a blind man who constantly asked you to blease zdob geebing on and on aboud zumthing thad zimbly zdared you in the vaze darling, too. I say, I believe there's a filthy demo going on up there.'

'What? A what?'

'A demo. A march. You know, placards and slogans. People

with a grievance. I seem to have missed all that. Missed out on it, as they say. And it's not at all that I've been short of grievances. Have you ever been to one, Richard? Or is it *on* one? A demo.'

'No, never.'

'There, you see. It happens to some people but not to others. Like finding God.'

After a few minutes, Richard said, 'I thought you were supposed to have left Cordelia because she couldn't have children or wouldn't or whatever it was.'

'There was a stage of some of that, before I got to know her properly or realised I was never going to or whatever it was. Then I sort of revived it when Nancy turned up. I must have thought it would go down better with the family. Just as well, the way things turned out, or failed to. Imagine being Cordelia's child, if you can. Oh no, I do believe it's that stinking demo again. How can it be?'

'It's still bloody awful, isn't it?' said Richard. 'Her.'

'As she is at the moment. Oh yes. Not too good the whole time, come to that.'

'It was absolutely terrible, her saying what she did.'

'Indeed it was.'

'Whether she meant what she was saying or not.'

'What actors say can move us to tears although we know perfectly well they don't mean a word they're saying or even understand most of it. Strange.'

'Not only that, Godfrey. What else could she say? She could have meant all those things just now without ever having meant anything like them in her life before. One just can't tell. Whatever she'd said she could have felt it. A lot of people would have felt a lot of what she did say. Even the worst and silliest and most affected and self-centred people in the world.'

'This is getting rather fine-spun, my dear fellow. My advice to you is to do your level best to treat Cordelia as you treat everybody else, on her merits. Who was that woman with the husband, what was her name again? Hobbs? Nobbs?'

'Dobbs. His is that too.'

'No doubt it is. I only saw him for an instant, but it was long enough for it to be made clear to him that I had formerly been married to Cordelia, and also long enough for him to betray his amazement that there should be two such men in the world, and if two, then why not more?' Godfrey snatched off his glasses and violently knuckled an eyeball. 'Her I placed immediately. The type I mean. An *acolyte* of Cordelia's. Or perhaps handmaid. She's always had the gift of attracting people like that to herself and getting them to do often quite troublesome things for her with no hope of any return. Once when we had our house in Iver we were giving a lunch-party, or rather she was giving one of her lunch-parties, and everything was done down to polishing the front-door knob by, oh, it must have been five or six at various times assorted females. Who were not only not invited to the party but *had never expected to be.* Think of it.'

What Richard was thinking was that nothing like that had happened around him since his marriage to Cordelia. He made no reply.

'Some of them were, well, sentient beings too. I've always wondered what the attraction can have been. Because what's there? A wilderness. A tundra.'

Godfrey paid the taxi-driver with effortless mastery and unhurriedly. Watching the operation, Richard marvelled at the way that, without any gross facial movement and of course any superfluous syllable, the man was able to register so plainly his complete contempt for Godfrey and everything he might have stood for. Maximal immobility, and jaws open but lips closed, did some of it. Richard was just coming to suspect it might be his imagination after all when he got a special two-second dose of it himself.

'Funny chap, that cabbie,' said Godfrey as he and Richard walked up to the Dom Radetsky. 'It's the house, I think. He doesn't like the idea of anybody at all going in there. Except . . .'

'If it had been her he'd have been out of his bloody cab and opening her door and helping her down and bowing and scraping and kissing her hand.'

'And quite likely refusing to take any money.'

'Right.'

Godfrey stopped just short of the house and the two looked at each other.

'What did you marry her for, Godfrey?'

'Oh dear. Well, she was quite pretty, and things like that. I expect you found the same, didn't you?'

'Yes, but there must have been other stuff we've forgotten. Surely.'

'No way of knowing, is there?'

SIXTEEN

'Cordelia's the sort of woman – '

'If you mention her again I'm leaving,' said Richard quite violently. 'Not another word on that subject while I'm here. And by the way she isn't a *sort* of woman.'

'And it's even doubtful if she's a sort of *woman*,' said Godfrey.

'Oh Christ,' said Crispin, looking from one to the other. 'I was only trying to be helpful, wasn't I? But you do realise she'd – I mean that extricating yourself from it all would be like, I don't bloody well know, like taking off Nessus' shirt, what?'

'Incorporating a jock-strap lined with super-glue,' said Godfrey.

'He was always the one for thinking up the clever extra bits,' said his brother.

'Actually, getting the thing off wasn't the problem,' said Richard. 'The poison in it started killing Hercules the moment he put it on.'

'You're not in that common-room of yours now, you know,' said Crispin.

'Common-room, what common-room? And if there were one you don't think they'd have heard of Hercules in it, do you, surely to God.'

'Interesting about that shirt,' said Godfrey. 'It's an even better image than I thought.'

'It was Hercules's own poison too.'

'Better still.'

'Let's have a drink,' said Crispin.

'Not for me.' Richard was firm. 'And . . . Look, it's marvellous being here, such a relief, but I've got to do some thinking some time. The common-room, it reminded me, I mean . . . Among other things. Is there somewhere I could be, somewhere here? By myself, where I won't be in the way?'

225

Crispin was apparently disconcerted. 'Well,' he said doubtfully, 'there's the *garden*, of course,' seeming to imply that somebody like Richard might feel more at home in such uncivilised surroundings. 'Nice day for it, too,' he added.

'Could I make a phone-call first?'

'Telephone in the hall, snack lunch in the kitchen at two, all right?'

Richard, who had remembered a minute before that he was supposed to have this academic job, called the only Institute number he had in his head, that of the archaic miniature switchboard on which the departmental secretary could usually be raised. This time there was an interval during which a rough brutish voice, recalling in its timbre that of the sweetmeat-scoffing portress, made obstructive noises. Then the recognisable tones of Mrs Pearson were to be heard, saying at first that he was lucky to have got her, she had only happened to pop in for a minute, the whole place was on strike, at least that was what it boiled down to though naturally it was called something else these days. She had done her best to let him know by telephone but had somehow failed to get in touch.

'Yes, er, I was called away. Erm, has Professor Hallett been in?'

That was the other piece of news Mrs Pearson had been hoping to pass on – Professor Hallett was a little bit tired and had been advised to take a few days' rest, so that thanks to nobody concerned this strike thing had come just at the right time in one way. No, it was nothing more than putting his feet up for the rest of the week. He would be as good as new by next Monday, when the sit-in or whatever it was would apparently be over. Richard was not sure that Mrs Pearson was telling all she knew, but she rather liked giving that impression and it would not have been like her to gloss over anything seriously wrong with Hallett. As he had hoped when he first heard her voice on the line, she then asked if there were any little jobs she could do for him round the Department, and he managed to find her a couple.

Except for an occasional uninspiring glimpse from a window, Richard had seen little of the land behind the Dom, though his slight acquaintance with rich bits of London was enough to have prepared him for a prospect of rolling parkland, if not of snow-

226

capped peaks in the distance. But no, as far as he could see it was all divided up into quite small patches by pieces of wall, hedgerows, a line of young trees, a suggestion of shrubbery. There was a corner with a wooden seat evidently meant to be sat on and what Richard guessed was a herb garden. He was able to guess it from the vegetable nature of the plants and their individual size, too puny for them to be worth the trouble of eating on their own. The plot looked well cared for. Who cared for it? He could not imagine Crispin even taking the trouble to get somebody else to take the trouble. Nor Freddie having anything whatever to do with it. A child, perhaps, the daughter of thirteen or fourteen, away at school but presumably back for half-terms, etc. He had met her, more than once he thought, but had no memory of her. Her name, whatever it was, seldom came up.

Children had not come into Richard's life much since he had stopped being one of them himself, what with their absence from his own domestic life and the fact that he practically never saw his sister's children because he practically never saw his sister, which in turn was because of what his brother-in-law felt about Cordelia and by association him. Richard's brother, an assistant bank manager in Yeovil, had three children, also rarely on view but in no way through Cordelia, just through whatever it was that had constructed the Vaisey boys for life on different planets. For instance, Robert Vaisey liked punk rock.

Lucky old Richard having no kids, said all the fathers and stepfathers and godfathers and uncles and other children-connected persons he met, and so he himself devoutly thought on every apposite occasion. Nevertheless when off guard, as now, he found that the most oblique reminder of his childlessness was likely to throw in his face what seemed to him the appalling underpopulation of his life. He had had round him, had known, had met as many people as most people, but he had let them all go away and they had not tried to come back. These days he saw almost nobody he ever thought about when they were not there. He brought out his engagement diary. Work arrangements, a couple of tennis dates, lunch with who, oh yes – a man wanting to talk about Blok, car in for tracking but that was yesterday now, a dinner-party next week at the Dennises', at the whos', oh God – friends of . . . He could remember with hallucinatory vividness writing the two or three necessary words down against the date in question and having the Dennises as a man and a woman, as anything more than the half-dozen letters of a name, nowhere whatever in his mind. A small part of that mind had been occupied at the time by the hope that the tiny painful red patch under his right nostril was not going to come up into a major spot, and the other three-quarters or so by the uniform dark-grey mist that normally shrouded it outside working hours.

But of course there was now one person in his life who was a person even to him, who without having to be there could cause that mist to dissolve in an instant. It needed no exercise of the will, no mental knack to have her entirely in mind, prominent cheekbones but not unusually high ones with little concavities under the temples and a slight flush, a faint intake of breath before she spoke, gorgeous upper arms and rather schoolgirlish ones between elbow and wrist, a smile that came on at various speeds, a very clear soprano-register voice, total absorption in him whenever they were talking together, and most likely in anyone else she might happen to be chatting to, only so far he had been too closely taken up with how she looked and sounded meanwhile to have paid much attention to that. Greedy, lazy, stick-in-the-mud, dull, incurious, bet-hedging as he was, and more and worse too, he determined now to catch and hold on to Anna, and estimated that that might very well be induced to come about if a small distant cloud stayed distant or came no nearer. But oh God, how different things might have been if it had never been there.

So far so not so bad, but so far was not all that far, and no way at all into the bloody old real world. He got up and chafed his buttock. Well, nobody had forced him to sit there. Chives, now – yes, those undernourished-looking spring-onion things were almost certainly chives. A great yawn made his ears click and his mouth spray saliva. His thoughts of a moment before made him wish there had been a flower of almost any sort to be seen, but there was none, not even a weed.

Snack lunch in the kitchen at the Dom meant nothing very pinched in a place large enough for the roasting and serving of a fully grown bison and opening into a not much smaller room that held a table big enough for a dozen or more to have sat

228

down, beyond which there might well have lain a third eating-chamber reserved for the clients of servants' dependants. It was true that Crispin seemed to have dressed down slightly for the meal by getting into one of the shabbier of his belted Scottish tweed jackets, and for a moment he stared at the label of the Hermitage '87 they were to drink with their prime Aberdeen Angus sandwiches as if he rather wished he had brought up instead some Finest French Red Table Wine, say, should he possess such a thing. But apparently, even after all these years, his family had still not learnt to grind small groups of guests trapped in seclusion by feeding them half-sardines. Or perhaps he was just too greedy himself.

The three sat down to eat in an austere, metallic corner full of contrivances like part of an avant-garde warship. Godfrey, still wearing the whole of his elegant greeny-grey suit, took the stool opposite Richard's and said encouragingly, 'You look as if you've had your think. And reached some conclusions?'

'Yes. I'll be leaving . . . you-know-who as soon as reasonably possible.'

The brothers looked at him in varied but obvious disapproval, even consternation. Crispin stopped chewing his sandwich. Godfrey adjusted his glasses for a closer survey.

Richard said a little irritably, 'What's the matter with you two all of a sudden? Half an hour ago neither of you could stand her. You thought she was a monster. Neither of you had the slightest – '

'Oh, she's a *monster* all right,' said Godfrey. 'But lots of people marry monsters, and stay married to them for various reasons. Not only men do that, either, as perhaps you've noticed yourself. But that's by the way.'

'You didn't stay married to your monster. Our monster.'

'No indeed, I walked out on her as I've always said. But I didn't do it until Nancy was in place, very firmly in place, and not only that, until I was as sure as I could be that as far as I was concerned she was better in every way than I'd ever imagined the, the first one was even at the beginning.'

'In other words until you were sure of a much better life for yourself.'

'Yes. But again not only that. Until I was as satisfied as I was ever going to be that I had a substantial right to bring about the tremendous emotional upheaval of breaking up my marriage by walking out on my wife. And until I had someone else's interests it was my duty to consider. Someone as important as Nancy.'

'I don't understand,' said Richard. 'What difference could that make, any of it? The wife you were walking out on was incapable of telling the truth about anything or ever behaving honestly. You said so yourself. So what's all this about a tremendous emotional upheaval? Just her doing her stuff, saying things and acting accordingly.'

'That's not how you were talking earlier. You thought she might have meant what she said in the bedroom. The second time round. Just as she might really have felt what she said she felt at the upheaval. The first time round. You thought it was all absolutely terrible. And so it was when I told her. So you need the thought of a proper right. Not much good at the time. Rage and hate and fear get you through at the time. But they don't last for ever. Nothing can. Except remorse. Just now and then.'

Godfrey had spoken fast but steadily for the past half-minute or so. As soon as he had stopped he put his hand over his mouth and pressed hard, so hard the fingers seemed to shake a little.

'I'm sorry,' said Richard.

'Have a drink,' said Crispin. He was going to say more to his brother but did not.

'It's all right, I've got one. Just to finish this, Richard – the stuff about right and responsibility doesn't really come in till later but it's important then. Nothing to do with morality, just prudence. Did you get on to any of it while you were having your think?'

'No, that was all selfish.'

'Don't say that, no point in saying that. Just not sufficiently selfish. Now perhaps we might change the subject.'

'By way of a small further piece of intelligent selfishness,' said Crispin, pouring wine. 'It's very important, dear boy, that you should make a real effort to visualise what life will be like, what your life will be like, in the absence of quite a lot of things.' With what Richard thought or at least hoped was unintended histrionic effect, Crispin took an appreciative swallow of Hermitage, by way of illustrating the quite a lot of things that were going to be absent, and pushed a piece of crust round his almost-clean plate, symbolising what life would be like in that absence. 'But I honestly doubt whether you'll have managed even to – '

'I think I'm as fully prepared as I can be to meet all sorts of horrible things I'm completely unprepared for,' said Richard.

Crispin glared at him in a rather frightening way. 'If that's the level of responsibility you're going to approach this subject on, you'd better piss off home right away and do your best to apologise your way back in. You bloody fool. The results of cutting your standard of living to the degree you're facing, or rather seem to be refusing to face, would be just as painful as any of your emotional and sexual and personal . . . shambles. And just as serious. And it's not funny or cynical or materialistic or bourgeois or Czech or typical or anything else of me to think so and go on about it. You'd need everything you've got to survive and I very much doubt if you've got what it would take. You're too old and you haven't done enough and you've spent too long not having to think about it, right, and you're not practical enough and you're not imaginative enough either. To deal with it. You English twit. Unless you're hoping I'll . . . No. Sorry. This is just as upsetting a subject as the other, you know, though nobody's supposed to think so. Anyway, Richard. All well meant. Please take it to heart.'

'Now of course if only old Crispers were a woman,' said Godfrey musingly but also without delay, 'he'd have been able to get up and run out of the room towards the end of that little harangue, say round about, what was it, you English twit. But since he's not, he sort of can't. Now I suppose we can change the subject, assuming you haven't had second thoughts in the last ten minutes. Anna, isn't it? Very good, you like Anna enough to intend to go off with her permanently and that's an end of the matter. I thought she was rather fine myself in the small glimpse I had of her, genuine too, but that's neither here nor there. Neither is what anybody else thought or thinks of her here or there. Is it, Crispin?'

There was no direct reply. Crispin was just bringing an enamel dish and a wine-bottle from one of the comparatively small refrigerators. 'I thought they'd leave us something. Bread-and-butter pudding. Savour it, Richard. Château Climens to wash it down.'

'I'd better not have any of that,' said Richard.

'Don't be an ass, dear boy. Drink it while it's there.'

'All right. I mean thank you. Half a glass.'

'Ippolitov,' said Crispin. 'There is indeed a Russian policeman of that name on a visit to London at the moment. Is this the man you saw?'

It made Richard feel quite important and rather unreal and also a bit of a prat to be passed the underexposed photograph of a younger, beardless but unmistakable version of his drinking-companion at the Cedar Court Hotel. 'That's him,' he could think of no way of not eventually saying.

'Though we're as far as ever from knowing how true or significant his story about the brother may be. And will remain so. You are going to tell me about Kotolynov.'

'My God, so I was,' said Richard. As he went on he thought he saw that while Godfrey had known nothing of Ippolitov, something of Kotolynov had reached him. 'He was fine. Completely Americanised. On the surface. He now writes – '

'Did you sign him up?'

'No. He thought art should be kept absolutely separate from politics. Which in his case is very understandable.'

'And in lots of other cases besides, I hope,' put in Godfrey.

'He's an artist too, you see,' said Crispin. 'Had Kotolynov heard of little Miss Tchaikovsky?'

'Oh yes, very much so.'

'Knew her work?'

'Enough.'

Before Crispin could ask if Kotolynov had given any opinion of that work, an intermittent humming noise began and a soft purple light pulsated in time with it. These proved to signal not a missile homing on the kitchen but a telephone call, one Crispin had been keenly awaiting to judge by his speed out of the room en route for his lead-lined command bunker.

After a moment Richard looked at Godfrey and said, 'Has he told you what he thinks of Anna? As, well, as somebody for somebody like me to go off with.'

'That's rather a lot of questions wrapped up in one, don't you think? Altogether, anyway, he doesn't much care for her because she's a Russian and the Russians have been bashing the Czechs about for forty years just in the first place, and he sympathises with her and wants to help her because she's a Russian and the Russians have been bashed about by their disgusting govern-ment for seventy years, and he thinks she's lower-class and he

232

also quite fancies her which is partly tied up with thinking she's lower-class.'

'How do you make that out, those last two?'

'It's like that because he's English.'

'Oh Godfrey, give it a rest, can't you?'

'I'm perfectly serious, I mean what I'm saying, I mean. Don't forget there's never been a time when I haven't been his brother. He doesn't only think he's an English aristocrat, he thinks he's the sort of English aristocrat you read about and didn't particularly exist in the nineteenth century. Well, he does a bit, you know. And you mustn't mind my answering your original question after saying that, but he seems to think that if you went off with anybody then Anna's quite a suitable person for somebody like you to go off with. Have some coffee.'

Godfrey was just producing coffee when Crispin reappeared as blithely as he had left. 'Well, that is satisfactory,' he said. 'Most satisfactory. Anybody care for some brandy? No, I agree, it is a bit of a killer in the middle of the day. Thanks, I'd love some – just half a cup.'

'Let me guess,' said Richard, who was relieved to find that the bad part seemed to be over and to hear that, for whatever reason, Crispin thought there was something to be said for Anna. 'Prince Charles has agreed to be signed up.'

'Indeed he has, and for many a good cause too, but I don't instantly see – '

'Our petition. For little Miss Tchaikovsky.'

'Alas, I'm sure HRH would deem it constitutionally inadmissible to lend his name to anything of that sort. No, I'm afraid I was exulting over a more selfish concern – my efforts among others' have successfully forwarded some sort of *scheme* down in London's dockland. A technical triumph on my part, largely. Not wholly, of course. The bad news is that I shall have to leave quite shortly. But before I do I'd like just to bring you up to date with petitional developments, which I'd soonest do in the, the something-else room . . . I'm sorry, Godfrey.'

'De nada, I too must take myself off in a few minutes. I'll finish my coffee and let myself out.'

All stood. Richard said to Godfrey, 'Well, it was quite a morning.'

'As you say. I don't think either of us has anything to apologise to the other for, do you? Not now.'

'No, I don't. In fact I want to say thank you.'

'That's handsome of you. Don't you think so, Crispin?'

'Not *wholly* uncharacteristic.'

The brothers continued side by side for a moment, looking at Richard. Then they embraced, briefly but warmly, something he had not seen them do before.

'He's a Czech, you see,' said Crispin.

Richard was almost sure he had been in the something-else room before, no more than almost because of Freddie's habit of starting to change one sort of room into another sort and then stopping or changing back. Wallpapers and such came and went with similar but separate irregularity. Whatever its momentary status the room Crispin took him to, though not large by most standards, had a desk in it and one or two upright chairs. At a second try Crispin found some papers in a drawer and spread them out on the desk.

'It's all there,' he said. 'These are the people and the things we've got, and these are the – '

'Sorry, Crispin, what are the things?'

'What? The, the, institutions, the bodies with nobody in particular at the head. Do try not to interrupt, dear boy, I haven't got too long. The committees. You know. Anyway they're there, and these are the ones who've said they can't or won't, and these are the ones we haven't managed to get hold of yet, rather a lot of them, yes, but I think we've done brilliantly in the time. Now you take these off and go through them, and then you've met Quentin Cohen in my office, haven't you? First-class chap, works twenty hours a day, I've put him in charge of the purely mechanical side now we've got the list together. So. Oh, while you're on the spot there is just one small but not unimportant thing you can do.'

Richard felt a twinge of uneasiness. He had recently heard a similar phrase used in troublesome circumstances, but nodded his head to indicate receptivity.

'Here' – Crispin pulled out of a squareish envelope a sheet of heavy paper with a ruled red-and-blue border, an elaborate heading, some lines of outsize typescript and a short column of assorted handwritings with lesser typescript accretions – 'here is the hallowed text in penultimate form, substantially as you saw it before, with some carefully selected signatures, more to come, space for yours at the top, if you'll just slap it down I can fax the whole thing along to Quentin and he can get on with getting it out.'

'Out? Out where?'

'Just the Press. Sort of progress report. Not the final clarion call.'

'A poet of major achievement and international importance,' Richard read out. 'I couldn't commit the Institute to that.'

'Really? Anyway, you won't be. See page 2.'

'Have I got to sign it now?'

'Why not?' Crispin half closed his eyes and for a moment looked all Slav, parched by the winds of eastern Europe, barely down from the Carpathians. 'Come off it, Richard. Come clean, dear boy.' He was the English gent again now. 'It's not the Institute you don't want to commit, it's you. Oh, the lady may be a poet of international importance, whatever that is, and no harm done. But major achievement, oh dear. Still, we had to say something like that. But you don't think what she writes is any good, do you?'

'No.'

'Russian policemen have their uses after all. You know I got a horrible feeling about this the very first time you told me about her at Rocky's. I asked you casually if her stuff was any good and you told me it wasn't your cup of tea but she was jolly highly thought of. Oh dear. Every time any other writer's come up you've made a point of saying straight out anything from bloody good to absolute piss, or, you hadn't read it, hadn't seen it on the page so couldn't judge it. Well, I thought it might be a case of that this time, only you were too shy to say so. Yeah. So I let it go, because I liked the petition, which didn't require merit in its subject, and it wasn't until Inspector Ippolitov turned up and explained to you she was part of a criminal conspiracy and you hoped he was right that I was sure something was badly wrong. It was obviously nothing at all to do with the lady as a lady, so what could it be? It didn't click absolutely until just now, when the witness showed unmistakable signs of embarrassment and discomfort. You were terrified of being asked what Kotolynov thought of her poetry. Because . . . Go on, Richard.'

235

'Because he thinks it's shit.'

'Your last hope destroyed.'

'I thought you were supposed to be in a hurry,' said Richard.

'I've made time for this, and we're nearly finished anyway. Now. You can sign that petition, top or bottom makes no real odds, and sacrifice your integrity, eh? You can not sign it, and the Press will want to know why not, and unless you lie convincingly to them, and almost certainly even if you do try to lie to them, the truth will emerge and the petition will be weakened and endangered. It might still succeed without you, just as it might very well fail with you, but what do you say to poor little Anna? The third possibility is a diplomatic illness, and I can fix you up with a real cracker,' – Crispin gave his first smile for some time – 'and that'll keep anybody from publishing anything but not from saying anything, and you'd still be stuck with your young friend. That's it, unless you can suggest another approach.'

'It's still got to be now, has it?'

'There are these names Quentin will go on trying to reach. You have six days yet, but nothing will change in that time. Well, I must go and put on some clothes. Good luck, Richard.' No smile now. 'Keep in touch.'

As he took his time peeing in the hall cloakroom, Richard did his best to shake off a feeling of petty exasperation at having been singled out by fate so unerringly. There were doubtless others in the kingdom who held that their view of artistic merit was in no conceivable circumstances to be lied about or made to take second place to anything or paltered with, but any such persons had taken good care not to put themselves in his position. The necessary brief handling of his penis in stuffing it back into his clothing reminded him, in a sort of theoretical way, of what he would merrily have been up to with Anna in no time if things had been just that much different. He stood stock-still with his hand on the cistern lever. Only one man had been entirely safe from Richard Vaisey's present predicament since the Creation, since very soon after that event, in fact. Adam in his unfallen days would not have given a fuck if Eve had written the lousiest poetry ever, with his ability to get the horn at will. But even that happy state had ended as soon as God noticed the grave threat to the survival of mankind posed by lack of food and rest, not to speak of more specialised complaints.

That was enough thinking to last him for a bit. He had got as far towards leaving the house as a yard short of the front door when a little flurry of feminine voices from its far side, accompanied by the sound of a key in its lock, sent him haring back whence he had come. Secure again in the cloakroom, he realised there was nowhere he much wanted to go at the moment, and that even if there had been he had no immediate way of getting himself there. He should have asked Crispin for a few hours' loan of some disused gunroom or deconsecrated chapel in one of the more distant parts of the house. Too late for that now and, with Freddie and possibly Sandy and what had sounded like three or four equally chatty chums now passed out of earshot, go he must.

He taxied home and there was his car where he had left it. Head down, keeping his back to the house, moving like a man in a film sequence about a military or criminal night-operation, he got inaudibly into the driving-seat and, right foot to the ground, managed most creditably to propel self and TBD a good halfway to the road before starting up. He drove south for some minutes hoping for inspiration about where to go. Nothing on that scale came along, but one thing or another must have been propelling him towards the place where he might have hoped to find Anna, because it was into that long gloomy terraced street that he eventually turned the car. Then at once he saw Anna herself in a mackintosh walking towards him on the opposite pavement, dark, beautiful, contented and inspiring fear. He hooted, but other hoots were also to be heard, waved, but too late, could not stop, had to drive eighty slow metres before he could stop, back, turn, go after her, and by then she was nowhere to be seen. He found a vacant stretch of gutter, halted the car, lowered his face and closed his eyes.

Immediately, it seemed, sharp knuckles rapped on the window. The face of an elderly man peered in.

'You all right, mate?' asked an appropriate voice when the window was lowered, concerned and yet with a touch of officiousness.

Richard started to draw in his breath for what by now would have been an almost involuntary burst of Russian vituperation, complete with hostile emergence from car and pursuit if appropriate. Then he relaxed and said, 'Yes thanks, I'm fine.'

'You're sure now, mind? You don't look too good, you know.'

Nor did the man standing on the pavement, not even to the quickest glance, the skin of his face with a thinner appearance than Richard could remember ever having come across before and a papery quality, his eyes seeming to lack normal moisture. 'It's all right,' said Richard. 'Thank you very much.'

'Because . . .'

No more was said. Richard shut his window and drove off without delay, knowing now where he must go.

SEVENTEEN

Richard's route took him more or less diagonally across central London in a direction more or less unfamiliar to him. In an attempt to avoid traffic, he was coming up a by-way near Trafalgar Square when he soon ran into more traffic that brought him to a dead halt for a couple of minutes just outside the entrance of a large building of Victorian date. A small party came laboriously through the swing doors and down the front steps of this place, consisting of a young porter and a not-so-young porter, each in dark-blue livery, and an old man in a grey suit they were supporting. The old man was weeping copiously, the tears running down his face. As Richard unwillingly watched, the three halted on the pavement and the junior porter stayed by the old man while the other looked for a taxi. His eye caught Richard's and turned unfriendly for a moment before passing on. Then the line of vehicles began to move and the group were no longer in sight.

Not long afterwards, Richard was walking from his parked car along a side-street near Russell Square. Soon he turned in at a small gateway and mounted a flight of steps much narrower than the one he had last noticed. At the top he pressed a button in the wall and waited while an amplified scratching sound was heard, followed by a bodiless voice that, if human, was probably female. When he had said who he was a prolonged snarling buzz came from the door and he entered.

At the top of a great many stairs, there stood waiting for Richard a man he had never seen before, the fourth or possibly the fifth man so describable he had confronted in the past twenty-four hours. Something awful happened to various parts of his mind in the second or so it took him to realise that actually he had seen this chap before, and that he was Tristram Hallett without his beard.

239

After involuntarily informing Hallett of this change in his appearance, but saying nothing of the fact that he looked rather ill, Richard said, 'How are you, Tristram? Mrs Pearson said something about – '

'Apparently it's called a heart *episode*,' said Hallett. 'Nothing so two-a-penny as an attack. I didn't know I'd had it till they told me.'

He led the way into a smallish and far from underfurnished sitting-room where a woman of about his age and general size and shape sprang up and hurried to embrace Richard. This was Tania Hallett, who, despite her first name and a fondness for colourful sashes and for headscarves, had never pretended to be anything more Russian than the wife of a professor of Russian. Even so she was apt to wear what might have been one or another set of alleged pre-Christian Rus earrings at any hour, though she was not doing so this afternoon, and that was as far as she went.

'So sweet of you to come over, Richard.'

'I was just passing.'

'I should perhaps tell you,' said Hallett, 'that any notion of a few days' rest and suchlike is rather telephone talk. I shan't be going back to the fount of enlightenment in Caret Street. Or perhaps you'd already surmised as much.'

'No I hadn't, and I'm sorry to hear it now, and a lot of other people will be too.' Richard kept quiet about the more selfish things he had felt on hearing this news, including a foretaste of loneliness and some concern at the loss of an ally and disquiet about the future.

'Mind you, I think these doctors tell you to stop doing everything in case you fall down dead of an ingrowing toenail next week and somebody asks them if they remembered to tell you to stop doing everything. Not that I intend to stop doing *everything*, I'll have you know. I intend to re-read certain Russian classics at my leisure and record such observations as occur to me. In fact I reckon I'm lucky to have got out of that place down the road while the knives were still in their sheaths. As to my successor . . .' If Hallett knew anything for sure about this question he left it unstated. 'You and I, Richard, have certain administrative matters to go over together, but for the love of God don't let's even discuss when we might discuss them, even now.'

'I expect you'd like a cup of tea, wouldn't you, Richard?' asked Tania Hallett. 'We usually have one round about this time.'

Richard said he thought that was a fine idea and Tania left him and Hallett alone together.

'About my little trouble, it's no use you or me saying anything. You'd tell me I look fine, and I'd tell you that according to the doc there's no reason why given reasonable care I shouldn't live for another, er, well, as many years as I fancy. When the chance comes, you put it over to her as convincingly as you know how that you thought I seemed in very good spirits, just that. Don't go on. The trouble is, the more attached you are to each other, the harder it gets to tell the truth. Starting with what the doctors really said and continuing with everything else of importance. Sorry to have gone on like that. You spread it around, if you would, that we won't have to move and we're all right for money. Well now, I don't think you and I have seen each other to speak to since the evening young Anna Danilova recited her poems at the Institute. A remarkable evening, in several ways. The two of us agreed it was a success.'

'Yes. There were good reports of it later.'

'Considered as a step in the mildly bizarre campaign Miss Danilova is evidently waging against the Soviet government.'

'Well . . . yes.'

'A campaign in which you yourself are taking a prominent part. In fact I gathered from your charming friend Crispin Radetsky that it's a *leading* part. In among others the literal sense that your name's destined to head the list of signatories to the proposed, er, petition.' Hallett smiled and looked sad for a moment. 'Congratulations, Richard. I didn't know you carried quite such weight with these people.'

'Thank you, if it's a matter for congratulation. And if it's true.'

'Oh, I'm sure. Now. To go back to the evening in question. You were upset or in a state about something – which we won't go into, but it wasn't that you were staggered by the high quality of the poetry you'd just heard, was it? No, of course it wasn't. After all these years you don't need to say a word to let me know how you feel about a thing like that. You thought they were bad, didn't you?'

'Yes, and so did you, and I could tell before you'd said anything.'

241

'Yes. Now, Richard, you must forgive me for going fast over the next point, perhaps for going over it at all, but there is something I want to say after it, and, well, you and she are having an affair, aren't you?'

'Yes, Tristram. What a lot I seem to be giving away with my mouth shut.'

'Oh, I didn't get it from you, I got it from her, at that dinner. Every time she opened her mouth except to eat or drink, which latter was parenthetically quite often, it was to ask me a question about you, and not the sort of question a hostile or random inquirer would ask, either. She can't have had many chances of talking to someone who knows you and speaks Russian. Now before you allow yourself to become altogether overwhelmed in fatuous complacency, let me remind you or even perhaps point out to you the seriousness of the position you've landed yourself in through the unhappy confluence of three things. Namely your attachment to Anna, your part in her campaign and your view of her work – unless perhaps you think some parts of that work are all right? No, of course you don't – nobody could be that bad some of the time and not too bad some of the rest of the time.'

Hallett raised a hand to smooth his hair across his forehead, but found that his post-academic self had combed all there was of it up and back, and he desisted. To Richard's eyes he was still not very recognisable without his beard. Now out of an inner pocket he took some folded sheets of paper, typewritten with manuscript additions. He gave an apologetic glance and went on,

'I've had a couple of days to do some thinking about this problem, which has some general applications.' As anybody who had known him professionally for more than a short time would have found quite unsurprising, he began without more ado to read from his papers. 'The eclipse of merit. Beginnings. The role of modernism in the rendering irrelevant and passé of artistic merit and questions of merit. As soon as originality became important, the days of artistic merit or excellence were numbered. The question *Is it any good?* had always been hard to discuss, and only to be settled after a lapse of time and by the judgement of the wider public. This irritated intellectuals, who found it easier and more agreeable to ask *Is it new?*, together with *What does it mean?* and *Is it art?*, questions easy to discuss and never to be settled. Examples from: music, visual arts, verse, minority performing arts, minority prose writing such as to exclude the wider public. There have been more recent encroachments from political or quasi-political art, such that it is agreed to be irrelevant or unseemly or even actually dangerous to ask *Is it any good?*. Example,' and at this point Hallett refrained from doing what he might well have done and change his style of delivery, however briefly, 'the poems of Anna Danilova, which although not or not systematically political in themselves are to be used for a political purpose, and the question of their merit is irrelevant and to raise that question unseemly among other things. To further their use for this purpose is to participate in, and to spread further, the attack on artistic merit.'

'Half a minute,' said Richard when Hallett paused. 'You and I saw Anna's stuff was no good the moment we set eyes on it. Or ears. Artistic merit's safe enough as long as there are people like you and me around. Oh my God.'

'Exactly. I've retired and you've capitulated.'

'I haven't capitulated. I'll be back.'

Hallett compared his watch with the vaguely Slavophile clock on the mantelpiece.

'If you're right,' said Richard, 'it's a hopeless struggle anyway.'

'What of that?'

'Do you imagine I haven't been over this a thousand times already?'

'Of course not. I want you to go over it a thousand and first time and realise what it is you propose to do. I also don't imagine there are no other considerations.'

Getting up from his chair, Hallett rested his hand on Richard's shoulder for a moment and moved with rather short steps to the door. Here he put out his head and asked what about that tea, which arrived in ten seconds and all complete. The three of them talked for some minutes of the Institute and of other, forthcoming matters. Quite soon, bearing various messages and commissions and promising to keep in touch, Richard left. Not to his surprise, Tania Hallett caught him up at the foot of the stairs.

'What did you think of what he had to show you?'

'What? Sorry.'

243

'He said he wanted your opinion on something he was writing.'

'Oh. Well, I thought it was very good, very well argued. And true, too.'

'What did you think of him?'

'I thought he seemed in very good spirits.'

'Thank you, Richard. Thank you for coming.'

'If there's anything I can do, even if it's – '

'There is something you can do, a couple of things. Keep ringing him up and coming to see him and talking to him and telling him about the Institute, and write to him, drop him a line even if it's only to send on a circular, and keep on doing it. I must go, I told him you'd left something behind, he didn't ask what. Now please don't say anything to me, don't say anything at all, and thank you for coming, and come again as soon as you can, and ring up.'

Tania shut the front door quickly after Richard. He stood for a few minutes in the little porch at the top of the rather steep flight of steps that led up to the entrance of the flats. A light rain had started to fall, and some of its drops were running more slowly down the thick leaves of three or four evergreen bushes that someone had planted and presumably took care of in the garden. Richard had misled Tania, or had tried to, about his impression of her husband, who he thought had been looking very frail, more so on subsequent inspection than at first sight, so much so that he had had trouble keeping his attention on what he had read to him from his papers. But then he, Richard, would have acknowledged that he had had limited experience of these matters. His parents and others of their generation had gone from being poorly to gradually getting worse till after some time they had had to go to bed and die there.

The rain had grown less. Richard forgot about it after walking a few yards and slowed down, then noticed it again and speeded up. He took his car and drove home, arriving there at twenty minutes past five. As he always did he went first to his study, where a note awaited him on his typewriter, the envelope addressed to '*Richard*' in Cordelia's elegant, barely readable writing. The sheet inside told him without preamble that she was staying in her room and would go on staying there until further notice and was not to be communicated with in any way. Well, he thought at once, that would simplify his life a little longer. At a second glance, he saw that what he had taken for a cabalistic sign at the foot of the recto was actually a form of PTO, or pTo. He turned it over and managed to read,

> which will be jolly conveniant for you but do'nt imagine your going to get away with it forever,

a notification that might have chastened him more if he had had more room for chastening left in him just then. He sat at his desk and read several times the Cyrillic titles of some of the nearer books on his shelves. Now was the time for the telephone to ring and a rather rough voice to tell him to drop all that Russian crap and see he was in the Viscount Rhondda by six o'clock. But unfortunately there was no such person known to him, not that for the moment he could remember one from the past either.

Richard waited. Nothing happened, nothing seemed to be happening anywhere. Even the street outside was quiet. To have something to do he looked through his book and called a number. An American woman's voice answered.

'May I speak to Mr Andrei Kotolynov?'

'I don't believe I know the name. Who is this, please?'

Saying who he was did nothing for Richard, and he was about to hang up when he thought to ask, 'Is Andy Cottle there?'

The distant voice, which had turned cold, warmed up again. 'Well, he often is, Andy Cottle, but not right now. Not for another two days. Do you want to leave a message?'

'It doesn't matter, thanks,' and again Richard nearly hung up.

'If it's urgent he's in London. At least he should have gotten there by now.'

He had. In no time those ridiculously authentic, even slightly underplayed American tones were ringing out on the line from quite a posh hotel in Piccadilly. Until he heard them, it had not quite dawned on Richard how dashed he had been just now on finding their user apparently beyond his reach. He announced his name.

'Good to hear you, Richard. What can I do for you?'

'I ... I'd like you to confirm something you said that day I came to see you.'

'Oh yeah. How's that nice little Russki poetry chick you brought with you?'

'Oh, she's fine, thanks. Now soon after we'd arrived you told me – '

'Is this about her?'

'Yes.'

'Ah. I'm sorry, but I make it a rule never to discuss questions involving ladies over the telephone. If you want to talk about her you'll have to come around here.'

'But it's only a matter of – '

'I'm sorry.'

To Richard's conscious relief he had no trouble in identifying as Kotolynov, or Cottle, the man who opened the hotel-room door. Once more he was not fully prepared for the satisfaction he felt at setting eyes on the man. Whatever it was he wanted from him, he did seem to want it rather badly.

'Just before we start – does your wife really think you're called Andy Cottle?'

'No, that's just for unknowns on the telephone or wherever. Also before we start, I thought you'd prefer to talk up here, which is the only reason we're not in the bar and doesn't interfere with us drinking.' Kotolynov gestured to a nearby bottle and accessories. 'You like Black Jack, don't you?'

'I don't want one now, thank you.'

'Horseshit, you've never wanted one more in your life. Don't get worried, I have to go out in half an hour. For Christ's sake sit down, Richard.'

Richard sat, on a chair and among a style of decoration that recalled one or another Empire. It would certainly have interested Cordelia, or she would have had something to say about it. When the glass of whiskey came he accepted it without demur.

'So you just refused to support little Anna's petition to the KGB and she won't have anything more to do with you,' said Kotolynov, 'but where do I come in? It won't help if I go and tell her you were right.'

'It's me I want you to tell. But before we get there – we're well on our way, of course, only we haven't quite reached that point yet. There are a couple of things in between.' He touched on a couple of the things, including what Hallett had said to him an hour before, notably his prepared statement, which proved to have been memorable enough despite any distraction. 'So it seems I have a strong duty not to sign this bloody document.'

'It does. It most certainly does that.'

'So I have your unequivocal support there.'

'You always had it. But on different grounds, political grounds or rather anti-political grounds. My support for your duty doesn't really – '

'But you said you thought her poetry stinks.'

'I did and do. But as far as my argument's concerned that's incidental. In a sense it weakens it. In a sense it doesn't matter what anybody does with total dreck.'

'But it is that?'

'What? Richard? You know it's total dreck.'

'I want to hear a Russian say so.'

'This is an American sitting here, but we won't insist on that. All right. Anna Danilova's poetry is junk, it's trash, it's all the bad names you want. No virtues, not even accidental ones. Wait a minute, that's not strictly true. It does have one such virtue your professor missed, can you guess what it is, of course not, well, most of her contemporaries write in such a way that makes it as hard as possible to judge their merit, she doesn't, she does nothing to hinder you from answering the question *Is it any good?* with a flat and unhesitating *No*. But don't let that bother you. More Jack? No, okay. Oh, now, one thing you might care to hear from an ex-Russian, the stuff is insensitive to idiom, to the natural run of words and phrases, it doesn't use the language and its qualities in the intimate loving way good poets always do even when they're writing way below their best. But I'm sure you knew that already.'

'I still wanted to hear a Russian say it. Thanks.'

'Is that all you wanted from me? For me to say something like that?'

Richard left this question unanswered. If he had been a different type of man he might have sprung up from his chair and done something mildly stagy, like crossing to the window and looking 'unseeingly' in the direction of Green Park. But he sat squarely on, hands clasping knees, eyes still not all that seeing in the way they gazed towards the empty glass in front of him. Finally he said, 'Do you think . . . would you say her poetry's morally bad?'

'*Morally* bad? How in hell could it be *morally* bad? Well, in a way I suppose you could call it fraud, but I never heard any of the clientele objected.'

At that Richard grinned briefly, so as to establish he knew a joke of sorts was being made. 'What I meant . . . do you think . . . what she writes shows a female full of conceit and vanity and affectation, not interested in other people, just putting on a sort of act, showing how different she is from everybody else, how extraordinary, how . . .'

'Hey Richard. Dear boy. Hold it now. Pull yourself together. Have another drink. No obligation. What Anna Danilova writes shows me somebody who's no good at writing, somebody with no feeling for literature, and *that's all*. Which ought to be quite enough in the case of somebody who gets to be called a poet. But, well, the time's gone by when the poetry was supposed to show you the kind of person the poet was. It can't have lasted more than about a hundred years from first to last. Now let's see, in your literature, there's Byron, who comes on like a self-righteous bastard, right, and is it Keats, a real nice little guy who didn't know a goddamn thing. Then there was some fellow who'd have you know he liked screwing women. But not all that long after, it was just ideas and stories, and then nothing much of anything. Any kind of person at all could have written it, in fact it got so you could hardly believe the stuff had come out the end of a human arm at all unless it happened to be Sylvia Plath's. Conclusion of lecture. But – '

'You don't think Anna shows herself up as vulgar and shallow and complacent and a victim of herd-instinct and all sorts of other things?'

'Richard my dear – those are faults of her *poetry*. Can you understand that? She may be all you say and worse in her own nature but there's no evidence for it on those pages. It could be they'd be better pages if there were some.'

Kotolynov had been speaking quietly for some time but at this point it was he who got up and moved a few paces off. He had apparently regarded it as perfectly natural to have been sought out like this and no less so that two men so briefly acquainted should have settled down to the purpose in question within a minute. But now it seemed as if some of the agitation Richard was still trying to suppress had communicated itself to him. He began to ask a question but stopped again.

'Her poetry means a great deal to her,' said Richard. 'She's not the kind of person to give it up for any sort of external reason. It wouldn't be right for me to even want her to. I feel about her quite differently from how I've ever felt about anybody else. I've had girls, but that was just a matter of having girls. I didn't see that at the time – I thought they touched me, but I see now they didn't, though I know that's a cruel and ungrateful thing to say. I thought my marriage was breaking up, but after what's happened it's perfectly obvious to me it was never a marriage at all like other people's, and I know saying that's cruel and ungrateful too. I can't ever have been much good at this kind of thing and it's amazing I've managed to find someone. So if I'm to give her up I'd better make bloody sure it's necessary.'

'Richard . . . please . . . who said anything about giving her up?'

'The only thing I've had, ever really had, is whatever you care to call it, my professional self-respect, my devotion to my subject, my determination to stick to the truth as I see it – I'm sorry, perhaps I'd better switch to Russian.'

'No no, go on in English.'

'Everything I've learnt and tried to live by tells me not to say Anna's any kind of poet except a bad one, so no signature, so I go and declare my disbelief in what she regards as the most important part of herself, and declare that disbelief in the most unambiguous, ineffaceable and public way. How could anybody live with anybody after that? You surely understand that. And if you do, Andy, you'll understand why I need a bit of moral support.'

There was silence in the room. Richard found he was taking not his first sip from the glass Kotolynov had recharged unseen. None of the things he had just said were new even to his thoughts, like how he had behaved to earlier girls with something not far enough from heartlessness. But he felt all of it had been true and accurate, and very much hoped he would be able to remember it.

'All right.' Kotolynov had gone back to his chair. He spoke earnestly even for him. 'Moral support coming up. I realise why you felt you should switch to talking in Russian just then, but I'll stick to English too. Your professional self-respect is the only thing of its kind you have, right, and it's quite a rare thing for anyone to have. If you surrender it for even the best of reasons, it's gone for certain and for ever. There seems to be no rule telling what happens to people who put themselves in that position, but it's unlikely to be good for them. So don't you do that, Richard. Commit yourself next time you meet her – sorry . . . no . . . signature. That may mean the end of her as far as you're concerned. On the other hand it may not. If it does, you may meet someone else and then again you may not. With human beings nothing is for certain and nothing is for ever. They die, some of them. Not all of them. Of course without Anna you'd probably be very unhappy for a long time, but if you're like some of the other Englishmen I've met you don't care too much about being happy. As to doing what you somehow feel you ought to do, that's something else again.'

Richard waited a moment. 'Is that the lot?' he asked.

'Just, it may sound kind of funny to be putting a principle before a human being, but in this case the human being's yourself, so that's all right.'

'What about Anna? Wouldn't I be putting my principle before her too?'

'I guess so. How would you feel about her in a couple of weeks as the human being you'd put before your principle? And if somebody tries to tell you, somebody like you it would have to be, that you already compromised your integrity by screwing her after you knew she was a lousy poet, you tell 'em from me nobody's perfect, you hear?'

Before they parted, Richard had time to ask Kotolynov what he was doing here in London.

'Well, I'll tell you. My American publisher's in town. He's called Clint Kautski, would you believe. Can you imagine how American he makes me feel? Old Clint has a very nice wife. No, Richard, no, Colonel Tomski is about to ride again, that's all. Mrs Cottle doesn't like London too well, no more than that. I've finished with the other. Good-bye and the best of luck. Next time you fill me in on what I don't know about cricket.'

Richard left the hotel in a state of mind too fixed and certain to be called determination. It was settled that he would refuse to sign Anna's paper, would do so as unmistakably as possible, with no diplomatic escape-hatches as indicated by Crispin after lunch that day. Actually it had been Crispin's summing-up then of the courses open that had decided the issue. Or had that come earlier, much earlier, too far back for him to reach or see, at some stage where answers were established before the questions came along?

This was not the kind of thinking Richard went in for very often and he soon gave up this time. He was troubled a little by seeming for the moment to suffer no special gloom, no desolation at the impending loss of Anna, or if not that then at the painful damage to be inflicted on what was between them, not even much in the way of ordinary selfish uneasiness, hardly more than the mild almost subliminal sort he was used to carrying round with him. Why not? He was sure he knew – it had not hit him yet. He remembered in his boyhood how his father had told him he could not after all go on the summer camping holiday he had been looking forward to, and how he had managed to keep going for over an hour afterwards saying it was all right and he quite understood. And he remembered, from years later, an aunt telling him that his dead uncle had once been given some very unpleasant news at the hospital and had apparently just not taken it in till the following day. Richard had thought he had forgotten that.

Uneasiness from another source was lavishly available to him as soon as he came within sight of home. Indoors all was quiet, or was it? No, it was not, at first not quite, a few seconds later far from it, as on the floor above a pair of female voices rose in altercation, one of them certainly Cordelia's, the other recognisable but not suggesting a name. This was supplied a few seconds later when a pair of female legs came into view descending the stairs at speed and quickly revealed their owner to be Pat Dobbs. She was carrying a tray of used crockery. At the same brisk pace, and without any sign of knowing Richard was there, although he stood in full view, she took this tray into the kitchen, from which there soon came a medium-sized crash as she presumably laid down her burden. When Richard joined her she was throwing away leavings and washing out dregs with great vigour and intentness. Although he made some suitably noisy noises on arrival and greeted her by name, she did no more than send the briefest of glances somewhere in the quadrant of space he was occupying at the time.

As if moved by some recalled example he stepped forward, saying gently things like, 'Oh now, whatever's the matter then, love?' and, 'Surely it can't be as bad as that?' and also gently laying his arm across her shoulders. With a readiness that made him feel as much of a shit as he had felt at any time in the past day or two, Pat stopped her demonstrations, lowered her head and started blinking fast. Her shoulders relaxed a little.

'What's the trouble?' he asked again.

Still not looking at him, she answered his question in full with another. 'Just who does that woman think she is?'

'Ah, that would be something to know, wouldn't it, who Cordelia thinks she is. What exactly – '

'It's the last time, I can tell you, it's bad enough in the ordinary way, I don't know why I come, Harry thinks I'm mad to, I'm just somebody for her to order about, what's in it for me, could I possibly be an absolute angel and slip round and throw a tiny light meal together . . .' The last phrase began in attempted imitation of Cordelia's mode of speech, but this soon faded away in tact or fatigue. 'And then it's did I have to absolutely *smother* it in butter and what took me all that time, no wonder this is stone cold, and where's the pepper and it was there all the time which made it *worse* and what on earth had possessed me to pick that tray when there were so many nicer ones . . .'

'Leave it and come and sit down.'

'And surely I might have been expected to show a tiny bit of consideration in the circumstances . . .'

'I'll finish this later. I think you need a drink.'

Richard was more used to receiving than uttering this kind of invitation and hoped he had used one of the acceptable forms. It looked like it. Pat accepted a gin and tonic and sat down with him in the drawing-room. To his eye she seemed mollified some of the way, in parts only.

'You'd think she'd be grateful for a little attention but all she seems to feel is indignant,' said Pat, still showing something of the latter herself. 'Which in her case means indignant with anybody who's ill-advised enough to come her way.'

It occurred to Richard that it was not at all long since he had had a go at Pat for being indignant with him because of his treatment of Cordelia, who had been represented to him then as terribly and justifiably upset. But he had the sense merely to offer further mumblings of sympathy and support.

Perhaps some of that previous conversation was going through Pat's mind too. She sipped her drink and said, 'Anyway, you're back now, aren't you? Or are you?'

These few words seemed rich with possible meanings and answers. Richard said, 'I can't tell you how much I appreciate your holding the fort here. I'm only sorry you've had to put up with all this – '

'No, I meant are you sort of back from having gone away from Cordelia. Of course I quite see, if you don't want to discuss it . . .'

'No, I'd like to tell you, if you think you can bear it. Things are still all over the place, but however they finally turn out I can't see me and her going on with our marriage. No matter what else happens or doesn't happen.'

'M'm,' said Pat, and nodded gravely. Then she went on with more animation, 'What else might happen or not happen?'

'Well . . . Anna, you know, the Russian girl . . . there are problems there, or going to be, to put it mildly. It's, you remember this poetry of hers? Oh Christ, it came up this morning, I'm getting completely – '

'I'm sorry about what I said then about that, Richard, I was upset.'

'That's all right, we were all a bit strung up. Anyway, that time we talked about it before, the day we met on the doorstep here, I told you I was absolutely sure Anna's poetry was no good and that raised a very serious problem. You remember that?'

'M'm.' This time Pat spoke non-committally.

'Well, since then, this document I'm supposed to sign, it says she writes great poetry, and in all conscience I simply can't bring myself to support that.'

'What document's this? Oh yes, I think I read something about it somewhere. So – the problem is you'd be saying officially you think her poetry's marvellous when in fact you think it's bloody awful, and you don't much feel like saying that. Correct?'

'Well, yes, and I've made up my mind I'm not going to.'

'Which – Anna? Anna will take it as a slap in the face and a terrific blow to her self-esteem and all that. Serious enough to break up with you?'

Pat was still being non-committal, had perhaps moved some way towards being strictly objective. Richard supposed that was on the right lines, though he could have done with a further instalment of her more conciliatory manner as seen just before. It might have helped to make his stand seem less capricious. 'Very likely,' he said to her question. 'I don't really know. And whatever happens she'll go on being a lousy poet.'

'In your opinion.'

'Of course it's my opinion, what else? But it's not like my opinion of a pair of slippers, it's the truth as I see it.'

'Oh yes. And if you go against that, then you're, you're doing what exactly?'

'Compromising my professional honour. Like a doctor breaking his Hippocratic oath. I'm sorry I've got to say it like that.'

'I don't see why you should be, if that's really what it is. But let's face it, Richard, that professional honour of yours is a bit shifty, isn't it? I mean, it didn't stop you from going to bed with the girl in the first place – I don't say it should have, or even could have, but it didn't. But that was when it was all under the counter kind of thing, just between you and her and whoever you cared to let in on it. Now it looks like going all public you suddenly start getting on your high horse about your professional standing and integrity and what-not.'

'I realise I must sound as if I am. I can't think of anything else to do at this stage.'

Pat's demeanour was now very far from non-committal, and it would have been called objective only by a select few. 'I can,' she said in such a way that Richard wondered how he could ever have seen anything attractive in the way her lower lip jutted slightly forward. 'Whatever you think of Anna's poetry is just your opinion, a very expert opinion, highly trained, all that, but just an opinion. And you love Anna enough, or fancy her, whatever you please, anyway, enough to run off with her and reduce your wife to a state of collapse and face the break-up of your marriage, but you *don't* love her or whatever it is enough to keep quiet about an opinion of yours.'

'To tell a lie,' said Richard.

'For the first time in your life? Really? No, what you won't do is tell a particular lie – all right – at a particular time in particular circumstances. And supposing what you'd be giving up was ten times as important as you say, how could that be too much to give up for somebody you love? How did it go? You were sorry you had to put it like that?'

Richard thought of saying that, whatever Pat might have seen him as before, for the time being he was still the husband of the woman who, he was quite convinced, had just now been intolerably rude to her. But of course he thought of saying it no more seriously than of flying in the air.

Meanwhile Pat had put on a good piece of dumb-show by having an intent look round Cordelia's luxuriously appointed drawing-room and then an appraising one at him. Now she said, 'Most convenient. Very neat. We've had our fun, we've got a bit out of our depth and we're a bit windy, and now, right on cue, we have an acute attack of professional integrityitis. Oh, it'll be a long and tough job, recovering your lost ground with the lady upstairs, and you'll never get all of it back. But worth some effort, eh, Richard?'

EIGHTEEN

'I think you'd better come round as soon as you can,' said
Freddie on the telephone. She spoke with unwonted urgency.

'But I've just told you I'm due to see Crispin at eleven-thirty
anyway. Is he there?'

'Not at the moment. I think you'd better come round straight
away. It's Anna.'

'Oh God,' said Richard into the telephone in his study. 'She's
supposed to be there at eleven-thirty too, but – '

'Well, she turned up about twenty minutes ago. She's lying
down at the moment.'

'What? Why, what's the matter with her? She's not ill?'

'I don't know. I don't think ill. But something. You'll see.'

Richard had passed an uneasy night, uneasy not only because
of his own thoughts and feelings but also, so to speak,
externally. Doors far and near were wrenched open, then shut
either with a vigour that fell just short of slamming or
inaudibly if at all. One clearly audible shutting, with its
distinctive bong, came twice over from his shower, where
Cordelia sometimes but by no means always washed her hair.
There were of course several trampings up and down the stairs,
and two sets of kitchen noises separated by some puzzling
interval like half an hour. Once from beneath him there spoke
for minutes on end the huge voice of a fiend or ogre, on
eventual second thoughts that of some nocturnal broadcaster.
Some noises remained unidentified, like a sharp crack as of a
small-calibre firearm, a prolonged inorganic groaning that
suggested lock gates or a locomotive turntable, a less comparable sound that made Richard think perhaps a large disabled
creature was dragging itself slowly and painfully along the
corridor outside his room. Soon after that, human footsteps
came and halted for a time at his shut door, then retreated. All

256

in all he had been feeling in less than top form for his appointment at the Dom even before Freddie's accelerating call.

He spent a small but measurable part of the journey there wondering whether he had heard real rebuke in her voice or a mere conscience-induced simulacrum, and a comparable part rebuking himself for such selfish fancies. Fancies or not, Freddie's aspect on meeting was not of the warmest. She had her hair piled on top of her head in a far-fetched way and was wearing a low-cut purple velvet dress with expensive edging, and altogether looked to him as if she had prepared herself for taking part in a costume ball, but in view of the hour among other things – still only mid-morning – he decided that this could not be the case. On her wrist, however, encrusted with jewels, was the smallest watch he had ever seen. She led him into the something-else room where he had last been, the one with Crispin's desk in it.

'She's in a funny state, that girl,' said Freddie. 'Rather worrying, in fact. Looks as if she hasn't been to bed all night.'

'Where? I mean where's she being in her funny state?'

'Just through in the sitting-room. She was stretched out there when I looked in just now, with her eyes closed but I don't think she was asleep.'

It was already hard to resist the impression that any strain Freddie was showing came simply from concern for Anna and some distress at not knowing how to help her. Richard would not have taken Freddie for one who felt ordinary things like that. Such people had grown rare in his life, though once it had seemed to be full of them.

'Is there anything I can do?' he asked.

'You can talk to her. When she got here she wanted to see Sandy.'

'Sandy? But . . .'

'She seemed to think she lived here. I told her she was still in Tuscany.'

'From what you're saying you were talking to her all right. What language was this conversation conducted in?'

'Anna knows quite a few words of English now, and she's got that phrase-book of hers. But she couldn't seem to tell me what she wanted Sandy for.' Freddie's expression showed doubt whether there could be an innocent reason for wanting Sandy. 'Or she wouldn't.'

'Did she try to explain what was the matter?'

'I don't think she wanted to, to me anyway. I found a phrase in her book about feeling ill or being ill, but she just shook her head.'

While she was speaking, Anna came into the room. The door and Richard's seat were at an angle such that he saw her a moment before she saw him, long enough for it to strike him that she did indeed look ill, or tired at least, and pale. But then at the sight of him she smiled and looked less bad but still not all right. On a different sort of day he might have noticed that her get-up went counter to Freddie's in being severe, faintly masculine, with a dark high-necked jacket that only just possibly might have come from the market near Professor Léon's house.

'I heard your voice,' she said in Russian as they reached out to each other. Near them Freddie mentioned coffee and by the time they looked round she was no longer in the room. Out of sight a door shut.

'I don't feel very well,' said Anna. 'Can we go somewhere outside?'

'I was just going to suggest it myself.'

'But I think I must be sick first. Where should I go?'

Both announcement and inquiry disconcerted Richard. Luckily Freddie was soon found again and at once took Anna away. As well as feeling sorry for her and concerned about her, Richard was conscious of irritation in himself. He traced it to a feeling that there was something self-consciously Russian about trooping off to be sick like that, or at least about baldly stating the intention. After further thought had failed to suggest what else she might have done at any point, he told himself that his first reaction was exactly the kind of thing he was going to have to get out of quite fast, like much else.

When Anna reappeared she was looking much better and smelling like a not very distant pine-forest. Richard took her out of the house and past the herb garden where only the previous day he had sat and thought about his life and about her. Beyond the trees and the half-grown shrubbery they came to an L-shaped piece of wall. Vegetable matter grew or was trained up parts of this, but there was a bench-like affair in the angle where a couple of people could sit without discomfort. No building could be seen from here. Richard prepared himself for the odd remark about how similar or dissimilar this or that was to one Russian matter or another before pulling himself up for wrong thinking. And in the event all he got was an irreproachably leaden, almost British offering that drew his attention to the ambient peace and quiet.

They, the peace and quiet, would be gone soon enough, Richard guessed. He found he could also guess in some detail what was to follow. So be it. He took Anna's hand.

'I'm afraid I had rather a lot to drink last night,' she said.

'Oh, were you at a party?' He must have been trying to be funny.

'No, I was by myself. I didn't telephone you because I was afraid of what I might say to make your situation bad or worse than it was or need have been. That was one reason.'

'I didn't telephone you,' said Richard, and as he spoke found himself unable to think of even one reason why he had not, so he was relieved when she hurried on,

'You wouldn't have reached me. I walked for hours, then I sat by the river and drank a lot of vodka out of a bottle Hamparzoumian had got me, then a policeman found me. I don't think he can have arrested me because I woke up lying on my bed in my room and it was four o'clock in the morning. I couldn't sleep again, so eventually I went for a ride on your Metro and I went to sleep there, and then again in a sort of park. Then I came here because I knew you were coming later.'

Yes, the hangover was real enough but no more than a by-product, as Freddie had evidently seen. Richard listened for insects and waited.

'Freddie is very kind,' said Anna as if she had followed his thought.

Richard would not have minded discussing this point one day, but said only, 'She told me you wanted to see Sandy. I didn't know you'd even met her.'

'Only once, and I didn't think she was very nice. Yes, that was silly. By the time I got to ask I didn't really want to see her any more.'

'What did you want her for originally?'

'I wondered if I could get some drugs off her. She seemed – '

'You wondered *what*?'

'I said it was silly. I had all kinds of funny ideas in my head.'

'Well, I hope that's one that's gone for good.'

A small bright wasp that had been hovering to one side of them moved nearer in a single spurt. Anna swiped at it vaguely and said, 'It's about my poetry.'

'Yes, I thought it was.'

'I'm sorry you don't like it. That's what I am – sorry. Disappointed. Sad. Not angry or bitter or complaining, and least of all wanting to hurt you.' And nothing she said in the next few minutes had a trace of any of those in it. 'You understand?'

'Yes.'

'Just after we'd made love the first time I gave you a book of my poems, a book you hadn't seen before. You've never said anything to me about it or them. Have you ever read any of them?'

'Yes.' He remembered looking through some of them standing on the pavement outside the Léon house, and never going near them since.

'Did you like any of them?'

'No.'

'No, well, that made me start to think, you see, when I realised you were going to say nothing even though I'd given them to you that day. Being a poet is as important to me as being a scholar is to you. And the scholar doesn't like the poet but Anna loves Richard. So what can Anna do? Stop loving Richard? No. Kill herself? No. Then stop being a poet.'

'Anna, that's impossible.'

'Not at all. I stopped last night. I asked Professor Léon if I could borrow a trashbin and then I just burnt all the poems, all the new ones that haven't been printed or published. Some of them I can't stop from appearing but there'll be no more.'

This was not among the news Richard had foreseen. It horrified him more than any possibility that had occurred to him so far. Nobody had the right to silence a poet of whatever sort. Even bad poetry had to exist, if only to heighten good poetry by contrast, to make the good poets shine out as even better. But he could not say that now. 'Don't forget you have a duty to Russia,' he said. 'Where a poet has always been more than a poet. The Russian poet has spoken for the people, for all those who've been forbidden to speak for themselves. You mustn't give that up.'

'It's too late, Richard.'

'I won't let you give it up.'

'Among what I burnt were the scripts of those poems I read at your Institute that evening, you remember. The ones you said you liked so much. In a new style, you said. They made you cry, you said. I don't know what you meant.' For the first and only time her voice faltered. 'But whatever it was you meant, they're gone now. Words lost upon the indifferent air,' she said, with an unfortunate reminder of what sort of poet she was.

'Actually they're not lost. They're all on tape. All those readings go on to tape automatically. I mean without any special instructions being necessary. The standing arrangement is for six copies to be made in the first instance. They'll probably be at the Institute now, or on their way there. You'll get a proof too, for printed copies. There's always a bit of a delay. But those poems aren't lost, Anna, be sure of it.'

'Oh.' She sounded disappointed.

'You couldn't have known that, but it will all happen as I say. And now let me tell you what you must do as soon as you've received your proof.'

'But please, how can there be such a thing? I gave nobody any written record. Your Professor Hallett asked me for one but I forgot, so much was happening.'

'They have transcribers who work from the tape and they're very good and you spoke very clearly. Your words are safe, darling. Make any corrections you wish, but be quick about it and let me have a text the moment you can.'

'How is it so urgent?'

Richard looked at her and away again and breathed in deeply. 'Well. Now you ask me I don't think I really know. Except that like Tristram Hallett I'm a professor. And I hope a scholar. All my professional life I've been accustomed to read poems myself, from the printed page, rather than have someone else read or recite them for me. It's the way I was trained to understand and judge a poem. So I've been waiting till I could read the poems you recited that night before I finally . . . But this, now, it's too important for that, and I'm too certain. And after all what is training? Only a guide. A crutch. So.' He reached out towards Anna and then sat back on the bench. 'In my, in my judgement these poems of yours are of high quality, as high as any written in our time. They have haunted me ever since I first heard them. Whatever you may or may not write in the future you are a fine poet. But let me have copies as soon as you can, please, my love, because I want to read them and get to know them.' Now he took her hand.

She stared at him. 'You wouldn't . . .' she said in fear.

'No, I wouldn't. Say what I don't believe about a thing like that. As you know.'

Leaving her hand in his, she nodded her head. Nothing more.

'It's eleven-thirty,' said Richard.

'Thank you for stopping me from feeling afraid. If you thought I was staying away from you these last days, one reason was because I was afraid you'd tell me I was a bad poet and would always be one no matter what I did, like a soul destined for hell. Now you've set me free. I don't know what else to say.'

'Then don't say anything, just give me a kiss.'

'Except I think I'd like a glass of champagne,' she said, leaning towards him.

Well, they had come to the right place for that, he thought to himself as they walked back across the sunny garden. Crispin, ever punctual, was waiting for them in the room with the bookshelves where he and Anna had first met.

'Richard says to me I am good poet,' she told him with great emphasis in English.

'Does he, by George,' said Crispin rather heavily. He had put on a little weight recently and sported some unnameable purple flower in his buttonhole that suggested, to Richard, the variety of his life and concerns. Then he roused himself to express delight at the news. 'Splendid! Magnificent! And quite right!' He added some words in German, embraced Anna and wrung Richard's hand. 'About time too . . . So no crisis. In fact, cause for a little celebration, surely.'

Richard smiled back. 'Anna mentioned a glass of champagne. I doubt if her English would run to asking for it herself.'

'Good idea.' Crispin pressed a bell and looked at his watch. 'As far as it goes. Now I think we might just pop next door and complete the formalities, don't you? No time like the present. You know, stick your monicker on the old petition, then I can fax it down to Quentin.'

'Oh. All right. Yes.'

'I don't think we need bother Anna with the details, do you?' To go with the mention of her name he gave her a cheerful smile and a wave. 'Or would you like her to see it?'

'I'll explain to her later.'

'You'd better explain something to her now. I would myself, but I don't imagine her English would run to it.'

There was a knock at the door and the man Enrique came in. Unlike other butlers Richard had seen in recent years, he was got up as neither a footballer nor a TV producer, more a butler. While Crispin gave his orders, Richard made some explanation to Anna. In the half-minute or so it took him and Crispin to move into the next room, he had time to ponder on the fluency and the solid B-picture-dialogue quality of the lies he had told Anna in the garden. He also reflected that she had seemed measurably less bowled over by what he had said than he had been counting on, the first really nasty thing he had ever thought about her, as opposed to her poetry. Overall he felt a kind of relief, the kind he remembered from hearing that he had definitely not got the scholarship or the job.

'There,' said Crispin after another half-minute. 'Now that wasn't so bad, was it?' He did things to his fax machine.

Richard made no reply.

'I thought perhaps lunch for four at Boulestin's – we can settle about the Archbishop and so on there. I hope you won't mind if I ask Freddie along. You'll be very popular with her when she's taken in your declaration of faith and has worked out some of its probable consequences – well, perhaps when I've helped her to appreciate the difference it'll make to your life. And to some other people's.'

But he made no direct reference to Cordelia, and he had already affirmed without the use of speech that whatever had led Richard to his decision was not and never would be something of concern to him. That was a relief too, so much so that it was hard to explain the slight chill that came with it.

NINETEEN

Richard drove his TBD into the space in front of what he would still have called his house and parked it there as usual. After letting himself in he went straight into the drawing-room, Cordelia's drawing-room, fully hers today in that it had her in it. She was sitting not in her usual chair but one with its back nearly to the door, so that all he could see from the threshold was a bit of white sleeve, a wink or so of gold from a bracelet or two and a three-quarter-rear view of most of a fair head, which did not move. Going round to the front of her, he noticed that a fresh jigsaw puzzle, evidently bearing some archaic picture of a pastoral scene, had been laid out and begun on the polished table by the window. Not the chessboard and men, though, nor the crossword. She had never been properly interested in those.

He sat down briskly facing her. What he saw before him was much as usual, shirt or whatever she called it on this warm day, expression one he had seen a few times when she had not known she was observed, faintly gloomy but apathetic more than thoughtful, mouth on the point of falling open.

'Hallo, Cordelia.'

'Hallo darling.' The voice was as normal, firmer than the look. No sort of collapsing act seemed on the cards.

'I've come to tell you, with the greatest reluctance, that I feel I can no longer – '

'Oh please don't keep us both hanging about, say what you've come to say Richard, oh I know it would be quicker if I said it for you but I'm not going to let you off saying it yourself.'

'Fair enough, I wouldn't want it any different. No – things have reached the point where – '

'Oh you're like some horrible old musty professor on one of those university committees of yours. For goodness' sake put it in words of one syllable.'

'I'm leaving you. I'm afraid that's not quite – '

'Surely you can't have imagined I wasn't expecting it? That I haven't prepared for it?'

'That's not the point. It would have been wrong of me not to have come along here and tried to – '

'Oh it would have been wrong of you. It would have infringed the code of the Vaiseys just to sneak off without a word and go to your Russian girl just like before but this time not come back. It's funny how I used to long to meet her and have a look at her and now I don't want to at all. I'm sure I know what she's like anyway. She's *your sort*, and I'm not.'

Cordelia was staring at him. He knew that what she meant by his sort was someone as lower-class as himself, and he could tell that she knew he knew. At no time in the past had she ever reminded him of her superior social origins, and the clear fact that she would say no more now was a kind of victory for her. He had no words to say.

'I expect you'll quite enjoy your new life,' she continued. 'Of course it won't be as nice as your old life in some ways, you know. There won't be as much money in it for one thing. In fact there won't be any money in it at all that I can stop getting there. Other things too. But one point I do want to impress on you darling. I'll never harm you personally, or your Russian girl either. I'm not that sort of person. Now apart from wishing you the worst of bad luck that's all I've got to say. Good-bye Richard.'

'Cordelia, we can't just go off like this without – '

'Oh yes we can darling. That's exactly what we can do, go off like this, and it's what we're going to do. You wanted one last thing from me, a lovely great scrumptious scene with you being really sorry and almost broken up but determined just the same and owing all sorts of things to this person and that person and me being fed up and cross and tearfully accusing you and whatever, and *you're not getting it*, okay? No scene. Nothing. Just if you'll excuse me I have some arrangements to make.'

She got up as if called by a dentist's receptionist and went. Richard sat on for a time, thinking of the blue eyes it was too late to look straight into and the body he could not remember at all except like an engineering diagram, and himself left the room without any such show of purpose. In his study he took in the existence of books, papers, files. Soon the task of shifting all this stuff would have to be faced, but not yet. Clothes and stuff, too. Upstairs he threw some things into a zip bag, came down again at the same stroller's pace and moved out to his car, where he put in another minute or so of unprofitable sitting. Then he pulled himself together and drove through lightish traffic to the Cedar Court Hotel, in which about the time of the dawn of the Christian era he had had drinks with Superintendent Ippolitov. This time he had only a solitary drink, which he made last only as long as it took him to decide that grieving over the end of his marriage was something he could put off for a bit, like shifting his books. He also made one telephone call from the hotel, to tell Anna he had done what he had come out to do, and this took a little longer. But altogether it was quite a short time before he returned to where he had left the TBD, in a couple of straight lines on this occasion.

Standing near the car rather than by it was a man he had never seen before, which surprised him greatly. Like Ippolitov this man was a policeman, though unlike him he wore uniform. Rather undersized for his job, some might have thought, and wearing a scanty moustache, he watched openly but in silence while Richard opened the driver's door. Then he spoke.

'Excuse me, sir, are you the driver of this vehicle?'

'Yes. Yes, officer.'

'I'm sorry to be a nuisance, sir, but it might save us a lot of time if you could tell me who you are. What we call establishing your identity.'

Richard gave his name and brought out a couple of letters from his breast pocket, one of which happened to be addressed to him in full academic style from the Librarian of the Institute. The policeman made a check against a small paper he now held.

'You wouldn't happen to have your driving licence with you, sir, I suppose?'

'No, I keep that locked up at home.'

'And where would home be, sir?'

'About a mile back up the road.' He mentioned the address.

Although he seemed not to have done as much as turn his head, the constable was now joined on the pavement by a slightly larger and older colleague who had perhaps been crouching unseen behind one of the potted shrubs in the forecourt of the hotel. He nodded shyly to Richard.

The first policeman performed introductions rather cere-moniously. 'Oh, er, I'm PC Blackett, sir, and this here is PC Freely. M'm. Freely, this is, uh,' – he suppressed a cough or eructation –'Dr Richard Vaisey.'

'Morning, sir,' said Freely in a noticeably thicker voice. 'Or I suppose strictly it's good afternoon now.'

'I expect you're wondering what this is all about, sir, aren't you?' said Blackett. 'Only natural, after all. Yes, what happened, somebody calling himself Dr Richard Vaisey rang in from the address you've just given us to report the theft of this car. Now I take it it wouldn't be you who made that call, sir?'

'Of course not.'

'No, I didn't really think it would have been, sir. Well, seeing we were in the area, we came on down the obvious way, like, keeping our eyes well and truly open, and then, what do you know, there she was, plain as the nose on your face. We'd just confirmed identification when you came into view, sir. All over in a matter of minutes. We don't normally reckon to be as quick as that.'

'How many minutes?'

'I'm sorry, sir?'

'How long has it been since the supposed theft was reported?'

'Ah, well that's quite an easy one, sir.' PC Blackett consulted the paper in his hand. 'From time of origin, that's when the call was received, until now, it's just coming up to . . . thirty-nine minutes. Remarkable.'

'It's even more remarkable than you think,' said Richard.

The two policemen probably missed this as they consulted each other, not saying a great deal, just a mutter or two. Then Blackett said in his reedy tones, 'It's nothing more than a detail really, sir, but I think the best thing now would be if you drove back to your house and produced your driving licence et cetera. We get a lot of these hoax calls, you know, sir, but you'll understand we have to follow them all up. That's life.'

'Of course.'

'I'll come in front with you, sir, if I may, I haven't seen the inside of a TBD much, and Freely'll bring up the rear in our old jalopy.'

'Hop in, officer.'

On the way, Blackett asked, 'Do you know anybody, sir, who might have made that call out of malice or mischief?'

'Oh yes.'

'Bothered you in that sort of way before, have they?'

'No, not in that sort of way.'

'I'll leave you to concentrate on your driving, sir.'

Between them they got both cars satisfactorily off the road in front of the house. Richard inserted his latchkey into the lock of the front door. It went in all right, though a little stickily, but would not turn. Instead, the recorded sound of some fancy keyboard instrument, like a celesta, came from inside the letter-box playing molto marcato an air distantly known to him as 'Balls to Mr Banglestein'. After sixteen bars and a full twenty seconds the music had finished, Richard had recovered his key and the policemen still showed no hint of surprise or amusement, but the door stayed shut.

'Do you know of any other legal mode of entry to these premises, Dr Vaisey?' asked PC Blackett.

'I'm afraid not. Well, er, we could go round the side if you feel like it and help each other over the wall and try and get in through the garden door, but quite frankly I don't see us having any more success there than here, do you?'

'No, I must confess I don't sir.'

'Could this be some kind of practical joke, sir, would you say?' asked the other policeman.

'The answer to that depends a bit on what you call a joke. It's true I've been having a certain amount of difficulty with my wife.'

This went over like the sound of a great cease-fire. 'Oh well, sir, there we are then, oh I see, sir, say no more, that's it, sir, end of story,' said the policemen as they melted away. 'As a matter of form, just produce your licence and insurance and road-tax certificates, sir, at the Bolitho Street police station within three days if you would,' Blackett went on, adding 'if you ever see them again' as he got in beside Freely.

As another matter of form, Richard pressed the bell and did no more than nod his head a couple of times when no sound came. Nothing of interest was to be seen through the windows he could see through. He went and sat behind the wheel of the TBD no longer than it took him to reflect that Cordelia's will and ability to organise what she evidently had organised had come as a total surprise to him, and that if he had caught even a hint of it in the past they might have had a nicer life together, or at least a different one. Then he switched on his ignition, with appreciable relief that doing so failed to cause the car to blow up under him, and drove away.

When he came back a couple of hours later he had some food and drink inside him and Anna standing on the opposite pavement. She crossed over, gave him a thumbs-up sign and waited on the doorstep while he positioned the car for a quick getaway if necessary. When he had done that he went to the part of the house wall up which she had climbed some days earlier.

'Right,' he said, 'are you ready?'

'Aren't you going to try the key again first?'

'No point in that.'

'How can you be so sure? It might just have got stuck the first time, or your wife could have had the locks changed back, I don't know.'

'What on earth would she do a thing like that for?'

'I've no idea, darling, but from what I know of her she's obviously a very eccentric lady.'

Anna went on waiting on the step. It occurred to Richard that she must have somehow known he had an undeclared reason for not wanting to put the key in the lock. He thought of substituting a different key, saying this time it would not even go in, but too late. 'Balls to Mr Banglestein' (, dirty old sod)' sounded clearly and in full from what must have been a small loudspeaker fixed inside the door.

Meanwhile Richard pluckily fiddled with the key. 'You see?' he said. 'Hopeless.'

'But what's the point of this tune?' Before he could answer she went on, 'I know it, it's an old German song, "Ach, du liebe Augustin", I think a children's song.'

'Is it?'

'But why should she have troubled to arrange for it to play like that when you put your key in the lock?'

'I can't imagine. As you say, she's a very eccentric lady.' It sounded most unconvincing, so he hurried on, 'Let's get moving. It shouldn't take more than a couple of minutes. Now you're quite sure she didn't go into the house while I was away telephoning?'

'Unless she burrowed in from underneath it. Are you quite sure you gave her long enough to answer?'

'Absolutely.'

'And you're also sure she'd answer if she was there, in the house?'

'Yes. Even surer. It would be psychologically out of the question for Cordelia to hear her telephone ringing and not pick it up.'

'Very well.'

With a little start-off from him she scaled the front of the building as readily and successfully as she had before. He was looking to his rear, to check whether any passers-by were paying her activities special attention, or whether a squad of armed police had perhaps started to converge on them, when a tremendous uproar broke out, it seemed at first all round him. Only after several seconds did he succeed in provisionally locating its source as inside the house and its nature as the barking, snarling and growling of a pack of very angry dogs, animals the size of ponies to judge from the noise they seemed to be making. He reached out towards Anna but she was already most of the way back to him.

'Right, into the car,' he said. 'Walk, don't run. But don't hang about either.'

'Were those things, were they really dogs?' she asked when they were moving. 'Do you have dogs like that in England?'

He glanced back and saw that several passers-by had stopped passing by. 'They'd have been on a tape. Kind of burglar alarm.'

'You said there wasn't a burglar alarm on the upper floors.'

'There is now. Sorry.'

'How long will that noise go on?'

'Probably till the police come and switch it off. Which won't be long because an alarm will also have gone off in the police station. Another reason for not staying around.'

'I can see why you want to avoid the police.'

'You never know.'

'Where are we making for now?'

'I thought Professor Léon's. We can sort of regroup there.'

But when they approached Professor Léon's they found a

police car parked outside it. Ignoring Anna's cries of alarm and protest, Richard drove past and round a couple of corners before stopping. She continued to protest and made to get out of the car.

'We can't just leave them,' she said.

He found he had to swallow several times before he could speak. 'Could anybody in that house be in trouble with the law? – immigration, anything at all?'

'Certainly not. Uncle Alyushka is most punctilious. Out of the question.'

'What about yourself? All your papers in order? Entry? Exit?'

She was calmer now. 'Yes, everything. Of course. I swear.'

'Wait here. If I'm not back in fifteen minutes take a taxi to Crispin.' He gave her money. 'You know the address. Good, say it. Speak slowly. All right. Darling.'

When he got to the door of the Léon house Richard found there a man he had seen before. Not only that – he remembered their having parted not much earlier that very same day.

'Good afternoon, Dr Vaisey. Well, well, we seem to keep bumping into each other, don't we? Just a moment, sir, hold it, there's no need to go charging in there like a bull at a gate.'

'PC Blackett. Good Lord. Whatever brings you here?'

'I might ask you the same question, sir, but perhaps it'd make more sense if we got yours out of the way first, like. So, we've had an anonymous tip-off to the effect that there's a cache of illegal drugs at this address. Now of course – '

'We? You?' Richard looked rather wildly round the narrow hall. The place seemed smaller and also less dowdy than on his last visit. 'Aren't you, aren't you out of your, away from your manor in these parts?'

'My what, sir? Oh I see what you mean, out of my jurisdiction, as you might call it. In a sense yes, so I am, but they've had quite a few people off sick round here. That summer 'flu, oh, there's a lot of it about, you know. Yes, I was just going to say, sir, we sussed this out as a hoax call right from the start, but of course we have to double-check everything. Still, now you've turned up, I was wondering, could this be your good lady's sense of humour at work once more?'

'It could. Indeed it could. Officer.'

'These old people here, as unlikely a bunch of drug merchants as I've ever seen, they'd be friends of yours, would they, sir? Russians, I gather. I noticed when we met before you're an expert in Slavonic, which is Russian, am I right? Very good, well, I think now if you'd kindly step this way you could meet Sergeant Widdowson he seems to be called, and we could wrap this lot up and I could get away to my tea.'

Sergeant Widdowson, introduced in Blackett's courtly style, turned out to be even smaller and younger than his subordinate and on that account, perhaps, the readier to accept his view that there was nothing here to interest the police. While this was being concluded Richard crossed the sitting-room to the four elderly Russians grouped by the fireplace in a defensive position, ladies to the rear behind Léon and Hamparzoumian. They were all pleased and most relieved to see Richard but hardly surprised – of course their English friend had come at once to their help.

'It's all right,' he told them, holding his fists out in a gesture meant to stress the point. 'All a mistake. Fortunately I happen to know one of the policemen and I have his assurance that no further steps will be taken in the matter. I should say they'll be leaving very soon, so there's no need to worry.'

The old ladies had not been worrying – of course English policemen would do them no harm in connection with something they so clearly had not done. But they smiled and nodded their heads in thanks, saying nothing as if Richard would not have understood if they spoke their language back to him. These and other things made him feel rather ridiculous, but that feeling changed when he saw Hamparzoumian, who had been unobtrusively clasping Léon's hand, release his hold.

After conferring with Blackett and a man in plain clothes, Widdowson seemed to conclude that he and the others could indeed afford to leave without further delay. He said to Richard in his unexpected big bass voice, 'Well, Dr Vaisey, a stroke of luck for us all you happened to be passing. Thank you for your help.'

'My pleasure, sergeant. Actually I was calling here.'

'I take it we can reach you through your Institute if required? Excellent.'

Apologies were offered and accepted. On the way to the hall again, Blackett lagged behind his colleagues. He said, 'I didn't think there was any point in dragging Mrs Vaisey into the matter, sir. Only confuse the issue.'

'Absolutely.'

'I'm glad you think I did right, sir.' He looked speculatively at Richard, who would not have been greatly surprised to be asked if there was not some fifth member of the household who, in a manner of speaking, had been involved in the affair. But what Blackett did ask was, 'Would you care to make a small contribution to our police charity, sir? I could assure you they do a lot of very good work.'

Richard gave him a £10 note.

'Thank you very much, sir. Er, would you like a receipt?'

'Don't bother, officer.'

'That's very generous of you, sir. Well, good-bye now.'

'Isn't PC Freely with you?'

'Fancy you retaining the name, sir. No, Freely's off till tomorrow, the lucky so-and-so, but I'll be sure and tell him you were asking after him, he'll be tickled pink. Coming, sarge.'

By the time the police party had disappeared and Richard, having taken his own leave, had got back to his car it was to find Anna still in it, even though nearly twice the specified fifteen minutes had elapsed.

'I knew you'd be back,' she said. 'But what happened?'

He told her after they had begun to drive away.

'I should go back and see Alyushka and the others,' she said.

'No need. They're all right now.'

'But they'll expect me.'

'I didn't mention you and they didn't ask. Telephone them later.'

'Where are we going so fast?'

'To a hotel. One we've never been to before in our lives.'

They soon found such a place, though any place at all where he could be alone with Anna would have suited Richard then. It was some time later that she called the Léon house. During her conversation Richard tactfully went into the adjoining bathroom. When he came out she said,

'I presume it was her again? What was the point? They've done nothing to her.'

'They're an extension of you and you're at least an extension of me.'

'You're not excusing her, I hope?'

'Of course not, just reading her mind or whatever you call it.'

'She is English, is she?'

'Yes, I'm sorry to say, as far as I know. Why?'

'The way she sounds on the telephone. And all this, it doesn't seem like the work of an English person.'

'No, nor of a person much. Like her voice. Do you mind if I make a couple of calls now?'

Not for the first time Richard rang Crispin, but got only his answering machine. Then he tried for Cordelia and rang his own number, but with no result. Then they did some shopping for Anna. Then they had a drink in the hotel bar and Richard thought for a time. Finally he made some more telephone calls, successful ones, instructed Anna not to go out for any reason except in the unlikely event of a message from him, which must in any case contain the name Lermontov in its first phrase to be accounted genuine, and left, saying he expected to be back in about an hour.

Twenty minutes later he was sitting in a stationary taxi a few yards down a side-street diagonally opposite his former house, at a point where he could just see the approach to its front door. The time was shortly before eight o'clock and there was still plenty of daylight. Presently the figure of Pat Dobbs descended from another taxi, moved towards the house and was lost to his view. When she did not reappear he made his own way there in a series of indirections. To get within reach of the door he had to pass along some yards of wall low enough to have revealed his head and shoulders to anyone watching from within, so he lingered until that part of the pavement was more or less clear and covered the distance in a fast bowed waddle, his hands pressed to his lower guts for verisimilitude. He edged up to the door. For several minutes there was silence on the far side of it. Then, at precisely eight-twelve, he caught the faint trill of the telephone. Good old Colonel Tomski – right on the button. Another two minutes went by, followed by a very faint click. The door opened an inch. In a flash he had entered and was in his study.

The room was empty even of furniture, so of course there were no books to be found, no papers, no typescript of the book on Lermontov or the hundreds of accompanying hundreds of pages of notes, no Institute documents, no address-book, no telephone-book, no car documents, no income-tax, VAT, bank, insurance or any other records. He stood there holding the

274

plastic bags he had brought to take away the more essential stuff and felt a large unfocused consternation which sharpened in no time when behind him Cordelia said, 'Hallo, Richard.'

He was breathing in at the time and so failed to manage a full-throated yell, but got off quite an impressive dose of sound none the less. 'Oh God,' he sort of said. 'My God . . . you've . . . I've . . .'

'Every piece of paper with any connection with you has disappeared,' she said, making sonants of all the p- and k- and s-sounds as meticulously as ever. 'Gone for recycling heaven knows where. Every stitch of your clothes too, but they'll stay much as they are until they reach their new wearers. Likewise all shoes, slippers, gumboots and such. Nothing to bring you here again. So you might as well leave now.'

'How did you know I was here?'

'Poor darling Pat is really quite a good actress on the TV screen but let's face it she's not much of a one in the flesh I'm afraid. I say I do so hope your American friend isn't still hanging on. I'm sorry to say I simply took my telephone off the hook and left it.'

Cordelia half turned away in the manner of a courteous hostess seeing a visitor off the premises. Though breathing about normally by now, Richard hung back for the moment.

'Come along darling,' she said affably.

'But I can't just leave . . .'

'If it's dear Pat you're worrying about you've honestly no need. As I told you I don't actually hurt people ever. I don't even stop guaranteeing their safety. Just their peace of mind, which I think I am actually quite good at interfering with.'

'How long will it be before I can – '

'Some time yet. Now out.'

Cordelia's next abrupt and gross interference with Richard's peace of mind, as distinct from its steady low-level erosion, took place the next morning. Perhaps superstitiously, perhaps on more substantial grounds, he decided it would not be safe for him and Anna to continue where they were. Accordingly after breakfast at the pleasant little Bayswater hotel he made ready to leave. Their bill was ready for them at the desk and he duly presented his silver Vantage credit card. The dark voluptuous-looking young lady there took it away and shortly afterwards brought it back again.

'I'm afraid this is not valid, sir,' she said in her little squealing voice.

Richard had always been one of the stoutest opponents of the phrase, 'an uncanny sense of déjà vu', pointing out that it should be reserved for times when the user had probably never seen before the sight in question, but now he felt he might have been hidebound, unimaginative. 'How do you mean?' he asked.

'The credit limit has been exceeded.'

'So I can't use it.'

'Our terms are spot cash, spot credit or cheque with sufficient card.'

His thoughts moved to the cheque-book and card in his pocket, but his hands stayed where they were. He could imagine too clearly the look that would come into the young lady's lustrous eyes if he went very far along that track. Quite a bit of the look turned up there as it was when, looking at his watch like a man with a badly sprained shoulder, he said he had an urgent call to make and would be back shortly to settle his bill and pick up his wife and luggage if that was all right.

'My credit card is out of date, expired,' he told Anna. 'I must go and get a new one.'

'From where?'

'From the place where they issue them. Not far away. Well, not too far.'

She nodded without speaking. Though perhaps not got up quite right for the part, she brought to his mind one of those prize-winning photographs that show a solitary figure on some empty quay or railway platform with a caption talking about the uncomplaining endurance of a thousand years of persecution that looked out of this woman's eyes. Then the real woman yawned reassuringly.

For once, Richard correctly forecast what was to happen at the end of his journey. A man told him that his bank account had had all the money taken out of it.

When he got back to the hotel the young lady said there had been a telephone call for him. He thought he recognised the man's voice that answered his return ring. It turned a little embarrassed, he fancied, when he said who he was.

'Oh – thanks for calling back, Richard. It's Harry Dobbs here.'

276

'How's Pat, Harry? I tried to ring last night but, er, I couldn't seem to find your number. Is she all right? I'm afraid things didn't . . . Can I speak to her?'

'No, I'm afraid you can't. That's just it. She's, well, she's not actually under arrest, but the police are holding her for questioning. I'm going round there as soon as I've finished up here.'

'What's it all about?'

'Shoplifting.'

'What! But she'd never do a – '

'Of course she wouldn't. She's been framed, hasn't she? And we all know who's fixed it.' Some strength had returned to Harry's voice. 'Your wife.'

Richard had got there already. He said, 'What happened, you know, last night?'

'Well . . . all Cordelia said, apparently, Pat heard voices, anyway Cordelia said somehow or other you seemed to have made your way into the house and wasn't that extraordinary, and Pat thought the less said the better, which I think was very reasonable under the circumstances, and so she just got away as soon as she could. But after all from what she told me and everything the whole scheme was your idea.'

'Where did this happen, I mean the supposed shoplifting?'

'At the big K & P just round the corner from us where we always go.'

'Oh yes I know it. What do you want me to do, Harry?'

'Sorry?'

'Well, I mean it's not going to help if I just charge into the police station saying this business was all fixed up by my wife to punish Mrs Dobbs for letting me into my wife's house when my wife wanted to keep me out. Is it?'

'Well, of course, put like that . . .'

'How would you put it?'

After a silence, Harry said, 'I'm sorry, I was upset and I wanted to complain to someone. And Cordelia is your wife.'

'For the moment. By the way, how do we know it isn't just an honest mistake on the part of somebody at the store?'

'Do you think there's any real chance it is? Pat told me what you'd told her about those policemen and your car.'

'Yes. No, not the faintest. Now listen, Harry, where's this

questioning going on? Right, you go on down there and I'll ask around and come along as soon as I can.'

'Thanks, Richard.'

'I haven't done anything yet, mate.'

Richard had not thought of Anna for several minutes, since being sent to the telephone immediately on his return. She looked up rather guiltily from the cup of coffee she had evidently had brought to her in the lobby.

'All well, darling?' she asked without anxiety.

Richard summarised his conversation with Harry.

Anna laughed heartily. 'Your wife's mad. I thought so when you first told me about her.'

'Not mad enough to be put away, unfortunately,' said Richard, who had laughed too, only with less conviction.

'You got your money card all right.'

'No. Cordelia's taken all my money away.'

'Can she do that? I see she can. That's not funny.'

'No. I must do some more telephoning now. You order yourself some vodka if you feel like it. While you've still got the chance.'

'Are you ready to settle your bill, sir?' squealed the young lady.

'In just a few minutes.'

This time Richard got Crispin straight away. 'A certain amount has happened since we last talked but the first priority at the moment looks like getting somebody off a shoplifting charge.'

'A piece of cake, I assure you, but I could be better placed knowing a bit more.'

One bit led to another and quite soon Richard was saying, 'Literally every page. It'll just be air pollution by now.'

'What about all your stuff down at the – '

Richard's eyes suddenly expanded and he said very fast, 'I must go now. Cordelia's taken all my money away. Anna's here.' He gave the number of the hotel and hung up.

Not long afterwards he was getting out of a taxi close to the forecourt of the building that housed the Institute, and very soon after that Mrs Pearson was saying to him, 'They were dressed like gentlemen and very well spoken. One of them was carrying one of those document-case things. You'll be calling the police in, will you?'

278

'No, it's a private matter. May I see the note they brought?'

'Of course, Dr Vaisey. I thought it was very suspicious, you needing all those papers so urgently but not being able to pick them up yourself, and then I found I couldn't get you on the telephone but your wife seemed to know all about it and she said it was all right. Where did I put that note?'

'My wife? What did she say? Tell me what happened.'

'Well, I told the men before they touched anything I'd have to get your confirmation, and they said naturally, and I rang your number and your wife answered straight away and said if it was about those papers would I please send them up as soon as possible because you were desperate to get off to your conference and you'd sort everything out on the train and you were so busy at the moment she didn't dare interrupt you. Here we are – I knew I'd got it somewhere.'

Richard took the note, which was a sheet from his own pad and just like him down to the hasty signature. 'I see,' he said.

'I've never spoken to your wife much on the phone. I suppose that wasn't really your wife, was it?'

'No.' He managed a rueful grin. 'I've a pretty good idea of who it was, though.'

'Oh, you mean . . . this was some sort of joke?'

'Well, you'd have to have a pretty weird sense of humour to see the point of it, but yes, I suppose you could call it that. Good God,' he added as at some inner reflection.

'I suppose it was part of the same thing that made you miss your lecture yesterday, Dr Vaisey. We're working normally now as you know.'

'Miss my – oh yes. I didn't get a chance to ring you until it was too late.'

'But you'll be there in the morning for the second-year people?'

'Oh yes. Wait a minute – on second thoughts no. Say I'm indisposed.'

'Don't worry, Dr Vaisey, I'll see to it.'

But Mrs Pearson, who had almost ceased to worry about the abstracted papers, was starting to do so afresh. Richard left her to it, removing himself after a bit more Good-Godding and a reference or two to what some people could get up to.

What had gone, he saw from a glance round his office, was

mostly lecture-notes and the like, replaceable after what laid end to end would have been several months of hard work. All the books and pamphlets seemed to be there still. None of the rare or important ones. They had lived in his study at home.

Later, Richard drove himself and Anna off in the TBD, which he had parked in a busy street a hundred metres or so from the hotel Cordelia had had no imaginable way of finding out they had been staying at.

'Well, that's it,' he said. 'Rounded off nicely. Nothing left for her to do.'

It was over a minute before a fearful rumbling vibration started to shake the car. Richard pulled in to the side and slowed right down. The offside front wheel continued on its way at a smart pace, entering the opposite line of traffic and bringing down a motor-cyclist in its career, fortunately without doing him any more damage than a broken collar-bone and cuts and bruises.

TWENTY

'It must have been a coincidence,' said Anna. 'Pure chance or bad luck. How many cars did you say were parked in London at any one time?'

'Did I say? Anyway it's obviously millions. But one of her gang could have spotted us when we were passing Professor Léon's, say, and followed us from there and noticed where I parked.'

'But I thought you went out after a while and moved your car from near the hotel up to the end of that long street.'

'Well, whoever it was must have hung about.'

'And posted the rest of the gang at strategic observation points. Pfui!'

'Somebody unscrewed those nuts.'

'Cordelia herself did it with special radio waves from her study.'

'I just can't shake off the feeling that it was her . . .'

'Go on. But you won't, will you? You're afraid to say "her last blow" in case it brings on another one, which you think was what happened the time the wheel came off just after you'd said something about there being nothing more she could get up to. What a fine mind you have, Dr Vaisey.'

'Very funny, comrade.' Richard spoke with some bitterness. He was thinking of the horrible if short-lived inquiry into the traffic accident, at which he had been exonerated as one who took all reasonable care of his car's roadworthiness but after which he had felt obliged to pay the motor-cyclist what had seemed to him a sizeable sum in compensation. There had been some attendant publicity.

'You don't really imagine she has any kind of supernatural power, do you?' Anna pursued.

'Not exactly, it's more – '

'I can see the advantage to you of believing in a thing like that.

The more of a monster you can make her, the less of a bastard it makes you feel for running away with me.'

'Not quite as funny as your last one, comrade.'

'Sorry,' said Anna, and stroked his hand. 'I've touched a point, though, haven't I?'

'Though? Of course you've touched a point. Not much of one all the same. And do you think it matters, half-believing a bit of rubbish like that now and then?'

'Oh no, not as long as you know what you're up to. But I think it might be good for us both if you'd say something.'

'All right. Here goes. We're free of her now.'

The two had been over most of that ground several times in the past few days without ever having reached such a declaration. After it there was a small but marked silence at the breakfast-table, during which both might have been assuring themselves that of course there was no conceivable turn of events that would bring an errant live shell from the not so far-distant artillery range to land plumb on their rented cottage. The moment passed, but was at once followed by a small sharp crash from the adjacent hall.

'The post,' said Richard, and added nastily, 'What else?'

The rubber-banded packet, besides pieces of mail for various other addresses not totally unlike this one, included letters for him from Cordelia and from Tristram Hallett. Before he could stop it, Richard's mind had turned to wafer-thin state-of-the-art anti-personnel bombs and nerve-gas containers. He soon hauled it back again, but he still opened the Cordelia envelope with unnatural care.

Inside were a cheque made out to him for £23.17 from a literary magazine and a single sheet of notepaper. Put into normal English, this read:

Darling,

I thought you'd like to know I know where you are. So you'll get your post forwarded, I mean. Dear Pat will be seeing to that but she seems to be away at the moment. Filming somewhere, perhaps.

Well, I gave you a fine old run for your money, didn't I? Actually it ran *me* into quite a lot of cash to organise – you wouldn't *believe* what it costs even to *find* a couple of bent actors. Still, worth every penny. Oh and by the way it's all over now. Your run, I mean. Oh just while I remember *poor* Pat and her sweet husbands had a burglary yesterday. Luckily hardly anything was taken, only some old picture though worth a bit according to *her*. And a ring or two. Of course they'd be insured wouldn't they?

Sorry about the cheque, I opened the letter by mistake. Of course you'll get all the money that's actually yours, like this. Very little that isn't, though.

Oh dear, what a lot about money.

My love as always,
Cordelia

Richard wished she had not written the four words above her name, whatever she might have meant by them.

'How much of it do you believe?' asked Anna.

'Oh, all of it. Particularly about its being all over. She wouldn't say that unless she meant it.'

'Why not? She might just be softening you up for the next one.'

'No, that would be cheating.'

'An idea like that, that's just you being English.'

'Cordelia's English too, as I told you.'

'Oh, merciful God. Do you believe she didn't have the burglary done too?'

'No way of knowing. People do get burgled in London without having let offending husbands in where they're not supposed to be.'

'Just as they get wrongly accused of shoplifting.'

'All right, I know what it looks like, but a what, an innocent burglary would look just the same and come in very handy. And Harry hasn't got hold of me to complain.'

'What would be the point of his doing that?'

'He's Pat's husband.'

'I'm glad I'm just a simple Russian girl,' said Anna, rising from the table. 'See you keep that letter by you and read it to me again later.'

When she had gone, Richard read his letter from Hallett, who after saying that all was well with Tania and him went on to say:

This morning I got a letter from my pal at Corpus which rather confirms one's impression that Debbie Abernathy will be my replacement in the autumn. I further gather that we had underestimated if anything the strength of the lady's determination to bring the Department into line with modern reality, as she might express it. I think we can expect full Russian-language study of texts to become at most an option for As and Bs, if not an altogether separate special subject. I don't expect you'll need any pressure from me to start looking elsewhere. We might discuss possibilities when you're in these parts again.

Richard had started looking elsewhere, so far inactively, since Hallett's departure first came in prospect. It would not have been easy for somebody of forty-six with his record of publication and a book on Lermontov still needing more work to get an equivalent job in his line. The same chap with a book on Lermontov in an advanced state of pulverisation would find it measurably harder. In a flash of foresight Richard saw himself in a room with strip lighting and wire-reinforced windows teaching businessmen and bureaucrats the Cyrillic alphabet. With his Skoda 1100 parked in the yard outside.

Time to make a move. He put the two letters on the small corner table that for the moment represented his study. Already there, principally because it had to be somewhere, was his copy of the transcripts of the poems of Anna's that she had recited at the Institute. The sight of it now reminded him with a sharp pang that it was two days since she had asked him to propose a title for the sequence, and not a single possibility had suggested itself to him. Instead, names for parts of the body and physical functions, some of a disturbing coarseness, had come flooding in. He had to boot a couple of them out that very moment.

His mood switching to self-pity, he remembered the tremulous eagerness with which, having contrived to be alone, he had snatched up the sheaf of text, half sure that his first sight of it would reveal a miracle in the style of the one that had saved St Elizabeth of Hungary, and that the words would send beauty and truth streaming into him. Alas, he had found nothing but a slightly different form of bullshit from before, not different enough to be any the less bullshit. A shaft of purest sunlight fell across the pretty but rather stuffy and uncomfortable little kitchen. How could it be, he tried to ask himself, not for the first time, that a beautiful bright girl like that could . . . could not just simply . . . could not prevent herself from . . . Ah, but anyone capable of answering a question along those lines would have had precious little trouble reshaping the world to suit himself.

Silence from upstairs, and recent experience, indicated to him that more of what he could cheerfully have done without was being created in the tiny spare bedroom that gave such an inspiring view of neighbouring fields and distant woods. How different would his life become if by another miracle the poems Anna Danilova produced from this moment forward were to be not too bad just there and there, quite interesting, competent, very sound, striking, brilliant, the equal of anything being written today, really good? Well, he would presumably be happier. He could not think he would love her more. He hoped that having to go on pretending to see merit in her poems would never make him love her less. No sign of anything like that at the moment. Early days yet, though. Perhaps she would stop writing in the end, not for any dramatic reason, just realise she had no more to say, had found something else. Like getting married? Like having a child?

Time to make a real move, further than across the room. While chewing over these matters he had been clearing away the breakfast things and tidying the kitchen. Now he tried to settle down in the sitting-room with Pasternak's volume of 1943, *On Early Trains*, but found he could not. At this time of the day and week he was used to working, not reading, however seriously. It could not be what it seemed to be, that the poems themselves, which he had reread in their entirety a dozen times, had lost a touch of their old immediacy. He remembered with a twinge of disquiet a story by some inconsiderable person of the Russian eighteenth century, about a scholar who had made a pact with the Devil, highly advantageous to him as he thought until he found he had irrecoverably lost the power of seeing beauty in any work of man. Time for a further move still.

He could not settle to anything because there was nothing for him to settle to. Going for a walk, going out of doors and moving hither and thither for the sake of it, had always seemed to him the nearest thing to voluntary boredom that life had to offer. He glanced again at the letters from Cordelia and Hallett, changed his tie and walked the mile and a half to the village. On the way he thought to himself that the present mildness of his consternation at the prospect of having to tolerate Anna's poetry for the foreseeable future arose from the more engrossing prospect of having nowhere to live, work, be. The cottage would be theirs till the end of the month, the rent-free loan, needless to say, of some Crispin connection. After that, presumably, Professor Léon's not very suitable roof would shelter them while they looked for somewhere. Somewhere? Somewhere where? What sort of somewhere? Somewhere, in any case, devastatingly, uncontrollably cheap. Just how cheap in pounds and pence Richard had a very poor idea. Cordelia had always handled everything to do with the money. To date, his efforts to cope with his new financial situation had been confined to accepting a loan from Crispin and trying unsuccessfully to remember the name of the accountant who looked after the joint Vaisey estate. Crispin would supply it. He would have other tasks too.

He, Crispin, was of course staying somewhere in the neighbourhood and would be along for lunchtime drinks at the cottage, foreseeably accompanied by Freddie. When the two appeared they less foreseeably had with them Godfrey, who was unaccompanied by Nancy.

'Well, he wasn't a thousand miles away in the first place, you see,' said Crispin irrefutably, and added a little later that he had told his brother something of the troubles Richard seemed to have experienced at the hands of Cordelia, but not enough, it seemed. The other three had hardly left on a visit to the outdoors when Godfrey rather closed in on Richard. He conveyed by his manner that his interest was sympathetic, but that they would come to that part later. He incidentally wore a zip jacket with an oriental motif on it and only days earlier had received a severe haircut.

'Well,' said Richard, 'the first thing I knew – '

'No,' said Godfrey firmly. 'From the start, and as it happened, and in detail.'

'But I still can't be absolutely sure that even that wheel wasn't her doing,' Richard was saying twenty minutes later.

'You never will.'

'Cheers. What's your feeling about it?'

'Oh, I think the odds are very heavy that it was her, but then I would. I agree no one will ever know how she managed it.'

'M'm. But somebody might have been killed. Somebody nearly was.'

'Yes,' said Godfrey, nodding his shorn head to show he had taken the point.

'What did you mean just now, you would think the wheel was her?'

'No more than it sort of fits in with her character.'

'Come on, Godfrey, what did she do to you?'

Now Godfrey shook his head and sighed. 'I was hoping not to have to tell you this, but I suppose I'd better. It might even cheer you up. I left her three days before the first show I'd had a real hand in designing was due to open at Goldie's. It burnt down on the second night. In fact it burnt down rather more thoroughly than might have been intended, in the sense that some wretched caretaker or watchman person was trapped and suffocated. The fire was started deliberately. They never found who did it but I've always been as good as sure she was behind it.'

'I remember. What was the next one?'

'There wasn't a next one. That was the lot.'

'She must have thought she'd done enough. And to spare.'

'Afraid of getting caught, more likely. The police turn frightfully nasty and go all energetic over things like arson and murder.'

'You went to them, did you? And they laughed at you.'

'They were too polite to in front of me, but they clearly thought I was mad. I probably looked and sounded a bit mad. Felt it, too, I seem to remember.'

'Godfrey, what made you so sure, or what did you say, as good as sure it was her? She made no bones about it with me, I mean she couldn't very well, but you had nothing to go on. Or had you?'

'Nothing very much, it's true. She looked at me in a way I'd never seen before when I told her I was off, but then you could argue I'd never told her I was off before.'

'No veiled warnings that she was ready for you?'

'No. She wouldn't have been at that stage anyway. No, the real thing was it did seem to tie in with her character. I remember we discussed that before, but I don't think either of us got as far as saying this.' Godfrey looked at his watch and said, 'The others won't be long but we've a few minutes yet,' thereby reminding Richard of Crispin. 'Er, I mean in more than the usual sense she has no character. An egotist to the point of emotional solipsism and on the brink of what was called psychopathy in my youth though no doubt they call it something else now, but with no interests or drives. Rather as if Hitler couldn't think of anything particular he wanted to happen in Germany when he came to power, and thought the frontiers he'd inherited were just about right. A zealot without a cause. Though that's another word you don't come across very often nowadays. Zealot, I mean.'

'Yes, I didn't think you meant cause.'

'Sorry. Anyway, more than most affluent women she has trouble filling the day. Hence the obsessive telephoning and collecting things she doesn't want and getting other people to do things for her, which takes much longer than if she did them herself. As I say, she's not interested in anything. Sorry. Again. I mean you must have noticed that about her yourself. It's ghastly, I keep forgetting you've been married to her too.'

'Don't worry, I can understand that. Go on.'

'Then suddenly, boom, wham, she's got something to do. Powie. Fucking me up. I truly am most terribly sorry for the bad language but I can't think off-hand of another way of putting it. A tremendous amount of what people get up to they get up to so as to have something to do, you know. Even really bad things. Like Iago. But she managed only one caper with me before she had to stop. She had a longer go at you but now she's had to stop that too.'

'How can you be certain?'

'Too risky to go on. She'd have felt she was in very deep water if that chap on the motor-bike had been killed. Daring, but inclined to caution too. Goes with being stingy.'

'She wasn't stingy when it came to financing her campaigns against us. It must cost quite a bit to persuade somebody to burn a theatre down.'

'True. Spending a lot of money on such things was very likely . . .'

'Her only extravagance.'

'Ten out of ten for that.' Godfrey had strolled over to the window and now looked out. 'Here they come.'

'Godfrey.'

'Yes?'

'How did you find her in bed?'

'Oh, absolutely marvellous. Until the time she was doing

something fairly unusual and I noticed her expression, and her thoughts, feelings, all that, were miles away. Or rather she wasn't having any thoughts et cetera at all. Like a theatre person not listening. Well, I suppose much the same sort of thing must have happened to you.'

'I should imagine so, yes, one time or another. I mean I don't think I'm the sort of man who's quite up to noticing things like that, but I'm sure it was just the same with me.'

Godfrey's shoulders heaved under the questionable jacket. 'Nice of her to take the trouble, what?' He waved to the returning party. 'Do you know, Richard, I've never told anyone that before, not even Nancy. Incidentally she was doing something else today anyway. Which is just as well, as I thought at the time.'

Behind him, Richard said nothing. He was not clear why, but this moment did seem like the end of Cordelia. He felt remorse and, for the final and perhaps only time, grief. Not for the life they had had together but for all they had not had. But he forgot about that completely when Anna came into the room. He greeted her as though they had not met for weeks and had not made love for days. If any of it came as a surprise to her, she concealed it well.

Not looking at them, Crispin said rather fast, 'I've booked lunch at the pub but you two needn't feel you've got to come along.'

Richard appeared to hesitate but was actually beating down a rather juvenile wish to remain. Pretending to consult Anna by eye, he said they would love to join the party. Freddie saw some of this and suppressed a snigger. She had started to get on really well with Anna almost from the moment of Richard's bit of perjury, and by now, with the aid of Anna's growing English eked out by her phrase-book, they were on excellent giggling and face-making terms. When the group got to the lunch-table the two women at once moved to sit together.

They ate in a private room, or in what quickly amounted to one, after Crispin had delightedly recognised one of a pair of solicitors in a comfortable corner about to order their meal and, after a minute or so of chatting over old times, had warm-heartedly required him and his companion to get fed somewhere else. All went uneventfully well for a time, but Richard knew that something was coming – Crispin never went anywhere without a reason. After unexpectedly allowing Richard to pay for the meal, he looked across the table and said, 'Have you heard anything about your new boss? I remember you sounded somewhat unhopeful.'

'She's turning out to be worse than I thought. I haven't met her yet.'

'Got anything else lined up?'

'Very much not.'

'Well, of course if you insist on staying in the academic racket that's your affair. Or funeral. Now I know you read and write Russian, but how well do you speak it?'

'Excellent,' said Anna in English.

Godfrey laughed and gave Anna a friendly look.

'I see,' said Crispin. 'Because one of my mates' mates is evidently looking for a Russian-speaker to do simultaneous translation for his nest of craps in Brussels. I said I'd see if you could be lured. Hard work, I imagine, and boring enough to suit anyone, but even I would call it reasonably well paid. Which'll come in handy for a fellow with your expensive tastes. First reaction?'

Richard looked grave. 'It'll need a lot of thinking about.'

'Fuck your mother, you English prick,' said Anna, not in English this time. 'You know so much Russian you've forgotten how to say yes please in your own language.'

'I don't think anyone needs a translation of that,' said Crispin. 'Shall I tell my mate you'll have a drink with his mate, Richard?'

'Yes. Sorry. Thanks.'

No one objected when Crispin suggested a final drink then and there. On the way out he drew Richard aside, brought out an unsealed envelope and took from it a sheet of paper which he unfolded before passing it over.

'What's this? Oh, I see.'

'Yes, it'll be handed in tomorrow at the Soviet embassy or whatever it calls itself nowadays and it'll be in the papers too. As things have developed it probably won't make all that much of a stir. Here or over there. Anyway, your name's on it. Nothing can change that.'

'No,' said Richard, putting the document away in his own pocket. 'I'll show it to Anna later. Well, thank you for all the work you've done.'

'Mostly delegated. This time next year the whole bloody issue will probably have collapsed into civil war. Still, whatever happens I'll be glad I got my blow in while there was still something left to hit at. It's rather rough that chaps like the unfortunate Sergei Danilov are going to be worse off when everybody's got something else to think about and there's nowhere even to send a petition to.'

'Er, what was in your mind when you decided to help Anna?'

'Well, it gave me something to do. That's Godfrey's theory, anyway. Then I thought Anna might make a nice pal for Freddie, but to be honest that only occurred to me the other day.'

'She won't be much use to her in Brussels.'

'That's where you're wrong. They'll be writing and ringing up and popping to and fro all the bloody time. Anyway, you should walk into the job. Distinguished academic, Russian, well, girl-friend. Pity in a way it's not a boy-friend, but there, you can't have everything.'

Freddie too got in a relatively quiet word while Hanni was bringing the car up. 'She's a really nice girl, that, and good value. You take care of her and mind you do better with her than with that sodding Cordelia. Be thankful you're free of that old bag and leave it at that. I know people don't want to be told how lousy their previous spouses were because it makes them look bloody fools for marrying them in the first place, but I'm telling you because you *were* a bloody fool, weren't you?'

'Any news of Sandy?'

'But after all Godfrey married her and he's not . . . What? Oh, Sandy's in a place called Oaxaca in Mexico with an American tinned-fruit man of some sort. I was glad she never caught up with you. She wouldn't have done you any good at all.'

'Oh. No, I suppose she wouldn't. No, of course not.'

That evening, Anna gave Richard a longer version of the special newsy look he had caught a glimpse of a couple of times earlier that day, making him wonder if she might be going to declare herself pregnant. She came sidling up to him while he sat over a newspaper rather unconstructively trying to remember what he had read and heard about Brussels.

'What a delightful party that was,' she said. 'All the more so for me because I had had a very successful morning.'

'Oh good.'

291

She now displayed a piece of paper, less grand than Crispin's, and gave it to him. With an immediate sinking of the heart he recognised what was a poem in her language, handwritten with a few corrections. Not quite a year later he was to see it in an English translation, a remarkable one in his experience for its fidelity to the letter and no less to the spirit of the original. It ran in part:

> man of all men in Shakespeare's island,
> eyes that shine through the rain in my heart,
>   where I came as a stranger,
> finding a hand grasping as firmly as time,
>   knowledge that burns like fire
> and makes my heart round and red again,
> music in unity in my snowflake veins,
> thanks, all thanks be in my eyes clear for seeing,
> and I
>   can face
>   the dawn mounted on our love
> which is you and my love and I and your love,
> quickcatchitbeforeitdisappearslikethenight
> over the river   never let go,
> spreading through the world like a boy's tear,
> to turn all the blackest dogs away,
> and you
>   have spoken
>   and I have listened,
> until like a spring the world runs down,
> and never fear the dark.

Richard stared at the manuscript for minutes on end without being able to think of anything whatever to say. Almost at once it was too late for professional bullshit about further study needed for definitive judgement, all that.

She had moved away almost as far as she could in the undersized sitting-room of the cottage. Looking away from him, but gently, she said, 'It goes on over the page.'

'What? Oh.'

He had hardly had time to turn over when she went on, 'You must take it as the best I can do and the only way I can pay tribute to you. I hope you can tell that at least I mean what I say in it. Perhaps at some time in the future you'll come to think my poetry's tolerable, or at any rate harmless. I know you think everything I've written up to this moment has no merit at all, including what I recited from that platform. When you told me that you thought those poems were good, I knew within a few seconds that you were lying. But that lie told me how much you loved me, and it means I'll always love you. I don't think I could put that into a poem, but I'll probably have a shot at it one day.'

Both were now in tears. They put their arms round each other and held on tight.

TWENTY-ONE

'What's she like?' asked Tristram Hallett.

'You've had a look at her, haven't you? I mean she must have been round here.'

'Actually not that, though we have met a couple of times. I mean to work – is it with or under?'

'To be fair, with rather than under so far.' Neil Jenkins accepted a second cup of tea and a kind of pan-Slavic biscuit from Tania Hallett. 'Cheers – lovely. She's not bad at keeping the riff-raff down at meetings either, it must be said.'

'You mean Duncan and his cohorts?'

'Son of Duncan is there now. The principle is unchanged, i.e. getting more democratic and worse all the time.'

'Does Prof encourage you to call her Debbie?'

'Yes, but "Professor Abernathy" warms her heart more. As regards the syllabus – well, you'll have seen. Richard is well out of it.'

'I suppose so. I wonder how he feels about things.'

'Well,' said Jenkins, 'if he's got any sense he should feel pretty good. Walking out of the ISS into a plush job with the lovely Danilova on his arm.'

'From what he told me before he went it wasn't exactly walking. And it was a great shame that all that fuss about the petition thing came to nothing.'

'What there was of a fuss. Well, yes.'

Tania's Slavophile clock on the mantelpiece chimed the half-hour between four and five. Jenkins stirred his small shape and looked at his watch. Hallett said quickly,

'Did you ever hear what actually happened about that over there?'

'My dear Tristram, you know very well that nobody ever hears what actually happened about anything over there. Now as then. Whether they're there or here. And I'd left Moscow by then anyway. One thing that came to my critical ears was that the brother of the noted Danilova seemed to be dead of something. Lead poisoning. Natural causes. There are quite a few of those around in Mother Russia, as you know, and these days they're on the increase if anything. The only bit of rumour that seems to be more than that is that wherever he may be he's not going anywhere else for some time.'

Hallett said, 'So Richard signed away what he must have seen as his good name for nothing.'

'Oh, I don't know about that, it probably helped him to collect the divine Danilova, and there can't be more than about five people in the world qualified to judge what was at stake when he put his name to that piece of piss.'

'I dare say. Unfortunately they're the only five whose opinion he cares about.'

'You're one of them, of course, Tristram.'

'I'd like to think I was.'

At that, Jenkins raised his eyebrows in a theatrical way, but desisted when he saw Tania's glance moving towards him. 'Well, now he's got her poetry coming at him all the hours God sends, poor devil. By the way, do you remember his wife? The Big C. Clytemnestra or some such name.'

'Cordelia, wasn't it? I must have met her.'

'She had a way of talking that was all her own, thank God. After about two minutes it made you want to scream and run out of the house. Extraordinary. Perhaps he needs something like that.'

'I'm not sure I see what you mean,' said Hallett rather coldly.

The telephone rang in the next room, on the far side of a communicating door. Tania jumped up and went to answer it. As quietly as he could, Jenkins put his cup and saucer down next to his plate on a low table, the tiles of which eccentrically presented the pictures in Moussorgsky's *Pictures at an Exhibition*. It was rather hot in the small sitting-room and Jenkins found it oppressive. He had been just about to leave when the telephone detained him.

Hearteningly soon, Tania was back, looking cheerful. 'For you,' she said to Hallett. 'Richard.'

Hallett got up at what was no doubt his best speed and shuffled out.

When he had gone, Jenkins said, 'How is the old boy? You know.'

'About the same. Listen, Neil, while we've got a second, do please come and see him as often as you can. He does so long to be kept in touch. Richard's very good but of course he's in Brussels practically all the time.'

'Naturally I'll do my best, Tania, but I'm afraid this is rather a busy time for me. New boss and one thing and another.'